ONE HOT ITALIAN SUMMER

KARINA HALLE

For my muse

ONE HOT ITALIAN SUMMER

A writer looking for inspiration in Tuscany.
One hot Italian single dad.
This summer is going to be a scorcher.

ONE

GRACE

They say writing is the loneliest profession.

It's said so often it's become a bit of a cliché. I never really understood it, because, until now, it's been the opposite for me. Writing has been the greatest journey, a dream career, a chance to be with my best friend day in and day out, working together to create something magical. It has never been lonely—it has never been anything but a shared discovery of the unknown. Me and Robyn against the world.

But now that world is unfamiliar to me. The lights have dimmed. It's just a maze of shadows, hard to find your way in and impossible to get out.

And I'm standing in front of that dark maze, knowing I have to go it alone, knowing the journey I'm about to go on —if I can even open up my laptop most days—is going to be dark and strange and terribly sad. There is no joy here, only fear. Fear that I alone will not be able to find my way with Robyn gone.

I stare at the blank page before me, this bright, flashing

thing that stares right back. It dares me to write a word. To start.

But I can't.

I reach over and slam the laptop shut then push back my chair a few inches, the sound of the wood scraping on the floor loud and definite. I want to put distance between me and the work but I know I can't do this forever. This is my career, the path I chose, and either I give up on it now and move on to something else, or I forge my way forward.

For now, though, I'm moving on.

Just for today.

Because it's easier this way.

I sigh and get to my feet, stretching from side to side. You'd think I just put in hours of hard work from how sore I am, but the truth is I've been sitting here since this morning, just staring at the screen, lost in thought and often paralyzed by it.

It's the end of May and I have a book due at the end of summer.

The first one I'll have written on my own.

A book with what feels like the entire world riding on it.

Because my world is.

I walk over to my bedroom window and gaze out. From here, I can see Dean Cemetery and people walking along Dean Path, their brightly colored umbrellas popping against the monochromatic background. So far, spring has settled on Edinburgh in a grey mist, and I can't remember the last time I saw the sun. It certainly hasn't helped my mood, turning writer's block into a solid concrete wall.

I sigh and rub my hands up and down my arms. The flat is drafty and damp, the kind that sticks to your bones. It's the top level of a stone house, and I've been renting it since university. There are wood beams along the ceiling, one stone wall in the kitchen, and wind that whistles through the thin windows, bringing in the chill and the musky scent of the River Leith.

Also, it was this cemetery across the street that changed everything for me. I stumbled upon a gravestone that only gave a hint of a woman's rich past and then my brain was off and running. A cozy mystery about an elderly lady who used to be a member of Scotland Yard and her long-lost American niece. Both of them teaming up to solve mysteries and fight crime while running a cat café.

Too scared to write alone, I approached Robyn, wondering if she'd want to write it with me. She said yes and the two of us jumped into it without a second thought.

I met Robyn Henry in my university's creative writing class. I was studying history at the University of Edinburgh in a vain attempt to make my professor father proud, and decided to indulge in something more freeing. Though I'd often spent my childhood alone, I'd lose myself in books. They kept me company when I had no one, and I'd pen silly little stories to pass the time. A creative writing course made sense for me.

It made more sense when I met Robyn.

Robyn was unlike anyone I knew. I was shy and quiet, keeping tightly to myself, and she was loud, quirky, and gregarious. She took a liking to me, kept on bugging me to hang out with her, wanting to read my stories before anyone else. She saw something in me that many people dismissed, and in turn I was enthralled with her. I wanted to be just like her.

My mobile rings, jolting me out of my thoughts. Honestly, there's only a few people who call me regularly and I have to say I don't feel like talking to anyone at the moment.

I go to my bedside table where it's charging and look at the number.

My heart goes cold.

It's my agent, Jana Lee.

I'm terrified of her.

I stare at it for a few moments, thinking. If it were my mom or dad I'd wait for them to text or leave a voice message, but I can't ignore Jana.

I pick it up.

"Grace speaking."

"Grace, darling, how are you?" Jana's throaty voice comes through. "How's the writing coming?"

She doesn't even take a moment before she barrels right into it. That's her, straight to the point, even if it knocks you over.

I can lie. I've been lying for the last couple of months, essentially as soon as Jana signed me as her client. But I'm not sure if she'll let it fly this time.

"Uh," I stammer.

"Please, please, *please* tell me you've made progress. Tell me you at least have a quarter of the book done." This is more of a command than anything.

"I do," I lie. I glance guiltily at the laptop on my desk, as if it's going to jump up and protest.

Jana sighs heavily. "Grace, listen to me. I need to know the truth. I need to know if you can finish this manuscript by September first. If you can't, then we're in some serious shit here with the publishers and I'm not about to put my neck on the line for you. I need to know now so I can either have the deal cancelled or we can move forward, as it is in your contract."

This was what I was afraid of. I always thought it was dumb luck that I managed to land Jana as my agent, after my last agent, Maureen, dropped me. For Maureen, Robyn was always the one she believed in. Robyn was her star. For the last six years that Robyn and I wrote the *Sleuths of Stockbridge* series, the only contact I even had with Maureen was through Robyn.

Then, when Robyn died, Maureen decided she couldn't represent me. Gave me the excuse that she was grieving, but I was grieving too.

I still am.

Jana represented another author friend of mine, Kat Manning, who put out her feelers, managed to snag me a phone call with her. I even took the train down to London to have a meeting.

Here's the thing about Jana Lee: she's as infamous for her brash, bold, volatile personality as much as her talent in picking and nurturing writers. She's one of the most, if not *the* most, powerful literary agents in the U.K. She's been responsible for everything from bestsellers to Pulitzer prize winners, and for whatever reason, she decided to take me on, even when I didn't have a book to show for it. All I had was a proposal, a three-page outline for a women's fiction novel, and she managed to sell it for a nice sum.

Now, of course, I have to follow through and write the damn thing.

Which has been next to impossible.

Time for me to finally admit it.

"I don't want the contract cancelled," I tell Jana. I need it. I need it to not just give me money to pay my rent since royalties are so unreliable, but to prove myself as a writer. To prove I can do this without Robyn's help, that I can do it alone. "I'll make it work. It's just been ... harder than I expected."

Jana's silence is deafening. Finally she says in a clipped voice, "What seems to be the problem? Writer's block?"

I don't think Jana gets very personal. In fact, she doesn't know much about me at all and I know barely anything about her. Everything so far has been strictly business and she's only mentioned Robyn a handful of times. Being honest feels like it comes with a price. I don't want her to think less of me.

"I guess so," I tell her hesitantly. "Fear, really. Fear that the book won't be good enough, fear that I don't know how to write without Robyn."

More silence. I can hear the fridge in my kitchen kick on.

"You can't edit a blank page, Grace," she says after a moment.

"I know. I just can't seem to..." I trail off, wondering how to explain. "Aye, I guess it's just writer's block then." Seems easier to say it like that.

"That's understandable," she says. "You've been writing a cozy mystery series through twelve books, with someone else no less, and now you're moving on to a book with romantic elements. I'm guessing the weather up there has been as shit as it's been down here."

"The gloom helped with the Sleuths of Stockbridge," I admit, peering out the window at the cemetery.

"Of course it did. Even with the lighthearted tone, it still dealt with murder, crime, and the noir-like atmosphere of Scotland. It fit the genre."

"Well, it's not like I can change the weather."

I'm met with silence again.

Finally, Jana clears her throat. "Listen, I know we don't know each other very well, not that I have a close personal relationship with any of my clients. I don't believe it's necessary to represent them, and actually, it lets me conduct business better. But I am empathetic to your predicament, Grace. I know what loss is like and I understand. However, we are both in this to make money and jumpstart your career, and I am getting concerned that this might be getting out of hand."

My cheeks burn. I hate being talked down to like this. My father was a pro at reprimanding me. He still is.

"I'm sorry," I say quietly. "I'm trying. It's just, this is a creative process and—"

"Yes, yes, the creative process. You're not a machine and you can't switch it on or off," she finishes, obviously mimicking what her other clients tell her. Writers, no matter the genre, are all peas in a pod. "But we can't wait around for your process to start. If you can't find the muse, we have to produce the muse."

I frown. "What do you have in mind?"

"I think you need to get away," she says. "Go somewhere hot and sunny where there's nothing to worry your pretty little head about. Find inspiration somewhere other than dreary old Scotland, because I guarantee you're not going to find it where you are. You're haunted by ghosts, Grace, and they're holding you back."

"I don't think I can afford it," I tell her. The advance I got for this book was fifty thousand pounds, which sounds like a lot until you break it down. I got fifteen thousand for signing, then I'll get another twenty when I hand in the book, then another fifteen when the book publishes, whenever that is. Jana takes ten percent of all that, so that amount has to last me until I hand the book in.

"I figured as much," she says. "How about this? I have a house in Italy, in Tuscany, right outside the city of Lucca. You can use it for a month, free of charge, so long as you work on your book. I want at least twenty-five percent of it completed in that month and I don't think that's too much to ask."

I stare at the floor, trying to think. "I can't … you have a house in Italy?"

A pause. "Yes. It's a wonderful place. You'll have it all to yourself. The only person you'll see is Emilio. He tends to the olive orchard and the pool and gardens."

It sounds like *heaven*, but still. "That's far too generous."

"I'm not doing this to be generous, Grace. I'm doing this because this is my ass on the line. Now, do you think this will help you get the book done?"

Say yes. Say yes, because if you say no, that might be the end of all this.

I swallow. "Yes."

"Good. Then it's settled," Jana says with such finality that I know there's no way I can go back on this. "Let's see … how about June first to June twenty-eighth? That's almost a month."

I briefly wonder why the twenty-eighth, since wouldn't it be easier to make it from the first to the first?

"Are you planning on using the house?" I ask her. "Maybe after me?"

"Ha," she lets out a dry laugh. "You think I have time for a vacation? No, my dear. I work. Work is my vacation. And remember, this is work for you too. I'm not letting you stay there so you can lie by the pool all day and work on your tan."

"No, of course not."

"So, are you in? Does this all work for you?"

"Sure, that works," I tell her. June was just a few days

away, which made it very last minute. "Hopefully I can find a flight."

"There are flights to Pisa all the time. It'll be no problem. In fact, I'll book them for you. Cheap. It'll probably be Ryanair or Easyjet, so don't get your hopes up. It's just a step up from flying cargo."

I'm so overwhelmed that I feel like I'm going into autopilot, like none of this is real.

"Are you sure you want to do this for me?" I ask her.

"Darling, I'm doing this for *me*," she says. "Now, I'll email you the plane tickets once you've got them. Emilio has a key, so I'll arrange for him to meet you at the airport. He's an old fart, but he's dependable."

"Okay. Well ... thank you so much, Jana."

"Don't thank me yet. Let's just hope this pays off."

"It will," I tell her before we say goodbye and hang up.

I stare at the phone in my hand for a moment before my eyes sweep across my flat. Jana is right about being haunted. It's not about being across from a cemetery. It's that all the memories in this flat are tinged with shades of Robyn. From our character and plot breakdowns over copious amounts of coffee (Irish Breakfast tea for her) while bundled up in blankets on the couch, to me texting her from my desk as I feverishly wrote and immediately emailed her chapters. I feel like there's no escape from her.

And for the first time, I realize the only way I'm going to be able to move forward is if I physically, then mentally, make the change and leave her behind.

I put the phone back on the charger, then head into my bedroom to start packing.

~

When Jana first told me about Emilio Bertuzzi, her villa's groundskeeper, I was expecting, well, an old fart (her words). But the Emilio that meets me at the airport in Pisa is anything but.

Yes, Emilio is old, at least eighty, and he has a forest of hair growing out of his ears, but beneath his bushy brows are kind and sharp eyes. He walks at a fast pace and practically wrestles my suitcase from my hands, hoisting it into the back of his beat-up truck with ease (and considering my suitcase is absolutely stuffed with clothes, that's no small feat).

The only problem is, Emilio barely speaks English, which makes me realize that Jana must speak fluent Italian if she's able to communicate with him at all. Who knows, maybe by the end of all this, I'll be speaking Italian too.

You don't need another distraction, I remind myself as Emilio takes a corner at breakneck speed. *Focus on the book, not learning a new language.*

Or at least focus on not dying. I don't know if Emilio used to be a race car driver or what, but he's been driving like he's in it to win it ever since we left the airport. Actually, everyone on the road is keeping up, like pace cars, which makes me think that driving aggressively fast may just be an Italian thing.

I've only been to Italy once, to Rome, on a book tour with Robyn. I had food poisoning the night before, in London, so I don't remember much of it. I do know it was for book number five, and that Robyn had a great time at the bookstore party, whereas I went right to the hotel room after the signing was over. Didn't get to see any of the sights, or eat any of the food, which is the ultimate shame when it comes to Italy. I hope to rectify it with this trip.

Except you'll be writing most of the time. Remember

Jana's words. You didn't come here for a vacation. You came here to work.

Which means no day trips to Pisa.

Or Florence.

Or Siena.

Or Cinque Terre.

And I probably won't be eating out often either. Jana assured me there was a large kitchen and that Emilio could drive me to the grocery store.

I steal a glance at him, marveling at both his ear hair and the amount of concentration he's giving to the road. At least I know I'm in capable hands.

I wonder if I should attempt to talk to him again but decide it's probably not for the best when he's driving, considering the amount of hand gestures we had both used earlier trying to understand each other.

Playing it safe, I bring out the Translate app and start prepping the list of questions I have for him when we arrive at the villa.

Then I take out the email that Jana sent me with all the information I need for the next month and look over it for the hundredth time.

The official name of the villa is Villa Rosa, a nineteenth century hunting lodge that's eight kilometers outside of Lucca. Aside from Emilio, who comes every other day, I will have the place to myself. There's an old chapel across the road that belonged to the previous owner, and after about a ten-minute walk there's a really nice restaurant. There are bikes I can use as well.

That's pretty much all the info she gave me, and I'm trying to imagine what an old Italian hunting lodge would look like, when Emilio takes the truck off the highway and onto a narrow rural road. We zoom around curves framed by olive groves and the low hills beyond, and I close my eyes when it looks like we're about to collide with a tractor trailer.

When I dare to open my eyes again, Emilio is trying not to smile.

Finally, the truck begins to slow for the first time, and we pull into a gravel driveway.

"*Siamo qui*," Emilio says in his deep, crackly voice. "We here."

TWO

GRACE

THE TRUCK PULLS TO A STOP AND I'M ALREADY gawking as I get out.

This place is *stunning*.

First my eyes are drawn to the villa.

Villa Rosa is three stories tall, the palest yellow color with a rust-tiled roof. It has quite an unusual façade, with two staircases leading to the same glass door on the second floor, the landing lined with window boxes of red geraniums. There's also a door on the main floor below it.

Then my eyes are drawn to the grounds, which seem to have been immaculately tended by Emilio.

To one side of the villa is a grove of lemon and fig trees interspersed with flowering potted rosemary and violets, and to the other side is a gravel path that cuts through cypress trees and under an arch of blush pink roses, showing just a hint of blue swimming pool.

Behind me, between the house and the road, is a large, closely-shorn lawn and I can see the tiny chapel beyond that, olive trees surrounding it as they rise gently up a hill.

"Wow," I say out loud as Emilio hauls my suitcase and duffle bag out of the truck. "Bellisima!"

I said that right, right? But he just nods and smiles and drags the bags across the gravel.

"Oh, let me," I tell him quickly, reaching for them, but he shakes his head adamantly.

"No, no," he says. *"Lascia, lascia."*

He hustles the bags toward the house, and I continue to stand there, dumbfounded. The sun is peeking out from behind some clouds and making my wool cardigan feel too hot and heavy. I tip my head back to the sky to get the rays on my face and take in a deep breath, inhaling the scent of lemon blossoms and roses and sun on grass. I just got here but I can already feel the well inside me filling up, promising creativity and production and even joy.

Thank you, Jana, I say inside my head. Even though she sent me here because her arse was on the line, I can't help but feel eternally grateful that I feel the seeds of inspiration. I tend to feel things very deeply, and this includes my environment, and I already know that the decision to come here will pay off for the both of us.

An unfamiliar thrill runs through me at the thought. I can't remember the last time I had hope.

Emilio clears his throat and my eyes snap open. He's waiting impatiently by the front door, gesturing with his head for me to hurry along.

I give him a quick smile and step behind him as he opens the door to the bottom floor.

It's cool inside and I'm immediately taken by the old wood beams and rafters above, and the terracotta tile below. It looks more like a restaurant down here, with two round tables covered by checkered tablecloths, wooden chairs, and then a lounge area by a massive fireplace.

"Please," Emilio gestures. "You have."

He's pointing to an honest-to-god bar that runs along the wall across from the lounge. It's fully-stocked with every type of alcohol imaginable, plus wine bottles tucked behind white glass cabinets.

Dutifully, I keep following Emilio past the bar—a place I'll have to frequent with moderation—and into a hallway.

"*Cucina*," he says, placing his hand on a swinging door near the stairs and pushing it open.

I stick my head in. It's the kitchen, looking both homey and slightly industrial. I guess this whole bottom floor used to be the restaurant from when this was a hunting lodge.

I follow Emilio up the stairs to the second floor which is a gorgeous living area with couches and the biggest wood coffee table I've ever seen. It takes up most of the floor. The room is bright, and scattered throughout are sculptures, marble, clay, some abstract, some of half-clothed women. It all looks very refined.

A row of framed photographs along a polished mantle catches my eye next. The photos are mostly in black and white which make me think they're of the villa back when it was a lodge. I'm itching to take a look and get inspired by the history, but Emilio continues up the staircase to the third floor, despite the fact that there are more unexplored rooms on the second.

He guides me down a narrow hallway to a door at the end labeled "C," and opens it.

My bedroom is delightful. Bigger than I thought it would be, with pale blue walls that contrast with the exposed dark wood beams above, and regal red bedding on the queen-size bed. It even has one of those gauzy curtains that hang above the bed, the ones you can pull around like a mosquito net.

Emilio throws my bags on the bed. He's sweating now from hauling them all over the house. He gestures to the loo, and I poke my head in. It's small but there's a shower, so I'm happy.

"I come back," he says to me, heading for the door. "Saturday."

Which makes it the day after tomorrow.

For a moment a tremor of worry goes through me.

I'm going to be by myself.

"Okay," I tell him. "Thank you so much for everything. *Ciao.*"

He just nods, wiggles his nose, and leaves down the hallway.

I stick my head out the door and watch him disappear, then finally hear the front door close and then the grumbling engine of his truck.

He's gone.

I'm alone.

Time to settle in.

I open the shutters and the windows and lean out, taking in a deep breath. The bedroom is at the back of the house, overlooking a glass-encased veranda or atrium below, then a wide lawn with a few fruit trees and a crumbling old wall lining the back. Beyond that is a thicket of trees, and in the distance a distinctive looking hill that overlooks the valley.

It's growing hotter by the minute, even with the window open, so I peel off my cardigan and unzip my boots, taking out a pair of flip flops from my carry-on. My feet need a pedicure, having been encased in socks and boots for months on end, and I make a note to do my nails later. I know no one but Emilio will see them, but even so, I already feel like this is a good opportunity to dress up more. There's a reason I brought a million sundresses that Edinburgh only lets me wear two months out of the year.

I quickly use the loo, admiring the blue floral wallpaper and jasmine-scented hand soap, then I grab my plotting notebook and pen from my purse, sliding my phone in the back pocket of my skinny jeans, and head out to explore.

All the doors in the upper hallway are closed. I assume one of them belongs to Jana and the rest are for guests. I don't want to be nosy, so I leave the doors closed and head down the stairs to the living room, making a beeline for the mantel.

There are several framed photographs. The black and white ones show a family posing outside the villa, looking exactly the same as it does today, save for the 1940's style car in the forefront. Then there's a photo of a beautiful dark-haired woman posing amid roses, a mysterious smile on her face. There's another of two men holding up a dead deer, each hand on an antler and smiling proudly.

There's only one picture in color, a little boy, maybe two years old, sitting in a basket of lemons. He looks extremely serious, which makes the picture even cuter.

I step back from the mantel and look around the room. One of the things I need to do is find the perfect writing spot. This room is airy and bright but it won't do.

I go down the short hall, but there's only one door open. It's a small library with a desk in the middle. I figure if the door is open, then I'm probably allowed to be in here. I sit down at the desk, trying to see if the height of the chair is to my liking. I could write in here, but it doesn't feel as inspiring as it could be.

I get back up and go check out the bookshelves. Most of the titles are in Italian, with only a handful in English, and they all seem to be about art or are non-fiction. I also don't see any of Jana's clients' books, not even the big names. Okay, so maybe it's a little narcissistic that I'm automatically looking for my books here, but I don't even see them in the Italian translation. Huh.

Well, you're a new client, I remind myself. *And she probably hasn't been here since she signed you.*

It makes me wonder how long it's been since Jana visited. The place feels very large with me being the only one here, but there's a warmth to it, like it was occupied recently. Perhaps Jana Air B&Bs the place out most of the year. In fact, given what a big shot and busybody Jana is, I have a hard time imagining her here at all. It seems too relaxed and warm and easygoing for her. How would she get anything done?

I'm not sure how I'm going to get anything done if I don't find a spot to write.

I leave the study and my search continues.

IT IS THE *PERFECT* SUMMER DAY.

I'm not saying that casually.

I mean, it's the summer day of your long-lost youth. It's a summer day that captures all the feelings of how the world used to be. A summer day to write about.

If this summer day could be bottled into an elixir, it would consist of a freshly-cut lawn and blossoming roses. It's the soft warmth of the morning sun as it mingles into the heat of the afternoon. It's the freshness in the air, the kind of air that has never been intoxicated with car fumes or pollution, an air of the past. It's the angle of the sun as we approach summer solstice, powerful and steeped in eons of time, igniting something ingrained in us.

To put it simply, I'm reminded of being a child again, and what those summer days felt like. There was purity and freedom and joy. So much joy as we shed our shoes and ran across lawns and through sprinklers and leaped into bodies of water.

When did summers stop being like that?

When we had to work, I remind myself. *Like you should be doing right now.*

I sigh. I should be working. Instead I'm lying by the cerulean pool and the sun on my pale body is both strong and fresh. I know I should be working on my book, not working on my tan. In fact, I had planned to get up early and get right into writing mode, but that never happened.

Yesterday after I arrived, I spent the afternoon exploring the rest of the house and the grounds. I shot Jana a quick email to let her know I got here alright, since she and I aren't quite on a texting basis yet, and she let me know that if I needed food that I could take a bike ride for about five kilometers to a country corner store, or I could just check the fridge.

Turns out she had Emilio buy me just enough food to survive a few days, including a fresh loaf of bread, butter, loads of olive oil, brown farm eggs, plus pasta, tomatoes and pecorino cheese. I happily made myself a sandwich with cheese and impossibly red, juicy tomatoes, and it's probably one of the simplest and yet most delicious meals I've ever had.

After that I grabbed a bottle of wine from the bar and then went out onto the back veranda to sit on an iron patio chair and soak it all in. Which then led me to discovering that the glassed-in atrium is actually an artist's studio, with sculptures filling the space.

I had zero idea that Jana did art. Then again, I'm discovering bit by bit that I don't know much about her at all. If that really is her art, then she's incredible. From the style I can tell that the sculptures I've seen throughout the house, and possibly the paintings too, are all done by her.

After that, I went to bed early. Perhaps the half a bottle of wine had something to do with it.

This morning I had plans to get up and write. That meant both figuring out how the espresso machine worked and finding the perfect writing spot. I wasn't able to work it, so I just settled for instant coffee I found in one of the cupboards, and I still couldn't decide on a writing spot. I put my laptop on her desk in the office and tried to get into it there, but my mind kept wandering.

I swear not all writers are this fickle. I know that Robyn was able to write anywhere and everywhere, whether it was on her phone while lining up at the bank, or lying down in bed. I have to keep to the same spot in order to set a routine, plus I need noise-cancelling headphones at the ready with a certain playlist. It sucks. I wish I was a little more spontaneous but my muse needs certain conditions to appear.

Anyway, I decided that maybe getting in a few hours by the pool would be a good idea. Refresh the batteries.

So that's where I am now. Lying by the pool, relaxed as hell and feeling guilty for it.

I sit up and wonder if I should get in the pool again. I take a look at my arms. I slathered on a lot of sunscreen so I shouldn't be burning anytime soon.

Feeling daring, I get to my feet.

The place is just so gorgeous and the sun is so hot that there's this delicious hedonistic vibe in the air. The pool is fairly large and set into the lush green grass, giving it a wild feeling. It's surrounded by a long, thick hedge that completely shelters it from the road, and down one end there's a gorgeous rose garden that I spent a good part of the morning wandering through.

Emilio said he wouldn't be back until tomorrow, which means I have the entire place to myself.

Which means I'm totally alone.

And while that made me feel a bit scared yesterday, even though I'm truly a loner at heart, now it makes me feel free.

I peel off my bikini top and fling it onto the lounge chair.

Sunbathing topless is totally expected in Italy, right?

Then I take it further and step out of my bathing suit bottoms.

Now I'm completely naked.

I giggle to myself.

I don't have a perfect body (what is that, anyway?) and I try not to look at myself in the mirror if I can help it. I know I could be leaner, I know I could have more muscle tone. I'm soft everywhere, the result of sitting on my arse most hours of the day. But here, now, my toes digging into the warm grass, the bright sunlight on my pale body, I feel more in tune with myself than I have in years.

I feel like I'm doing something dangerous and naughty and completely free, something Grace Harper of Edinburgh wouldn't normally do.

I walk around the pool, heading into the rose garden to smell some of the pink and yellow blooms at the entrance. I close my eyes and inhale. It smells like a lemon drop martini, utterly entrancing.

A *crunching* noise makes me whirl around.

I'd heard a few cars drive by earlier on the road, but I know for a fact that they can't see me. Was that noise from the road or...?

Cautiously I walk back to the pool area and step out from around the giant fig tree that lines the gravel path to the house.

There's a man standing there.

"Ahhhhh!" I scream.

"Ahhhh!" he screams.

What do I do, what do I do?

My first thought is that I'm totally naked and that I have to cover up immediately but my bathing suit is on the other side of the pool, and all I can do for now is cover my breasts and cooch with my hands, staring at the stranger, mouth open.

Then, before I can turn and make a run for the hedge or, god, something, anything, a young boy appears beside the man, staring at me with the biggest eyes I've seen.

Oh. My. God!

Without thinking, I run and launch myself into the pool, an awkward cannonball bordering on belly flop. I hit the water hard and then let myself sink to the bottom, in absolutely no hurry to surface.

Who the hell was that? Why is there a man here? And a boy. Oh my god, he saw me naked. They both did. What's he doing here? Am I in any danger? Is he here by mistake, here to rob the villa?

Eventually I have to resurface, because, you know, air.

I break through, gasping for breath, and once the water is out of my eyes, notice the man has stepped even closer, peering over the edge of the pool in concern. Guess he thought I wasn't coming back up.

He takes a step back and then motions for his son, who is still staring at me mouth agape, to turn around. Who knows how much of me he can see?

"Wh-who are you?" I manage to say, hoping they understand English, hoping I don't start stuttering.

"Who am I?" the man repeats incredulously, his brows raising. Somewhere in the back of my mind I recognize that he has perfect eyebrows, dark and shaped with a distinctive arch, a strong frame for his intense brown eyes. "You're asking who I am?"

Okay, well at least the man with the perfect brows speaks perfect English.

I continue to tread water, hoping he can't see my body clearly. To his credit, he's not looking. He seems too shocked and borderline angry to do that.

"My name is Grace Harper," I tell him, finding my voice. "I'm a guest of Jana Lee's. This is her house."

Isn't it? Now I'm second guessing everything. I mean, that was Emilio at the airport, right? He had a sign with my name on it but he never actually said his name was Emilio. Oh lord.

The man watches me for a few moments, his brows drawn together, and I can't figure out his game. Jana never said there would be any guests coming. Maybe he's a friend of hers? Perhaps even a boyfriend, though he does seem a couple years younger. Then there's the kid, who must be around ten years old, who is still facing the other way, though I catch him looking over his shoulder at me and frowning.

The kid rattles off something in Italian, and the only word I understand is *"Papà,"* so I guess this is the kid's father.

"Non lo so," the man says, and then glances at his son. He makes the gesture for the kid to turn around, which he does begrudgingly, huffing as he goes.

It's while his focus isn't on me that I'm able to get a

better look at him. The man is tall, perhaps six feet, and with a slim but muscular physique, like an athlete. His skin is bronze in the sunshine, his hair black, shorter at the sides and longer on top so it sort of flops onto his forehead, and his face is strong and well-defined like a Roman sculpture.

He's wearing dark jeans, a navy t-shirt and slip-on sneakers, with no socks. There's a large gold watch on his wrist. He seems like the epitome of Italian fashion, like he should be advertising Armani cologne or something. He's incredibly handsome, even though I push that realization to the back of my head because that's the least important thing right now.

"So, who are you?" I ask. "Unless I'm in the wrong house."

"Jana invited you?" the man asks, rubbing his jaw in frustration as he ignores my question again.

I nod. "Aye. Obviously. Or I wouldn't be here. She said to come down for a month so I can finish my book. She's my agent."

He nods slowly, realization coming over his eyes, though he still looks pretty pissed off. "I see."

I blink at him. "What do you see? You haven't even told me who you are."

"I'm Claudio Romano," he says to me with a sigh. "This is my son Vanni."

Vanni looks over his shoulder at me and says in perfect English, "And *you* are in *our* swimming pool."

THREE

GRACE

I CAN'T HELP BUT STARE, TOTALLY CONFUSED.

I shake my head and then swim to the edge of the pool, resting my arms on the grass. At least they can't see my body this way. "I'm sorry, your *what?*"

"Our swimming pool," Vanni says, louder this time, as if I couldn't hear him. "You're in *our* pool. This is *our* house. You're a ... a ... *intrusa.*"

I don't have to speak Italian to know he sees me as an intruder.

"Enough, Vanni," Claudio says. He gestures at the house. "Why don't you take your bag to your room? I'll handle this."

I don't like the way he says *handle this.* What, he's going to throw me out of the pool? Naked? I press my body even closer to the edge.

Vanni hesitates for a moment, then with sunken shoulders, walks off down the gravel path, throwing one more frowny glance at me.

"So Jana invited you," Claudio says, sounding tired.

25

"Funny, she never told me about it. Then again, I'm not surprised."

"I don't understand."

"Jana is Vanni's mother. She is my ex-wife."

I'm doing an awful lot of blinking in shock these last five minutes.

"Your ex-wife?" I repeat. "She ... she never told me she's been married. She never told me she had a son! And she definitely said I would have the place to myself. Why on earth would she leave that out?"

He shrugs. "I don't know. But Vanni and I weren't supposed to be home until the end of the month. Our trip got cut short."

"Well ... fuck," I swear. I stare at the rose garden, musing over how fast things can go from feeling free on the perfect summer day, to realizing you're intruding in some-one's actual house. "I am so sorry," I say, looking up at him. "I had no idea."

"I know you didn't," he says. "Otherwise I'm sure you would have been wearing clothes." A small smile curves his lips.

His lips.

My god, those are some pretty lips.

"Grace, was it?" he asks. I nod. "Grace, I'm going to take our bags inside. Take your time in the pool. We'll be in the house where we can talk about this further."

Then he turns and walks off, disappearing around the hedge, his footsteps crunching on the gravel path.

I wait until I'm sure he's out of sight, then I swim across the pool and quickly haul myself out of the water. I slip my bathing suit back on, which isn't easy when you're wet, then wrap the towel around me, taking a few moments to gain my breath, waiting for both the feeling of shock and embarrassment to fade.

Unfortunately, they don't. I feel like hiding out by the pool forever, stewing in my thoughts.

What's going to happen to me now? I'm going to have to leave. I can't stay here in someone else's house. I'm going to fucking kill Jana. How could she not tell me that her ex-husband and her son live here? Her *son*! You think that would have come up at some point.

Now it all makes sense. The fact that I had to be out of here by a certain date, the lack of photos of herself, which I thought was odd because her office is full of pictures of her with authors and famous people. The sculptures, the art studio, the fact that the place felt fully lived in.

How could she do this to me? The whole reason I came here was for the peace and quiet to write, not just the weather and change of scenery to provide inspiration. I get that she probably thought her ex and son were gone, but even so, that was a ballsy move.

And now her ex and son have seen my whole arse and then some. Heat flushes my cheeks and I plop down on the lawn chair, my body refusing to move. I'm mortified on every level. I can't imagine what it would feel like to come home and find someone else living in your house. In fact, I'm surprised they're taking my word for it and not calling the cops.

Unless that's what Mr. Romano went in there to do.

Shit.

Guess I better head inside and put clothes on before I'm hauled off somewhere.

I gather my towel tighter around me and slowly walk around the pool and down the gravel path, my flip flops slapping noisily. I had exited from the living room doors, so

I head up the nearest outdoor staircase, pausing halfway to notice a shiny black vintage Ferrari in the driveway. Damn. The man has money *and* taste.

I step through the glass doors to the living room and hear a commotion from upstairs, basically Vanni yelling in Italian at his father, probably about the crazy naked lady who appeared in their pool.

I need to get changed, but I also don't feel like going up to where the both of them are, so I head over to the mantel to look at the pictures again.

Now I'm looking at everything in a new light. The little lemon boy is obviously Vanni when he was younger, the black and white photos are probably of Claudio's family. In fact, as I look a little closer, I think I see the family resemblance. Those sexy eyebrows.

The sound of a throat clearing makes me whirl around, my fingers gripping the towel tighter.

Claudio is standing at the bottom of the stairs, another bemused smile on his face.

Damn, damn, *damn*. Now that we're inside and I don't have the sun in my eyes and I'm not naked, I can get a better look at him and he's somehow even more stunning than I thought.

"I certainly don't mind if you stay in your bathing suit all day," he says, his large hand palming the end of the railing. "Make yourself at home."

I flush again. I may not be naked but I'm in a small towel in his living room. At least I'm dry and not dripping onto the floor.

"I ... uh," I stammer. I gesture helplessly to the photos. "I was just looking at your photos." *Definitely not buying time because I thought I'd run into you upstairs and it would be awkward.*

"Ah," he says, walking over to me, sliding his hands in his pockets. He stops in front of the mantel and peers at it, as if he's never seen the photos before. He nods at the one of the woman in the roses. "That's my mother."

"Really? She's beautiful," I tell him. I steal a glance at him, now seeing the resemblance. He's so close that I can see his dark brown eyes are ringed with gold, seeming to glow beneath his thick black lashes.

He turns toward me, and I feel myself flush again. I didn't want to run into him upstairs while in my towel, and yet this is much, much worse.

"I better go change," I tell him quietly, quickly turning around and hurrying over to the stairs.

I head up, and just as I'm walking down the hallway, one of the doors opens across from me and Vanni pokes his head out.

"Hey," he says to me.

I stop and eye him anxiously, pasting on a smile. "Yes?"

"Are you a writer?"

Oh man. I really don't want to get in a conversation with this kid while a lot of me is still on display.

I nod and edge toward my door. "Yes."

"I ask because you said you were one of my mother's clients." He's like a miniature version of his father, although his eyes look like Jana's, so when he narrows his eyes in suspicion, the resemblance really comes through. "I've never met one of her authors."

"Oh, well." I would raise my hand in greeting except my towel will fall down and I don't need to traumatize this kid anymore. So I nod. "Nice to meet you."

"Vanni!" Claudio yells from downstairs and then says something in Italian.

Vanni rolls his eyes and then steps back in his room,

29

shutting the door. Pretty sure Claudio said something along the lines of "quit bugging your mother's client and let her get changed."

I quickly go into my room and close the door behind me, locking it for good measure, in case Vanni gets curious again and wants to ask more questions.

My heart sinks at the thought of having to leave so soon after I got here, especially after I put everything away last night, expecting to be here for a month. I'll have to do that later though.

I take out a dress from the wardrobe, figuring it's my last chance to wear one before I have to head back to gloomy Scotland with my tail between my legs. It's a spicy orange red with spaghetti straps, fitted at the bodice enough so it compresses my girls and I don't have to wear a bra, then flares out. I look myself over in the mirror, smoothing out the wrinkles, and then tie my wet hair back into a bun. I don't have any makeup on my face but it doesn't matter at this point.

I take in a deep breath but it does nothing to calm my heart, which has been oscillating between slow thumps full of dread and skips and hops fueled by anxiety. When I was young, I had a stuttering problem, which caused a lot of grief for me. Kids made fun of me, and I had no friends. I spent all my time alone, lost in books, reading or writing, creating my own little worlds. I did whatever I could not to speak up in class, where my nerves would get the best of me and the stuttering would get worse, but of course my teachers were dicks and always called on me.

That continued for a while until my father made me go to a speech therapist a few years after my parents' divorce. While my mother said my impediment made me unique, my father, who at that point had left us in Ullapool, starting a new family in London, said I'd never get anywhere if I didn't change things. As much as I wanted to fix it, I always thought that perhaps his love hinged on me being "normal."

The speech therapist changed everything for the better, though. I came out of my shell, just a little, just enough to get through high school relatively unscathed, enough to have a friend or two. My father, well he didn't change toward me at all. I'm still terrible at public speaking, which is why I relied so heavily on Robyn during our book events, and if I'm especially nervous or stressed, I tend to slip back into old ways.

And even though being here is not my fault, I still feel like I'm a burden to Jana's ex-husband and kid.

I don't know how long I sit on the edge of the bed, repeatedly smoothing out the wrinkles in my dress like it's a nervous tic, wishing Robyn was here to take charge of the situation, but eventually I know I have to go downstairs and talk all this over with Claudio. At least no cops have shown up in the meantime.

I cautiously open the door and step out into the hall, and then quietly latch the door closed behind me. The door to Vanni's room is shut. The last thing I want is to be asked more questions. He seems exceptionally bright and his English is perfect and his accent not as thick as his father's, but even so I'm unsure how to act around my agent's somewhat secret kid.

Is that what this is? I think to myself as I quietly go down the stairs, holding on to the railing as I go. *Is Jana trying to keep Vanni and Claudio a secret? Why?*

"There you are," Claudio says.

He gets up from one of the couches and comes over to me. "I was getting worried. Here, have a seat. Did you want a coffee?"

I do want a coffee, badly, and I know he'd probably make one from the espresso machine, but I don't want to be more of a bother than I already am so I just shake my head. "No, thank you." And then I sit down on the couch.

He pauses by the staircase. "Are you sure? I'm making one for myself."

Well, in that case. "Okay. Sure. If you're having one. I don't want to be a bother."

He tilts his head as he studies me, and even from across the room I can feel the weight of his gaze. "You're not a bother. You're just a mysterious stranger I found in my pool. I'll be a minute."

He goes down the stairs to the kitchen, and I immediately exhale when he's out of sight. Funny how a room can feel completely different depending on the circumstances. Yesterday I was marveling at this living room, the sculptures, the stenciled roses on the walls, feeling like a guest in a hotel given free rein. Now I feel like I've broken into someone's home.

I hear the whir of the espresso machine from downstairs, and it's not long before Claudio appears with two coffees in hand. He places both on the giant coffee table and I take an appreciative glance at his forearms and biceps, tanned and muscled in all the right ways. He must work out. A lot.

He sits down in a plush white armchair across from me.

"I'm sorry I couldn't get the right amount of crema," he says, gesturing to my coffee as he raises his to his lips. "The machine needs to be fixed."

"It looks great," I tell him, and it does look like the perfect espresso. I take a tentative sip and close my eyes in appreciation. I know the caffeine is going to make my poor heart skyrocket even more but it'll be worth it. This is *divine*.

"Now, Ms. Harper," he says, and I open my eyes to see him leaning back in his chair casually, dark eyes focused on me. "How about we start from the beginning?"

I clear my throat and get right to it. "Right. Okay. Well, as you know, I'm a writer. But more than that, I'm a writer on a deadline. There's a difference between the two. It's a pretty important book—the book that can make or break my career, and I signed with Jana because of this book. But it was only a proposal. I made the mistake of selling the idea and the outline before the book was done. Anyway, it's a new genre for me and of course Jana is my new agent, and I just need everything to go right. I've been struggling with writer's block for a while, and Jana suggested that maybe if I came here for a month I could get my writing mojo back. I'm from Edinburgh and the weather's been awful and..." *I'm lost in grief.* "...I just needed a change of scenery."

While I've been talking, Claudio has been listening intently, his brows knitting together in thought.

"I see," he says slowly and then breaks eye contact to have a sip of his coffee. It's only when he's looking away that I get a bit of my breath back. "So Jana said this place was unoccupied?"

"She just said she had a villa in Tuscany and I was welcome to use it. That's all. I swear."

He glances at me. "I believe you."

Another soft smile curves his lips, and for the first time it hits me that, wow, Jana was really married to *this* guy? He does seem a bit younger than her, in his mid to late thirties, while she's in her mid-forties. And not that Jana is bad looking or anything—she looks like Anne Heche with her sharp glasses and short blonde hair, but their personalities have to be the complete opposite, at least what I've seen so far.

"I'm used to Jana doing..." He gestures into the air with his hand. "Stuff like this, though not exactly like this. You should feel special. You're the only author to have stepped foot in here."

"None of her other clients have ever, erm, borrowed the house?"

He shakes his head, which does make me feel a wee bit special.

Then it makes me realize that she must have more riding on me than I know.

Or maybe no other author has ever struggled like you have, I think to myself.

"Vanni and I were supposed to be gone all month," he explains. "We have family friends that we go on a trip with every year. This year we were going to sail to Sardinia. Have you ever been? *Bella.* It's beautiful. Alas, my friend's son broke his leg falling down the steps of the boat, and we had to cut the trip short. The boy will be okay, but Vanni is a little crushed that our annual trip got cancelled."

"And I guess it didn't help to find a stranger in his house."

"Well, in his pool. But don't worry about him, he's nothing if not resilient."

"You speak perfect English," I can't help but say. "The both of you."

"Many Italians do," he says, almost as if he took offense to that. "It helps that we travel so much, especially when we visit his mother in London." He pauses. "So, she never told you she had a son?"

I swallow hard, feeling like I might get in trouble for saying anything. "No. She didn't. We, well, we very much have a client-agent relationship. I actually don't know anything about her and she doesn't know much about me either."

"I don't think that's so unique with her," he says. He finishes the rest of his coffee and then gives me another arresting stare. "So, now what?"

I shrink into the couch a little, hands folded in my lap. "I guess ... I go back home."

My focus is on my hands, but I can feel his gaze on me. When I finally look up, he's observing me like I'm a sort of puzzle, which I suppose I am. What to do with the writer?

"Do you think you'll be able to finish your book if you go back home?" he asks.

I shrug. "Who knows at this point? I know I won't give up on it."

He nods and then gets up. "If you'll excuse me, I have to make a call."

He starts down the hallway and I quickly yell after him, "You're not calling the cops, are you?"

I don't think he hears me though, because he goes into the study and closes the door.

Before I can dwell on it, there's a clamor of footsteps on the stairs and then Vanni bounces toward me. "You're still here."

He sits down on the chair his father was just in and takes such a similar pose that I bite my lip, trying not to laugh.

"I'm here for now," I tell him. "Pretty sure I'm going."

"Are you Irish?"

"Scottish."

"Outlander," Vanni says knowingly. "That show has got time travel all wrong. *E un peccato.*"

I can't help but frown. "The time travel is wrong?"

He nods, serious as can be. "Their time travel theory is based on timing, location, and the person traveling. There is no such thing as time traveling traits in people. Jamie Fraser can't time travel? Why not? It's not, how do you say ... prejudiced. Time travel is equal opportunity."

I blink at him, unsure what to do with that information. "So, I take it you know a few things about time traveling." I lean in, my elbows on my knees, and give him a mock suspicious look. "You wouldn't happen to be a time traveler, would you?"

I obviously don't have a lot of experience with kids, but they do like it when you humor them, right?

Maybe not.

He stares at me like I'm an idiot. "You think I'm a time traveler? *Mio dio*. No, no, *è il mio cavallo di battaglia*." He notes my blank stare. "It's my *forte*," he explains. "That's what that means. Anything about time travel, wormholes, the multiverse."

Jana's son is a Stephen Hawking in the making. Interesting.

He sits up straighter and puffs out his chest. "I am in science and physics class, three years ahead of everyone else. A thirteen-year-old level."

"That's very impressive."

"*Sì*." He sighs, sitting back. "I know." He stares off into the distance for a moment and I wonder if the conversation is over. Then he looks at me. "I hope you get to stay."

So do I, I think.

"I'm not sure that will work out," I say. "Neither you or your father were expecting me. Your mother invited me, but she didn't tell you."

He presses his lips together and nods. Perhaps his mother is a touchy subject with him.

Then he shrugs. "She's like that. She forgets things. One time I went to London by myself on the plane and she forgot to pick me up at the airport."

My eyes nearly fall out. "She what?"

"She was so sorry about it. She showed up a few hours later crying. I'd never seen my mother cry before, so I wasn't mad."

Jeez, Jana.

"Anyway," Vanni goes on. "If you stay, then I could have some company. I was supposed to be with my best friend Toni, but he broke his leg. It was kind of cool, until he started screaming, and then I realized we would have to come back home."

"You wouldn't feel weird about having a strange woman in your house?"

"You're not strange," he says. He frowns again. "I don't think. But you aren't a stranger. I know your name and what you do. You're Grace Harper and you're an author."

I'm Grace Harper and I'm an author.

Why did that sound like a lie?

Suddenly Claudio's voice booms from the office, yelling at someone on the phone.

With a sinking feeling I realize who.

Perhaps after this, I won't be an author anymore.

FOUR
CLAUDIO

"I said I was sorry," Jana snipes at me over the phone. "What more do you want, Claudio?"

She pronounces my name wrong sometimes. *Claw*dio instead of *Cloud*io, just to piss me off, and she's doing it now.

"Why the hell didn't you tell your client that you had an ex-husband and a son? I can understand me, perhaps, but Vanni? Are you ashamed of him?"

She sighs heavily, and I sink down into the chair in the study, feeling the weight of my words in my heart. I don't talk to Jana on the phone very often because it never goes well, even after all these years apart. But that's more on her end than mine. It's better for everyone if we communicate by text.

"I'm not ashamed, I merely forgot. I'm a busy woman, Claudio. It happens."

"You didn't forget," I remind her. "This isn't even your house anymore. Your name isn't on it. Any claim you had to it dissolved when we got divorced six years ago."

"I didn't think you'd be home."

"I can see that."

"Look, this girl has been through a lot. I felt sorry for her. I thought I could help her. And she has potential to go further than she has so far. She needs me to do it, and I provide the right motivation."

"Uh huh," I say, squeezing the bridge of my nose. Jana touts herself as a miracle worker when it comes to authors and deals, though this is the first I've ever heard of her feeling sorry for someone. "What happened to her?"

"She wrote with another author. Together they were Robyn Grace. Robyn died, so Grace is now on her own."

No wonder I sensed sadness in the girl. Her blue eyes don't hide anything.

"And so now her muse is gone," I say quietly, knowing all too well how that feels.

"I guess," Jana says. "Though the muse should be money. I've never understood that about you artists." She pauses. "Lucky that you don't have to worry even if your muse never shows up again."

I ignore that. She's always bringing up money, trying to see how much I'm making, even though she's doing well for herself.

"So, what will you do?" she continues. "Force her on the first plane back home?"

"No," I say slowly. "I think I need to talk to her."

"You know you would be doing me a favor if she stayed there."

"And what makes you think she wants to stay here?" I can see how spending a month at a villa in Tuscany would entice anyone, but when you realize you have to live with a brainy kid and a moody artist ... that's not what she signed up for. "We'll be a distraction."

"Well, you'll have to figure that out. Just, please, if she

wants to stay, let her stay. There is so much room there. You'll barely see her. She'll keep to herself, you'll keep to yourself. You spend so much time in your studio anyway." She mutters that last part under her breath, reminding me once again that my art takes up too much of my time. "And maybe down the line she can even watch Vanni some days. The company would be good for him."

"All right," I tell her. "We'll see."

"Great. Okay, I have to go, I have an important call in a minute."

There's always an important call.

"Okay. *Ciao, ciao.*"

I hang up the phone and stare at the desk for a moment before I get up.

I have to admit, the idea of someone staying here isn't that bad of an idea. Grace seems nice, albeit quiet and somewhat shy, though I suppose that's not strange for her profession. I don't think she'd get in the way of my work and I don't see myself getting in the way of hers either. And what Jana didn't say, but what I know, is that it would be good to have a woman around the house, for Vanni's sake. He loves his aunts, but I think he's at the age where he's getting sick of their cheek-pinching and meddling.

It doesn't hurt that Grace is easy on the eyes as well.

I only saw her naked for a moment, but the image is seared into my brain, whether I want it there or not. She's on the short side with soft curves, and this luminescent pale skin, white with a touch of peach, the kind that immediately makes me think of my art, like she's made of a marble slab before I chip away at it. Pure and timeless and full of potential. Her hair is thick and dark, the color of teak, and her face is rather unusual in a beautiful way. Full upper lip, a gap between her teeth, big blue eyes that don't hide everything that's going on behind them.

They're the eyes of an artist, that much I can see.

I slip my mobile phone into my pocket and open the door, hoping that they didn't hear any of that. I was yelling at Jana earlier, a bad habit of mine that I've tried to lessen for Vanni's sake. I'm fairly even-keeled, but my temper can get the best of me, especially when it comes to my ex-wife.

But as I enter the living room and see the grim look on Vanni's face, plus the chagrined expression on Grace's, I know they at least heard my raised voice.

"*Va tutto bene, Papà?*" Vanni asks me. *Is everything okay?*

"Everything is fine," I tell him. Grace looks so uneasy, her hands constantly smoothing out the bottom of her dress. "I just got off the phone with Jana."

She gives me a stiff smile. "I figured."

"She's very sorry about the mix-up. Sends her apologies."

Of course, that's not what she said at all. She was sorry that we came home early and ruined the little writing retreat. But I won't throw Vanni's mother under the bus in front of him.

From the way her brows pinch together, she doesn't look like she believes it either. She may not know Jana that well, but she knows her reputation at least, and Jana isn't one to apologize for much.

In fact, the more I think about it, the more I realize that the whole reason Jana probably kept me and Vanni a secret from her client isn't so much that she's ashamed of us, but that she's embarrassed. Of herself. I know she loves Vanni a lot, as much as she can, but we did have a short, albeit complicated, marriage, which then led to a divorce. Jana is all about image. Even though the divorce was amicable and wanted by the both of us, she still views her marriage as having failed, and failure is something she'll never admit to. There's too much pride at stake.

I wonder if Grace will come to that conclusion on her own.

"So now what?" Vanni asks. "Can Grace stay or does she have to go back to Scotland?"

"Grace is welcome to stay if she wants to," I say, looking at her.

She's surprised. I suppose she didn't think that would be an option.

Her forehead crinkles. "Are you sure?"

I nod. "You're more than welcome to. If you think you can finish your book here, or at least get good headway on it, then I think it's worth it. Don't you?"

"But you don't know me."

"Jana vouched for you. Besides, I'm a good judge of character." Usually. "So long as you don't mind us in your writing retreat. I'll of course be busy in my studio, and Vanni is good at occupying himself." I give him a stern look. "Which means not pestering us when we're working," I warn.

"Oh, he's not pestering me," Grace says.

I smile. "You say that because you don't know my boy. He will in fact start talking about the science behind the movie *Interstellar* when you're about to chip away at the pinky toe of St. Paul for a church's commission."

"I take it you're the one who made all this art," she says, eyeing the statues.

I nod just as Vanni bowls on through. "Have you seen *Interstellar*?" Vanni asks her. "Because if you haven't, then we need to watch it, right now, and then discuss."

"Vanni," I warn him again. "She hasn't made her mind up to stay or not, and you are not helping." I'm used to dealing with Vanni's impulsiveness and intellectual demands, but Grace isn't.

"I would love to stay," Grace says, her smile genuine this time. "But if you ever need me to leave, I will. I won't be offended. You're incredibly gracious for letting me stay here when you have every right to make me go."

I'll admit, it will take some getting used to having her here and I have to do what I can to ensure she doesn't interfere with my art. Not that I've got a handle on anything so far. I was supposed to take this month off when we were on the boat, hoping that at some point the salt air and open sea would reel in inspiration, pulling up creativity like creatures from the depths, but that didn't happen. Now that I'm back here, I have no idea how I'm going to get back into the swing of things.

It seems Grace and I might share the same struggles with a slippery muse.

"I think the only thing we need to do is lay down some ground rules," I say. "For the most part, this house is yours. I'll give you the formal tour, so you know what is what. But my studio is off-limits *if* the door is closed."

"That's the glassed-in room?"

"Yes. It used to be the dining room for the lodge. All the glass panels slide open when I need air, especially for drying, but there are also curtains I can pull down when I need no distractions. I'm sure it is the same for you—sometimes a beautiful view is more distracting than it is inspiring."

She gives me a small nod.

"We also need to find a suitable workplace for you, if you haven't already." I go on. "You're welcome to use the study if you wish. There are plenty of tables in the dining room downstairs. There's also the table outside under the pergola and one in the veranda. But if the scenery distracts you as it does me, it may not be the best place."

"I'm sure I'll find something."

"The kitchen is yours, so help yourself. Later I'll get groceries—just let me know if there's anything you need specifically. I'll be making the meals as I always do, since Vanni is helpless in the kitchen, and then has the courtesy to eat everything in sight."

"I'm a growing boy," he says with a roll of his eyes.

"You're lucky you have your mother's metabolism," I tell him. "When I was your age, I was a round little thing."

Vanni manages a rare smile and gives Grace a conspiratorial look. "I've seen pictures. My nonna still calls him *piccolo zucca*. Little pumpkin."

That boy. I shake my head, ignoring his betrayal, and ignoring the bemused look on Grace's face. "*Allora*," I say loudly. "So it goes, you are welcome to join us. We eat breakfast at nine, lunch at three, and dinner at eight. I'm quite strict with these times when we are at home, just so I can get into the right, how you say, headspace? My work requires a lot of patience and a lot of focus. I need the structure. Perhaps you are the same."

"I need *something*," she says quietly. "I would love to eat you." She stumbles over her words and blushes. "Eat *with* you," she fills in quickly. She clears her throat awkwardly, fidgeting in her seat. "The schedule might help me. Though I may ask for your help with the espresso machine. I tried to work it but I gave up pretty quickly."

"That won't be a problem. And I'm sure you know that you are free to use the bar as well. I take it that's part of the bargain when you're a writer."

Grace's cheeks flush a darker peach which makes her glow.

Hmmm. Now why do I have the urge to make her blush more often?

I clear my throat, not willing to let myself be distracted. "So, what do you say? You'll stay?"

"I'd be honored to," she says. "Thank you. *Grazie.*"

"*Grazie,*" I say, correcting her flat pronunciation. "Not so much a zee at the end, but a zee-a."

"*Grazie,*" she says, now overdoing it.

"*Grazie!*" Vanni yells.

I chuckle. "Don't worry, Ms. Harper. By the end of it, you'll be fluent, whether you like it or not."

"I could give you Italian lessons," Vanni says eagerly. "What's the point of knowing both languages so flawlessly if I can't share them?"

"I might take you up on that," Grace says to him, smiling. Her smile makes her look younger and impossibly pretty, like a living doll. "Perhaps I can teach you some writing skills in exchange."

Vanni waves her away. "Please, I am already *so* good."

I shake my head, never not blown away by my son's confidence, even in things he doesn't do well. With his love of science and his logical, analytical brain, writing and anything creative has fallen to the wayside with him. But he'll never admit it.

Grace laughs at that, her laughter reminding me of birdsong in the spring.

A peculiar feeling tightens in my chest, a warning of some kind.

Of what, I don't know.

But I hope I'm making the right choice in letting her stay here.

FIVE

GRACE

Even with all the commotion of the morning, lunchtime rolls around fairly quickly. After I was given the go-ahead to stay, I went to my room to get out of the way. Though Claudio seemed genuine in his invitation, I also know that Jana must have argued with him to change his mind. I know she wouldn't back down if she could help it, and me leaving here would look like a failure to her and damage her pride. And the thing I'm still afraid of is that Jana might want to distance herself from me, just because she's embarrassed over the supposed mix-up. She's so volatile, who knows what will set her off? I once heard she refused to take on John Grisham as a client because he called her Janet. Of course that could all be hearsay.

So, just in case, I decide to keep to myself for a while and stay out of the Italian's hair. I sit in the velvet armchair in the corner of the bedroom and take out my plotting journal, trying to force my brain to focus on the task at hand.

I have the first few chapters done and a detailed two-page outline of what happens in the story. But even with that as a guide, none of it seems to fit. It's like the story I thought of all those months ago, the story Jana sold to the publisher, isn't the story I feel pulled to write anymore.

I sigh and look over the outline, wondering how much I can change before it turns into a book they didn't agree on buying.

Here is the gist of what I have so far:

There's a woman, Annabelle, who is grieving the death of her estranged mother. She decides to travel to the Shetland Islands to learn more about her since her mother grew up there and was very secretive about her past life. Once there, she discovers a few secrets, including a half-sister she never knew, and she has a romance with a burly fisherman who gets her to open up. At the end, the burly fisherman disappears at sea, but Annabelle is forever changed for the better.

I guess what I'm caught up on is the fact that her love interest dies at the end. If it was a romance, he would live and there would be a happily ever after. With women's fiction, it feels like the more sorrow and depth the character goes through, the better, at least to the publishers. Besides, the focus of the book isn't on her love interest—he's an enigma most of the time, closed off to her and the reader. The focus is on her personal growth.

And yet, why shouldn't my character have a love that lasts? Why isn't she worthy of it? Did my book only sell because I promised that conflict and a bittersweet ending? Or is it possible that I can change it to a happily ever after? Would that cause it to lose all credibility?

I don't know anything about writing romance. In the *Sleuths of Stockbridge*, my character never had a romantic arc. Robyn's character did because she was younger, and she was often dating a different guy, but it was never the focus. I guess it doesn't help that my own love life is completely lackluster. The adage goes, "Write what you know." I always suspected that was bullshit, but I still think I'm deeply unqualified to write a romance.

A knock at the door pulls me out of my dilemma.

I sit up straight. "Yes?"

The door opens and Vanni pokes his head in, straight-faced. "Here is your first lesson, Grace. *Pranzo.* It means lunch. *Il pranzo è pronto.* Lunch is ready."

I get to my feet and repeat the phrase after him. "*Il pranzo è pronto.*"

"No, no, no," he says with an exasperated sigh. "You have much to learn."

I bite back another smile and follow him out of the room and down the stairs to the first level.

The glass doors to the backyard are open. Beside it, the door to Claudio's studio is closed. Vanni leads me outside, past the bar to the patio where the table and chairs are set, leafy grapevines growing over the pergola, giving just enough shade. The heat is in full force now, strong and heady.

The table is set for three, with a small bottle of mineral water, two wine glasses, and a bottle of chilled white wine in the middle, condensation running down the sides. My mouth starts salivating at the sight.

"Ah, you're here," Claudio says, appearing behind me in the doorway, carrying a giant bowl of salad. He places it on the table and then waves at me to sit down.

"Please sit.

I sit down beside Vanni and peer into the bowl. It's definitely not a salad you'd find in Scotland. There are big pieces of red tomatoes, onions, olives, basil, cheese, and hunks of bread glistening with olive oil.

"It's all we had left," Claudio says. "And luckily it was all we needed to make *panzanella*."

He leans over and using ceramic tongs, piles the salad onto the plates, then sits back and pours us both a glass of wine.

When he's done, he gives me an impish smile that makes him look positively boyish. "I suppose it would have been polite of me to ask if you wanted wine. I just assumed."

"Well, you assumed correctly," I tell him, lifting my glass. "Cheers to that. And for letting me stay *and* for being so understanding."

Claudio's eyes are soft as he stares at me. He raises his glass, gaze locked on mine, and I feel strangely exposed. I'm not used to this much eye contact with a stranger, and while I guess he's not so much of a stranger anymore, it still feels a lot more intimate than I'm prepared to deal with.

"It's *cin cin*," Vanni speaks up. "Not cheers. And when can I have wine, *Papà*?"

"When you can drink it and not make a face," Claudio says to him while he continues to look at me. "*Cin cin*, Ms. Harper. *Buon appetito*."

"Please, it's just Grace," I tell him, taking a sip of wine. It's so cold, and so good. "Ms. Harper makes me sound like my mother."

"You don't like your mother?" Vanni asks.

I almost laugh at how earnest he sounds. "No, I love my mother. But, I don't know, it makes me sound ... old. *Older*."

"How old are you?"

"Vanni," Claudio chides him. "That's not polite to ask."

"Why not? I'm ten. And *you* are old."

"I am not old," Claudio counters.

"I'm thirty," I tell them.

"Ah," Claudio muses as he spears a tomato and munches on it thoughtfully. "You seem both older and younger than thirty."

"That's the first time I've heard that."

"It's a compliment," he finishes. "You look young, but your eyes, they are the eyes of someone who has been through a lot, someone who is wise beyond her years."

I'm not good with compliments, and I want to correct him because wise is the last thing I feel, but I manage to shove some of the salad in my mouth, letting the flavor explosion take me away. My god, why do simple tomatoes taste so good here?

"Thirty is old," Vanni says after a moment.

I nearly choke on a hunk of vinegar-soaked bread.

"Vanni," Claudio warns him. "*Smettila*. Enough."

His son shrugs. "You're at least fifty."

Now Claudio is laughing. "Hey. What is with you? I'm thirty-six."

"Then *Mamma* is fifty."

"Your mother is forty-five." He gives me an apologetic look. "I'm sure Jana shivered just now without knowing why." I smile at the image. "She would probably kill me if I gave out her real age."

I make a motion to zip my lips. "Her secret is safe with me."

Meanwhile, I can't help but be impressed. Jana would have been, what, thirty-five when Vanni was born? Claudio would have been twenty-six. Sooner or later I'd have to get to the bottom of how they got together because there's definitely a story there. Perhaps Claudio likes older women. Maybe he's attracted to the strong, confident, and assertive types. You know, the complete opposite of me.

But asking "how did you and your ex-wife meet?" isn't

the best conversation to have while eating, so I busy myself with more food and wine, which suits me just fine.

"How are you liking the wine?" Claudio asks.

I glance up at him, and he's staring at me curiously, his dark eyes glittering as sun streams between the vine leaves, making the gold in his irises shine.

I swallow, totally aware now that I must have been making my food orgasm face. Robyn has pointed it out to me many times when I'm enjoying food I like. Pretty sure it's *not* flattering.

"It's really good," I tell him, trying to compose myself. "Did you make it?"

He shakes his head. "No. I got that from the store. I don't have the agricultural thumb that my mother and uncle had. The best I can do is keep the roses going when Emilio isn't here."

"Emilio?" I perk up. "He picked me up from the airport."

"Yes, Jana told me as much."

"He's very nice."

"He's my uncle," Claudio says. "His brother, my Uncle Giovanni, whom Vanni is named after, died. He owned this place before, when it was a hunting lodge. Emilio always has his hands on this property. He's the one who planted the olive grove and the roses. Why we call it Villa Rosa. All of this." He twists in his seat to gesture to the sprawling lawn behind us. "It was all roses. His wife, Lucia, she would grow them and sell them to the local stores. It was her way of making it feminine, to balance. She didn't like the idea of hunting. Too barbaric."

"She was right," Vanni says through a mouthful. "But she's dead now. Just like Zio Giovanni."

The boy is so blunt.

Claudio gives him a lingering look before flashing me a quick smile. I know that look. It's when you're so used to someone acting a certain way, you forget sometimes that other people might not understand.

"So, Emilio," I prompt, wanting to skirt past any awkwardness. "I guess he still loves the property if he comes here every other day."

Claudio takes a gulp of wine and I watch his Adam's apple bob in his throat, finding that strangely mesmerizing.

"He does. Sometimes he stays for dinner, sometimes he stays over after that if he's had too much wine. I'll show you his room later when we're on our tour, just so you're never surprised to see him. Otherwise he lives in the next village over by himself. He has his own plot of land, still keeps working it at his age."

I glance at him and then at Vanni.

"What?" Claudio asks.

I shake my head. "Nothing. I just find it interesting that three generations of men can have such wildly different interests."

Claudio's angled brows come together for a moment, his full lips pursed as he thinks, another distraction. Then he grins at me. "You're right. That's terribly observant."

I shrug. "One of my few gifts that only sometimes works."

"What do you mean?" Vanni asks his father.

"*Allora*," his father says, which I'm now guessing means *so* or *well*. "Grace pointed out that your interests are science, while mine is art, and Emilio's is agriculture and growing things. Of course there is some overlap."

"Yes, Zio Emilio loves your cars. And you take care of his roses. And you also make olive oil."

"Cars?" I ask.

"Sì!" Vanni says and starts to get up from his seat. "He has a car collection. They're all old and cool and expensive. You must come see."

"Vanni, sit down," Claudio warns him.

Vanni sighs and sits back down, cracking open the mineral water.

"I saw the vintage Ferrari in the front," I tell Claudio.

He nods and gestures to the next property over where there's a big barn. "That's where I keep them."

"Oh. I assumed that was someone else's place."

"No. We own about thirty acres here, though twenty of it is the woods. That barn is ... multipurpose. It's a garage for my vintage cars, a small olive oil pressing plant, while the upstairs holds all my models."

He seems to expect me to know what he means when he talks about models, so I just raise my brows. "I take it you don't know much about sculpting."

I obviously don't.

I obviously also didn't realize that being a sculptor meant you could afford this place plus a barn full of vintage cars.

"Finish up," he says to me, swallowing the rest of the wine. "So I can show you around. I'm sure Emilio didn't tell you much."

"Just that he'll be back tomorrow."

But even with Claudio telling me to finish up, lunch lingers on. The two of us finish the bottle of wine after we've eaten all the food, while Vanni tells me about an Italian scientist called Enrico Fermi and his views on quantum theory.

"One day I'll have to tell you all about Gio," Vanni says after he's talked for about ten minutes straight.

I look at Claudio for answers. "Gio?"

Claudio suppresses a smile at his son.

"Yes, Gio," Vanni says. "He's me but in another time-line. As you know now, Giovanni is my real name and I was named after my dead uncle. So, I'm Vanni and he is Gio, and we are both me."

My head spins a bit. The sun and wine don't help. "I'm sorry, another timeline?"

Vanni frowns at me. "You are familiar with the multi-verse, yes?"

"Okay, okay," Claudio says, getting up. "Vanni, this is too much for after a meal. Could you please clean up while I take Ms. Har–*Grace* on a tour?"

Vanni grumbles but says, "Yes, *Papà.*"

Claudio walks over to me and grabs the back of my chair, pulling it out.

"Thank you," I tell him, momentarily taken aback at the old-fashioned gesture, just as Vanni noisily piles the plates on top of each other. "*Grazie!*" Vanni corrects me.

Claudio puts his hand out for me, and I stare at it for a moment, admiring it, while I'm wondering what's going on. Then I put mine in his, the warmth of his palm and his calloused fingers as they close over mine causing a current of electricity to run up my arm, making me feel like I'm standing at the edge of a thunderstorm.

He helps me to my feet, which is just as well because suddenly it feels like I have no feet.

Then he drops my hand, because all he was doing was being gentlemanly and polite and oh so Italian, and starts to walk across the grass. "Come. We'll start with the garage first."

I take a deep breath before I walk after him, using the moment to get my head on straight. I'm going to be with this man for a month, the last thing I need is to have any sort of feelings, physical or otherwise, every time he's around.

I mean, he ticks all my boxes, and that's not just a euphemism. He's handsome as hell. Incredibly sexy. Built like an athlete, trim with broad shoulders, muscular and strong. Charming as sin. All of our lunch, I couldn't keep my eyes off him, and yet I had to keep looking away. He's like the sun, where giving him too much attention might be dangerous, and yet your gaze is drawn there anyway.

There's nothing wrong with admiring his looks, I tell myself as I walk alongside him. *You admire hot guys all the time.*

Though not when they're your agent's ex.

And not when you'll have to be in close proximity with them for a month.

I steal another glance at him as we walk, and his eyes catch mine. I know that for all the staring I was doing of him, he was doing the same as me, though he seemed completely unapologetic about it. Might just be the way he is.

I'm sure you'll get used to him in a day or two. Then he'll be old news.

I'm counting on it.

He leads me to a path lined with potted cypress, then through an old iron gate along the stone wall. We step into what looks to be another gravel parking lot, perhaps where guests would park back in the day, and then to the barn.

He motions for me to stay where I am and walks to the barn doors which he unlocks with a key he pulls from his pocket. Then, in an impressive display of strength, he pushes one of the heavy doors open, the muscles in his arms and shoulders popping, and flicks on a light.

"Here we are," he says, waving for me to come forward.

I slowly approach him and peek inside.

There are five cars, four of them vintage sports cars, then a modern green Range Rover SUV. The vintage cars are all two-door, one of them a convertible. I don't recognize all of them, but from the insignias I see a Maserati, a Lamborghini, and an Alfa Romeo.

"Wow," I say breathlessly. "This would be my father's heaven."

His brows raise appreciatively. "Your father likes cars?"

"Yes. Growing up he had a 1968 Jaguar and I think now he might have an Aston Martin. I'm not sure. I haven't seen it."

"You don't see your parents very often?"

"Uh, well, not really. I live in Edinburgh but my mother is in Ullapool. That's on the West Coast, the Highlands, and my father lives in London. He remarried a long time ago."

"Ah," he says.

"So this is all yours?" I can't help but ask.

He shrugs. "More or less. My father had the Maserati Ghibli there and the Lancia Stratos. He gave them to me. Has no room or no need for them anymore."

"But you collected the rest? Including the Ferrari out front?"

He nods, scratching at the stubble on his strong jaw. "I know what you're thinking."

"What?"

"How does someone in the arts afford all of this."

"You're right. I am thinking that. No offense."

He gives me a lopsided smile. "No offense taken. But it all started with my father. Have you ever heard of Sandro Romano?"

I shake my head. "I know Sandro Botticelli."

56

"Personally?"

I burst out laughing, and without thinking, I reach out and smack his arm playfully. "No. Not personally. Anyway, go on."

His grin widens, seeming to appreciate my outburst, and I have to wonder what's wrong with me, because I am definitely not one of those *reach out and smack someone playfully* people. I keep my arms and legs inside the vehicle at all times.

"Sandro Romano is my father," Claudio says. "He's a famous painter here in Italy, and I guess around the world in certain circles. His paintings are worth a lot of money."

"Oh," I say softly. "That's where you get it from."

He lifts a shoulder. "Maybe. I paint sometimes, but it looks pretty amateur, especially compared to him. He opened an art gallery in Lucca a long time ago, and now I run it. He's somewhat retired and living on the island of Elba with my mother." He pauses. "I say this for context, because if it wasn't for my father, I wouldn't have had the training and education and exposure to do what I do. And what I do is create art that people pay large amounts of money for."

He's downplaying his success and talent, attributing it to his father. "I'm sure you have talent that would have come out some other way, had your father gone on a different path. Don't sell yourself short."

Claudio runs his fingers along his jaw, pinching his square chin as he studies me. "Let me ask you something, Grace, from an artist to an artist."

"I'm a writer," I interject.

His brows raise, his face looking like I just slapped him. "*Nooo*," he says in a hush. "A writer is an artist. You don't agree?"

I shrug and look down at my feet. "Honestly, I don't feel like much of a writer right now anyway. So I definitely don't feel like an artist."

"Just because you don't feel it, doesn't mean that you aren't. Which brings me to my question. You say I am selling myself short because my father paved the way for me. This is your first novel on your own, correct? You had a writing partner before?"

I glance at him sharply. "How did you know?"

"Jana," he says.

"Oh. Right."

"Do you feel like you deserve to be where you are had Robyn not been there?"

Robyn's name sounds so foreign coming from Claudio, like the image of her, the idea of her, the ghost of her, didn't have a chance of existing here until he brought her up. Hell, for the first time since her death, I had gone more than twenty-four hours without succumbing to my grief. It feels ... wrong. And yet I know it's needed at the same time.

Claudio takes a step toward me. "I'm just saying," he says, his voice lower. "It is hard for us to own our success sometimes because we're afraid if we do, we'll lose the magic. Perhaps the muse won't show for us because she thinks we don't need her. But we do. At least I do."

I manage to look at him. "You have muses?"

"Of course. What kind of artist would I be if I didn't have inspiration delivered by some unpredictable force of nature? What kind of Roman would I be, for that matter? I have the deities in my blood, and they are elusive creatures."

I'm pretty sure Robyn was the one who supplied the muses for the both of us. Or maybe she was my muse. Maybe the two of us together created this magic that could never be bottled up or duplicated again. The thought makes my heart sink right to my knees.

"Come on," Claudio says gently. His eyes search mine as he reaches down and briefly presses his fingers to my wrist, sending another current through my veins. "I have more to show you."

He turns and I follow, my skin warm where he touched me.

SIX

GRACE

When I wake up it takes me a moment to realize where I am. Not back in my drafty flat across from the cemetery, but in a comfy spacious bed with fancy linens and morning light trying to slip through the closed shutters.

I'm in Villa Rosa.

I'm in Tuscany.

And there's a knock at my door.

I slowly sit up, wondering if it was the knock that originally woke me.

"Y-yes?" I say, clearing my throat.

"*La colazione è pronta!*" Vanni yells from the other side. "Vamoose!"

Okay, so I know what vamoose means. I lean over and grab my phone from the dresser. Nine o' clock on the dot. Claudio wasn't kidding about his schedule.

I exhale thoroughly and swing my legs over the bed, taking a moment for my brain to settle.

I stayed up late last night, which accounts for why I feel so tired.

But it was for the best reason.

After Claudio showed me the garage, he took me through an area where they do their own olive oil pressing, generally to give as gifts and sell at the art gallery, plus a small gym (which accounts for Claudio's muscles), then he brought me to the top level where he keeps his clay models and spare statues.

After that, I felt something rumble through me, like the creativity that had been percolating since I landed in Italy was finally coming to a boil.

Claudio showed me the rest of the grounds a little more thoroughly than when I was left to my own devices, telling me the history of the place, and I decided that the table in the covered veranda at the outskirts of the pool area was the perfect place to write, at least at that moment.

I went to my room, grabbed my laptop and notepad, and then hunkered down for the afternoon and evening, only going inside to get water and use the loo. I didn't even have dinner since I was running on creative adrenaline and didn't want to stop, and Claudio totally understood.

Then later, I came up here to my room and wrote until about three a.m.

Which explains why I'm both exhausted *and* starving.

I quickly slip on a pair of joggers and flip flops, pulling on a bra and tank top. The only bad thing about having two men in the house with me is that it has ruined my plans for a braless June.

The table is set up outside again, and I guess it will be the designated dining area until the weather sends us inside. It's another gorgeous day, with soft morning sunshine that hints at the heat to come.

Claudio puts his newspaper down the moment he sees me, and gets to his feet, flashing me the kind of smile that makes my head spin.

"You're up," he says. "I felt badly about getting Vanni to wake you, but I figured since you didn't eat dinner last night, you should at least have breakfast. Espresso?"

"Please," I say emphatically as I sit down and look over the spread.

The food looks glorious. Poached eggs, slices of cold cuts and hard cheeses, a loaf of crusty bread, cooked prosciutto, melon. Yesterday while I was writing, Claudio went to the grocery store and so now we are obviously spoiled for choice.

Vanni, meanwhile, is slathering a slice of toast with a disturbing amount of Nutella. He grins at me cheekily as he bites into it, chocolate smearing on his face.

"Here we are," Claudio says as he places the espresso in front of me. "I must apologize for the crema again. I'll take a look at the machine later."

"*Papà*, you've been saying you'll look at the machine for a year now."

Claudio pauses, his coffee halfway to his lips while he shoots his son a look that could kill. "Vanni," he says calmly. "Have you ever heard of the expression, throwing someone under the bus?"

"Have you ever heard of the expression, the wheels on the bus go round and around?"

I snicker to myself and both of them look at me. "Sorry. It's just, that's an old nursery rhyme."

Vanni raises his chin. He would look haughty if he didn't have Nutella on it. "It also means that you keep saying the same thing over and over again, like wheels on a bus going round and round."

"You just made that up," Claudio says, reaching forward with a napkin and wiping the Nutella off his face. Vanni squirms in response. "I have to say, it's very clever."

Vanni shrugs. "*Naturalmente.*" He goes back to munching the bread.

I can't help but be a wee bit smitten by the two of them together. They seem to have such a good, easy relationship. Obviously I know nothing about parenting, but the love between them is more than noticeable.

"Grace," Claudio says, turning his attention back to me, his eyes sharpening in intensity. "I take it you got some writing done yesterday. Your muse finally showed."

I nod as I finish chewing on a slice of melon. "I think so. I just hope the muse returns. I'm a little at a loss as to where to go with the story today."

"You're making progress, that's what matters."

I exhale through my nose. "Yeah. But I didn't do a lot of writing. It was a lot of rewriting. I basically went through and rewrote my whole proposal and outline, and then rewrote the first few chapters."

"That's not easy to do."

"No," I say, shaking my head. "And to be honest, I don't know if I'm allowed to do that."

"But it's your art."

"But someone bought that specific art and now I'm changing it."

"I see. What did you change?"

"Well, for one, my book was supposed to be set in the Shetland Islands. I've been there with my father when I was really young. It's cold and isolated and desolate. And while that setting made perfect sense for me when I was in Edinburgh, now that I'm here ... it doesn't feel right. I want to be here in person and in the book. In both worlds."

Vanni straightens up suddenly and leans toward me. "You experience both worlds too?"

I give him a pointed look. "*No.* Not like you do with

your parallel universe timelines or whatever. I mean, when I'm working, that's one world that I create, and that I occupy. And when I'm not writing, then I'm in reality. That's another world. Sometimes you want both worlds to be as different as possible. That's usually the case when, well, when you're trying to escape something. Other times, you don't want to escape. This place, here, this *is* my escape. And I want the book to reflect that, too."

"So you went from the Shetland Islands to ... Tuscany?" Claudio asks.

"They say to write what you know. I'm here right now. Why not?"

"I absolutely agree," Claudio says, flashing me another warm smile that makes my stomach flutter.

Argh. It's too early in the morning for this reaction.

"Right," I say slowly, averting my gaze. "I just don't know if Jana will agree."

"Yeah, she probably won't," Vanni admits.

Thanks for the vote of confidence, kid.

"Ignore him," Claudio says. "I'm sure it will work out. They need a book, don't they? This is the book. And whatever magic you work, they'll see that too. Have faith."

I give him an appreciative smile. Little does he know that the setting isn't the only thing that's changed. I've turned the sad ending into a happily ever after. I have no idea what I'm doing, but at least I'm excited to find out.

"Well, I know you are busy today with your writing," Claudio continues after he drains his coffee cup. "But later, Vanni and I are taking the bicycles and going to Lucca. It's not too far. If you want to join us, we have an extra bike for you."

That does sound like a lot of fun, even though my balance on bikes is chaotic at best.

You're here to work, the voice speaks up. *Not to meander around the Tuscan countryside on bikes with your agent's son and ex-husband.*

"I'll see how things go," I tell him.

But as disciplined as I try to make myself, the frantic energy I experienced yesterday as I rewrote everything disappears once I officially start on a blank page. I try writing outside, I try writing in the study, but the looming realization of what I had done and how I have to grapple with a whole new story and plot, weighs too heavily on me, and every other minute I'm distracted by the beautiful day and the idea of going on a bike ride with those two.

So, in the end, the bike ride wins.

Or perhaps my procrastination does.

I close my laptop with a sigh. Maybe a bike ride will clear my head and I can get back to it later. I bring out my phone and check my email out of habit. I expected Jana to email me at some point to apologize for the mix-up over the house, but I haven't heard from her. I guess I'm not surprised.

It's probably for the best. If I heard from her, I'd be tempted to tell her what I'm doing with the book, and if she balks at the idea, then that will send me into a spiral that I'll never recover from. I have to stick to my guns and write this book my way and not care what anyone says until it's done. I know it's either that or there won't be a book at all.

And you won't have your second chance. The world will know you were nothing without Robyn. That's why Maureen dumped you, isn't it?

I push the negativity out of my head. It's not going bike riding with me.

I zip into one of my favorite casual dresses, a knee-length red and white number with a tight bodice and full skirt, then slip on a pair of hot pink shorts underneath since I'll be on a bike. On my feet I go for a pair of beige linen high tops for traction and comfort, then I grab a crossbody purse (my notebook stuffed inside in case I'm struck by inspiration), and head down the stairs.

Music comes blaring out from the bottom floor, a familiar staccato drum beat that gets louder until I realize it's INXS "Need You Tonight."

I follow the music and find the door to Claudio's studio open, the song blaring out along with Claudio singing loudly, "I'm lonely, can't think at all."

I pause by the doorway and look in. He said I couldn't disturb him if the door was closed, but if it's open, it's fair game. His back is to me and he's grooving slightly in front of a table, a stereo on top of a sheet-covered stool in the corner of the room.

It looks less like a museum in here and more like a workshop, curtains drawn over most of the glass windows, clay stains on them. There are small slabs of marble and stone scattered around, as well as a lot of equipment, such as calipers, rulers, chisels, saws, goggles, gloves, and the like.

"So this is where the magic happens," I say, loud enough to be heard over the music. Last thing I want is for him to turn around and find me staring at him like a creeper. And I am a creeper, because he's been giving me a great view of his ass in his paint splattered jeans. The man knows how to fill them out.

Claudio turns around, but instead of looking embarrassed (I would be mortified if someone had caught me dancing and singing), he gives me an apologetic smile. "I am so sorry," he says. "Is the music disturbing you?"

"Not at all," I tell him. "Actually, I came down here to take you up on that bike ride."

He gazes at me for a moment, the smile turning soft, a wicked curve to the corner. He's got the most expressive lips, conveying so much emotion with the smallest movement. Don't mind me. I could wax poetic about those lips all day.

Save it for your book.

"I'm glad to hear that," he says after a moment, a very long moment in which he just smiles and stares at me and makes my stomach do that fluttery thing again. "I think it would be good for you. Have you been to Lucca?"

"I haven't been anywhere in Italy," I tell him. Except for Rome, but that's not even worth mentioning.

"Well then," he says, clapping his hands together. "Let's go."

"I don't want to interrupt anything," I tell him, nodding at the table.

"Oh," he says, and then steps aside to show me a lump of red clay. "I wasn't doing much. As you can see, my muse hasn't visited me today. When that happens, I put on music. Do you like INXS?"

I shrug. "I haven't really listened to them much. I'm not a fan of the saxophone." His expression crumples and I quickly add, "I *do* love 'Never Tear Us Apart.' I think it's an amazing song."

"You know they are coming to Lucca in two weeks," he says.

"Really? Who is the singer this time?"

He shrugs. "I don't know. Does it matter? They can never replace Michael Hutchence. But I may get tickets today when we go into town. Would you like to go with Vanni and I? It's for the Lucca Summer Festival. They have concerts on the weekends in June and July, big names."

"Aye. That sounds like fun."

"*Aye*," he repeats in a mock Scottish accent, which sounds funny when combined with an Italian one.

"You making fun of my accent?"

"Never," he says, his sable eyes gleaming. He steps toward me and stops, looking me over. "I like your outfit, by the way. Very cool."

I glance down at the dress and high-top sneakers combo. It doesn't really go together, but I'll have to take his word for it if he thinks I look cool. I mean, he's the one who looks cool with his paint-splattered jeans and thin grey t-shirt with a faded yellow logo on it. I can't tell if it's purposely distressed and threadbare as is the fashion sometimes, or if he's had it forever. Either way, it shows off his upper body perfectly, clinging to every taut curve. The man sure knows how to dress for maximum impact.

"Thanks," I tell him, blushing.

He studies me for a moment, eyes resting on my cheeks, which makes the burning intensify. Then he looks away and strides past me out of the studio.

Okay. That was a strange little moment.

I follow him into the dining room, and he tells me he'll meet me out front. He runs up the stairs shouting for Vanni, and I step out the main door to the gravel lot in the front. His vintage Ferrari is still parked there, gleaming in the sunshine. It's gorgeous and I find myself secretly hoping he'll take me for a ride in it one day.

Yeah, that will help. The two of you cruising around in a hot car is one step away from turning you into a lovesick teenager.

Hmmmm. Probably not a good idea.

"Here," Claudio says from behind me, bringing out two bikes from the corner of the house. "I have a bike for you. I hope it will be okay."

I head over, my shoes crunching on the gravel, and Vanni appears behind Claudio, holding on to the handles of his own bike. Vanni's bike is a cruiser which is a lot more my speed, but I guess I'll have to make do with the bigger bike that Claudio thrusts toward me.

"You can manage?" Claudio asks.

I nod, my smile tight.

"Do I really have to wear my helmet?" Vanni complains, holding it in his hands.

"Yes, you know you do," Claudio says, placing his palm on top of his son's head. "Your genius brain needs all the protection it can get, *si*?"

Vanni doesn't buy it. "Gio doesn't have to wear one."

"How do you know? Can you see Gio right now?"

It takes me a moment to realize they're talking about Vanni's alter-ego in another dimension.

"I just know these things. I feel them," Vanni says. But he reluctantly slides the helmet on and sighs. "*This* is the darkest timeline."

We get on our bikes. Mine is a little shaky on the gravel, enough that I can't get my leg around it.

"You sure you're okay?" Claudio asks me, brows together in concern.

I give him a dismissive wave. "I'm fine, I'm fine. I'll get on where it's flat."

I walk my bike down the driveway to the smoother pavement of the road, trying to hide the shame. I don't know the last time I went bike riding, but I'm obviously not very comfortable with it anymore. I hope the old adage "it's like riding a bike" is true.

Once the bike is on the flat road, it's much easier to swing my leg around and get on. Though the bike wobbles a bit as I try to peddle through and there's a terrifying moment where I'm sure I'm about to eat shit, I manage to keep myself upright.

"Maybe *she* should wear the helmet," Vanni calls out, happily biking ahead of me.

"I'm fine," I say again, louder.

With my legs slowly pumping I glide past Claudio and give him a shaky smile. "See. Like riding a bike."

Claudio pulls his aviator sunglasses down over his eyes and smirks. "You're going the wrong way."

Right.

Somehow I manage to do a wide circle on the road, wobbling here and there, and then we're all riding off in the right direction.

The weather is so beautiful, a continuation of that perfect summer day, that I can't help but beam as I ride, taking my place between Claudio and Vanni as we head down the country road, passing by rolling hills of tawny grass and grapevines, dotted with towering cypress, sprawling farms, and quaint villas.

I catch Claudio looking over his shoulder at me, and my first instinct is to stop smiling, because I feel like a kid. But he looks amused by me, so I decide to keep smiling instead. The grin he gives me back matches my own.

It's disarming enough that I turn my eyes down to the road in front of me. If I keep staring at Claudio, I'm going to fall in a spectacular fashion.

Why does that feel like a metaphor for something?

SEVEN

GRACE

USING THE BACK ROADS, IT ONLY TAKES JUST OVER HALF an hour of biking before we see the old city of Lucca rising before us like a massive fortress, just the tops of the buildings showing beyond the towering walls.

"See those walls," Claudio says, pointing to the brick ramparts. "They have been there since 1650. That's where we'll be biking."

"Up there?" I ask incredulously. They have to be at least thirty feet high.

"Don't worry, there's plenty of room."

We cross a busy intersection and then head down a gravel path that takes us to an arched gate. I can see glimpses of ochre buildings and narrow cobblestone streets full of people and restaurants, but we're heading up a path now to the top of the wall.

"And the linden trees are in full bloom right now," Claudio says as we reach the top and find ourselves on a wide path lined with benches and trees, people biking or pushing strollers past us. "They have the best smell in the world."

I'm not sure what linden trees smell like. The trees here on the wall look like old chestnut trees, but the view is stupendous, looking over the grass fields just outside the city, and then into the bustling, colorful streets of Lucca on the other side.

We bike around on top of the wall with ease, and when Claudio motions to a set of trees as we're about to ride under them, I'm hit with a strong blast of their perfume. This must be linden, a mix of honey and lemon that sinks right into me. He wasn't kidding when he said it was the best smell in the world. Somehow I know that in years to come, if I ever smell linden blossoms again, I'll be brought right back to this moment.

There are plenty of things to look at along the way, and I sheepishly stop every few minutes to take a picture with my phone, but neither Claudio or Vanni seem to mind. There's a lush botanical garden, ruins of bastions, and sprawling palazzos, in addition to all the towers and churches.

It seems we're about halfway around the city when Claudio slows and asks if Vanni and I would like to get something to eat.

I'm starving at this point (I'm still not used to these late lunches), so we walk our bikes down a path that leads into the city and lock our bikes up against a pole, while Claudio leads us into an open square.

Now this is the Italy I missed out on when I was sick in Rome, the Italy everyone is always talking about. There's a large circular square (I get that it's an oxymoron) with street musicians in the middle and restaurants sprawling out on all sides. It's so much hotter down here where this isn't any breeze or shade from the trees, and I immediately feel sweat prickling at my hairline.

"This way," Claudio says, and to my relief he leads me to the first restaurant we see. My legs feel like jelly from biking and now the sweat is causing my dress to stick to my back, the heat making my head feel dull.

We plunk down at a table at the edge of the piazza and Claudio quickly signals the waiter.

"A bottle of pinot grigio?" Claudio asks me.

I mean, I'm not used to splitting a bottle of wine at lunch but I definitely *could* get used to it.

I nod shyly while Vanni puts in an order of mineral water. Sometimes I wonder if that's just Vanni's mature personality or Claudio's parenting because most ten-year-old kids I've seen would be clamoring for some sort of sugary soda. When I was young my diet consisted of Irn-Bru that I'd sneak behind my parents' back.

I look over the menu while we wait for the wine, my attention stolen by the violin player in the plaza playing along to Metallica that comes from a portable vinyl player. He's wearing a plague mask, which somehow suits the music.

"He's good," Claudio says appreciatively. He reaches into his pocket and pulls out a ten Euro bill and hands it to Vanni. His son takes it and then runs out to the musician and stands by him, watching him play, totally into it.

"What's he doing?" I ask.

"He likes to contribute," Claudio says. "I think he feels it's his contribution to the arts, even though it's my money."

I flash him a warm smile. "That's nice." I pause. "He's a really good kid."

"He is. I can't say I take all the credit."

"What do you mean?"

He sucks on his lower lip for a moment and stares across the square. "I do what I can, but I know I could be a better

73

father. How he turned out this way, I don't know. His mind works in ways that mine never did, even now. Physics? Layers of the universe? No, I just know what's right in front of me. I have trouble understanding that enough as it is."

"You're selling yourself short again."

His lips twitch as he fixes his eyes on me. "Making art and raising a child are two very different things. Vanni is a great kid, but I know I could do more for him. It's my art that makes it difficult. You said that you are often straddling two worlds, and it's the same for me. When I'm working ... it's all I can think about. I turn into a very moody bastard, so just watch out."

I let out a soft laugh. "I'm sure being a single parent doesn't help either." I want to ask why he has custody of Vanni and Jana doesn't, since usually the child goes off with the mother by default, but it feels inappropriate considering the circumstances and I don't know Claudio well enough yet to get so personal.

"No, it doesn't," he says. Then he sets his palms flat on the table. "So, have you had a look at the menu?"

Ah. So Claudio doesn't want to talk about the single dad life. Fair enough.

I pick up the menu and decide on fried eggplant and goat cheese before Claudio makes me order a pasta dish as well. Apparently in Italy, pasta is more of an appetizer than the main dish since the portions tend to be small, which bodes well for me, since that means I can have pasta and more yummy stuff. I settle on one with pancetta.

Eventually Vanni tires of the musician and triumphantly places the bill inside the man's case before running back to us.

The wine is good, the food is great, the heat becoming something of an afterthought as the afternoon wears on.

When we're eventually done (I'm noticing Italians love to linger over their meals), we get our bikes and start riding them through the city.

For me, this is a wee more challenging since the path on the walls was wide and cool. The streets here are busy, narrow and hot, and full of restaurants and people. We wind our way past several churches and towers that Claudio points out to me, and I know my history professor father is shuddering right now because I don't know the names of any of them, then finally we come to a stop outside a bookstore.

Here's the thing about me and bookstores. I used to love them, as you would imagine. My mother used to own one in Ullapool when I was young. My father actually bought it for her after I was born, which I always thought was very sweet and romantic.

That was until they divorced and he left her with nothing, gave his new family all his time, attention and money, and my mother was forced to sell her store to make ends meet for us.

But that's not actually why they make my anxiety go up.

It's that my books can be found in those stores.

I know, I know, that's every author's dream. And as much as it was a goal post I had, a box I needed to check, I didn't realize how weird it would be until it happened. It's like I can't go into a bookstore now without wondering where my books are, what the placement is, if someone will recognize me and make me sign them. Or at least it was that way, until Robyn died.

I haven't stepped foot in one since.

"You think your books are in here?" Claudio asks me as he locks our bikes up outside. Vanni is already heading inside, rubbing his hands together eagerly. Something tells me he's heading right for the science section.

"Maybe," I tell him as he opens the door for me, the bell jingling loudly above our heads.

"Your books are translated into Italian, so they should be," he says.

I slip him a curious glance. "How do you know?"

"I looked you up, of course," he says without missing a beat.

The bookstore is bigger on the inside than it looked on the outside, but it still feels claustrophobic. Everything is a little haphazard, books shoved onto dark wood shelves, stacks of them taking up the corners. A couple of fans whir above us but do nothing to disperse the heat inside.

"Come," Claudio says, placing his hand at the small of my back. I suck in my breath, trying not to lose it over the fact that he's touching me again. In hindsight, I probably should have gotten laid before I got here because I can't keep feeling this way every time he touches me, and he's probably going to be doing a lot of that considering he's Italian, and everyone here seems very touchy feely.

With his fingertips pressing against me, seeming to burn through the back of my dress, he leads me through the nooks and crannies of the store until we come to the mystery section in the back.

"They would be here, yes?" he asks, finally taking his hand away.

I let out a shaky breath and then try to focus on the shelves in front of me.

"Aye," I say.

He goes to the shelves, his eyes skimming over them until he gets to the G section. "Found them."

Another flash of relief goes through me. There's nothing

worse than being in a bookstore and not finding your books there. You're always hit with the feeling that perhaps you're not a real author after all. I know most of us suffer from imposter syndrome anyway, so it's like a real kick in the pants, another reminder of "you suck, you're done, it's all over."

Claudio starts thumbing through them. "There are only six of them ... which is number one?"

Since I only know the English titles, I say, "It should be The Mystery of Princess Street."

"Hmmm," he muses, and I take a moment to appreciate the muscles in his back. "I don't see anything like that." He pulls one out and turns to hand it to me.

It's a hardcover, which is a nice change from the mass market paperbacks we are known for in the UK and North America, and feels heavy in my hands. The cover is glossy, and the art is of a door in the snow, which tells me nothing. "Dopo Tutto Sei Arrivato Tu," I say, reading the title. "What does that mean?"

"It means You Came After All."

I let out a laugh. "Well, that makes no sense."

If anything, it sounds a little dirty.

He shrugs. "I know. Sometimes our translations don't. I'll be right back." He then walks away, disappearing around the corner, probably going to check on Vanni.

I examine the book, feeling the thrill of having it in my hands (I have boxes of foreign editions I haven't unpacked yet) while being in a bookstore in the country of the translation. Yet my heart feels heavy as I stare at the title. And when I flip the book over to the back and see both Robyn's headshot and mine, my chest swells with grief.

"This isn't right," I whisper to the book. "You should be here." I shouldn't be in Italy at all. I should be in Edinburgh, either working at my flat, or at the café down the street, or at the house Robyn shared with her fiancé Jack. We should be finishing up on edits for the thirteenth book by now, a book we were halfway through writing when she died.

But that book will never see the light of day, because I couldn't bear to finish it on my own, even though the publisher asked me to. As a result, I had to pay back my half of the advance, which is why I'm not in the best financial situation at the moment. Meanwhile Jack, who acts as her estate, had to pay back Robyn's half.

That's probably why he wants nothing to do with me. Also probably why Maureen didn't want to be my agent anymore. She got to keep her cut, of course, but I was no longer dependable if I couldn't even finish the last book.

A presence behind me pulls my mind back into the bookstore, and before I can turn around, an arm shoots out from behind, holding a pen. Claudio is right up against my back, nearly touching me. He might as well be because I can feel the heat of his body radiating outward, and I'm immediately wrapped up in his scent. I automatically close my eyes and breathe it in. It's subtle, but it's sweet and warm ... like almonds and sunshine.

Forget the linden blossoms, Claudio might be the best smell in the world.

"Here," he says, his voice sounding low and rumbly, sending shockwaves right into my ear. "Sign them."

I open my eyes and see him shaking the pen at me. I swallow thickly. "I can't."

He takes the pen away and steps to the side to look at me closely, putting space between us. "Why not?" he asks, his eyes searching mine, once again feeling too much and not enough.

"I made a promise not to do any book signings," I tell him, giving him a guarded look.

He flips the pen around in his fingers while he scrutinizes me. "Who did you make that promise to? Why?"

"To Jack. That's Robyn's fiancé. Or ... ex- fiancé. Either way, I promised I wouldn't."

"So you're never allowed to sign these books?" Claudio crosses his arms across his chest, seemingly bothered by this.

"Well, more like I can't have a physical signing. An event. She should be there, you know? And I wouldn't want to do a signing on my own. It's not right."

He purses his lips, thinking, and then tries to hand me the pen again. "This is not a book signing. You are signing books. There is a difference. Please." He nods at the book. "Sign it."

"Why?" He's being strangely persistent.

"Because," he implores. "It is important. I want you to sign them, all of them, because these books are a part of you and any store is honored to have them. At the very least, sign this one and let me buy it."

Claudio looks so damn sincere that it's overwhelming.

"You don't need to do that," I tell him.

"You need to take pride in your work."

My brows shoot up. "Who says I don't?"

"You lack confidence."

Now my hackles are rising. "That's a pretty ballsy thing for you to say when you don't know me, and you haven't read my work."

The corner of his mouth twitches. "I am a ballsy man, that is true. But I *will* know you, and I *will* read your work. And if my assumption turns out to be false, then I am happy for it." He waves his hand at the book. "Please. Sign it."

I frown. I don't know why I'm resisting so much. Hesitating, I take the pen from him, our fingers brushing against each other in a way that makes the air around us feel hotter and heavier than it already is.

Then I sign my name.

It looks strange on the page without Robyn's signature next to it.

Lonely and wrong.

Oh.

Maybe that's what I was afraid to see.

"May I?" Claudio asks, holding his hand out. "I am going to buy it."

"Are you sure?" I ask as I place it into his hand. "I don't know what book this is. You might read it out of order."

"Then I'll get the rest," he says. He clutches the book to his chest in a gesture that makes my stomach feel alight, and then waves at the books on the shelf. "Let me buy this. You sign the others."

He leaves and I exhale harshly through my nose. Man, he is *bossy.*

But I do what he says. That resistance is still there but somehow I power through. By the time Claudio comes back, this time with Vanni in tow, I've signed them all, each one easier to sign than the last, until my name looks like it belongs in those books.

Maybe this is a part of moving on.

Maybe Claudio knew that all along.

"*Perfetto,*" he says after I put the last one back on the shelf.

I balk at the giant paper bag in his hands. "Did you buy the whole store?"

He looks a bit sheepish and he glances down at a triumphant Vanni. "He had to have some new books that came in. Who knows how I'll bike home with it all."

Vanni just grins. "I got a book about the Tipler Cylinder."

I don't know what the Tipler Cylinder is, but I have a feeling I'll hear about it.

"Also," Claudio says, reaching into the bag and handing me a ticket. "This is yours. For the concert on the thirteenth. INXS, remember?"

Not like I could forget. He only told me this morning. "*Grazie*," I say, slipping the ticket into my purse.

"*Grazie*," Vanni corrects me, even though I know I said it right.

I ignore it. "How much do I owe you?"

"Owe me?" Claudio looks borderline insulted. "You'll never owe me anything. Come on, let's go back. Emilio should be home and I need to start preparing dinner. He eats as much as Vanni does." He pauses and says under his breath, "And complains even more."

WHEN WE GET BACK TO THE VILLA, EMILIO IS DEEP IN the olive grove, tending to the trees. I'm exhausted from the bike ride, so I excuse myself to go have a nap. I end up sleeping so long that once again Vanni has to knock on my door to tell me it's time for dinner.

I get up, feeling groggy, and chastise myself for sleeping instead of attempting to write. I only just got here and it feels like the days are slipping through my fingers, and along with it, my chance to finish this book.

I slide on a pair of leather sandals and a cardigan in case the evening gets chilly and head downstairs and outside to the veranda.

Everyone is already there, Emilio and Claudio on one

side of the table, Vanni and my seat on the other. In the middle is a bottle of mineral water, plus two bottles of red wine. I suppose with Emilio here, we're going to hit the wine harder. Everyone's plate already has food on it and there's a basket with a small loaf of brown bread in it.

"Sorry I'm late," I say, and I nod at Emilio as I sit down. *"Buongiorno,* Emilio."

The old man gives me a slight smile and nods, eyes twinkling. He's wearing the same plaid shirt he was wearing when he picked me up but now it's caked in dust.

"Ciao," Emilio says.

"It's *buona sera,"* Vanni whispers to me. "Good evening. *Buongiorno* is good morning."

"Ciao is what we usually say," Claudio points out. "Much less formal."

I nod, distracted by the food. It looks amazing and elegant, even if I don't know what it is. It's also a rather small amount. "What is it?"

"It is just antipasto," Claudio says, reaching for the wine bottle and pouring me a glass. "The starter. That's mashed celery root with some asparagus, a poached egg, and those are truffle shavings."

Holy shit. My mouth is already watering.

"Please, please eat," Claudio says. "Dig in, that's the saying, right?"

I nod and dig in.

One bite and I'm already in heaven. Then I have the wine and my eyes practically roll back in my head.

I catch Claudio watching me, his eyes glinting, and I know I'm making my food orgasm face again. Thankfully he doesn't call me on it.

I finish the course in no time and then Claudio brings out the next dish, placing it in the middle of the table.

"*Pronto*," he says. It looks to be a small chicken basted in a dark sauce, surrounded by slices of pickled red onion, fennel, and oranges. The smell is out of this world and I've never seen a prettier, more elaborate looking dish.

"Grace, would you like a choice of meat?" he asks, bringing out a sharp knife.

I'm usually boring and go for the white meat or breast when I eat chicken but I say, "Whatever you think is best. I like chicken."

"Ah, but this is *cappone*," he says, flashing me a wicked smile. "The cock."

I blink, feeling heat between my legs.

"It's rooster," Vanni adds quickly. "And it's very good. Usually we eat it around Christmas, but I'm not complaining."

That makes more sense, yet my mind is wrapping around the way that Claudio said "cock," particularly how his lips looked.

Sheesh. I need to get a grip.

I busy myself with a sip of wine as he puts slices of meat and a leg on my plate.

"Go ahead," Claudio says. "Try it."

There is a teasing quality to his voice.

He's trying to get me to make that face again.

With everyone watching, I slice a bit off, rubbing it in the orange and fennel, and take a tentative bite.

Holy crap.

While I try not to let my eyes roll back in my head, I'm unable to stop from grinning. "Wow."

"Really?" he says, brows arched. "Good." He starts to slice pieces off for Vanni.

"This is *incredible*," I say through another bite. It's far more tender than any chicken I've ever had. "Are you even for real?"

"I hope so," Claudio says, his overly earnest expression making me smile. "Or perhaps I am a figment of your imagination."

Impossible. My mind could never dream up someone like him.

I turn to Vanni. "Tell me, is your father as good of a cook in the other dimension?"

"In Gio's universe?" Vanni asks. "No. He is even better."

He gives his father a pointed look. "Because in Gio's timeline, his father isn't an artist. He doesn't work at all. He has all the time in the world to spend with his son."

Oh boy. An awkward silence stretches between father and son while Emilio gulps his wine, seeming to pay no attention.

I clear my throat, hoping to smooth it all over. "If Gio's father doesn't work, then how do they make money?"

"His mother," Vanni says. "She's an agent in that timeline, too."

I want to ask if his parents are still married in that timeline, but I decide against it. That would probably be opening a can of worms.

"Well, that's not the timeline you live in," Claudio says hastily, pouring himself a glass of wine. "And in this timeline you better eat your food before it gets cold."

Vanni shrugs, seemingly unaffected, and shoves a piece of *cappone* in his mouth.

Despite that minor blip, dinner is wonderful. I savor every morsel of food (who knew fennel could taste so good?) and sip of wine, and there's still room in my stomach when Vanni brings out a wooden slab arranged with sliced fruit, cheese, and half a honeycomb, the honey oozing across the board.

When we're done, Vanni and Emilio start to bring the empty dishes inside and I'm about to do the same when Claudio comes out holding two small antique glasses of bright yellow liquid. He stands at the end of the table and motions with his head for me to get up.

I get out of the chair, leaving my cardigan behind on it since the evening air is warm, the sun close to setting. Then I go over to him, taking the glass from Claudio and raising it to my nose to smell. "Limoncello?"

"Sì. I made it myself."

That brings a smile out of me. "Of course you did. Is there anything you can't do?"

He lifts one shoulder in a half-shrug. "Probably. I'm not sure I can write."

"I'm sure you can write." I take a sip of the liquor. It's blissfully sweet and cold.

"I can't write *well*." He takes a sip of his drink, my eyes focused on his lips, the quick flash of pink tongue. He swallows, gazing at me, and raises the glass. "It's a digestif. Perfect for after dinner, along with a walk. Would you like to keep me company?"

I hesitate, though I'm not sure why. "Sure."

He picks up on it and frowns. "I'm not keeping you from your writing, am I?"

That's not it.

"Probably not. I'm not sure I'll get back to it tonight."

"Ah," he says as we start strolling across the lawn. "You work more in the morning, yes?"

"More like I need to have a lot of time prior to physically writing just to let it percolate. You know, simmer in my brain. I mean, I guess I could force it right now but..."

"But art can't be forced."

"Not for me," I admit. "A lot of authors have this ability to write on demand but that's never been my method. I don't even have a method, I just know I have to feel it, live it. It takes a lot out of me, so going into it is like going into battle sometimes."

"I know how that feels," he says. "And I'm guessing it can be a battle to be pulled out of it."

I bob my head. "Aye. If I'm into it. If I'm not, well, it's a little too easy to hit save and leave it and go and do something else. Some authors have the urge to write all the time. I find it much easier to just … not. Sometimes I think that makes me bad at what I do."

He glances at me, a look that makes me feel strangely appreciated. "I doubt that. You're just human. Every artist is different."

I try and take that to heart instead of pushing it away. I've so rarely had the chance to talk about writing that it's a relief to find someone who seems to understand.

We turn up a pebbled path that runs parallel to the villa, lined by potted lemon trees and pink oleander, and the occasional marble statue. I pause by one of them, a woman covered in roses. She's not only life-size, she looks so lifelike, as if she was once real and turned to stone, like a victim of Medusa.

"How do you do it?" I whisper, running my hands over the roses, feeling their hard grooves, the petals as smooth and velvet soft as a real rose. They seem to glow in the coral light of the setting sun.

"Do what?"

"Make *this*," I say. "My brain can't wrap itself around this kind of creation."

He has another sip of his drink and runs the back of his

hand over his lips. There's something intensely sexual about it that for the second time this evening, my body feels like it's betraying me, heat pooling inside my core.

"It's easy," he says after a moment, his gaze leaving mine and drifting over the statue. "I should say, it *can* be easy. It depends. I create statues for people, churches, cities and towns. Those are commissioned. I make replicas of other works, more or less. Those are easy. That is just based on skill. If you have the skill and the training, then it is easy to do as they say. I'll admit, easy sometimes means boring. But it's money."

"Which one was this?" I ask.

"This was for me," he says. "I have an idea and then I work with it. You know, for her, the lady of the roses, I could see her in my mind. But I was unsure of how to free her. Sometimes it's already there in the marble or the clay and you just have to unearth it. It already exists in this world and you're uncovering it. That is the best. You feel like an archeologist unearthing dreams."

An archeologist unearthing dreams. I like that.

He sighs, sucking in his lower lip for a moment. "And sometimes it's blank. You're not sure what to mold, what to sculpt. You need to create it. You need to create the idea. That can be hard. That is when you are waiting for the muse. Perhaps writing is the same?"

"Pretty much," I say as I finish the rest of the drink, a nice buzz picking up. "Sometimes the book is there, some-where, already." I gesture to the space above my head. "It's already a thing and you just need to transcribe it. You're like a medium, writing down messages from some other life. And other times..."

"It sucks."

I laugh and give him a sly smile. He gets it. It's so rare to find someone who knows exactly what I'm talking about. "Yes, sometimes it just sucks."

He tilts his head, eyes raking over my face, then raises his glass. "Here is to our muse, then. May she bless us both."

I raise my empty glass and he finishes the rest of his. He swallows and then plucks my glass from my fingers. "I shall get you a refill."

"Actually," I say quickly as he starts toward the house. "I think I'm going to make another attempt at writing tonight. I'm inspired now." Or at least determined.

His face falls slightly. "You can still have another drink for inspiration?"

I shake my head. "I better not or I'll be tempted to go to bed. But perhaps I'll have another espresso to take to my room."

"Of course," he says, and we head inside the house, the sun setting at our backs.

EIGHT

CLAUDIO

DESPITE MY BLATHERING ON ABOUT THE METHODS OF my art to Grace a few nights ago, the muse has been refusing to show her face today and every day before. Oh, she's here. I can tell. It's brewing, this need to create, even if I can't identify it, even if I can't see it. I can feel the vibrations in my bones.

The door to my studio vibrates on its hinges from frantic knocking.

I shut my eyes, drawing in a long breath. I know it's Vanni. Grace would never dare to disturb me when my studio door is closed. I've learned that about her these last few days. She knows creation is sacred. She's been keeping to herself, writing, while I've been doing what I can in here. If this was a competition between us, however, I'm pretty sure I'd be losing. She has found her muse, but mine is still shy. It doesn't help that it's my job to be a father first. Art must always come second.

"What?" I say loudly, trying not to sound angry at the interruption.

The door opens and I look over my shoulder to see my son poking his head in.

"Sorry," he says, though he doesn't *look* sorry.

"What is it? I'm trying to work."

Vanni looks at the lump of clay and the mess of sketches across the table. Generally the clay would have taken shape by now, but it's just a giant blob with my knuckle indents in it.

"That doesn't look like anything," he comments glibly, walking over.

"Because I keep being interrupted," I tell him. "What is it, Vanni?" I repeat, trying to sound more patient this time.

He throws his arms out, his head back, and wails, "I'm booooooooored."

I exhale and spin around on the stool to face him. "You've read all your books already?"

"The Tipler Cylinder is bunk," he cries out. "It's impossible, physically impossible, to create an infinitely long cylinder! In space!"

I have no idea what he's talking about, but it doesn't matter, because Vanni whines a lot when he's bored. His brain needs constant stimulation or he just sort of falls apart. This is why I wish his school stayed in session all summer. Instead, they get out earlier than they should.

"Okay, well, we can get Emilio to come over and you can help him—"

"Nooooooo." He throws his arms dramatically against the table, burying his head.

"Look, I need to create something," I tell him. "You know I do. This is work."

"Maybe Grace will pay attention to me," he mumbles.

"No," I say sharply, enough that he lifts his head in alarm. I clear my throat. "No. Grace is here as our guest."

"She's Mom's guest."

"Regardless, she is our guest now. She needs to write. I need to work."

"You weren't supposed to be working right now anyway," he points out, his fingers tracing over the abstract sketches I've made. "We should be on a boat on the Mediterranean with Toni. Like we are every year."

"Last year we were in a cabin in Austria."

He shoots me daggers. "And this year was supposed to be on a boat. But no, Toni had to break his stupid leg."

"Hey," I tell him, putting my hand on his arm and giving it a light squeeze. "That's not very nice. This isn't Toni's fault."

"It is! He's the klutz who fell down the stairs."

"You're a bigger klutz than he is."

"Am not!"

"You are. That could have been you."

His face is starting to get red. A meltdown might be imminent.

Which means I need to stop my attempt at working.

"This timeline sucks!" he snarls and then storms off.

"Vanni!" I yell after him.

I get up and walk into the house, which is a lot cooler than my studio, thanks to it being a literal greenhouse, even with the curtains drawn and panels open. I can hear Vanni stomping up the stairs to his room.

I pause and pinch the space between my brows, warding off a headache. I know how he feels, but I also need to take this opportunity to work.

But that's what being a parent is all about. The balance that keeps you running from one side of the seesaw to the other.

I do what I can to work, though my mind keeps wandering, feeling guilty about Vanni. Then my phone rings.

My sister Maria.

"Claudio," she says. "How are you?"

I sigh, finding it too hard to lie. Besides, she knows me too well.

"Uh oh. That sounds like a frustrated artist," she says.

"It's Vanni."

"I see. And you are the frustrated artist."

"I feel bad that I need to work..."

"That's what I thought. Listen, Sofia here has been moping around, bored. All her friends are on vacation, but of course I am working, same as you. But my job has reduced some hours for the summer and anyway...how about Vanni comes and stays with us for a few days? Sofia would love the company."

Maria's daughter, Sofia, is the same age as Vanni and they get along quite well, especially as she likes science and things like that.

"Are you sure?" I ask suspiciously. "Because I don't want him to get excited over nothing."

"Yes, of course."

She's agreed to come by and pick him up in a couple hours. She lives in Livorno, which isn't far.

I head upstairs to tell Vanni the news, hoping he'll be excited.

Luckily he seems to want the escape.

"Maria will take you to the fair," I tell him. "She said so. Maybe you can go for a boat ride. You might even be able to see your Nonna and Nonno on Elba. A ferry ride, that would be fun."

Vanni knows that only one of those things is likely to happen since Maria also works, but he seems happy enough to have someone his own age to play with.

I sigh, and as he starts to pack for a few nights away, I close the door, feeling the guilt throb deeply in my heart. This never gets any fucking easier. I know it was Maria's idea to pick him up, but I still feel bad that I need this time and space to work on my art.

The sound of a door creaking open brings my attention across the hall to Grace peering at me with those big eyes of hers.

My god, she's a stunning creature.

"Everything all right?" she asks quietly.

I nod, rubbing my hand along my jaw, the stubble scratching my skin. My frustrated artist beard is starting to come in, which is what happens when all my energy goes into getting a project off the ground. "It's fine." I pause, noting that she's wearing a pair of glasses. She looks unbelievably sexy in them. "Sorry, we disturbed you, didn't we?"

She shakes her head and takes her glasses off. "Not really. I was taking a break. On Twitter." She adds that last part sheepishly. "What's going on?"

"Vanni is going to go stay with his aunt for a couple days," I tell her.

Her forehead creases. "Oh. Why?"

"Maria's daughter is as bored as he is. He needs to be with someone his own age right now," I say, not wanting to get into the tribulations of being a single father who doesn't have enough time for his son. As if I don't feel awful about it already. "They both get along well, and Vanni wants to go." I glance at my watch. "He's leaving in an hour, then I'll start lunch, if you're interested."

Her eyes gleam and she gives me an enthusiastic nod. "Wouldn't miss it for the world."

Her words, plus the look on her face, makes something twitch in my chest. I've been feeling that more and more around her these last few days. My eyes are often drawn to her, especially when she's not looking, taking in every inch of her face, her neck, her hair, down to the swell of her full breasts, the dip of her waist. There's a pulse in my palms, an itch in my fingers. I want to touch her skin, feel her curves, let my hands glide over every soft part. This isn't completely sexual, though naturally it's that, too. It's not easy to ignore that my dick feels a certain way about her, that even her scent gets me hard.

But it's more than that. I have this thrumming urge to turn her into art.

Perhaps she's your muse. Perhaps she's what you have to create.

I bury that voice and abruptly turn away from her, heading down the hall and down the stairs, not letting myself glance back at her. This is the second time I've had to leave her awkwardly, as if the distance between us is the only way to get that voice to shut up.

But of course, it talks about her when she's not there.

It's not long before Maria pulls into the driveway and Vanni and I head out there to meet her.

"Thank you so much," I tell her as Maria leans out of her window. I kiss her on both cheeks, and she glares at me. "What?"

"You're lucky I live so close," she says, while I give my niece, Sofia, a wave as she sits in the passenger seat. I'd embrace her too but she, like Vanni, is at the age where they want as much physical distance from their relatives as possible.

"I'm lucky that you're so good to me," I tell her. "Veronica, Giada, they don't care."

"Hmmphf," she glowers, but there's a lightness in her eyes. "Perhaps I should have moved to Rome, too."

"Bah," I say, waving my hand. "You are a Tuscan girl."

Vanni opens the back door, throws his backpack on the seat, and gets in without saying goodbye or even looking at me.

"Drive," he tells my sister.

She is having none of it.

"Vanni," Maria says, eyeing him in the rearview mirror, throwing up her hands. "First you come in my car without saying hello, then you expect me to drive away without you saying goodbye to your father?"

Vanni rolls down his window and says, "Ciao," and then rolls it back up.

Maria and I exchange a look that says *kids*.

She gives a wave and reverses back onto the road, and then they're gone. Even though it's just for a few days, my heart is in knots over it.

I find myself wandering over to the pool, wondering if I should have another swim. I do laps for an hour first thing in the morning, and not only does it burn calories, but it puts me in a Zen-like state, letting me concentrate on the coming day.

Instead I step into the rose garden, inspecting the flowers, wishing I had a pair of shears on me to do some deadheading and snip some blooms. I'm thinking that perhaps a bouquet of them would be nice in Grace's room, when she appears from behind the building, slowly walking over to me. She's wearing a short white dress, and with the sun beaming down on her, she looks like an angel.

"Ah," I tell her, straightening up. "I was thinking about you and then you appear." I make a motion with my hands. "*Poof*. Like magic."

She gives me a veiled glance, stopping at the entrance to the garden. "You were thinking about me?"

Her tone is quiet, curious, shy. Sometimes I get the impression that she doesn't know what to think of me. Even though we've been living in the same house for nearly a week, she still regards me with a bit of distance, and I'm not just talking physical, though I have noticed that when I touch her, she tends to stiffen. I'm not sure if she's uncomfortable with me, or just people touching her in general.

I hope it's the latter, though she'll have to get used to it being here in Italy.

I step toward her and pause by a tall, flowering bush. "I was thinking these roses would be perfect for your room. Here. Come smell them."

She gnaws on her bottom lip for a moment, looking incredibly sexy, then comes over. I hold the stem (this variety doesn't have many thorns) and direct the open bloom toward her. She dips her head, closing her eyes and taking a big whiff.

"Mmmm," she says appreciatively. "Like ... tea. Apples and tea."

"This rose is your namesake."

She straightens up and blinks at me. "It is?"

"Grace," I tell her. "It's called Grace. And it couldn't be more fitting." I run my fingers along the silky petals, reveling in the feel. Each flower has close to eighty of them, giving it the appearance of a dahlia. "See how many layers it has? Like you." I pause, licking my lips. "And probably just as soft."

I knew those last words would send a flush across her cheeks, her pale skin giving way to apricot, matching the color of the petals.

She averts her eyes, studying the rose with forced concentration, and I know the compliment was a bit too much for her.

Take it easy on her, I remind myself. *She is the client of your ex-wife. She's here because of her. The last thing you need is for Jana to call you up screaming because you drove her author away.*

"*Allora,*" I say, pressing my palms together. "Are you taking a break?"

She nods, frowning. "I was hoping to say goodbye to Vanni before he left."

That makes my heart grow warm. I've gotten so used to it just being the two of us. "I'm sorry. He wasn't really in the mood. It was quick."

A wash of sympathy comes across her face. "It must be tough. You know, trying to balance everything."

"It is," I say, putting my hand at the back of my neck, trying to gather my feelings, which often feel too complicated to put into words. I'm not sure why Grace would even understand them when she's not a parent herself, yet there's something inside her that tells me she would. When I look at her sometimes, I see part of myself in her.

"If I had a kid, there's no way I'd be able to write," she says. "I'm so amazed you've been able to do what you can."

"It helps that Vanni is very independent."

"You never had a nanny?"

I shake my head adamantly. "No. I know I can afford one—my parents tell me all the time to get one. But that's not the way I want to raise him. I would rather put my art to the side and raise him myself, if I must, than have someone else do it. He's worth more than everything."

She's silent for a moment, taking a step toward me to touch the next rose. I should move backward, but I don't. I find myself breathing in, the orange scent of her shampoo mingling with the roses. My dick jumps to attention and I have to will it to back down.

"If you don't mind me asking," Grace begins, shooting me a wary look, "and please tell me if it's none of my business. I *know* it's none of my business…"

"What is it?"

"Why doesn't Jana have custody?"

I've been asked that a lot. People tend to assume that Vanni's mother is dead, and when I tell them the truth, I can see them hardening. They don't understand. Sometimes I don't either, but I'm trying.

"She did. For half a year, after we divorced. By then she had fallen in love with this other man. Her agency was just getting off the ground. She wanted to hire a nanny." Grace makes a knowing sound. I continue. "Yes. And I didn't like that. I didn't like that he was with her just so someone else could take care of him. So I asked for custody and she gave it to me. He's been with me since he was four."

Grace's nose wrinkles slightly, and I know she's probably getting the wrong idea, as most people do.

"You have to understand, Grace, that she never wanted to become a mother. It wasn't in her. I was the one who pressured her into keeping the baby. I was the one who asked to marry her. It was all me. Had I not … Vanni wouldn't be here."

"You don't regret it, do you?"

"Of course not. Vanni is my world. But I know people are quick to judge Jana, especially other women. Not saying that you are, it's just that I know Jana very well, and she's not maternal. She loves Vanni and she gives him what she can of herself, and she tries, which is the most important thing. But I was the one who wanted her to have him. I thought, naively, perhaps, that after the baby, after marriage, we would fall in love. But it didn't work that way."

"I'm sorry," she says softly.

"Don't be. It went both ways. I never fell in love with her, she never fell in love with me. We were two people brought together by accident, really, and with my upbringing, I thought I was doing the moral thing in marrying her and being a father. I had no idea that perhaps not everyone is meant to be a parent." I run my fingers over a rose petal. "I know that I *am* supposed to be a father, though. So there is that."

"I guess this makes more sense to me now," she says after a moment. "I couldn't imagine how you two got together. You seem so different."

"We couldn't be more different," I tell her. "Though we both have tempers, and that certainly doesn't help. I met her one night. I was young and I had just taken over my father's gallery. She had come in to look at the art. She was so bold and assertive. Anyway, need I go on?"

She shakes her head quickly. "No."

Good.

"Speaking of the gallery," I say, switching the subject. "How about we have lunch in Lucca again? Might as well since I would only be cooking for the two of us. Then I can show you the gallery."

Her eyes dance as she looks up at me. "Can we take the Ferrari?"

"The Berlinetta Lusso?"

"Whatever that shiny black thing you've been driving is."

"I thought you'd never ask."

A joyous smile spreads across her face. "Let me just grab my purse," she says, then runs toward the house.

I stroll toward the car, a little more spring in my step. It's silly to feel like I've been able to impress her with my car, and yet I can't deny the feeling. It's been a long time since I've had anyone I've even wanted to impress. Every corner of my life has been wrapped up in Vanni and in art, for as long as I can remember.

It's not long before she's locking the door behind her with the skeleton key and running toward the car, still smiling. If I'm not mistaken, she's added a bit of makeup to her face. She looks radiant, sexy. Of course she looked that way before too.

"Get in," I tell her, opening the passenger side door.

She gives me a grateful smile and steps in while I close the door and go to the other side.

I buckle myself in, watching in amusement while she runs her hands over the supple leather of the camel-colored interior. "This ... now this is a sexy car," she says.

"She gets sexier." I grin at her and start the engine. It roars to life, purring underneath me.

Then I'm slamming the car into reverse, whipping it around the gravel lot, and tearing off down the road.

Grace lets out a girlish yelp, immediately gripping her seatbelt as we burn it around a corner. I know I shouldn't be showing off like this, but I can't help it, especially as she's jostled in her seat and her dress rides up, showing off her smooth legs.

I try to keep my eyes on the road, though it's hard when there's a gorgeous giggling girl beside me having the time of her life.

The only problem with letting a Ferrari really open up is that the drive is that much shorter. We're at a pay parking lot outside the city walls in record time.

"So?" I ask her as we get out of the car. "What did you think?"

She laughs, a sound that makes me feel like I'm floating. "I think you're a menace to society."

Now it's my time to laugh. "Maybe. But still sexy, right?"

"You? Or the car?"

"Why not both?" I shrug.

She doesn't answer, but from the coy turn of her lips, I take it she means both.

This time I decide to take her to a different, quieter part of Lucca for lunch. We find a spot on Piazza Napoleone under the shade of a giant chestnut tree, and instead of wine, I insist she has an Aperol Spritz.

"Like all the Instagrammer influencers have," she says as the waiter plunks the orange drinks down. "Always wanted to try it but ... since I usually drink wine alone at home, that's never happened."

"Not much for the bar life?"

Her face scrunches. "No. I'm a proud hermit."

She raises the glass to her lips, and I keep my eyes glued to her, watching for her expression as she takes her first sip.

She starts smiling, then laughing, hiding her smile with the drink.

"Tastes funny?" I ask.

"No, tastes great. You're making me laugh, watching me like that. Stop it." She giggles and waves her hand in my face.

"I'm sorry. It's just that your facial expressions give me life."

She rolls her eyes and shakes her head. "Believe me, I heard that a lot growing up. No surprise that I'm a terrible liar."

"As am I," I tell her. "I don't think it's such a bad thing." I raise my glass. "So here is to that. Here is to being terrible liars. *Cin cin.*"

She composes herself and sits up primly, clinking her glass against mine. "*Cin cin.* To terrible liars."

Our eyes stay locked while we sip.

Going out for lunch was a great idea. Not just to give myself a break from cooking, but to see Grace's very expressive face as she takes in Lucca. Even when we're sitting in a comfortable silence together, her eyes are watching everyone as they walk past, always observing. I guess that's what makes her a good writer, knowing how people behave, the way they talk, the way they act. She doesn't gawk either, she's very subtle. I know she studies me sometimes in that same way.

I have to wonder what she thinks, what she sees.

I hope, whatever it is, that she likes it.

After lunch we take our time strolling through the streets, getting gelato and peering in shop windows.

I have to say, I know it's not a date but it feels like one. Or, perhaps it just feels good to be with someone that I want to be around, someone I'm increasingly intrigued by.

"Claudio," a familiar voice calls out.

I turn around to see an old friend, Marika Nespoli, waving at me from a café table, sitting alone, shopping bags piled on a seat.

"Marika," I greet her as I walk over.

She gets out of her seat, and I grab her lightly by the shoulders, kissing both her cheeks.

"It's been a long time," I say to her.

"It has," she says, wiggling her fingers at me. A diamond ring on her left hand catches my eye.

"Congratulations," I tell her. "I assume Daniele is the lucky man."

"He is," she says, beaming.

I realize that Grace has been standing a few feet away,

watching curiously and not understanding a word, so I gesture for her to come over. "Marika, this is Grace," I say, switching from Italian to English. "She's an author."

"An author," Marika says, her English fluent enough. "That is cool. What do you write?"

Grace seems to shrink before my eyes, getting a painfully shy look on her face. "It's just fiction."

I step back and put my arm around her, giving her a squeeze. "Stop being so bashful, Grace. Just fiction? You're a New York Times bestselling novelist." I look to Marika. "Us artists are so humble, aren't we?"

"You're not," Marika says with a laugh.

I let go of Grace's shoulders, wishing I could have kept hold of her for longer. If it gave Marika the impression that we were together, I wouldn't have minded.

"So, what is your author name?" Marika asks.

"Grace ... Grace Harper."

Interesting.

"I'll have to look it up on my Amazon," Marika says. She smiles at me and says in Italian, "She is very beautiful. You're a lucky man, Claudio."

I don't correct her. Because it's all true.

"We won't keep you," I tell Marika, switching back to English so that Grace doesn't feel left out. "I'll see you soon, yes? I am having a gallery night next Saturday. You should come. And bring Daniele."

"I will," she says. "*Ciao, ciao.*"

"*Ciao, ciao.*"

Grace and I walk off toward the bustling plaza around the church, Chiesa di San Michele in Foro, one of the top sights in Lucca. Away from the shadows of the buildings, heat shimmers off the white tiles and perspiration tickles the back of my neck.

"You never told her you wrote under Robyn Grace," I mention. "I take it that Grace Harper, your name, will be your pen name for your upcoming book?"

She nods, looking guilty. "Yes. I know the book isn't out yet but ... I didn't ... I wanted..."

"You wanted to be known by your future, not your past?"

"Something like that." She glances at me. "What's a gallery night?"

"Oh, sometimes I have these invite-only parties at the gallery. After hours. Sometimes to showcase new work, sometimes to have an excuse to drink around friends. I'm a hermit too, as you say, but it's good for me to be social."

She nods at that and then stops in her tracks once she realizes we're walking toward the church. "Wow," she whispers as she stares up at the white monolith that was built in the 1100s.

I'm so used to the church that I pay it no mind. "You know, you're invited to the gallery night as well," I tell her. "I'd be terribly hurt if you didn't come with me. Of course, you'll be with me at the concert the night before, so it depends whether you're sick of me or not."

Please don't be sick of me.

It takes her a moment to tear her eyes away from the massive building. "I don't have anything to wear," she says feebly.

I almost laugh. "You? You pull out a new dress every day. Don't get me wrong, I'm not complaining, but I am sure you have something. I won't take no, Grace. You're coming with me."

She just nods and then slips me a quick glance. "Marika is very beautiful. How do you know her?"

"She is my ex-girlfriend," I say matter-of-factly.

Her eyes go wide, lips pulling together to make an "O."

"A couple years ago," I go on. "She's engaged now, as you saw."

She mulls that over for a few moments. "You would have made a great couple. Both of you are so ... you know..." She gives me the once-over and gestures with her hands.

I grin. "Grace. Are you trying to say I'm good looking?"

"Only if it doesn't go to your head."

"Too late."

"So what happened?"

"Between us? It was nothing dramatic. Actually, we were pretty good together. But it wasn't meant to be."

"Why not?"

She seems awfully interested in my ex. Hopefully I won't read too much into that.

"Because of Vanni, actually."

She jerks her head back. "Really?"

I nod. "He didn't like her. I never could figure out why, but he didn't like her and he didn't like me dating her. So I ended it."

Grace continues to stare at me, processing that.

I go on. "Look, obviously I wasn't head over heels in love with her if I gave her up that easily. If I was, I would have fought for her. But in the end, my son mattered more and I had a choice to make, and I chose to make him happy."

"But you were happy with her..."

I shrug. "It's the way things are sometimes."

"Is he like that with all the women you date?"

I wipe the sweat off my brow. I can't tell if the sun is getting hotter or if the questions are getting more intense. "To be honest with you, I don't really date."

Her mouth twists in surprise. "That's hard to believe."

"Is it?" I ask. "You've seen the way I live. Where would

I find the time? Come on, let's go to the gallery before it gets any hotter."

We go toward the gallery which is around the corner from the church, and thankfully back in the cooler shade of the buildings.

The sign outside says Romano Gallery, and I push open the door.

There are a few tourists inside, looking at some of my sculptures and my father's paintings (the gallery only carries our art), and I head over to the register where my employee, Carla, is working.

"Mr. Romano," she says in a hushed voice, not wanting to alert the customers that the man who creates the art is on the premises. She thinks they'll bug me, but actually they often end up actually buying the art. As is the case here, weeks can go by without a single purchase. "I wasn't expecting you."

"I just wanted to show a friend around," I tell her in English, turning to smile at Grace.

She is a friend, isn't she?

"Grace, this is Carla."

"*Ciao*," Grace says.

"*Ciao*," Carla says warmly. She's about twenty-five, with black hair that swoops over one side, and an undercut, plus a plethora of facial piercings. She intimidates some but she's very soft-hearted. "And where are you from, Grace?"

"Edinburgh, Scotland," Grace says, her accent becoming more apparent.

"*Edinburgh*," Carla rhapsodizes with a smile. "I have been to the Fringe Festival twice already. I love it."

"Oh, I actually took part in that one year," Grace says. "Well, actually it was in university and my friend was in it. I just helped."

I let Carla and Grace talk while I walk around the space, inspecting the pieces to make sure some child hasn't been let loose in here and scribbled on my statues with crayons (that happened once), and checking to see if anything has sold. It hasn't, but I'm not too worried. Or at least, I won't be once I can create my next piece.

Perhaps it's the pressure that's causing my muse to stall.

"Is this your father's?" Grace asks, appearing beside me.

I glance up at the painting hanging above a statue of an eagle that I made. "It is an original Sandro Romano."

"It's beautiful," she says softly.

And it is. There is no denying that my father has the gift of interpreting beauty in the world. His paintings are often of flowers or the ocean, hyper realistic with pastel colors. This one is of a cove on the island of Elba. I've heard people say his work makes them feel like a baby, I guess because there's something so pure, peaceful, and soothing about looking at them. His art makes people feel cradled and protected.

However, that's not what I see when I look at them. I look at his talent and what he's been able to do, and I realize that I will never be enough no matter how much art I create. He likes to remind me that I wouldn't be where I am if it wasn't for him. He doesn't mean harm by it—he's just a boastful man, and he aims to keep me humble.

I just think it works a little too well.

Even now, Grace is staring at the painting with awe, and I have this bitter pinch inside me, almost like jealousy. It doesn't matter that I've caught her looking at my work with that same expression. I feel replaceable. Like my art is forgotten.

Or maybe I just want her to look at *me* that way.

NINE

GRACE

THOUGH I'D ONLY BEEN AT VILLA ROSA FOR A WEEK, not having Vanni around for the last two days has been weird. It's not just that I miss being around the kid, because he definitely keeps me on my toes, especially with his impromptu Italian lessons, it's that being alone in the house with Claudio has made things ... well, complicated.

There's much irony in the situation. The house should feel bigger, emptier, but instead it feels smaller and more intimate, like there is no escape from each other. Every corner I turn, I find I'm running into him, and every time he sees me, he smiles as if I'm a Christmas present under a tree. He makes me feel wanted, which, considering my upbringing, is hard to come to terms with, and when I'm not finding moments to write, he's by my side, asking me questions, becoming a constant in my days here.

Which brings me to the other irony, that he sent Vanni away so he could work with less distractions, but I'm the one who is more distracted now.

How can I not be?

I know my experience with men is quite limited

compared to others. I am by no means a virgin, but I didn't have my first boyfriend—or have sex—until I was in university, and since then there's only been two relatively long-term relationships, both of which just sort of fizzled out. I know with my writer brain I can be spacey and forgetful, and I think the guys just expected more from me. Maybe it's not in me to give, maybe it's the way I'm built. Or maybe they weren't the right guys.

Whatever I felt for them, sometimes I think it must have been love (but it's over now, ha), but I never had that jolt. I never looked at them and had my heart skip, never had the kaleidoscope of butterflies unleashed in my belly.

With Claudio, I do.

I shouldn't. I know I shouldn't. I know that encouraging any feelings toward a man that is completely off-limits is a bad idea and I've done what I can to ignore it, but it's getting to the point where it's a battle. A battle against my body. I don't want to lust over Jana's ex-husband—but I do. I don't want to feel this bubbly sensation, like my body is flowing with sweet champagne.

But I do.

And so, being around Claudio has gone from being this easy, comfortable thing, to being something heavy and weighted, strung tight as a piano wire.

Oh, who am I kidding? It was never easy around him to begin with. While his personality is charming and the way he moves through the world is so confident and effortless, from the beginning I've felt overwhelmed by this man. I feel like a shy young girl, blushing at the drop of a hat, looking up at him in quiet awe.

He intimidates me, the way he stares into my eyes, so bold, so unapologetic, so completely at ease with himself. It's like he wants me in a way I can't figure out. Sexually, yes. Maybe. I know how his gaze feels when his eyes linger too long on my chest, on my legs, on my lips. And maybe I'm reading too much into it, but it's like he wants more from me.

Like you're the art he needs to unearth.

I swallow that feeling down and focus my attention back on my work. Today I'm outside in the covered veranda, a tall glass of mineral water beside me garnished with a slice of lemon from a tree on the property, effervescent fizz emanating into the air. Dinner will be ready soon, though I've told Claudio he shouldn't have to cook for just the two of us, that I'll easily be satisfied with some wine and bread.

Last night Emilio came over, which was nice and a bit of a reprieve from the strange tension that's brewing between me and Claudio. But tonight, Claudio's insisted on cooking again.

At least my book is coming along—when I'm not being distracted. I've only written two chapters but those two chapters are symbols of the biggest hump I had to get over.

Of course, tonight I've stalled again, but it's on purpose. I think, when it comes down to it, I'm a method writer, and my heroine is facing her mother's death. I know what to pull from, I know what to write. I know exactly what she's going through. Except there's a block inside me, a wall that refuses to let the bad feelings out. I need to access them, and I know I can if I push, but I'm afraid.

"Am I interrupting?"

Claudio's voice pulls me from the page and I instinctively hit the save icon.

I twist in my seat to look at him.

This evening he's dressed in cream-colored pants and a black dress shirt, untucked, his collar open, showing a slice of bronze skin. His chiseled face is taken over by scruffy beard, the dimple in his chin barely visible. He calls it his "frustrated artist" beard, so I guess I won't see him clean-shaven until he's broken through.

He looks good with the beard. More rugged, slightly wild. Sometimes I imagine what his face would feel like on my skin, the roughness tickling between my legs.

Stop that.

"I was just finishing up," I tell him, quickly snapping my laptop shut. "Is it time for dinner already?"

He nods, jamming his hands in his pants pockets and rocking back on his heels, watching as I get up and grab my laptop, cradling it under my arm.

"Stop," he says quietly.

I halt, halfway between him and the veranda. "What?"

He holds out his palms as if he's framing me. "I wish I could paint this."

I look behind me. The veranda's ochre pillars seem to glow in the evening sun, pink oleander framing the corners.

"It is very pretty," I comment as I look back to him.

"*You* are very pretty," he says, his voice husky and low, and the compliment makes me feel as if I've become unanchored from the ground. "I wish I could paint you. Here. Just as you are."

Damn.

I smile awkwardly. "I bet you could."

Paint me like one of your French girls...

He shakes his head, his hands dropping to his sides. "No. I couldn't. I don't possess the talent. I don't even think my father does. Besides, he would color you all wrong. He would capture your softness, but he wouldn't do justice to the rest of your colors. You are too vivid, too real."

I feel the heat creeping up onto my chest, my cheeks.

The tension between us keeps winding and winding, and I don't know how to be free of it. I don't know what to say.

"You are very beautiful," he adds, and my stomach flips again. "You know that."

I want to laugh, but his eyes are burning with sincerity. "I don't know what I know."

"This makes you uncomfortable?"

I shrug, my eyes focusing on the tops of his shoes.

"Is it the compliment?" His shoes start to move as he walks toward me. Stops just a couple of feet away. "Or is it because *I* said it?"

"Because I don't believe it," I admit, looking up at him. Actually, it's both. It's all of it.

"How can you think that?"

"I don't know," I say. "I have a face like a lemon." I grab my chin. "There's too much of this."

He bursts into laughter. "A lemon? Well, then you are lucky you are in Italy. We love lemons here." He gestures with his head toward the villa. "Come on, we'll have lemons with our dinner."

He turns and starts walking, and it's only then that I notice my legs are shaking, my knees feeling like water. What is this man doing to me? Does he even know?

Dinner is as intimate as you would imagine, just the two of us sitting on the patio. But Claudio switches from being enigmatic and intense to easy and charming, putting me at ease. At least, as much as I can be at ease when I'm in such close proximity to him.

When we're done with the food, we linger over panna cotta with fresh plump raspberries, the perfect mix of creamy, sweet, and tart, and enjoy a glass of brandy-colored Amaro. Actually, Claudio seems to enjoy the Amaro—I find it horribly bitter and medicinal, but I have to admit I appreciate the buzz.

"So tell me," Claudio says, leaning back in his chair, hands behind his head, facing the lawn, the sunset reflecting on his face. "I need some good news. What did you manage to write today?"

I sip the Amaro and make a face at the taste. "I finished a chapter. I should have started the next one but ... I'm stalling."

"Why are you stalling?"

I rub my finger around the rim of the glass, watching it, gathering my thoughts. "I don't know," I eventually say.

When I glance up, he's staring at me calmly. "You do."

He's right.

"I guess ... I have to access some emotions that I don't want to face today."

"Which emotions?"

I briefly suck my lip into my mouth. "Grief."

"Grief." He surveys me, his eyes roaming my face. "Tell me about Robyn."

Just the sound of her name, and I feel the bottom drop out of my chest, my heart plunging into something cold. "What is there to say?" There is too much to say.

"How did she die?"

I think Claudio knows it makes me uncomfortable to talk about her, that it's too raw, and yet he's pressing the question anyway.

When I don't say anything, he gives me a small smile. "You can talk to me, Grace."

"Why do you want to talk about her?"

"Because she is important to you. And if she's important to you, she's important to me."

I can't help it. Tears start pricking my eyes. Ever since

she died, I've had no one to talk to about her, no one who cared. My own mother tried but she didn't understand. I think she may have thought we were lovers, but that wasn't the case at all. We were just close in so many ways. People thought I needed to get over it.

"She was hit by a drunk driver on Christmas Eve," I manage to say, my breath shaky but my tears under control. "They hit her and took off and she ... she was left on the side of the road for hours until Jack found her. They had been fighting, something stupid, like what to make for Christmas dinner, and she had gone for a walk to clear her head and ... Jack told me that he thought she went to see me. He called me, asking if she was there. When I told him I hadn't heard from her, he went out on foot to look and..."

I take in a deep breath, trying so hard to hold it together.

"It's okay to cry," Claudio says softly.

I pinch my lips together, my chin quivering, and nod. I know it's okay.

But I don't want to cry now.

I gulp in another breath, and my heart slows. I swallow. "I just can't stop thinking about her on the side of the road, for that long, all alone. People must have driven past her, the police said that she was in a snowbank and wouldn't have been seen. She died there alone. Jack found her, called the ambulance, but there was nothing they could do. Her internal injuries were too much. And still I think ... I think how could anything have been too much for her? She was so strong and bold and brash, she took on the world. Life was a ride to her, and she brought me along. And yet she died. It still doesn't seem real." I blink, looking down at my drink but not really seeing it. "How could this be real? How can this world go on without her? And how could she leave me here all alone?"

I've never admitted that last part. The feeling that she left me here. That she moved on without me. It feels selfish and wrong to grieve someone's death and yet be angry that they left.

A moment of silence passes between us, the only sound the soft chirp of the evening crickets.

Eventually, Claudio sits up straighter and lets out a melancholic sigh. "I can't pretend to know what you're going through, but I understand how you must feel. She sounded like a pretty special person. You were lucky to have had her in your life."

"And unlucky now that she's gone." I exhale noisily, feeling like I can't get enough air out of my lungs. "I don't know what I'm going to do without her. She saw something in me that no one else did. You know, my parents ... my mom tried her best as a single parent but she didn't know what to do with me half the time. My father, he never even cared to make the time. But Robyn ... sh-she cared. She gave me confidence, she made me a good writer, made me a better person."

"You didn't need Robyn to become more confident, to become more talented. Robyn was merely the artist and you were the work."

I bite my lip, trying to understand. "What do you mean?"

"You were already those things. You were like ... when I have an idea for my sculpture. You know how I said it's sometimes already formed, already existing. You already exist, Grace, you just had Robyn bring it out of you. She was an archeologist and you were the dream." A flash of intensity comes across his eyes and he looks away. "Robyn helped you realize these things about yourself, but she didn't make you. She only helped."

It feels like I have a lump of bread stuck in my throat. "But what if…" My voice sounds weak and shaky and I hate it. "What if I'll remain buried now? Without her?"

He looks to me and gives a slight shake of his head, his eyes soft. "No. You are in the midst of uncovering yourself. Right here, right now. You will discover who you are. You will flourish." He twists in his seat to face me, reaches over and places his hand on mine and just that simple gesture makes the whole world tilt on its axis, my eyes drawn to the sight of his tanned skin against my pale hand.

"I see it happening before my eyes. And it's all you." He gives it a squeeze, causing heat to curl down my spine.

Then he takes his hand away and I feel like I'm left hanging on an edge.

"Come on," he says, getting to his feet. "I know what to do."

I stare up at him blankly, my heart drumming so fast and loud in my chest that it's making it hard to think. "What to do about what?"

He walks around and pulls out my chair. "What to do about Grace Harper."

I get up, my feet feeling unsteady, and I've never felt so unsure about anything, and follow his lead into the house.

He goes behind the bar and grabs a bottle of red wine, inspecting the label before putting it back down and grabbing another. Then, having second thoughts, he grabs both, tucking one under his bicep, while grabbing two wine glasses with his free hand.

It's a beautiful sight to see.

He nods toward his studio.

"In there," he says, an order more than anything.

I feel somewhat honored to be invited into his studio, so I walk inside, looking around. Aside from mounds of unsculpted clay on the table and some sketches, there doesn't seem to be a lot of work being done in here, at least nothing more than the last time I was in here.

He places the wine and glasses on the table, right on top of the sketches, then heads to the corner of the room where he grabs an old portable stereo from the corner, then throws a sheet off a stool. With his other hand, he picks up the stool and brings it over to me, placing the stereo at the edge of the table.

"Sit," he says.

I sit down on the stool, feeling a rush of trepidation run through me.

He gives me a quick smile. "Don't look so worried," he says. He takes hold of my shoulders, his hands feeling large and impossibly strong on my bare skin, and then spins me so that I'm facing the table.

Then he pours us both a glass of wine and hits play on his stereo.

I'm not surprised to hear INXS blast out, a song I'm not familiar with.

"Ah," he says, reaching over and turning it down. "Too loud, too loud."

He leans across and grabs the first hunk of clay and drops it in front of me.

"We are going to sculpt," he tells me.

"We?" I look up at him over my shoulder as he stands behind me.

He grins, a little bit charming, a lot devious.

He places his hands on my shoulders and spins me around again, this time giving me the once over.

"You will have to change," he says. "I don't want your beautiful dress to get ruined."

I glance down at my dress. It's strapless, with pink and white stripes. I think I got it from a cheap store like Primark.

I'm about to tell him I don't care if it gets dirty, even though I'm still not quite sure what tonight is about to entail, when he starts unbuttoning the rest of his black dress shirt.

"Wha—" I say, my voice catching, unable to take my eyes away as he opens his shirt and takes it off.

Oh my *lord*.

I cough, nearly choking on my own spit since I'm salivating over him.

I know Claudio goes swimming early in the mornings, but I have yet to catch him in the act (I mean, I should, considering he's seen me *naked*, something I hate being reminded of), which means I've never seen him without a shirt, which means despite my vivid imagination, I had no idea how hot he really was.

He's ridiculously hot.

Like, footy player, movie star, rock star hot.

He's got the V on his hips, the treasure trail, the six pack, the wide, taut chest with a dusting of chest hair, the sinewy shoulders and muscular arms, and the world's most gorgeous skin tone. He's got it all and he's just standing there, like his unveiling is no big deal. He should have at least warned me.

"What are you doing?" I manage to ask.

His plush lips curve into a smirk.

"You have a problem?" he asks playfully. "Put this on over your dress." He reaches over me, placing his shirt on my shoulders, holding out a sleeve. "My shirt is already a wreck."

I glance down at his shirt. It looks spotless.

I reluctantly put my arms through the sleeves. I expect

it to feel hot and damp from sweat, but the shirt is cool, and it smells like him, like spicy almonds. I busy myself by buttoning it up, then rolling up the sleeves, averting my attention from his chest.

"You're not going to put on a shirt?" I comment after a moment, trying not to look at him.

He shrugs. "I can if it makes you uncomfortable. I often work like this. It gets hot in here, and dirty. Messy." He says *dirty* and *messy* with husky deliberation, drawing the letters out, exploring each word. I fight the urge to squeeze my legs together to quell the throbbing. "I figure, I've already seen you naked. It's only fair."

Thanks for the reminder.

"So what exactly are we doing?" My voice is practically squeaking.

"We are going to make art," he says. He perches on the edge of the stool and gestures to the clay. "Go for it."

I stare at him, agape. Go for it? Go for what?

"I see," he says after a moment. "How about you tell me what you'd like to create."

"Uh, nothing?"

"Is that so?" His brow quirks up. "If you could create anything right now, put something into this world that wasn't here before, make something exist, give birth to a creation, you wouldn't know what to make?"

I rub my lips together, trying to think.

"Okay," he says with a chuckle. "How about some wine first."

Aye. Wine. What a good distraction.

I reach for my glass and take a hearty gulp. He does the same with his and then takes out a lump of clay. I watch him as he palms it over and over again, and I can't help but imagine those same hands doing the same to my body. Then his fingers do the work, expertly pushing and prodding and stroking and...

I have another gulp of wine. The fact that he's shirtless in front of me and handling that clay like I'd want him to handle my body is too much. Add in the fact that his face is creased in concentration, his tongue occasionally sliding out of his mouth, and I'm a goner.

This was a mistake.

I mean, what am I doing here? I should go upstairs and try to write. Hell, I should go upstairs and put my vibrator to work. Anything but the torture of watching him do this.

I never thought I'd ever be jealous of a piece of clay.

Then he pauses, his fingers hovering in front of his creation. I can't tell what it is— it's an abstract oval with curved holes and slits. Naturally my mind is making it sexual.

His fingers trace over it, but he's no longer pressing hard. It's like he's thinking with his fingers.

Can you imagine what those fingers would do to you?

Okay, I'm going to need to step outside and take a breather.

As if sensing this, he leans back and turns his head toward me. "See? Easy."

I snort. "Easy? You were making love to that thing."

"Make love? I like that." He laughs. "Well, isn't that the secret to any great piece of art? You equate it to sex some-how. Sex and art are always intertwined."

"Maybe in sculpting."

"Not in writing? Aren't you writing a romance?"

"It's supposed to be women's fiction..."

"But there is a romance, no?"

"Yeah..."

He gives me a weighted look before he says, "Perhaps you need to add more sex."

"That would be a first," I say. "And anyway, that scene doesn't come until later. I was going to fade to black it anyway."

"Fade to black?"

"You know ... imply they have sex but don't actually show it."

His brows knit together in pure confusion. "Why the hell would you do that?"

"Because..." But I don't really have an answer.

Because it's easier that way?

Because I don't want to have to live vicariously through my character?

Because I don't think I have what it takes to write a convincing love scene since my own experience with sex has been ... lacking, at best.

"There is no need to shy away from it," he goes on, his voice lower. His gaze seems to bore into me. "I know perhaps back in Scotland and England things are modest, but here sex is ... well, it's more than natural. It's a way of life. It's the *joy* in life."

How did this happen? How did I end up in his studio incredibly turned on, with him shirtless, talking about sex?

I open my mouth, not sure what I can say to that, when he suddenly slaps his palm down on the table and goes, "Ooh!"

He reaches over and turns the volume up on the stereo.

I exhale internally, unsure where the conversation was going to go.

The moody opening strings of INXS "Never Tear Us Apart" fills the studio.

"You know this song, yes?" Claudio asks me. His eyes have completely lit up, looking almost manic. I nod.

"Two worlds colliding," he sings softly, more to himself than anyone. "And they will never tear us apart." Like his lyrical speaking voice, his singing voice is just as smooth. Then as the guitar hits the familiar notes, he raises his hands in the air, pausing for a moment before he plays an imaginary drum roll.

"Ah yes," he says as the rest of the song kicks in. "That right there. Goosebumps."

He grabs my hand and places it on his forearm where his flesh is raised and hot. "Feel that. Have you ever had music do that to you?"

Well, fuck. Now *I* have goosebumps.

But it's not from the song.

"You have them too," he says appreciatively, eyeing my skin. "You will see, when the concert comes, you will have them all the time."

"Can't wait," I manage to say, taking my hand away from his arm. The concert is in a week. I don't know how I'm going to survive until then. I don't know how I'm going to survive the rest of the month. Thank god Vanni is coming back tomorrow and I can go back to hiding and working. I shouldn't be alone with this man. I'm getting too confused. It's too much.

"What's happening here?" he asks, gesturing to my face. "You're thinking and it's not good."

"That's what I do," I remind him.

"And maybe that's why you can't create. You think too much."

"Well, we can't all be visited by the muse."

"Oh, that?" he asks, looking incredulous as he jerks his thumb at his sexy abstract thing. "That's not a product of the muse. That is just me messing around. That's what I do. I create just to create and then I destroy it. See?"

He reaches over and pounds his fist into the clay sculpture, flattening it, and I actually gasp at the destruction.

"What did you do that for?" I cry out.

"It's nothing," he says. "And that's how you need to go into it. It's okay to make mistakes, it's okay to not know where you are going. You can always mash it up and start again."

He gets to his feet. "Here," he says, coming over to me. He stands behind me, his hands on my shoulders and ... shit.

He's massaging them.

His touch feels hot, even though his shirt.

"First, you need to relax. You are too tense. Drink more wine."

I reach for the glass and finish it, though the reason I'm tense is because he's fucking massaging me. And I'm not about to tell him to stop.

"Okay, good," he says, and then leans down, his mouth at my ear. My eyes flutter shut, my body poised to shiver from his breath at my neck.

Dying. I'm already dying.

"Relax," he murmurs, resting his chin on my shoulder. He takes his hands and runs his palms down over my biceps, over my forearms, all the way to my hands. He guides my hands to the clay in front of me, placing my fingers along the edges, moving them as he would move.

I know there's a different INXS song playing now, but all I hear in my head is The Righteous Brothers "Unchained Melody" because Claudio is full-on Patrick Swayze right now and I'm a pixie cut away from being Demi Moore. If he starts kissing my neck, I'm going to lose it.

But he doesn't. He just stays pressed up against me, guiding my hands.

"Let me show you," he says softly into my ear, sending sparks down my spine. "Then you will know."

I try to do what he says. I relax back into him.

And the moment I surrender, the more my fingers begin to move on their own, kneading, creating.

"See," he murmurs, "you just need to stop thinking so much. Let go."

But it's too hard to let go. I cling to my worries like a battle axe. I worry about what this means. I worry about what's next.

I worry that this man might want me. And if he wants me, I don't know what I'm going to do.

Because I want him, too.

And nothing good can come out of hooking up with my agent's ex-husband. Not if I truly want to start my career over. Not if I want to stand on my own two feet. I don't care if the divorce was a long time ago, if there is no love lost between them. You don't do that. And you especially don't do that to Jana.

She would make me pay.

"Grace," Claudio says softly, pausing my fingers. "Do you see?"

I kind of zoned out, so I blink and look down at the clay.

I see a face looking back at me.

At first I don't know whose face it is. Naturally, I don't have the skill to make anything lifelike. And yet I know who it is.

It's my heroine.

"Do you see?" he repeats, and I can hear the smile in his voice.

I nod, a flush of pride moving through me, and turn my

face slightly to his.

His eyes are right there.

His mouth is right there.

It would take no effort for his head to dip down one inch and press his lips to mine.

Oh lord. He's going to kiss me.

He has to.

My eyes drop to his beautiful lips and they part slightly.

But when I look up, he's staring deep into my eyes instead, and I can count every thread of gold in his dark irises, every black lash that frames them.

"You just needed to let go," he whispers. His gaze turns hot, desire flickering across his face.

Then he straightens up. "More wine?"

He removes his hands from my arms and grabs the bottle, pouring us both another glass. With space between us, it feels like all the air has come back into the room, sobering me up a little. I sit up straight, remembering to breathe.

"Thank you," I say, grabbing the glass.

"*Prego*," he says. He sits back on his stool, hooking his feet around the legs. "Now you know how to create. Now you can do it on your own. You just needed someone to show you. Just like Robyn showed you how to be an author. Now you are an author. Just you."

I take a sip of wine and give him a grateful smile. In some ways I feel like Claudio has taken it upon himself to fix me, help me face some things about myself, help me deal with moving on.

And that's all you are to him. Just a project, something to mold. You're like another piece of clay, ready for transformation.

Nothing more than art.

TEN

GRACE

A KNOCK AT MY DOOR PULLS ME OUT OF A DEEP SLEEP.

"Grace." Claudio's voice sinks into me like I'm still dreaming. For a moment I'm confused, because I could have sworn I dreamed about him, a dream that was vague and nebulous, but the feeling still remains. The feeling of having a heart so swollen with love that I still feel it coursing through my veins, leftover fragments of my imagination.

Then the feeling turns into one of pain.

Ow. My damn head.

I sit up slowly, the room spinning slightly, and tap my phone on the side table.

Nine-thirty.

I've slept in.

"Grace," Claudio's voice comes again, soft, supple.

I could listen to that man say my name all day long.

I clear my throat. "I-I'm awake."

There is a long pause, long enough for my ears to pick up on the beat of my heart in my head, and then, "Time to get up."

I hear the floors creak outside the door as he moves

away, and my stomach growls at the thought. I sure had a lot to drink last night, though at least I remember everything.

I turn my hands over in my lap. Red clay is caked under my nails, while there are smudges of it on my arms, the clay having dried to a shade of rust.

That clay is from his fingers.

They are memories of his touch, imprinted on my skin.

I don't want to wash them off.

If I do, I might forget what it felt like to have his arms around me, to have his calloused hands hold me.

Good lord, last night was a doozy.

After our attempt at recreating the pottery scene from *Ghost*, we drank the rest of the wine and continued to work on our own stuff separately. I have to admit, it was still a lot of fun. We just talked about everything, Claudio coming through with his wicked sense of humor. We stayed up until midnight, at least, and at the end we both had created and smashed about four different works of art.

Well, at least his were all works of art. Mine were blobs and they never turned out as good as when he had his palms pressed against my hands, guiding me. Perhaps I wasn't able to let go the same way, perhaps I could only do so when he was holding on to me.

I close my eyes, my mind drifting back to how it felt. When was the last time I had someone touch me like that? I've been starved for affection for far too long. Now that I've had a taste of it, I'm craving it.

I'm craving him.

This isn't good.

I get up, slip on joggers and a t-shirt, not bothering with a bra, and then head down stairs. I'm bleary-eyed by the time I get to the bottom floor, almost running right into

Claudio who is standing in the middle of the room, wearing a fucking *Speedo*, holding a couple of towels.

"Catch," he says, throwing a towel at me.

The towel whacks me in the face and falls to the floor. I'm too stunned by the Speedo, to be honest. I mean, it's black and it looks fucking amazing on him, something I never thought was possible, but also, what the fuck?

"We're going swimming," he says.

I blink at him, finally snapping out of it enough to bend down and pick up the towel. "What?"

"Come on." He nods to the front door.

I wave at the back door to the patio. "But breakfast?"

He grins, shrugs like he doesn't make the rules. "I slept in and missed my swim. I can't start breakfast until I go swimming. That's the schedule."

"But why do I have to go?"

"What do you have against swimming? I saw you do it before."

I ignore that. "Besides," he adds, "it will make you feel better. I know you're hungover, too. You got me drunk last night."

My eyes bug out. "I did not! You got *me* drunk!"

Another sly grin, another quick shrug. "Whatever you say, naked girl."

"Naked girl? Is that my nickname now?"

"If you keep it up, maybe?"

I groan. "Let me go get my bathing suit."

"Go in your underwear."

"I'm not wearing a bra."

His eyes move to my chest. He raises a brow. "That's not a problem. One step closer to naked girl."

"I'm going to go get my suit."

He gives me a wry smile. "I'll be by the pool."

He turns and walks to the front door, and I take a millisecond to appreciate his damn fine arse, before I go running up the stairs to my room. I quickly slip on my bikini, a red high-waisted one, then go back down and outside.

Claudio is already in the pool, doing laps back and forth in the crystalline blue water. The birds are chirping softly from the trees, the morning sun soft and hot, the air fragrant with the opening roses.

I throw my towel down on the lawn chair beside his and sit down on the edge of it, watching his body cut through the water. The muscles in his back and arms are strong and rippling, his skin looks extra dark against the crisp light blue, and he moves like a shark, smooth and calculated. The way he slices through the water reminds me of the way he is out of water, both at ease and in control.

Eventually he pulls up at the end of the pool and looks at me, water dripping down his face. "What are you doing?"

"Watching you," I admit.

His face lights up playfully. "Is that so?" He starts swimming toward me and pauses at the edge right in front of my chair, a lock of black hair stuck to his forehead. "And do you like what you see?"

Oh, how do I answer this?

I could tell him yes.

But that would be too bold, too bare. I don't have it in me.

I decide to hedge it. "You look like a professional. Did you ever swim on a team?"

His eyes narrow thoughtfully at me and he spits out water. "No. But I did spend my youth swimming off of Elba. My parents' house is right on the beach. The water is beautiful." He pauses, licking his lips. "I should take you there."

My heart feels like it stutters. I swallow. "To Elba?"

"Yes. You can meet my parents."

Oh shit.

"They would love to meet an author," he goes on.

"I should probably stay here and write," I manage to say even though there's a voice buried deep inside me that's yelling at me, that I should say yes, that oh my god, why am I passing this up?

"I see." He gives me a small smile but it's not hard to see that he's disappointed. "I suppose if I'm already dragging you to a concert, then gallery night, that's a lot of time spent with me. I can't blame you for being sick of me."

"I'm not sick of you," I say quickly. "Not even a little."

He seems skeptical. "Are you sure? I do realize that when you planned to come here, you weren't planning on being around someone else all the time. I more than understand that you need space."

"I don't need space." I mean, I kind of do, because I need to write, but shit, I also *want* to be around him too. I need it.

I'm a mess.

All I know is if I go away with him somewhere ... I don't know. Here, I'm barely holding on. It feels like I'm constantly skirting the edge, and one wrong turn and right look and I'm going to go over. He's making it hard to breathe properly, to think properly, and I barely have my wits about me. The only thing I have is this villa, a sense of structure. If I go away with him, I'm afraid I'll fully let go.

You're assuming he wants to sleep with you, the voice tells me. *He's Italian. He might be that way with everyone. You might be getting the entirely wrong idea, and then how embarrassed are you going to be when you throw yourself at him?*

"Grace," Claudio says. "Get in the pool."

I realize I've been staring at him like an idiot the whole time my mind has been tripping over itself and going in circles. Suddenly the pool seems too small for the both of us.

"Grace," he says again, a warning tone. He lifts himself out of the pool with ease, the water sliding off his body, and walks toward me, his hand out. "Get in the pool."

I stare up at him. "I-I'm fine."

"You're doing that thing again," he says, shaking his head in disapproval. "The thing with the thoughts. What did I tell you about letting go?"

Don't let go, don't let go.

He reaches down and grabs me around the waist.

I yelp, and before I know what's happening, he's hoisting me up and carrying me over to the edge of the pool, my legs dangling in the air.

"Oh my god, Claudio!" I yell, laughing at the same time. "Put me down!"

"Okay," he says simply.

With one easy motion he throws me in the pool. I hit the water with a giant splash, then hear Claudio diving into the water next to me.

I burst through the surface, gasping for breath, and see him treading water, grinning at me.

"You arse!" I yell, doing a haphazard swim toward him, splashing water.

He raises his hand to shield himself from the splashes, laughing. "Arse! That's a new one. I have been called an ass before, never an arse. I am honored."

131

"You shouldn't be!" I splash him again. "I could have drowned."

"I would have rescued you."

"I don't need rescuing," I tell him, the words coming out harsher than I meant. I swallow. "I'm going to get you back for this."

His right eyebrow raises. How does he do that? "Hmmm," he muses. "You are a murder mystery writer, perhaps I should be worried."

"Aye, you should be. Lock your door when you go to sleep tonight."

I turn around and swim for the shallow end until I feel the bottom beneath my feet, then twist so I'm facing him.

He stays where he is, treading water, and damn it, I wish he didn't look so damn sexy right now. "I will lock my door, but not because of you. We have guests tonight."

I stare. This is the first I'm hearing of this.

"My sisters," he goes on. "I just talked to them this morning. Giada and Veronica, they live in Rome. They're driving up today to see Maria. All three will come over here for dinner when Maria brings Vanni back. They'll be staying overnight, but as you can see, there is plenty of room."

He must read the anxious look on my face because he adds, "Don't worry, you'll like them. They are very nice. I mean, they will be nice to you. Not to me. See, I am the youngest, the baby, and they never let me forget that."

I smile at the idea of Claudio being bossed around by three older sisters.

"Ah, see," he says, splashing water toward me. "I told you you'd like them. I have no doubt the four of you will gang up on me. Even Vanni won't come to my side."

"I'm sure you can handle yourself just fine," I tell him.

He starts swimming past me for the stairs and pulls himself up. "Sure, but that is a given," he says. He picks up a towel and starts toweling himself off, patting it over his thick, muscular thighs, his rippled abs, his sculpted shoulders.

And I do the pervy thing and watch him do it.

Fuck it.

If he's going to look like that, then my leering gaze is what he's going to get. It's only when my eyes start focusing on the thin quality of his Speedo and the flattering outline of his dick, that I realize it might be a bit much.

He stands at the edge of the pool and gazes down at me through heavy lids. "Do you still like what you see?" he asks me. There's a husky quality to his voice, all playfulness fading away.

This time he means it.

I just stare up at him for a moment.

I'm sure I'm saying it all with my eyes.

Then I dive under the water and swim nearly the whole length of the pool holding my breath.

When I pop back up, he's gone.

THE DAY PASSES BY SLOWLY. AFTER THE SWIM, AND breakfast, Claudio locked himself in the studio, the door closed. I took that as a sign to leave him alone and try to get my own head on straight. So I took my laptop to the study, wanting zero distractions. Writing outside is lovely, but too many times I find my attention being stolen by the birds or the smell of flowers and that pull to just wander through the rose garden, marveling at things.

Today I really wanted to put in the work. And though it

was hard at first to push Claudio out of my mind, I did. I tackled the scenes with my heroine, made her face her mother's death, and cried my eyes out. It was hard, and my soul felt like it was bled and smeared on the computer screen, but in the end I felt like a weight had lifted. It was cathartic, and more than that, it gave me confidence. If I could write that difficult scene, then surely I could tackle the rest.

Lunch was quick, and Claudio was both jovial and serious, his moods flitting between both. We had minestrone soup and crusty bread with olive oil, nothing too fancy, but satisfying all the same. Then we both went our separate ways for a few hours until I heard a bunch of shouting reverberating through the house, and I knew his sisters and Vanni had arrived.

I smile to myself. It was only me growing up, so I missed out on having that big family with lots of siblings. When my father remarried and had a daughter with his new wife, I thought things would change. But my half-sister Beth doesn't want anything to do with me, no matter how hard I try, so that didn't work out the way I hoped it would. I still have faith that when she's older (she's thirteen and going through stuff) that we'll finally have a chance to connect.

Regardless, I'm excited for the new distractions. Things got kind of weird at the pool, so the more people in the house, the better.

Especially people who know Claudio well. I want to learn everything there is about him, what he was like growing up, if there is indeed something that magic man can't do. I want the dirt. I want to know it all.

I get off my bed where I was working through some plot holes in my notebook, and get dressed. I pick—surprise— another dress, this one white with short sleeves, buttons down the middle, and oranges printed on it. I pull my hair back into a low ponytail, then slide on an orange headband. I've got this 60's Italian chic thing going on, so I play that up with my makeup, a wee bit of winged liner and mascara, a touch of blush. I look half-decent, even with my lemon face.

Of course, there's no point in denying that I'm not only looking good for Claudio, but for his sisters. I want them to say "who is that girl?" although that might be pointless considering the women that Claudio dates. I know he said he doesn't have time to date anymore, but that woman, the ex of his, Marika, was stunning. Perhaps he's known for dating tall, tanned and leggy blondes, basically everything I'm not.

Well you're not dating him, so why does it even matter? I tell myself.

The thing is, I can tell myself things, but it doesn't mean I'll believe it.

Even if Claudio tells me things.

Even if he says that I'm beautiful.

The thought makes something flicker deep inside me.

Hope, maybe.

I head out of the room and down the stairs, the yelling getting louder and louder.

"Grace! *Ciao, ciao!*" Vanni yells at me as he turns the corner on the second floor, racing past me on the stairs with his backpack. He's followed by a blonde girl in a pink romper, who gives me a shy look while running up the stairs after him. I'm assuming that's his cousin.

They disappear up the steps and I steel myself for the rest of my journey. As much as I want to meet his sisters, I do tend to get all awkward when I meet new people, and the yelling is throwing me off. I can't tell if they're actually angry or that's just how they talk.

When I get to the bottom floor, the bar looks like it's been ransacked and raucous laughter is coming from the patio. Okay, laughter. That's a good sign.

I take in a deep breath and turn the corner.

Three female versions of Claudio are sitting at the table, all three of their heads swiveling to look at me. I don't see Claudio anywhere.

Gulp.

"*Chi è questa?*" one of them exclaims. She's wearing cat-eye sunglasses.

"Ooooh," another one says, this one wearing a stunning shade of red lipstick. "*L'autrice!*"

Another one, the shortest, the most petite, also wearing red lipstick, gives them both a dirty look. "*Inglese!*" she scolds them.

Then she eyes me, a brow raised. Wow. Perfectly shaped eyebrows that move independently from each other must run in the family. "I apologize for my sisters being so rude. You must be Grace."

I raise my hand slightly. "That's me."

She points to herself with a red fingernail, the polish chipped. "I am Maria. This is Giada." She flicks her nails toward the one in sunglasses, who looks to be the oldest out of all of them. Then she points at the other sister. "That is Veronica. We are Claudio's sisters."

"It's nice to meet you," I tell them, feeling awkward on my feet. Do I do the whole kiss them on each cheek thing? Would that be too informal? I'll just stay here.

"Oh, come now," Maria says, getting to her feet. In seconds she's grabbed me by the shoulders, engulfed me in a cloud of lemony perfume, leaving lipstick marks on my cheeks. She pulls back and inspects me closely. "You are a beautiful woman."

Wow. Do all the Romanos throw compliments around like confetti?

Of course, I blush at that.

"Thank you. *Grazie*."

"Ah yes, Vanni told me he was teaching you Italian."

"He's trying. I'm not the best student at the moment."

"Of course not. You are writing, yes?"

She takes me by the hand and leads me to the table, sitting me down beside her.

"*Ciao*," Giada and Veronica say in unison.

"You must forgive," Giada continues. "My English is not so good."

"It's better than my Italian," I tell her, giving her an encouraging smile. It's then I notice they all have mineral waters, as well as espresso. "Where is Claudio?"

"Ah," Maria says. "We sent him off for some lemons."

Veronica frowns and mutters something under her breath, gesturing to her coffee.

"She is saying his espresso machine is not good enough," Maria translates. "And that normally he has the lemons all cut up for us."

"Is good for our blood," Giada explains, splaying her palms.

I can see why Claudio said they all picked on him. They just got here and already they're bossing him around. I have a feeling they were doing most of the yelling.

"Ah, you found her," Claudio's melodic voice booms. I look up to see him walking across the lawn, yellow lemons cradled in his hands. He pauses behind Giada, his eyes brightening as he looks at me. "I hope they've been kind."

"They're lovely," I tell Claudio, giving his sisters each a warm smile.

"I see," he says. "You've already joined their side."

KARINA HALLE

I laugh at the mock hurt expression on his face. The man can be completely adorable sometimes.

Maria clears her throat, and I look at her. She's watching both me and Claudio with interest, a touch of suspicion in her eyes. I immediately press my lips together, willing my face to go blank. I know my facial expressions give everything away, and the last thing I need is for his sisters to think I have some crush on their brother.

I mean, that's the only way I can describe it. A crush. There's something so juvenile about the term, but it is what it is. An infatuation. I never even crushed on anyone growing up (what was the point? I could barely talk to anyone, let alone look them in the eye), so this feeling is new to me, but it's there all the same.

But crushes go away, right? It's just based on attraction. Eventually it will fizzle out.

I've decided that's what I'll tell myself.

"What would you like to drink?" Claudio asks me, his voice warm, his eyes still fixed on my face, ignoring what-ever look Maria is giving us. "Aperol Spritz?"

I nod. "Please."

It's become one of my favorite drinks to have in the sun, just before dinner. Claudio says it's an aperitivo, which is meant to open up the appetite for dinner, but I'm just in it for the bittersweet buzz. One thing about being at Villa Rosa is that I'm always ready for whatever Claudio is cooking.

Claudio heads inside to the bar with his lemons, and I still feel Maria's eyes on me. I glance across the table at Giada and Veronica, and they are in the midst of communi-cating something to each other with their eyes. Then they look at me.

Uh oh. Why do I feel like they're thinking the same thing Maria is (whatever that is)?

They never come out and say it though and soon Claudio joins us with Aperol Spritzes for both of us, plus the slices of lemons for their waters (and it turns out Veronica's water contains vodka). We all toast to the summer and then the sisters get talking. Most of it is in Italian, with Maria translating when she can. A lot of it is just them picking on Claudio. They like to call him the "Golden Child" since he's the only one of them that followed in his father's footsteps and became a successful artist. There's a lot of love there, but I can tell they don't really take the arts that seriously.

Only Veronica has a mild interest in the arts, doing watercolor paintings of landscapes when she can. She doesn't sell them though, despite years of Claudio trying to convince her to let his gallery carry them. She says that would take all the fun away and it would no longer be a relaxing activity to her.

"If you sell my paintings, it is a job," she says with a dramatic wave of her hands. "It is no longer a hobby. It is no longer something I do for my soul."

Claudio and I exchange a knowing look. I'm sure he feels the same way I do, in that when I was writing stories for fun, it was a completely different experience. The pressure wasn't there, the creativity came easily and free-flowing. Now, well, here we are, lucky to be doing what we do, but terribly aware that luck runs out when you're not creating.

"So, Jana is your agent, yes?" Maria asks me.

Giada and Veronica exchange a dark look.

I nod. "She is. If it wasn't for her, I wouldn't be here."

"That's very interesting," she says carefully.

I raise my brows, wondering what she's getting at. I sneak a glance at Claudio and his face has hardened, a look I don't see on him too often.

"How so?" I ask.

"Well," she says, sitting back in her chair, holding two fingers in the air. She ticks off one. "For one, we haven't seen Jana here since ... well, I suppose since she went to London and never looked back." She ticks off another finger. "For two ... no, I suppose that's it. You're here on behalf of Jana, and yet that woman has nothing to do with our lives."

"Maria," Claudio says coldly. "She has plenty to do with my life."

A current of jealousy runs through me, catching me off-guard.

"Is that so?" Maria asks, not looking even a little intimidated by his steely tone. "Then tell me, why is it she never comes here? Tell me why Vanni so rarely goes to see her? The woman does not care for you, does not care for Vanni. So don't pretend like she has something to do with your life." She pauses and adds something in Italian. Judging by her tone, it's not good.

I sit there quietly, feeling extremely self-conscious, my eyes darting between Maria and Claudio's face-off. Veronica and Giada's eyes are doing the same.

Claudio looks like he's simmering, his face darkening, a deep crease between his brows. Is this a prelude to him losing his temper, which he has warned me about before?

"She is the mother of my child," he manages to say, each word hard and deliberate. "And anything you want to say, you better say in English so Jana's client can hear you."

Maria looks at me, nonplussed. "Does this bother you? You are friends with Jana?"

I shake my head, flashing my palms in surrender. "Oh, this is none of my business."

"Uh huh," Maria says slowly. "I think it is your business. If you and my brother are together, then well..."

Oh my god. She's not insinuating we're, like, a couple, is she?

I glance at Claudio in confusion, but he's not looking at me for once.

"Jana is still a presence in my son's life," Claudio says carefully, ignoring what she said. "Therefore, she is still a presence in mine. She will not be disrespected by you, or by anyone."

I stare down at the orange bubbles in my drink, a tense silence coming over the table. In the distance a rooster crows.

Knowing how complicated Jana and Claudio's relationship is, it's refreshing that he defends his ex-wife when I'm sure many men would not.

On the other hand, this is a stark reminder for me that Jana is very much a part of Claudio's life—contrary to what Maria might think—and that any feelings I have for Claudio, crush or otherwise, don't have a place here. No matter how badly I want Claudio to want me, I know that the two of us could never be a thing. It just couldn't happen. Jana makes a triangle, whether I like it or not, and there is no point in making my own life more complicated, let alone Claudio's.

Giada opens her mouth to say something to break up the ice that's formed between the siblings, when suddenly Vanni and his cousin come barreling out of the house.

"*Papà*," Vanni whines to his father. "*Sono molto affamato!*"

From the way he's clutching his stomach, I assume he's

141

talking about wanting dinner. I think everyone is just grateful for the interruption.

"Si, si," Claudio says, getting to his feet and heading inside. Again, he doesn't look this way, which leaves me feeling a little bereft.

Thankfully, Maria and her sisters move the conversation on to other topics, and we end up eating dinner at the big table on the veranda. Things seem easy again, with everyone in a good mood, and the wine flowing, and the sisters sparring on and off, but for whatever reason, Claudio never meets my gaze. I'm not sure what to make of it, but it's noticeable and I hate it. I feel like I did something wrong but I have no idea what.

It isn't until later, when I excuse myself and head up to my room, that I realize he never corrected his sister when she said that we were together.

ELEVEN

GRACE

Time is a funny thing.

It's been nearly a week since Claudio's sisters were here.

It's been the slowest week of my life.

Time has absolutely been dragging on by, which for a writer, is often a good thing because it always feels like we never have enough time to write.

But it's different now.

Claudio has put some distance between us. It's like what Maria said about Jana shocked him into remembering that I'm just as tied up in Jana as he is. Before he was all flirty banter and simmering looks, and now, well, it's not that he looks at me coldly ... his gaze is still warm, his smile still genuine.

It's that it's like he pulls his eyes away quicker, his smile fades before mine does, and before there were many instances of him getting in my space, asking me questions, always around me. Now he gets up and goes to his studio, and the door closes and that's it. I'll see him doing something with Vanni, but it seems like father and son bonding and I don't want to get involved. The only time I see him is during mealtimes, the only chance for us to talk.

But the problem is, once the meal is over, it all comes to an end. We go our separate ways again.

It shouldn't matter what Claudio does. It's his house and he has his own busy life, and I'm...just the guest.

But when you get used to something and it's taken away...

Well, sometimes you end up wanting it more.

And this week has dragged on because I know I have two opportunities to be with him again. There's tonight, for the INXS concert, although Vanni is coming with us too. And then there's tomorrow night for the gallery.

So, yeah. I've been reduced to pining for the moment to be alone with him again and it's fucking killing me.

Not to mention it's killing my book. It's hard to focus and concentrate when your mind keeps being pulled else-where. Which means I'm kind of screwed, because it's a damned if you do, damned if you don't situation. Either way, Claudio is on my mind too much for my own good.

"Are you ready!?" Vanni yells from outside my bedroom door, immediately pounding his fists on it.

I laugh to myself and head over to the door, opening it.

He's on the other side, wearing an INXS shirt that hangs to his knees that I assume his dad got him, and he's so freaking adorable.

"I'll be ready in a couple of minutes," I tell him. I just have to do something with my hair. Otherwise I'm ready to go in my jean shorts and black tank top. No concert shirts for me. "You know, you're not supposed to wear the band's shirt to the concert."

Vanni's nose wrinkles. "Why not?"

I shrug. "I don't know. It's an unwritten rule."

"Well that's stupid," he says, pulling at his shirt and staring at it. "Are we supposed to pretend that we're not there to see the band?"

I laugh. "Good point."

He narrows his eyes at me. "I don't think that's a rule. I think you're just jealous that my father gave me this shirt and you didn't get one."

Again, I'm grinning. "Okay, Vanni. That's it. You got me. I'm jealous."

He shrugs, raising his chin haughtily. "It's natural," he says with a flourish of his hands.

Then he turns and runs down the stairs.

I roll my eyes and head back into my room, deciding to pull my hair back into a high ponytail, my minor contribution to the eighties. I grab my crossbody purse and head down to the living room.

Claudio is sitting in the armchair, back to me, Vanni on the couch across from him.

"She's *finally* ready," Vanni exclaims dramatically, as if he wasn't *just* at my door.

Claudio turns his head to look at me, his eyes coasting up and down my body, leaving a trail of heat where they've been.

He smiles.

And *goddamn it*.

He's completely disarmed me with a simple look. He can't even exist anymore without my heart tripping over itself, without my knees feeling weak. I can't even be sure that my feet are holding me up.

You're a hot mess, Grace.

"No dress?" he asks, getting to his feet, stopping a few feet away.

I lick my lips, my throat feeling dry. "Sorry to disappoint you."

"You could never disappoint me," he says, voice dropping, eyes glinting with sincerity.

I swallow. I can't stop staring into his eyes, lost in this look, this voice that I've been craving all week like a junkie. Seconds seem to span into eons.

"Can we go?" Vanni whines, breaking through the spell.

Claudio turns to him. "Yes, Vanni," he says while my eyes flutter closed for a moment, giving myself space to breathe.

"Grace?" he asks.

I open my eyes to find both of them staring at me.

"Yes. Let's go," I manage to say.

Because there are three of us going to the concert, we can't fit in the Ferrari. Instead we get inside the Range Rover parked outside.

"This isn't as fun to drive," Claudio says as I buckle up in the passenger side, Vanni in the back. "And it's awful on fuel, and breaks down more than it should. But it is still sexy, no?"

I nod. I've always been a fan of these cars. "They're very popular back home. Lots of people drive them, especially around the Highlands."

"Ah," Claudio says, taking the car out onto the road. I watch his tanned hands on the wheel. The way he holds it is the same way as when he's making art. There's something so distinctive about the way he uses his hands, so much grace and skill and strength in them.

He turns his head and eyes me. "Perhaps when this is all over, we will come up there and visit you."

I manage a small smile, part of me thrilled that he would think of me when this is all over, the other part hating to be reminded that this is a short-term thing. I've got only two weeks left here in Tuscany. Two weeks to get most of my book finished. Two weeks to fall out of … well, whatever has been tied up in knots when it comes to Claudio.

"If we drive to Scotland, that means we'll have to take the car train from France!" Vanni exclaims. "Then we can go to London, pick up *Mamma*, and then come see you, Grace."

Yeah. That wasn't what I had in mind, but because that's what Vanni has in mind, it's a wee slap in the face. Serves me right for feeling the way I do.

I eye him in the mirror. "That sounds great."

It's not long until we're pulling into a parking lot outside the walls of Lucca. Already it's crazy busy, the concert itself being held on the long green expanse of grass just below the walls. It takes time to finally find a free parking space and then walk through the throngs of people all heading over to the venue. The band doesn't start for another two hours, but everyone had the same idea in getting here early.

It's exciting though. It's been a long time since I've been to a concert, and it was the opposite of this. Robyn insisted I go with her to a BTS show, and though my knowledge of K-Pop is minimal, it was a lot of fun. And I was keenly aware of being some of the oldest people there.

Here, everyone seems older than me and there aren't that many kids. There's an infectious buzz in the air, people chatting happily, drinking alcohol from plastic cups, the air heavy with sweat, the sun slowly creeping down behind the hills to the west.

We cross the road and head into the gates of the concert, giving the tickets to the volunteers, then squeeze past the lines outside of the merch tents.

"*Papà*," Vanni says, begrudgingly holding on to his

father's hand. "Look. You could buy Grace a shirt like mine."

Claudio stops and glances at me inquisitively. "Would you like a shirt, Grace?"

"No, that's okay," I tell him quickly.

"She thinks it's wrong to wear a shirt of the band when you go to see the band," Vanni explains.

Claudio's brow raises higher, a devious smirk on his lips. "Is that so?"

Uh oh. I don't trust that look.

"*Allora*," he muses, stroking his chin, "Grace thinks she's too good for a t-shirt, is that right?"

"No," I say carefully, but he's reaching over and grabbing my hand, pulling me toward the closest merch tent.

I'm both dreading what he's going to do and completely swooning at the feel of my hand in his. Giddy. That's what this feeling is. I'm giddy.

Over *hand holding*.

What are you, twelve?

He brings me right to the tent, in a five-person deep line, and waves at the t-shirts. "You pick. I'm buying."

"Really, it's okay."

"You don't want to match with me, Grace?" Vanni asks. I glance down at him on the other side of Claudio, and shit, he's looking up at me with big eyes. "It would mean so much."

My eyes narrow. The kid doesn't care. He's trying to embarrass me.

"Yes, Grace," Claudio says, dropping my hand to take out his wallet. "You want to disappoint my son like this?"

Oh *lordy*.

I roll my eyes. "Fine. I'll take that tank top over there."

"Tank top?" Vanni says. "We have to match."

"*We* will match, Vanni," Claudio assures him. "Grace can have the tank top."

"You're buying a shirt for yourself?" I ask him, eyes wide. "You wouldn't dare."

"Why not?"

I look him up and down, at his dark jeans, black t-shirt, black moto boots, the aviators pushed up on his head. He's the epitome of sexy cool.

"You would ruin your aesthetic? I mean, I know how much aesthetics matter to you."

He flashes me a wicked grin. "It will be worth it to embarrass you."

And so that's how I end up in a scratchy INXS tank top, pulled over my other one, with father and son in matching shirts. It is somewhat embarrassing. We look like a family of the biggest nerds but Claudio doesn't care at all. He's living off of my reaction.

What helps is a trip to one of the bar carts and getting some glasses of wine, and then heading over to the edge of the crowd where we find a patch of grass to sit down on.

"We can't see the stage from here," Vanni whines, trying to look over the people in front of us.

"Don't worry," his father says. "We'll get up and go into the crowd when they start. Do you want to stand for hours if you don't have to?"

"I thought you were going to put me on your shoulders." He sticks the straw from his Coke in his mouth and smiles sweetly.

"You are too big for that," Claudio says.

"But would you put her on your shoulders?" he asks, eyeing me. "She's not much taller than me."

"I'm not going anywhere," I tell Vanni. "I would break your dad's back."

"We'll see about that," Claudio says.

I give him a look, like don't you even try.

He merely sips his wine and slips his shades down over his eyes, smirking away.

A fluttery feeling passes through me, and I busy myself with my wine, looking at the crowd. The more I drink, the more I relax, and the more I'm hit with ... happiness.

We're sitting here on the grass, the blades tickling my thighs below my shorts. I'm extra hot because I'm wearing two tops, one of them with the smell that new concert tees seem to have, sweat pooling at the small of my back. My pinot grigio is growing warmer by the minute and the sun is just disappearing, the sunset reflected in Claudio's sunglasses.

Aye. That's what it is. I'm *happy*. It's not just because I'm buzzed. With the smiling crowd, the warm air, the fading blue sky overhead, I feel at peace. Like, for once, I know I'm going to be okay. And maybe that's not true, but for this moment, for tonight, I'm going to pretend it is.

We finish our drinks and then Claudio gets up to get another round for us. It's darker now and the band should start soon.

"Grace?" Vanni asks when Claudio has disappeared into the crowd.

"*Sì?*"

"Do you like my dad?"

Oh. No.

I glance at him, pasting a big phony smile on my face. "Like your dad? Sure I do. He's a nice guy. Just like you."

He purses his lips in thought, raising a brow. He's not buying it.

"I mean, do you *like* him. The way he used to like my mother."

I should be relieved that he didn't use the word *love*, but even so this isn't the best question to be caught up with, especially when I have such a hard time lying.

"I think he's nice," I say. "He's a friend. That's all."

He watches me closely, and I turn my attention back to the crowd, which is getting thicker as it grows around us.

"Hey, maybe we should get up," I tell him, getting to my feet and dusting the grass off the backs of my thighs. I hold my hands out for him and hoist him up.

"So you're just friends?" he asks.

"Yes, Vanni. We are just friends. Like you and I are friends."

Okay, so maybe not quite like that.

"Good," he says.

Oh boy.

Don't ask him what he means by that, don't ask him what he means by that.

I clear my throat. "Do you ... think that one day your dad will remarry?"

Vanni shudders at that, visibly upset. "No. He knows he can't."

"He ... can't?"

"I don't care if he has girlfriends," he says carefully. Then his brows snap together. "But I will *not* have another mother."

Ah, so Claudio wasn't kidding when he told me that the reason he broke up with the gorgeous Marika, was because Vanni didn't like her. I'm starting to think Vanni won't like anyone that Claudio ends up with.

Which is none of your concern, anyway, I remind myself. *Because it sure as hell won't be you.*

"There you are," Claudio says, brushing past the crowd, managing three drinks in his hands. Even with his concert tee, which doesn't fit him nearly as well as his normal tees do, he looks every bit the Italian stallion.

He hands me my wine and gives Vanni another Coke. The kid is going to be sugar high all night.

"I think they are just about to start," he says to me, then looks over my shoulder. "The crowd is closing in. We need to stay close so we don't lose each other."

I thank him for the wine, ever so conscious of Vanni's questions.

Why did he even ask?

Does he suspect I like his father as more than a friend?

Does he suspect that his father likes me?

Is he worried that we are going to get together?

Or is this his way of a preemptive strike?

I'm going to assume that he's just afraid of what *could* happen, and since I'm probably the first female who has consistently lived in the house, it's easy to assume that we're together or might be.

Suddenly, the stage lights go on, pulling me out of my head.

The crowd roars.

"It's starting," Claudio says. "Let's get closer."

He reaches over and grabs Vanni's hand.

Then he grabs mine with the other.

He pulls us into the crowd, squeezing us past the sweaty throngs of people, the swagger-heavy opening notes I recognize as "Suicide Blonde."

Of course Claudio is practically beaming. I can't really see the stage that well since we're all in a level field and, like, everyone is taller than me (I don't know why the tall people always stand in front of me at shows—I must have some strange gravitational pull.) I don't recognize the singer, but he's *good* and sounds close enough to Michael Hutchence for it to totally work.

But while part of me is bowled over by the sound and the lights and the crowd, I'm also acutely aware that Claudio is still holding my hand.

Not just holding it, holding it tight. I can feel his rapid pulse, and I'm going to assume it's because of the excitement of the show.

I sneak a glance at him.

He's grooving to the music, smiling, the stage lights reflecting in his dark eyes, making them dance too. There's something about him that feels otherworldly to me, like before I met him my life seemed lost and hopeless. And *dull*. It still does in a way. I'm still grieving. I'm still worried about my book. But at the same time, so much belongs to another life. The life I had before I met him.

Now that I'm here, I'm swept up in his charm, his essence, his view on life. It's not just that I find him ridiculously attractive, it's not that I don't dream about letting go of all my inhibitions and screwing him (because, believe me, I think that's exactly what I need).

It's that he makes *me* feel good. He makes me feel better about myself, like I'm somehow more interesting. When I'm around him, whatever zest and passion he has for life rubs off on me, until I see things the way he does, like the world is one big canvas waiting for me to paint it. Like I'm worthy of holding the brush.

As if he can tell I'm staring at him, he squeezes my hand tightly.

I squeeze it back.

We hold hands like that until the haunting strings of "Never Tear Us Apart" begin to play. My mind is automatically brought back to our session in his studio. He'd held me so close, not a care in the world. And I remember the feeling of letting go.

That surrender.

I want that again.

And I also want *more* than that.

"Vanni," Claudio says to him, barely audible over the music. "Do you want to come on my shoulders for this song?"

He shakes his head violently. "No. You said I was too old for that."

Then Claudio turns his head toward me, peering down. "Grace?"

I want to laugh. I can't get up on his shoulders. I might be short, but I'm heavy. I will break his back. Not to mention, the people behind us will probably get mad.

I look over my shoulder. Then again, the couple behind us is making out and not paying attention to the show at all.

"I..." I say. Wanting to say yes, needing to say no.

Before I can complete my sentence, he squats down low, like impressively low (those quads are beasts), and pulls me around so I have to get on his back like we're playing leapfrog, my legs around his neck.

His hands take a firm grasp on my thighs, his forearms pressing my calves against his chest. "Hold on," he says.

I immediately grab hold of his hair, though that's probably not what he meant, and he straightens back up, slowly. He does it with so much ease, it's like I'm not on his back at all. Meanwhile I'm not making it any easier with my wavering back and trying to get a grip on his head.

"Sorry, sorry," I tell him.

"Don't be," he says. "I like it when you pull my hair."

Oh lord.

And now I'm suddenly very conscious that his head is

154

between my thighs. Backwards from the way I've dreamed about, but still. He better do nothing to turn me on.

"Are you okay?" he asks.

"Yes," I squeak. I glance down at Vanni who is shaking his head in disapproval.

I do have an amazing view of the concert, but angry Italian gibberish from behind me grabs my attention.

I turn and the making out couple have ceased their tangled tongues and are giving me a dirty look.

"One song," I tell them, trying to think what that is in Italian. "*Una sonata.*"

"*Canzone,*" Claudio whispers, correcting me.

"*Una Canzone,*" I tell the couple. "*Per favore.*"

The couple shrugs and goes back to making out.

"Very good, Grace," Claudio murmurs.

He begins to stroke his thumb against my thigh, his rough skin against mine, making my veins course with heat.

Yeah, so much for not being turned on.

What is he doing?

Just shut up and enjoy it.

So I listen to that voice. While Claudio rubs his thumb along my skin, back and forth, over and over, I wind my fingers into his hair. It's very thick and strong and soft, and I can feel him relaxing beneath me. Every now and then I give it a playful tug, hoping he's as turned on as I am.

But eventually the song comes to an end.

It's time for me to come down.

And Vanni says, "*Papà,* I need to use the toilet."

"Okay," Claudio says, grabbing his son's hand while gripping my leg tighter with the other. "Hold on, Grace."

"Wait!" I cry out, my nails digging into his head as he starts to walk through the crowd with me on his back. "Put me down!"

But I'm drunk and I'm giggling.

I feel like I'm in a circus, riding an elephant, but in fact it's just a stupendously talented and handsome man, and I'm up here on display. I start waving to people, waving to the band, who are paying me no attention, of course.

I can't stop smiling.

By the time we reach the line of porta loos on the side of the field, I'm laughing hard, having a tough time staying upright.

As Vanni goes off into one of them, Claudio starts to stumble.

I shriek, still laughing, and he goes down on his knees.

"Ahhhh!" I wrap my hands around his face, blinding him, and pitch forward until my shoulder hits the grass.

The impact is soft, and I roll over onto my back, my hands clasped over my stomach, knees up, and I am laughing so hard that I think my ribs might give out.

Claudio is laughing too, a big and boisterous laugh that only fuels mine.

He grabs my legs as he crawls over to me, leaning over.

"*Mio Dio*," he says, chuckling. "Are you okay?"

I look up to see him looking down at me, hand at my face.

I can only grin at him, nodding. The stars are shining in the sky beyond him, one insanely bright star right behind his head, and my eyes keep going in focus between his face and the starlight.

Both are insanely beautiful.

"I am sorry about the crash landing," he says, his hand still at my cheek. "I tried very hard to make it gentle."

I bite back my innuendo.

"I imagine that's what riding a camel is like," I say through a laugh.

"Yes, but I would hope I'm less smelly and hairy."

"Much less smelly. You smell like almonds and sunshine," I tell him. The drunk in me is speaking now.

He blinks at me for a moment, then his smile deepens. "That doesn't sound so bad."

"It's really not."

I sit up and he puts his hand on my shoulder to help me. Then leaves his hand there.

His other hand is on my bare thigh.

I swallow, noticing the goosebumps on his arm.

"You have goosebumps," I say quietly. "That song really does it for you."

He glances at his arm and then slowly meets my eyes, giving a small shake of his head. Something in his gaze changes, no longer playful. His smile fades.

"No," he says thickly. "It's not the song."

His fingers press into my shoulder.

Eyes smoldering.

He licks his lips.

And for a moment, we aren't on the grass outside the loos at an INXS concert. We're nowhere at all. It's just empty space and it's him and it's me, and every wire that has tightened between us over these last weeks is close to snapping.

Once they snap...

"*Papà!*' Vanni's voice dissolves the world.

It was there, and now it's gone.

The roar of the concert comes back and Vanni is running over.

"*Stai bene?* Why are you on the grass?" he asks, looking down at us in surprise.

"Your father dropped me," I tell him, throwing Claudio under the bus so that Vanni doesn't pick up on the fact that we just shared one very strange and fleeting intimate moment.

Vanni looks heavenward. "I told you I was too old. Of course she is too old too! Come on, can we get another Coke?"

"We'll see," Claudio says.

He gets to his feet and then turns and hauls me up, fingers wrapped around my elbows. Our eyes lock, an expression that I can't read sitting deep within his eyes, and his hand trails down my forearm, over my wrist, over my hand, then finally lets go.

I swallow hard, feeling drunk and dizzy, all because of him.

He grabs Vanni's hand and they walk along the edge of the crowd to the food cart, me right behind them.

TWELVE

CLAUDIO

I AM NERVOUS.

I stare at my reflection, trying to decide if I should wear a tie with my suit or not, but I can't make up my mind. It shouldn't matter—I have nights like this at the gallery all the time. It's just me and my friends, and maybe one of my friends will bring someone with money who will buy one of my pieces of art and I can breathe easier.

Or maybe not.

But of course, it's not just business as usual this time. This time, I have company.

In another world, another universe, perhaps one that even Vanni isn't aware of, she would be a date.

But in this one, at least, she is a guest.

Grace is coming with me to gallery night.

And she's why I'm nervous.

She's why I can't decide on tie or no tie.

She's the one I want to impress.

La mia musa.

I'm starting to think she's my muse.

Outside, thunder rumbles ominously. After nearly two

weeks of sun and building heat, the tension has broken. Dark clouds gather behind the peaks of the distant hills with threats of rain. It would be good for the land to have some rain tonight. Perhaps it would be good for everyone, a reprieve of sorts.

The relationship between Grace and I has gotten more complicated over the last week. Prior to my sisters showing up, I was willingly pushing her, seeing how far I could go. I wanted to know if she felt what I felt. Something a bit more complicated than pure attraction. Yes, I lust for her but it's more than that. It's something inside me recognizing something in her. Perhaps the pull of an artist's heart for an artist's heart. Maybe it's just the potential of what we could be.

But my sister Maria reminded me that it wasn't just my feelings that were complicated. It was the situation. With Grace being Jana's client, with her being here because of Jana, because she needs to finish this book, I realized how selfish and inappropriate I have been. There's a part of me that physically aches for her, this need to be around her, to gaze at her beauty, and I can do all that without involving Grace.

I just haven't felt this way in a long time ... dare I say, ever. I'm not sure what to do with myself, and pleasuring myself night after night with thoughts of her hasn't helped—if anything, it's made it worse because my imagination is pretty fantastic, but it stops just short of being the real thing.

I want the real thing.

I want Grace.

I want to touch her, to explore her body from head to toe, discover everything hidden to me, lose myself in the way she's put together. She's art, I know she is, and if I can't have her, I need to create her. She inspires me to no end.

Slow down.

I stare at my reflection, at the dark eyes peering back. I can't let my mind run away on me because if it does, my body will follow.

I decide against the tie, tossing it on my bed.

Rake my fingers through my hair, adjust my cufflinks. Black suit, white shirt, no tie. I know I look good. But there's only one opinion I care about.

I grab the keys to the *Lusso* and leave my room, closing the door behind me.

Out in the hall, Grace is doing the same thing.

I stop, air seizing in my chest.

Grace is wearing a dress that would be fitting in a Dolce and Gabbana ad. White with a bright floral print—the top is like a bustier, with skinny straps and cups that push up her breasts, dangerously close to overflowing.

When I tear my eyes away from her chest, ignoring that persistent pang of need in my dick, I'm taken by her face, the red on her lips, the smoky eye, the way her dark hair shines, cascading softly over her shoulders.

"It's not too much, is it?" she asks, her voice quiet and anxious.

It's too much for me, I want to say. *Far too much for me to handle.*

I don't think I'll survive tonight.

Somehow I manage to speak. "You look beautiful."

I want to say more. She looks more than beautiful. There are no words in my vocabulary to describe her. She's the writer here, not me. I just know that if I were to sculpt her, people would be fighting over themselves to own her, to display her beauty forever.

In the back of my head, a risky proposition rears its head.

I ignore it for now.

"Okay, good," she says, eyes downcast so all I see are her lashes. "I was worried that I'd either be too overdressed or too underdressed."

"You're perfect," I tell her, licking my lips. If only I could get her to believe it.

I clear my throat, trying to regain some composure. "And me? No kind words for me?"

"Do you need me to tell you you're handsome?"

"*Yes*," I say emphatically. "How else will I know?"

She breaks into a smile that lights up her whole face. At least she still finds me funny. That's something. Maybe it's everything.

Last night was the most fun I've had in a long time. It wasn't just that the show was amazing. It's that I finally felt Grace becoming undone. She wraps herself so tightly, afraid to let go, afraid to feel because her feelings seem too big for her body. She's consumed with her darkness sometimes, as I suppose it can be for writers. And I can't blame her, because she seems to have gone through so much.

But she let herself be free with me last night.

It's probably too much to ask for it again.

I jerk my head to the stairs. "Come on. Let's get going."

I head down the stairs and see Vanni lounging on the couch, reading a book. When he sees us, he sits up straighter. "Are you sure I can't go with you?" he asks with pleading eyes.

"Was the concert not enough?" I chuckle. "And you have been before. You remember? Lots of adults, no kids. You're not allowed to touch anything."

"That's okay."

"No eating either. I don't trust you not to get cheese on all of my statues."

He nods at that, understanding. "Okay. At least here I can eat."

"Where is Emilio?"

He shrugs. "I think he's cleaning the pool."

"Okay, well you listen to your uncle," I remind him. Not that Vanni is ever a troublesome kid, but I know one day he's going to give me a run for my money.

Grace gives him a little wave. "*Ciao*, Vanni."

"*Ciao, ciao, ciao*," he says with a dismissive wave, then with a heavy sigh, picks up his book again and goes back to reading.

We head down the outside stairs to the Ferrari parked below. I open her door for her, and a vicious thrill runs through me, the sight of her, in that dress, getting in my car. Too sexy for words.

I shut the door and swallow hard, needing to compose myself yet again. Thankfully once we get to the gallery, we will no longer be alone. In some ways, I can't trust myself not to do or say the wrong thing when I'm alone with her, which is why I've been trying to give her as much space as possible for the last while. Even last night we weren't truly alone, and in the moments that we were ... well, we were close to something we wouldn't be able to come back from.

But perhaps you won't want to go back.

"I can see why you choose to drive this over your other vintage cars," she comments as I get in my side, buckle up, and start the engine.

I flash her a smile. "You haven't been in the others."

She blinks at me, her eyes gleaming. "Maybe you'll have to take me for a ride in all of them."

Damn. She's not going to make this easier on me, is she?

"If you're a good girl," I tell her as the car roars out of the driveway. "Maybe."

"A good girl?" she repeats, looking incredulous. "I'll have you know you can't get more of a good girl than me."

"I believe it," I tell her, my eyes flitting over her chest as the Ferrari bumps along the rough road.

Also, I believe I told myself to stop flirting with her.

It's fucking hard.

"Do you think it's going to rain?" she asks, staring out the window at the dark clouds. "The air feels electric."

As does the air between us, here in this car.

I'm about to answer her, but there's another crack of thunder, and like God was trying to prove a point, the clouds spill over.

We're immediately engulfed in a torrential downpour, rain soaking the streets, my windshield wipers working overtime.

"You are something magical," I tell her. "God listens to you."

She makes a snorting sound, gazing at the rain streaming down the windows.

"You really are, Grace," I go on, my hands feeling damp on the steering wheel. "You sell yourself short but your work is phenomenal. You're a true creator."

She shoots me a wry gaze, just as I knew she would. "You haven't read my work."

"But I have," I tell her. "I read every book, from Dopo Tutto Sei Arrivato Tu, all the way to your last, Tutti Muoiono a Volte."

Her eyes narrow. "I don't know what those are."

"Those are the Italian titles for The Mystery of Princess Street and To Catch a Killer."

She rubs her lips together, and I can see the wheels turning in her head. She doesn't believe me.

"Go on, ask me anything," I tell her.

"Oh, I'm sure."

"I mean it. I've read them all."

"Fine. What is Caroline's cat's name?"

"Mr. Claw."

"Okay. You could have read a review. What is the name of the guy that Susan dates in book three?"

I have to think for a moment because that character was all over the place. "George?"

"James," she says. "Nice try."

'That is not fair. Ask me something else."

"All right." She drums her fingers along her thigh, thinking. "Tell me what your favorite part was. In any of the books."

"I have many favorite scenes, but my favorite part is your character. Caroline."

"How did you know I wrote her?" she asks quietly.

"She has your stamp all over her. She's thoughtful and observant. That's why she's such a good detective. But she loves with all her heart. She cares very much for her partner. And she's not a, how you say, doormat. She's strong when she needs to be, and when she knows what's right. That is just like you."

Grace stares at me for a moment, her eyes growing wet with tears. Then she looks away, out the window.

Something about her breaks my heart. Something I wish I had the power to fix.

"You did read them," she says after a moment.

"Would I lie to you?" I say. "You know we are both terrible liars."

"That's true." She glances at me, eyes soft. "I can't believe you read them. Why?"

"How could I not? I have a famous author staying in my house, the least I can do is read her work."

She seems touched by that, her fingers resting gently against her chest.

Good.

It's not long before we've parked. Only problem is, you have no choice but to park outside the walls of the city, which means it's at least a five-minute walk to the gallery.

It's still pissing down with rain.

I turn off the engine and the sound of the rain hitting the roof engulfs us. The windows are already fogging up. The electricity outside the car is no match for the building electricity inside.

"Shall we wait it out?" Grace asks.

The space between us feels smaller and tighter than ever.

"We can," I tell her, my voice feeling too harsh, too loud, for this small space.

"You might be late for your event," she notes. Her pupils are wide, overtaking the pale blue of her eyes, and though she gives me a small smile, there's something strained about it.

"This is true. But we don't have an umbrella." I pause, licking my lips. "And it would be a shame if you got wet. No?"

She visibly swallows, eyes brightening for a moment. Then she puts her hand on the door handle. "I say we go for it."

So then we do.

I get out of the car and take off my suit jacket, running to her side, water splashing on my legs. I immediately hold the jacket high above her head, trying to protect the both of us the best I can.

"But you'll get wet," she protests.

I put my arm around her, pulling her right up to me, the only way the both of us will be somewhat sheltered. "It's not the end of the world. Let's go," I say, and we head off through one of the arches that lead into the city.

As we walk, the rain becomes less of an issue. It's still pouring, but the only thing I can think about is Grace, the feel of her body pulled close to mine. She fits against me perfectly, and it feels easy and natural and ... right. Like it's always been this way, like it should always be this way.

But, by the time we finally reach the gallery, reality comes rushing back. My shirt is soaked and she's quite wet as well.

She shoots me a grateful, albeit anxious, glance as I knock at the door to the gallery.

"Thank you for that," she says. "But you look like a drowned rat."

Carla opens the door, her eyes wide.

"*Mio Dio!*" she exclaims, holding the door open. "*Entra, entra!*"

We rush inside, dripping water onto the floor.

"You are soaked!" Carla cries out. "No umbrella?"

I shrug, taking my jacket and hanging it up on the coat rack by the front door. "All the hot weather has been misleading."

She looks us up and down, shaking her head. "Okay. So you need to go dry off. I need to run out and get some more Prosecco. We have everything else set up."

She gestures to the tall quartz table in the middle of the gallery where all the appetizers have been set up. Then she grabs the umbrella by the door. "I will be back soon.

Guests won't arrive for another half hour, so you have time."

Then she gives us another pitying glance and leaves, running out under her umbrella into the rainy cobblestone streets.

"Come on, let's towel off," I tell Grace.

Against my better judgement, I reach down and grab her hand, leading her through the gallery to the store room at the back. There are a few statues in here that there's no space for on the floor, and they loom around us like ghosts. Against one wall are stacks of paintings covered with paper—prints, not originals—and there's a shelf crammed full of shipping and packing supplies for orders.

I leave her in there for a moment and head across the short hall to the toilet where I grab some white fluffy hand towels. I know Carla had put them there for the guests tonight. She often does a great job in prepping the space on nights like tonight, though I know she didn't plan on me using them all to towel ourselves off.

When I come back to the storeroom, Grace's back is to me, studying a statue. It's life-sized, a copy of the Farnese Hercules.

I close the door behind me, taking a long moment to admire the curve of her ass in that dress, and she looks at me over her shoulder, nodding at the statue. "He's so lifelike. His beard. The skill you have..."

"It's a copy," I tell her, standing behind her. "I didn't create him. He was already created. I just copied. I wasn't the first one, of course. The Ancient Romans liked this statue so much that copies of it were found all over the world, a thousand years ago."

"You still need an insane amount of skill," she says. She

turns around to face me, a sly smile playing across her face. "Don't sell yourself short. Remember?"

I ignore that by reaching out with the towel and pressing it against her chest. "You aren't too wet," I tell her. A heavy sense of anticipation seems to pulse around us, and I can't be the only one who feels it.

"You're soaked," she says, her voice shaking slightly, breathless. Her chest rises and falls against my hands.

I press the towel against the soft swell of her breasts, and my dick immediately hardens against my fly, threatening to send me over the edge, an edge I've been flirting with for a long time.

I have a hard time speaking. "It will dry."

I pause with the towel at her collarbones, my eyes drifting up to hers. They're wide, glimmering with something I want too badly to believe. Then I look to her neck, her hair. Finally I glance at the statue behind her.

"I want to ask you for a favor," I tell her, my throat feeling thick.

She blinks at me, mouth parting. "What?" she asks softly.

I take the towel and put it over my shoulder before I place my hand at her neck, letting my fingers trail up the curve to her ear.

Her eyes fall closed and I reach back, winding my fingers through her hair before making a fist and pulling it off her neck.

"You have no idea how perfect you are," I whisper. "Your skin. Your bones. Your build. You're art, Grace. And I think you might be my muse."

Her eyes open, brows raising. "Your muse?"

I nod, sucking on my lower lip. Her gaze drops to my mouth. "Sì. *La mia musa.* But you do more than inspire me to work. You inspire me to make art out of you. I would like to sculpt you, Grace Harper."

Her mouth falls open. "Me?"

She really doesn't see it. There is something so beguiling about that, how someone who possesses so much charm and beauty can be so fully unaware of it. It's both a shame and a mystery.

"You," I tell her, taking another step closer until I'm pressed up against her, and I know she can feel how hard I am against her hip. I see it with the slight flare of her nostrils, the heat peppering her liquid eyes. "I want to sculpt you. I want to make a copy of your beauty, of your soul, for the world to see."

"I ... I don't..." she stammers.

"Yes," I tell her. There are dark smudges beneath her eyes where the rain has mixed with her mascara, and I cup her small face in my hands, running my thumbs gently under her eyes, wiping it away. "You, Grace. You."

I was so close to kissing her last night that I'm not letting another opportunity pass me by.

I lean in, my face closing the gap between us, and kiss her. It is soft at first, my lips pressing against hers, taking her in like fine wine. Her mouth is warm, beautiful, and relaxes instantly, her lips opening against mine. My tongue slides in, feeling her mouth, while the need that's been building inside me threatens to overtake us both.

I let it.

I press my fingers harder into her face, sucking her lower lip into my mouth like it's a piece of sweet candy.

My sweet Grace.

But I can't be so sweet anymore.

The desire crashes over me, like it just realized what's happening, that I have her in my hands, that my mouth is devouring hers. My lips grow hungrier, our tongues moving at a faster, more frenzied pace.

A hand drops to her breast, pulling down one side of her bustier, delighting in the soft flesh, while my other hand slips down to the back of her neck, holding her in place while our kiss gets rough and messy and wet.

Her hands have been static this whole time but now they reach for my collar, tugging on the damp corners, pulling herself to me. My cock rubs against her through my pants and she lets out a breathless moan against my lips.

"I'm back!" Carla's voice divides us like an axe swinging down.

Shit.

We break apart, breathless.

I don't think I've ever been so turned on.

Disoriented.

"Claudio?" Carla asks, her heels clacking across the gallery floor as I hear her approaching the room.

Grace and I stare at each other, wide-eyed, breathing hard. My mouth burns from her lips and I slowly rub my fingers across it for a moment before I yell back to Carla. "We're in here!"

Grace seems to snap out of her daze, and she immediately turns around facing the statue, discreetly tucking her breast back into her dress.

But me, I stand there like a man on the verge of becoming undone. The first threads were pulled, the rest of me is waiting to follow.

The door opens and Carla pokes her head around the corner and looks at us in surprise. "Oh, Claudio. How are you still wet? You're going to need another shirt."

At least it's keeping her attention from my pants, where

my dick is fighting to get out, aching for Grace and impossible to control.

"I'll be fine," I tell her.

"Ah, here," Carla says, walking across the room and pulling out a basket from the shelf. She hands me a blow dryer from inside it. "We have this in case any paintings get wet. Here, dry it off."

I take it from her hands. "*Grazie*, Carla."

"Grace," she says to her sweetly, "can you help me set out the Prosecco?"

"Of course," Grace says quickly. She follows Carla out of the room, shooting me a quick, furrowed glance as she does so.

I stare at nothing for a few moments, trying to compose myself. I then unbutton my shirt, taking it off so that I can dry it with the blow dryer. It's a shame Grace had to leave. I remember the way she looked at me when I took my shirt off around her before, back in my studio. She did what she could to hide the lust in her eyes, almost as if it shamed her. I want to bring that lust back, no shame, just surrender.

And yet when I was kissing her, she was giving herself to me.

She was surrendering.

I just hope that the kiss won't push us back.

I want to move forward with her.

But I don't know what she wants.

When the shirt is somewhat dry, I pull it on and head back into the gallery.

I thought that things would settle between us after we kissed, that I wouldn't feel as nervous anymore, but the anxiety is back and bigger than ever.

Everything is set up, with Grace and Carla having a glass of Prosecco and chatting. For a brief moment, I think about how they would make wonderful friends, and I picture a future in which Grace never has to leave.

It makes my anxiety wane, just a little.

Jesus, how will I ever get over that kiss?

"Here is the man of the hour," Carla says, plucking a glass of Prosecco off the table and handing it to me. "*Cin cin.*"

The three of us make a toast and clink glasses, but my eyes are locked on Grace. She's been such an open book, but right now, when I really need to know, I can't tell what she's thinking.

"Looks like we have our first guest," Carla says excitedly.

A little too excitedly.

Before I turn around to look at the door, I already know who it is.

I turn and see none other than Lorenzo Ducati step inside, Carla practically drooling on him.

"Who is that?" Grace whispers, her eyes expressively wide.

My heart seizes with jealousy. It's always been possessive.

"That," I say, gesturing to the giant man in a charcoal shirt who's walking toward us, "is Lorenzo Ducati."

"He's ... big."

She's not wrong. Lorenzo is taller and more muscular than I am, and covered in tattoos, so he intimidates most people. I've known him since I was young, so he's always been Lorenzo to me, and despite his appearance, and his quiet nature, he's actually a man with a heart of gold. Just takes a bit of digging to see it.

"Claudio," Lorenzo says in his deep voice, giving my

hand a strong shake. We quickly embrace and I slap him affectionately on the back.

He glances appreciatively at Grace. "Who is this?"

His eyes linger on her chest for longer than I would like. My jaw tightens for a moment, but I manage to say, "Lorenzo, this is Grace."

I should add that she's a guest of my ex wife's, but I don't. What I want to add is that she's the woman I nearly fucked in the storeroom. My muse. Somehow I manage to rein it in. He may be bigger than me, but I have no problems in asserting my territory.

If I need to.

"Nice to meet you," Grace says, then adds, "*Piacere*."

It's a pleasure. Her Italian is coming along nicely.

"Grace is an author," I tell Lorenzo. "She's extremely talented."

"Is that so?" he asks in English. "What kind of books?"

"Murder mysteries. So far."

"Any translations in Italian?"

She nods and gestures to me. "Claudio has read them all."

Lorenzo studies me for a moment and then nods. "Ah."

Yes. He understands now.

"Do you live in Lucca?" he asks her.

She shakes her head, looking forlorn. "I wish. It's lovely here. I'm just visiting for a wee bit."

Lorenzo looks at me. "You know, you need to come see me play. You have been saying for years you would."

"Play what?" Grace asks.

"It's called Calcio Storico," he explains. "We have our final match in Florence on our feast day for St. John the Baptist."

"It's like rugby combined with soccer and wrestling," I

add. "With some boxing thrown in. It's dangerous and it's crazy. And so, of course, it's very popular among the locals. Not many tourists know about it or watch it. But all of Florence comes together."

"It can get pretty violent," Lorenzo says with a wicked grin. "Everyone is covered in blood by the end."

"Lorenzo is one of the best," I tell her, patting him proudly on the shoulder. "He is a monster when he plays. They have no equipment either. They play in historical costume—nothing but an elaborate pair of pants."

Her eyes go even wider, no doubt picturing Lorenzo shirtless.

"It's not for a few weeks," Lorenzo says to her. "So if you're here, it would be great to see you. It's sold out but I have extra tickets."

I would love nothing more than to bring Grace to see Florence. Seeing the game would make it even more interesting. But Grace might be back home by then.

Plus, do you want to spend your last days with her there?

My heart sinks at the thought.

I can't even say what our last days will be like when I don't even know what tomorrow will bring.

Was that kiss we shared the beginning of something?

Or was it the end?

THIRTEEN

GRACE

IT STOPPED RAINING.

After gallery night came to an end, leaving me exhausted from meeting so many of Claudio's friends and potential buyers (not to mention all the Prosecco I had), Claudio and I walked through the shiny wet streets of Lucca, back to the car.

We talked about Lorenzo and some of the friends he had in the gallery, as well as Florence and other places in Italy. Claudio was upright, sober, and I was stumbling. Occasionally his arm wrapped around my shoulder, holding me tight, and other times I was left on my own.

But I didn't remember much of the walk.

My mind was locked in the past.

As in, a few hours ago when he told me he wanted to sculpt me, cupped my face, and kissed me.

The kiss that broke my world open.

It was better than I could have imagined, better than any kiss I've had before. A kiss that usually only lives in fiction, a kiss that's born of art. Obviously, I could write about it for days.

His velvety soft lips felt sinful, awakening something inside me I never knew was there. He was right in some ways about unearthing something that already existed. When we came together, it felt as natural as breathing, and I needed it like I needed oxygen.

But it was terribly fleeting.

One moment his tongue was sliding against mine, his fingers trailing delicately over a bare breast, his erection pressed against my hip, and I was feeling the full extent of his desire.

In the next, it was over. Carla, none the wiser, was dragging me off to help her pour the sparkling wine for the guests.

I had to spend the rest of the evening trying to focus on meeting new people and smiling and not feeling awkward, but all I could focus on was the kiss that we shared. How much I wanted it again.

And what it meant.

We were silent as the car sliced through the puddles on the rain-soaked road, the reflection of the streetlights bouncing off the windshield. Claudio seemed tense, and not in a good way. Borderline moody, the way he gets sometimes.

It feels like forever before we finally pull up to the house and I'm practically scrambling to get out of the car just to escape the tension.

This is so awkward.

The kiss was a mistake.

Are we just going to pretend it didn't happen?

All of these thoughts are flying into my brain—*ping, ping, ping*—and I feel like screaming as we enter the house through the bottom door, like I can't possibly go to my room after this, I can't possibly sleep. I can barely breathe.

So we stand there in the middle of the lounge, staring at each other.

And then Claudio says, "I'm feeling inspired. I'm going to go work for a bit."

He nods toward his studio.

My eyes fly to the old clock on the wall and back to him. It's past midnight. Is he asking me to come in the studio with him? Was that a hint?

I stare at him, but I can't read anything. And I don't trust myself to see the right thing either, not after a few drinks, not when it feels like nothing is certain and everything between us is on the line.

"Okay," I say. "I'm going to go to bed."

I say it despite the voice inside me that's screaming *noooo, tell him you want to see his studio. Invite him to your room!*

But the words were said.

I have to stick with them.

Claudio nods, and I swear I see a flash of disappointment on his brow. He walks closer to me, stops, reaches out for my hand, grabs it.

He raises my hand to his mouth, flipping it over, and as his eyes hold mine, he places a long, hot kiss on my palm.

"Goodnight, Grace," he says huskily.

I swallow, trying to respond but it comes out as a squeak instead, and his hand reluctantly lets go.

I pull my hand to my chest, staring dumbly at him for a moment. Then I run up the stairs as fast as I can.

I get to my room, close the door, and climb right onto the bed, knees brought to my chest, trying to breathe through it all.

There will be no sleep tonight.

THE NEXT DAY IT FEELS LIKE EVERYTHING IS BACK TO normal.

Vanni is lounging around, reading some science books.

Claudio is busy in his studio.

And I? Well, I'm doing what I can to write, though it's next to impossible when every time I close my eyes, I can still feel his lips against mine, the hard, feverish need he unearthed when he kissed me. How can he just go back to work like that? How can he just move on?

Didn't he tell me I was his muse?

Or was that just a line?

It's hard to know with these Italian smooth talkers.

It's also hard to know when my experience with the opposite sex is minimal and my brain tends to run away on me, always jumping to the most negative scenario.

The result? I wander around the house like a ghost, unmoored from routine, wanting to latch on to something, anything.

Finally, my wanderings bring me out to the rose garden.

Where I find Claudio with his back to me, holding a pair of clippers, his arm bundled with peachy roses.

The Grace rose.

"What are you doing?" I ask him, standing at the edge of the garden. My voice is quiet, barely audible above the hum of the afternoon crickets.

He straightens up and turns to me, eyes locking with mine.

To my relief, they are warm and familiar.

He's never a stranger.

"Ah, *la mia musa*," he says, the words coming out in a

lyrical rush. I never tire of him speaking his native language, and I'll certainly never tire of him calling me his muse.

Whatever that means.

"Just the person I wanted to see," he finishes.

"How so?" I ask.

Because you wanted to continue that kiss?

Because you wanted to talk to me about that kiss?

"Stay there." He holds out the bunch of roses, framing me in with them, his eyes scrutinizing the scene. "Yes. This is what I *want*."

Want. The word sounds honey-soaked coming from those lips.

I inhale the smell of the roses, feeling shaky. "What?"

"You. Remember last night?"

I stare at him incredulously. Like, which part is he talking about here?

I manage to nod. "Yes."

"Do you remember when I kissed you?"

I gulp, my stomach erupting in butterflies. "Y-yes."

"Do you remember before I kissed you, when I asked you for a favor? If you could be my muse, if you would let me sculpt you?" He pauses, his eyes gleaming. "You never gave me your answer."

"You didn't give me much time."

He grins. "Very true. So perhaps it is my fault. But you can answer me now. May I sculpt you?"

"You may do a lot more than sculpt me."

I can hardly believe the words that leave my mouth.

And from the way Claudio's eyes widen, I don't think he can believe it either.

He blinks. "You should be careful what you ask for. I might just give it to you." He swallows, a flash of pink tongue wetting his lips. I remember what that tongue felt like against my own, and my body stiffens at the thought of it everywhere else.

"But I need no distractions with my art," he adds huskily. "Having you as a muse is complicated enough. Please, tell me you'll consider."

"I've already considered it. Yes. You can ... sculpt me."

He gives me a wicked smile that makes my skin feel hot. "*Perfetto*. Tell me, do you have a dress with thin straps, something not so stiff, but loose, with lots of movement, something that drapes nice? Any color will do."

I nod. "I know just the one."

"I thought you would. Good. Now, perhaps after dinner you could put it on and meet me in the studio. I thought I would give you warning so that you can get your work in for the day."

I almost laugh. Work? There will be no work today, especially not now when I know I'm going to be a model for his art.

"Oh, and if you can go without a bra, that would be great."

I cock my head. "You pervert."

He shrugs, the roses bobbing. "Yes, it's true I am. But in terms of the art, it is much better."

"Right," I say slowly.

Then he turns around and starts snipping away at more of the roses, the bundle in his arms growing. Something tells me that I'll be seeing those roses later.

Of course, now that there's something I'm anxious about, time flies. Before long it's dinnertime, and the three of us enjoy a caprese salad and bruschetta. I drink more wine than I normally do, trying to drown my nerves which are growing tighter by the minute.

Finally, when it's over, I exchange a knowing glance

with Claudio and head up to my room. With shaking fingers, I flick through the dresses hanging in the small wardrobe, looking for the right one.

I find it. I pull it out and hold it up to myself. It's a Zimmerman that I splurged on last year but never had the chance to wear, though it's absolutely perfect for Italy. It's linen, hits mid-calf, with white and yellow stripes, and ruffles across it. There's a tie that goes around the waist, or you can let it fall freely. I think this is exactly what Claudio is asking for.

You know he's also asking for you?

I get undressed, glance at my body in the mirror, and refuse to dwell on the imperfections. Besides, I don't have to get naked for the sculpture. Since I'm not supposed to wear a bra, I forgo my knickers as well. Then I slip the dress on, tying it loosely around the waist to give it some shape. If he wants to untie it, he can.

I practically squirm at the thought of him untying me like a ribbon on a present. This isn't going to be easy, is it?

I head down the stairs, my pulse beating against my wrist, passing Vanni in the living room, listening to something on his iPad with his headphones on. He doesn't even look at me.

Then I'm at the bottom floor.

The door to Claudio's studio is open, music softly blaring.

"Mystify" by INXS. No surprise there.

I step through the doorway, overtaken by how hot it is, and the sweet tea scent of the roses, which are bundled in a beautiful pile on the table.

Claudio is in the corner, trying to set up a fan.

When he sees me, he stops what he's doing and stares.

Doesn't say anything.

I feel like I'm on display, being judged. I hold out my arms, jutting out my hip as if to say, *Ta-da*.

"Does this work?" I ask, feeling more anxious by the minute.

He nods quickly. I can't tell if it's desire in his eyes or awe. Maybe it's both. Either way, he doesn't look disappointed.

He straightens up and walks toward me, stopping close. His eyes flit from my face, down to my shoulders, to my breasts, then the rest of the dress. "Mmmm," he says, pressing his lips together. "*Sì, sì*. This will do."

His gaze comes up to meet mine, eyes holding me in place. "You are too much for this world, I think."

I look away, feeling embarrassed.

"Once again," he says, reaching out and placing his fingers under my chin, raising it so I meet his eyes, "you must learn to take the compliments. I won't stop giving them to you. I'll do it until you believe me, and then I'll do it some more. *Capisci?*"

I nod against his hand.

He slips it behind my neck, expression serious. Wraps my hair around his fingers and holds it up. "I can't tell if I want your hair down or not. I'm afraid I'll lose the lines of your neck if I don't. You have an incredibly sexy neck. Have I ever told you that?"

I'm silent. Manage to shake my head.

"I'm surprised I didn't have a taste last night," he says roughly, leaning in close until his lips hover just above my skin. "Very surprised," he whispers, his breath hot.

Then he pauses.

Pulls away, his eyes at the door behind me.

He walks toward it, and I let out a harsh breath. I'm

already feeling dizzy and this hasn't even started. The heat of the room is mingling with the heat between us.

I turn to see him close it.

Then he locks it.

"Models must have privacy," he says to me, walking over to the table. It's now that I notice a bottle of white wine half-hidden behind the roses, perspiration running down the side. It looks so deliciously cold.

He grabs the bottle and a glass. "I apologize for the temperature in here," he says. "It gets so hot during the day, even with the curtains drawn and the sliding doors open."

He hands me the glass of wine, the stem cool between my fingers, then pulls the stool over to me.

"Here. Sit."

I perch on the end of the stool, wine glass in hand.

He studies me from head to toe, brow furrowed, lips pursed.

"Are you planning on sculpting me with the wine?"

He meets my eyes and smiles. "It would be fitting, no? I could call it Portrait of an Author."

"Very funny."

"No," he says, leaning back against the table, running his fingers over his jaw. "The wine is for your nerves. So you relax." He tightens his shoulders, raising them up to his ears. "We don't want you like this." He lowers them. "We want you like this. Drink up."

At least he's honest about wanting to get me drunk.

After he's finished studying every inch of my body, my skin burning where his eyes have been, he straightens up and goes around what I'm guessing are a bunch of statues covered in sheets.

When he comes back out, he's pushing a slab on wheels. In the middle of it is a large mound of clay, about waist-high,

184

propped up by a rod which attaches to a base on the slab. Two more rods come out of the sides of the clay.

"This will be you," he says, placing it between us. He reaches over and takes one of the rods between his fingers, bending it. "These are wires, so that the clay has something to support it. I can move them to any pose. I will only work on your head and bust today. Eventually the whole thing will be encased in clay."

"So what should I do?" I ask.

"How about you move to the edge of the stool a little more. Is that okay? Are you comfortable? Perhaps hook this foot behind the stool leg. Yes, that's it. Now straighten up. Put your hands in your lap. No, you can hold on to the glass. Hold on."

As I get in position, he turns around and scoops up the roses, taking great care to place them in my arms, even while I hold the glass. I'm overwhelmed by the smell of roses and almonds, and the salty scent of his sweat, mixed with sun-warmed skin.

My hormones immediately go into overdrive.

As if he notices this, he reaches out and tucks a piece of hair behind my ears, his eyes then resting on my lips. "Yes, this might be quite complicated."

He's answering a question he already had in his head, and I don't have to wonder what it could be.

But if some tiny part of me thought he might kiss me again, I'm rebuffed when he pulls back and gets to work.

I wish I could see what he's doing, since the back of the clay model is to me, but it's just as good watching the expression on his face. This is where he's coming alive, his brows knitting together, his jaw tense, the focus in his dark eyes stark and brooding. He is the epitome of concentration, mixed with periods of mania, where his eyes look at me and light up, and I feel like I might be the most precious thing in the world to him.

I hope he'll still look at me like that when this is all said and done.

Eventually he pulls back, taking a break. He wipes the sweat off his brow and plucks the glass from my hand. He turns around to fill it up, his shirt damp and sticking to him.

"You can get up, if you wish," he says to me, handing me the glass back. "I need to direct the fans over here. It is getting too hot."

I stand up, shaking out my legs that were on the verge of falling asleep, then take a big thirsty gulp of wine. It's not as cold as it was, but it tastes just as good. He unplugs the fan and brings it over, aiming it at the floor.

"I don't want to disturb your hair or the roses too much," he explains. "But it is damn hot."

"When can I see?" I ask him, nodding at the clay.

"Not yet," he says. "Not until I have the basics. It is still a very rough draft."

That I get.

I sit back down, adjusting the roses.

He frowns and stops in front of me. Reaches out to touch my shoulder. He slides a clay-dried finger under the strap and lets it fall down my arm.

"Mmmhmm," he muses.

He takes his hand and then places it at my neck. Slowly trails his rough, textured fingers down to my collarbone, leaving a trail of clay in its wake.

His palm then slides down over my shoulder, over my arm, down to my hand, investigating each finger.

He takes the glass of wine from me and has a quenching sip himself before he places it behind him on the table. Then he takes my hand, holds it for a brief moment, fingers intertwined, before he places it on my lap by the rose stems, posing me.

"Do you know," he says slowly, the words spoken with deliberation, "that I didn't sleep at all last night?"

His hand goes to my waist, settling against the curve. He holds it there for a moment.

I'm almost too afraid to speak, like if I do, some magic will dissolve. "No?" I remember him going to his studio, right after he kissed my palm. "Too busy working?"

He shakes his head, eyes following his hand as it goes up my side. "Working? No. I didn't go into the studio to work. I went into the studio to take my mind off of you. But I could not." He wets his lips again, his hand now at my breast.

I instinctively hold my breath, my heart thundering in my head. *Woosh woosh woosh.*

His eyes skirt up to my mouth.

"I could not sleep because all I could think about were these lips. I wondered when I'd get the chance to taste them again. I wondered, perhaps, if I'd ever know what they'd feel like wrapped around my cock."

Holy.

He didn't.

My eyes go so wide that they hurt.

"My boldness makes you nervous?" he says, his thumb now brushing over my nipple, causing me to bite my lip, holding back a groan. My body betrays me, squirming, as my legs try to quell the building pressure.

"No," I say breathlessly.

"Does it turn you on?" he asks, his thumb circling, causing my nipple to tighten through the fabric, an arc of pleasure that radiates down the rest of my body.

I can barely swallow, barely talk. "Yes," I hiss.

"Just checking," he says, a hint of a wicked smile on his lips.

His fingers wrap around the neckline of my dress. With one fluid motion, he yanks it down, my breasts bobbing free.

He stands back, staring at me, at my chest, bare and flushed, nipples in tiny pink peaks, his gaze alternating between inspired and desire. Perhaps there's never been that much of a difference between the two.

"So fucking perfect," he says, holding out his hands as if to frame me, while I sit there, breathing hard.

I swear to god, if he tries to go back to sculpting...

But instead he bends down, placing his mouth over my nipple, and I almost fall off the stool. He sucks on one while he plays with the other, the other hand at the small of my back to keep me in place. It's like a jolt straight between my legs, making me buzz with electricity, causing my thighs to part.

Then his mouth comes up to mine, stealing the breath from me. He tastes like my skin, mixed with a hint of salty clay, and his lips engulf mine with the kind of passion that makes me ache. It's a wet, rough kiss, a little unrestrained, a little messy. The fevered intensity starts to rise inside me, intermingling with butterflies in my chest.

I want this man like I've never wanted anything before.

His hands disappear into my hair, holding me firmly at the back of my head, while I submit myself to him, to this kiss, to wherever this man is going to take me.

He pulls back, placing hot, wet kisses beside my lips. "*La mia musa*," he whispers hoarsely. "You are better than art."

Then he crouches down, throwing up the hem of my dress and ducking his head under it. So when I said I'd submit to wherever this man takes me, I didn't think he'd immediately put his head between my legs.

But I'm not complaining.

I gasp, his hands running up the insides of my thighs, spreading them with a firm grasp. He pauses, his stubble tickling my sensitive skin, inches away from where I'm bare and most certainly wet.

Next thing I know, his hands are gathering the hem and pushing it up and around my waist. Now I'm really exposed.

I grip the edge of the stool with one hand, shocked by the intimacy, the sight of his dark hair between my legs. Rarely did my boyfriends go down on me in the past, mainly because they never seemed into it, and I was always self-conscious of myself.

Looking at Claudio now, I'm in a state of shock, but it's a state that dissolves into want. It's like I never even knew what I wanted until I had it.

And I have it.

His fingers dig into the tender flesh of my hips, while his thumbs keep my legs open for him. I'm breathless in anticipation, the waiting turning into yearning, turning into dying for his contact.

When it comes, all the air leaves my lungs.

His mouth is soft and wet over my clit, tentative, taking his time. My back arches, pushing myself into his mouth, like I have no control over my body anymore. The only thing I can do is grip the edge of the stool with my own hand until my knuckles turn white.

Then...

Fuck.

He takes me into his mouth and sucks me gently and I'm crying out, "Oh my god," and I drop the roses. I absently watch as they tumble over his head and spill onto the floor, and then I'm gripping the edge of my seat with my other hand, like I'm afraid I might float right up to the ceiling.

He pulls back enough, his eyes piercing as they meet mine. "Does that feel okay?"

There isn't even a hint of irony in his voice.

Does it feel *okay*?

I can't talk. I just nod.

Then the sly grin appears on his lips. "Just checking."

His grip gets tighter, and this time he sucks me harder, causing me to moan. Loud. My hands go to his hair, holding him tight.

"Is this to go harder? Slower?" he murmurs against me, the vibrations spreading through me.

"Just ... keep going," I whisper harshly, my neck going back, my eyes falling closed.

Dear. God.

He alternates between kisses and licks, his tongue swirling until the pressure is at capacity and I can't hold back anymore.

"Oh god, yes," I cry out, my words sounding feverish and foreign, like someone else is speaking through me. I've never been someone who vocalizes during sex, and now, from him going down on me, I want to tell him all the dirty things I want done to me.

But my mind can't even form sentences. Not when his licking intensifies, when he starts sucking me harder, and harder and then ... then...

I'm coming.

The orgasm tears through me, making my limbs shake, my body on the verge of completely letting go and falling onto the floor. It's all too much, my thoughts and feelings are scrambled, and every physical part of me feels like it's been shot into space and back.

"You taste like sin," Claudio says to me as he gets up. He leans in, putting his hand at the back of my neck and kisses me, until I taste myself too, the salty and sweet. "Except I know your sin is heaven sent."

He steps back, and I sit there, trying to catch my breath, half off the stool, the roses at my feet.

He starts to unbutton his shirt, eyes locked on mine, brimming with raw lust. His shirt sticks to him with sweat, and he pulls it off, throwing it on the ground. He then unzips the fly of his jeans, slowly. Too slowly. And even though my body still feels raw from the orgasm, I'm getting turned on all over again, like the desire inside me is a switch that's never fully off.

"Are you on the pill?" he asks, voice low and husky.

I swallow. Nod. "Yes."

I'm actually on it for my skin, mostly, though I figured it would never hurt if I got involved with someone. Of course that opportunity never came. Until now.

"Good," he says.

Slides his jeans down until he's in his briefs.

My eyes are glued to his hands as they slowly rub down against his cock, which is large and outlined against the grey fabric.

I gulp.

Lord have mercy on me.

He steps out of his jeans, and since he works barefoot, he's already half-naked.

Then he pulls down his briefs, really making this into a show.

A show worth any cost of admission.

I've been taught that if you see a man's penis, you should politely turn your head. No one wants you to stare.

But I can't take my eyes off it.

And it's obvious Claudio *wants* me to look. He's proud ... and for good reason.

His cock is large, thick, and vaguely threatening. Like, if I don't treat it well, it's capable of some very sweet, severe punishment, the kind that keeps you coming back for more.

Eventually I close my mouth and look up and into his eyes.

Of course he's got the cockiest grin. A cock like his would do that to you.

I swallow, rubbing my lips together, my entire body tense and on edge, wondering what's going to happen next.

"Turn around," he says, his voice dropping, becoming rough. His smile fades. "Bend over the stool."

I stare at him, mouth agape again.

He stares right back, sliding his fist over his cock, his eyes squinting in pleasure as he reaches the thick base.

I am in trouble.

Somehow, I manage to get to my feet and turn around, bending over the bench so my behind is to him.

"No, no," he murmurs. "That won't do. Pull up your dress. Let me see your ass."

I reach back and start tugging up the hem of my dress until it's gathered around my waist. I have to say, it's a wee bit easier to be on display this way when I can't see his expression.

That said, I can *feel* it. His eyes are practically burning my skin.

Silence hums between us.

Finally he clears his throat. "I'm beginning to think that perhaps this is what I should sculpt."

"Don't you dare," I tell him, adjusting myself so that my boobs aren't as squished against the seat of the stool. "Are you just going to stand there or what?"

So bold, Grace.

And yet I don't care. I don't feel like myself right now. In fact, I haven't really felt like myself since I got here. It's all been leading to this moment, the chance to really do something freeing. To do something for myself.

Getting fucked by Claudio might be the best self-care possible.

"I don't like to be rushed," he says, his voice sounding like silk as it cascades over me. "I like to take my time. I have wanted this, dreamed about this, got off to this, and I am in no hurry for it to be over."

But then I hear him walk forward.

A grunt of appreciation.

He runs his hand over the smooth curves of my cheeks. "You have tan lines from being in the sun. I don't know why this is so sexy. Like I am seeing something I'm not supposed to."

He pauses.

Then...

WHACK.

I jerk up, my fingers gripping the edge of the stool as the sting from his slap shoots through me.

The bastard just spanked me!

"Did you like that?" he asks, running his hand gently over where he just slapped me. "Was it too much?"

There is so much rough desire brimming in his voice, but at the same time, I hear his concern. Like he's actually worried.

"Wasn't too much," I manage to say, licking my lips. "Do it again."

193

I practically *hear* him grin.

WHACK, WHACK!

Both cheeks get it and I let out a cry of pain and pleasure. The sting somehow makes me focus on him, on what's happening, on the feeling, instead of wondering. It's like it's anchoring me to this moment.

Anchoring me to him.

After a few more hits, he leans down and places his mouth where my skin is burning, soothing it with his lips and tongue, making me melt into a puddle of want. I want him inside me so badly, I'm positively aching for him.

"So," he muses, pulling back as I feel a hand move to my hip, encasing me in his large, warm palm.

I wonder where his other hand is going, and then I feel it between my legs, stroking me.

I gasp, unable to stop the sound.

"You are so wet," he says. "I was worried that I wouldn't fit, but perhaps I might now." He slowly inserts his finger inside me, one, two, three.

"Fuck," I cry out.

"Say it again."

"*Fuck.*" I pause. "Fuck *me.*"

He chuckles, a wicked sound. "I never thought I would hear you say such words, with so much desire. Of course, all you ever had to do was ask."

His fingers pull out and I tense up, just as I feel his grip tighten around my hip, and the hard press of his cock teasing my wetness.

Then he pushes in, achingly slow. I tense around him, unable to relax, trying to breathe through it. I think if he went any faster, I would be impaled.

"Does that feel good?" he asks, his voice breaking. "It feels *so* good, *musa.*"

I make a strangled noise, trying to nod. I take in a sharp breath through my nose, forcing my muscles to relax. I feel like I've been revirginized, it's been *that* long, and Claudio is a big boy to start with.

He pushes in to the hilt until I feel the soft press of his balls against me, and then he's slowly pulling out. Achingly and teasingly slow. His breath is long and steady, but while I'm breathing to relax, to accommodate his girth, he's most likely breathing to stay in control.

I like that he's in control here. I like that I'm bent over this stool in his studio, surrounded by his art, and he's taking me from behind like this. I don't have to think, I can just be.

I can just enjoy him.

"Fuck," he murmurs through a strained groan, then lets loose a few Italian words I don't understand. I don't need to understand them. Their dramatic cadence tells me it's all about desire.

He starts pumping in a bit faster now, his grip holding strong. In and out, his hips press against me, and my mind wanders to how this must look from behind, the bronzed strong muscles of his ass flexing as he pounds me.

I can't believe this is happening.

"Grace," he says roughly, but he doesn't say anything else.

We lapse into silence, the sound of his skin slapping against mine, the wet sound of his cock as the small thrusts get longer, harder. Delicious little grunts come from deep within him, turning me on even more, and then his hand slips under and finds my clit.

I moan loudly, and it seems to fill the room.

"You're so perfect," he says, his fingers stroking my clit in circles. "Your skin, your cunt. If you could see what I see, the way I move inside you..."

He picks up the pace, working me harder, his cock sliding against me with each pass, the pressure from his fingers increasing.

I won't be able to hold on for much longer. The ache is building, starting in my belly and moving to my spine, and I'm opening wider and wider.

"I'm close," I manage to say, not knowing if he needs a warning.

He just grunts again at that, going faster now, rougher.

Another *whack* as he spanks me, and it brings my mind around, and then his fingers go back to work. I feel like I'm the matchbook and he's the match, and if he strikes me just right one more time...

Suddenly the stool starts to rock, unable to keep steady from the unrestrained pounding I'm taking, and I'm almost falling off of it.

Claudio lets out a frustrated growl, and before I know what's happening, he's grabbing me by the hair and pulling me off the stool. He throws out his arm so it knocks the stool over, and it goes skittering across the floor.

Without the stool beneath me, I'm being held up by a large fistful of my hair for a moment. Then I'm quickly lowered to the floor where my elbows and knees are digging into the spilled roses. My face is pressed into the petals, and I take in the heady whiff of my namesake flower while Claudio continues to fuck me, still deep inside.

"Fuck," he cries out gruffly, the pace picking up again. "You feel so good, you are so good, so perfect, I can't help myself with you."

With this new position on the floor, my hips higher, another swift thrust of his cock slides against the right places and that pressure inside me expands, making me feel like I'm on the verge of going off like a bomb.

His fingers find my swollen clit again and that's all it takes. A few wet strokes of delicious friction, and the match strikes, an aching flame rolling down along my spine until it explodes at the base, licking through me, taking no prisoners.

"Oh god, oh god," I cry out. "*Yes.*"

Garbled nonsense follows as I come apart around him, feeling like I've been blown wide open. There's nothing left of me, except tender, spent pieces.

My upper body collapses onto the ground, my face crushed against the velvet soft roses, and I try to brace myself for what I know is coming, all while I slowly come back down to earth.

Claudio keeps pumping into me, the sharp slap of his hips filling the room, the feel of his balls as they whip against me. He is a voracious, relentless beast at this moment and I think he might just fuck me into the ground.

Then he stills for a split second, his breath sucked inward, before his fingers bruise my hips, and he comes inside me with a low groan.

His thrusts slow, and eventually his grip loosens and I feel drops of sweat fall onto the small of my back.

"Grace," he says, and I can still feel myself pulsing around him as my body tries to regulate itself. He lets out a shuddering breath. "*Mi hai distrutto.* You have destroyed me. Body and soul."

Likewise, is all I can think. *Likewise.*

He affectionally runs his hand over my back, smoothing out the sweat, and then pulls out. I immediately feel the space he leaves behind. I wanted him to stay buried in me forever.

He gets to his feet, while I slowly straighten up, on my knees, picking away the loose petals that are sticking to my damp skin. I hear him pull on his clothes, and then he walks around in front of me, just in his briefs, holding out a hand for me.

I give him a quick smile and put my hand in his, letting him help me to my feet.

I expected things to be awkward between us now, since we just had hot, sweaty sex in his artist studio, but it doesn't feel that way. He grins at me, his eyes glossy and sated, and then wraps a hand around my waist, the skirt of my dress straightening out.

Even after all that, the sight of that smile takes my breath away, making those little butterflies dance.

"Here," he says quietly, reaching out and touching my forehead. When he removes his hand, I see peachy rose petals in them. "I suppose I'll have to get more roses for next time." He pauses, searching my face. "And by that I mean the sculpting session. Let's see how far I get before you distract me again."

He leans in and kisses my forehead where the petals had been, his lips warm and lingering. We're both still trying to catch our breath.

"So," he says to me, as he pulls away. "Are you done being a model for the night or would you like to try again?"

To be honest, I don't think I could go back to staring at him for hours and sitting in one spot. I need to be alone to process what happened. I need to think about what this means.

"I might be ready for bed," I tell him, even though it's still fairly early. Vanni is probably still up.

But he just nods. "I thought you might."

Then he turns and grabs his clothes, getting dressed.

And I stand there, wondering how much my world has changed.

FOURTEEN
CLAUDIO

IT WASN'T A DREAM.

I wake up with a voracious hard-on. I roll over to my side, my legs catching in the sheets. I'm used to waking up like this, particularly after Grace arrived in my life, like a shining star caught in Earth's gravity. My dreams have been filthy with her.

But last night's dream wasn't a dream at all.

I close my eyes to the faint sun streaming in through the curtains, replaying the scene in my mind.

Her smell, her taste, the way she felt when I drove my cock inside. So tight, warm, it was like coming home. I saw the side of her I always wanted to see, the side that was buried under all her layers, coming apart like the petals of the roses as they crushed beneath her. I don't think I'll ever smell roses the same way again.

Fuck. That was *real.*

It happened.

Art come to life.

Granted, I didn't get that much work done, but that's hardly the matter. The work will come easy now, I know it will, now that she's given me permission to sculpt her. As long as I can keep my hands off her and on the clay.

That won't be easy, not when she looks the way she does, not when she takes me in with those baby blues of hers, looking at me sometimes like I'm a god.

At the very least, I felt like a god last night.

I get up, deciding to take a shower, thoughts of Grace rolling through me until I have to get off again. It's been a long time since I last slept with someone, and now my body is firing on all cylinders, a slumbering beast that's been awakened.

When I step out of the shower, I get changed, and glance at the time. It's seven thirty, perhaps a little too early to wake Grace. After we fucked in the studio, we ended up going our separate ways to sleep. I could tell that she had a lot on her mind, and I wasn't going to push it, especially as Vanni could easily catch us with the other in bed. The boy doesn't knock when it comes to me.

But when I head down the hall to her room, her door is already open a crack.

"Grace?" I call out quietly before pushing it open.

Her bed is made, the room empty.

Hmmm.

I head downstairs, checking the study, then go to the kitchen.

No sign of her.

I step out the back, thinking she might be in the pool for some reason, when I see her sitting at the veranda, her back to me. I don't think I've ever seen her up this early and it makes me uneasy somehow. As if last night disrupted something.

"*Buongiorno*," I say to her as I walk across the grass, hands in my pockets.

She turns to look at me, giving me a quick smile, before focusing back on her laptop.

"Uh oh," I say, coming over to her. "I've interrupted something."

I put my hand on her neck and lean in for a kiss, but she instantly jerks her head back.

Feels like I've been kicked in the stomach, to be honest.

"Sorry, sorry," she says softly, eyes darting everywhere. "I just ... Vanni could see us."

I look back at the house. Vanni is most likely still asleep.

But from the frightened look in her eyes, I'm not going to press her.

I drop my hand and step back, swallowing my discomfort.

"Forgive me," I say, displaying my palms.

Her face softens. "I'm sorry. I just ... I need to figure things out first."

I angle my head, staring at her, wondering where she's coming from.

"What do you need to figure out? We had sex last night, yes? There is no mystery there. Certainly no mystery of whether you enjoyed it or not."

I can still hear her low, breathy cries as they echoed around the studio.

She rubs her lips together, pink staining her cheeks. "I know."

"Don't tell me you thought it was a mistake," I say teasingly. I keep an easy smile on my face, though I know I'll lose it in a moment if she agrees.

Her eyes widen and she shakes her head, taking her hands off her keyboard and putting them in her lap. "Not a mistake. I just need to ... move past it."

My brows go up. *Move past it?*

"Don't tell me you want to pretend it didn't happen." I decide to push her, make that blush deepen. "I know my cock is all you can think about."

Yes. There it is, the pink spreading across her face and now her chest.

"Claudio," she whispers. "I..."

I walk around and sit down across the table from her, folding my hands on it, fingers steepled. "I am going to pretend that last night I fucked a few brain cells loose so that you don't know what you're talking about. Grace, why on earth would you move past *that*? Why not think about it? Revel in it? I know that's what I'll keep doing until it happens again." I pause, reading her tense body language. "I get the feeling that I might be waiting for a while ... if you feel shame."

She exhales loudly through her nose and gives me a pointed look before shutting her laptop. "I'm not ashamed. I'm sorry. I just ... I don't want to ruin what we have and I really don't want to make things complicated between you and me and Vanni. Not to mention Jana."

"Jana isn't a part of this conversation. Neither is Vanni."

"But he's your son."

"He is. And I love him. I would do anything for him. And I have. But right now, what you and I share, our bodies, it does not involve him. So you can stop worrying about him. Okay?" I place my hand palm up on the table, gesturing for her to give me hers. "This is about you and me, Grace. That is it. That is all. That is enough."

She hesitates and then puts her hand in mine, nodding her head.

I grasp it hard.

"I just need to go slow," she says quickly. "I don't want to ... lose focus."

She eyes her laptop.

"That I understand." But I'm not sure how much of that is the truth for her and how much is an excuse. "Your work comes first." I pause. "You also come first." I give her a weighted look so she can't escape my meaning.

I lean over and kiss the top of her hand before letting go. I straighten up.

"Then I shall leave you. I don't think I've ever seen you up this early."

"Yeah, well I couldn't sleep much," she says, looking coy. "And I figured this was the only opportunity to write out here before it gets too hot."

"That's smart," I tell her. "I'll go get breakfast ready."

I walk around the table and head into the house, but the spring I had in my step earlier has faded. I'm sure that Grace will come around, I just wish we were on the same page about this whole thing. Whether we're sleeping together, or whether it's something more, whatever we create is something just for us. And for now, it doesn't need the permission of anyone else, not even of my own son.

I just need Grace's permission.

And I can only hope she'll give it to me.

BREAKFAST WAS FAIRLY EASY. I MADE A FRITTATA AND put together a board of sliced meats and cheeses and bread. Vanni, of course, only had the Nutella. I swear he goes through two jars a week. Where does he put it all?

Grace was acting quiet and demure during breakfast, which I understood. She was trying to appear like nothing was wrong, like nothing had happened between us, and since she's a bad liar, I guess the best thing was to talk as little as possible.

Vanni, as observant as he is, didn't notice. He was too busy talking about a movie theatre in Lucca playing a matinee of *Back to the Future*.

"Can I go, please?" he pleads as I settle down with an espresso.

"Not with those crumbs on your face."

He grabs a napkin and aggressively wipes them off. "Okay, now can I go?"

I sigh. I did want to take part of today to work on the sculpture of Grace, providing Grace would volunteer as model again. But Vanni looks so sincere, and I still feel bad that he didn't have the vacation he wanted.

"Okay," I say. "Matinee? What time?"

"Two o'clock," he says. "It's in the city, you know the old theatre Cinema Astra? We can bike there and have lunch. Then I can meet Paolo. It was his idea."

Paolo is one of his school friends, also a nerd like Vanni.

"Are you sure? It's not too hot for a bike ride? Also, why not another movie, if you must? You have seen *Back to the Future* a million times."

"Gio's father would let him go."

I roll my eyes and exchange a dry look with Grace, who has a smile dancing on her lips. "Fine. If alternate dimension Vanni can go, then you can go."

"It's alternate *universe*."

"Okay." I turn to Grace. "Would you like to come with us?"

I expect her to say no, so I'm surprised when she nods. "Aye, that sounds like fun."

Hmmm. Always keeping me on my toes.

It's not long after that we get the bikes out and are set to ride off. We leave a little earlier than we should, trying to beat the heat, but it's no use. It's ten o'clock and we're already sweating. Luckily the road through the valley is flat and there's a breeze as we go. When I catch glimpses of Grace, she's smiling again.

That's something I wish I could sculpt, or at least take a picture of. Her eyes closed, lips spread wide and tilted up to the sun. She looks so happy and free. That's the Grace I saw last night, moments after she came around my cock.

Fucking hell, what am I doing? I'm falling for her a little too fast.

And I don't think there's anything I can do about it.

We get to Lucca, overheated, with our clothes sticking to us. We walk our bikes through the uneven streets until I find a nice restaurant that's open for an early lunch, in the cooler shade of the buildings.

We sit around an outside table, drinking Aperol Spritzes (a Coke for Vanni), while watching the world go past, waiting for the kitchen to open. We're silent for a lot of it, all of us just existing in the moment. There's this indescribable warmth in my chest, this feeling of contentment that I haven't felt in a long time. Perhaps my feelings are ridiculous, but just being here, the three of us ... it feels like family.

But you're not family. She's a guest and she will be leaving sooner than you think.

I feel cold at the thought. I've been doing what I can not to dwell on the fact that Grace's time at Villa Rosa has an expiration date. There's no good in counting the days, knowing how fast time will pass you by anyway. It's a fight that I won't win.

Soon the kitchen opens and we place orders for our food, sharing grilled eggplant, zucchini, and bocconcini as an antipasto, then moving on to pasta. Grace practically loses her mind over the spaghetti carbonara, demolishing it like she's starving.

There's nothing sexier than watching her eat. She does it with such enthusiasm, her face collapsing in pleasure, the same way she did when she came.

Then we take our time relaxing over espressos and then limoncello, before Vanni bids us goodbye.

"Remember, go straight to the theatre," I tell him. "I don't want you getting lost."

The theatre is around the corner, and Vanni has been to Lucca so many times, there's no way he will get lost. The city isn't that big, regardless.

"I will, I will," he says. I can tell from the look on his face that he's both annoyed and grateful I'm not walking him there. At least I know Paolo is a good kid, and his idea of a good time is studying (or watching *Back to the Future*, it seems).

"I'll meet you outside in two hours. We'll keep the bikes locked up here."

Vanni nods and takes off down the street.

"Must be nice to be in a city where your kid can do that," Grace comments, finishing the last of her drink.

I shrug. "Perhaps I wouldn't let him go in Rome, but here it is okay."

I've already paid the check, so I drum my fingers on the table. "So? Where to?"

She shrugs. "Anywhere would be nice. I guess we have to leave the bikes?"

"No, we can take them and keep his bike locked up here, as long as we don't leave our bikes out of our sight. Want to take a ride?"

She nods.

I get the attention of the waiter again and add a bottle of white wine to the bill. The wine is to-go. He brings it to me with two plastic cups.

Grace's brows raise appreciatively. I know the true way to her heart.

Biking through the city streets is a little complicated with the amount of pedestrian foot traffic, so at the first opportunity, we take the path up to the medieval walls again. Last time we didn't do a complete circle, so this time we go where she hasn't been yet.

It's still hot as sin and the shade of the massive chestnut and linden trees aren't doing much to cool us down. I decide for us to stop, and take a path down that leads to a wide expanse of grass, lined with crumbling ruins on the other side of the city.

"What is this?" Grace asks, getting off her bike once we get to the grass.

"This is history," I tell her, pushing my bike along. "These are the ruins of bastions. When this was built in the 1500s, they expected Florence to attack. When they didn't, these old walls became disused. It's the perfect place to enjoy a bottle of wine."

Hopefully in private.

We walk along the crumbling walls until we come to a nice spot shielded from view of the main wall where cyclists and walkers pass. I pluck the wine and glasses from the basket on Grace's bike, then throw our bikes down on the grass and sit down beside each other, backs against the wall.

The bottle is a screw-top, and I open it, pouring it into the cups.

"*Cin, cin,*" I tell her, raising my wine.

"*Cin, cin,*" she says, raising hers.

I know I'm staring at her too much, and I know I'm

possibly being too much, especially when she told me this morning that she needed space. But to change would be like changing who I am. I can give her space, but I can't pretend I don't ache for her.

I finish my sip and clear my throat. "So, this evening. Would you care to model for me again?"

She stiffens. Not the reaction I wanted, but one I expected.

"Tonight?"

"If you're not writing, but I understand if you are."

Understand, but I would still be disappointed, no matter how wrong it is to feel. How can she keep her focus on her work when I am here and losing my mind over her?

"Ummm," she says, staring down into her wine.

"Grace," I say to her. "You are my muse. I need you."

Her face softens, her eyes growing wet. Her mouth opens and then closes again. She has a sip of wine, licks her lips. "Look ... Claudio."

And here it comes. The blow. What she was trying to tell me this morning but lost the nerve, perhaps feeling sorry for me because I was too honest about what I wanted, too open with my feelings.

She sighs and looks down at her hands. "I'm ... I'm afraid."

This is news to me. "Afraid?"

"Yes." She swallows, eyes roaming the field. "I'm afraid that ... I'll lose focus. Not just with the book. That I'll lose focus on myself. Last night..." She sucks in her lower lip and my dick twitches, dying to have another taste. "It meant something to me. And because it meant something, it changes everything."

"Maybe it's okay if everything changes. And I would never let you lose sight of yourself."

"You don't understand," she snaps, then shrinks back. "Sorry. I'm sorry. It's just ... I don't know myself. I've only just begun to discover who I am and what I want. And I'm afraid that ... that I'll throw it all away for you."

"So that's what you're really afraid of? It's not about Vanni, it's not about Jana..."

She gives me a wry look. "Oh, it's about them, too. I'm just afraid that ... well, you always talk about how I need to discover myself. Unearth myself. What if I miss that opportunity because I'm with you."

I lean in close to her, putting my hand on her leg. "But what if I help you?" I whisper. "What if this is something we do together?"

She frowns. "You want to fix me."

"I want to help you."

"By fucking me?"

I can't help but grin. "You don't think it counts?"

She scoffs and twists slightly away from me.

I give her leg a light squeeze. "I'm not going anywhere, Grace. All I ask from you is to let yourself go. Let yourself be free. You did that last night. Last night you lost yourself to me. It's okay to surrender sometimes, let the current take you where it needs to."

She runs her tongue over her teeth and slowly nods, her attention off in the distance. I know I've just come on too strong and I wish I could take my words back, but they've been said and now I have to deal with them.

Then she gets to her feet, and I realize how much I'll have to deal with.

"Where are you going?" I ask her.

"I need to clear my head," she says, walking away. She finishes her wine and tosses the cup over her shoulder. It bounces in the grass beside me.

I watch her for a moment, blindsided. It's not like Grace to act like this, and the fact that I'm the reason is disconcerting.

I get up, march over to her, grab her by the arm and pull her around to face me.

"You can't run from me," I tell her, feeling emboldened. "You can't run from your problems. Maybe you thought you could by coming here, but you have to face them head on and you *are*. You are changing before my eyes. But don't pretend that I'm part of those problems. You're not that good of a liar."

"Let go of me," she says, her pupils pinpricks, her words harsh.

I drop her arm, feeling lost in all of this.

"Grace," I manage to say. "Let's talk about it."

"I don't want to talk to you right now," she says. "You're making everything so much more complicated."

I do the next best thing to talking.

I grab her face and I kiss her.

She presses her fist against my chest and I expect her to pound on me, like I'm King Kong and she's some hapless maiden.

But then her mouth is opening against mine, a whimper escaping her lips and flooding through me, and her hand goes from a fist to being open and flat against my shirt. Her fingers grab hold of the fabric, and my tongue slides into her mouth, eager and ravenous.

I spin us around, still kissing her, still holding her, pressing her against the ancient wall. My hands drop to the hem of her dress, and I yank it up, feeling her spandex shorts underneath. I let out a grunt of frustration; this is the equivalent of a chastity belt.

I take hold of her shorts and underwear, roughly tugging them down until she kicks them off her ankles.

Then I slip my arm under her ass and hoist her up until she's against the rough stone wall.

"Claudio—" she says, breathless, but I cut her off with my mouth, my lips devouring her, the wolf to the lamb. She's kissing me back, just as ravenous, and I can feel the push and pull inside her, the war to either continue arguing over something stupid, or to succumb to me, to let me fuck her senseless, and turn her world inside out.

I quickly reach down and fumble with my zipper, taking my cock out of my pants, positioning it against her cunt as her legs wrap around my waist. I suck in a deep breath — she's already *so* wet, and then I thrust up into her.

She gasps into my mouth, her head rolling back against the wall, and I pull down her neckline, sucking a perfect pink nipple into my mouth. Flicking, sucking, tasting her perfect skin. It makes her cry out again, hoarse and breathy and *god*, those sweet little sounds she makes will be the end of me.

I keep pumping into her, my cock lengthening with each thrust, until I'm sure I can't go on like this. Her nails are digging into my head, into my shoulder as she holds on, more of those hungry cries falling from her open mouth.

I lick up her collarbones, sliding my tongue across her neck, and reach down to tease her clit, knowing the best way to set her off. I want to make her come around me so hard she sees stars and we break right through this wall.

Of course, the fact that I'm fucking her in public, for all the world to see, hasn't escaped me. It just makes me harder. At any moment someone could come stumbling from behind the wall and see me screwing her, her legs wrapped around me, her breast bare.

I can see it now. I'm a lucky bastard.

And this woman is heaven. This woman will make me fall so damn hard I won't be able to get to my feet again. With each and every jab of my hips, each slick velvet pass of skin as I move inside her, it brings me to the edge, the place you don't return from. I'm not sure if I've ever been this close before, to that big unknown.

But I will gladly take the leap.

For her.

"Oh, fuck, Grace," I cry out hoarsely into her neck, biting and sucking and leaving marks and bruises, but she just grips my cock even tighter, grows even wetter. She likes this bit of pain, and from what I can tell, doesn't mind that I'm fucking her out in the open.

She tugs at my hair, harder and quicker now, and I feel her urgency. She's breathing heavier. I pull back to watch her face, her eyes half-closed, jaw slack. Her eyes open enough to hold mine, fear and lust and vulnerability washing over them.

I rub my thumb over her clit in a few hard, rough strokes.

Her eyes go wide, her hips trying to meet mine, and then she's coming.

I take it all in.

The sight of my muse in freefall.

Something in my chest drops, like I'm freefalling with her, like this is a journey only the two of us can go on, a journey that could take us anywhere.

Her mouth opens, her brows snapping together, and she's crying out my name, over and over, not caring that people passing on the other side of the wall can hear her.

Then she's shuddering around my cock, squeezing me into my own orgasm. It snakes through me as I'm fucking her hard, and then I'm shooting inside her, my pumps slowing, and every inch of my body is warm, so warm. Like slipping into a bath.

Mio Dio.

La mia musa.

My eyes flutter closed, sweat rolling off my forehead and dripping onto her chest. I kiss her again, dazed, the taste of wine still on her tongue.

"You..." I whisper, catching my breath. "You are full of surprises."

She swallows hard, breathless. "So are you."

I grin at her and quickly pull out, then I lower her to the grass. She moans a little, hand at her spine.

I grab her shoulder and turn her around, taking a look at her back. I wince.

Her nice dress is all roughed up from where I was fucking her against the wall, the stones tearing apart the fabric.

"I don't think your dress will forget this," I tell her, pulling at the back so I can see her smooth spine. "Your skin doesn't look broken though."

"I'm sure I will bruise," she tells me, turning around and smoothing her dress out. "And I have enough dresses anyway."

"That you do," I say, my fingers trailing down her arm until I'm holding her hand. "So tell me, Grace. Are we done arguing for the day? Do we need to talk some more?"

She looks flushed from the sex, or it could be the sheepish look on her face.

"We're done."

"And so...? You're not going to run from us, no matter how *complicated* I am? You're not going to let your mind conjure up things that aren't true? We can just ... *be?*

Claudio and Grace, two incredibly sexy people who like to fuck each other?"

She gives me a quick smile at that, and then wets her lips with her tongue, eyes roaming my face as she thinks. She nods. "We can just be ... and I'm sorry if I've been..."

"Nothing to apologize for," I tell her quickly. "I want you to talk to me, okay? About anything. Don't be afraid to do that. Both of us ... I think this is so new. I know I haven't been with a woman in a long time, and I certainly have never been with a woman like you. It will take some getting used to, and I am sure we are both bound to get afraid or say the wrong thing, but as long as we keep communicating..." I gesture between us. "Then we will be okay. Maybe better than okay?" I say gently.

She flashes me a pretty smile, a touch of relief on her brow. "Definitely better than okay."

Good enough for me.

FIFTEEN

GRACE

"Vanni, where's your father?"

Vanni doesn't even raise his head, his eyes glued to his iPad, where someone with a very serious voice is talking about something. Probably a scientist.

"Vanni," I say again, leaning against the railing. I had woken up late this morning since Claudio hadn't come to wake me. Neither had Vanni. I've been up and down the house, peeked at the pool, and haven't seen Claudio anywhere.

"*Parla in Italiano,*" Vanni says dismissively.

This kid, I swear.

"*Dove tuo padre,*" I say, pretty sure I'm saying it right. "*Dove tuo padre?*"

Finally, Vanni looks up at me and smiles triumphantly. "I am an excellent teacher, am I not?"

Truth is, it's been Claudio that's been helping me with my Italian lately. Though half the things he's said, I can't repeat in front of his child.

"Yes. Of course."

He turns back to his iPad. "He is in the chapel."

My brows shoot up. *The chapel?*

"He said not to wake you," he goes on. "Said you needed to sleep."

My face immediately goes hot and I'm grateful that Vanni is so involved with whatever he's watching. The truth is, the last few days here, the only time Claudio and I have had time alone together is at night, which means there's a lot of him sneaking into my room. We have sex for hours, feeling spent and exhausted, but he can never stay the night and sleep with me, just in case we get caught.

There's a dirty thrill about it, the sneaking around, the keeping our liaisons a secret. Not that it feels all that good to keep secrets from Vanni, but in this case, the less he knows the better.

Besides, I don't know what we are and I don't want to put a label on it. I'm well aware that my time here is ticking away. I only have ten days until I'm supposed to leave.

Ten days left of having Claudio sculpt me, with both his hands, and with his tongue.

Ten days of trying to get as much of the book finished as possible, before I head back home and lose my inspiration entirely.

With the weather getting progressively hotter, working on the veranda isn't cutting it anymore. I do what I can in my bedroom, with the fans whirring full blast, and some-times I'll go and write in the study. But the heat, plus the ever-present distraction that is Claudio, makes it hard to concentrate.

But in some ways it's also been easier. I'm able to put my feels directly into the book, as my character starts to fall for her love interest. The only difference is, I know my char-acters are going to have a happy ending and that won't be the case for me.

It can't be.

However complicated my feelings for Claudio are, I know deep in my heart that I'm setting myself up for a sad ending. This can never move beyond a temporary thing, a vacation fling. Even if I let myself fall deeply for him, if I remove the bars around my heart and let him in, give something of myself to him that's more than just my body, I'll be devastated when it all comes crumbling down.

Sleeping with my agent's ex-husband is one thing. I already feel as if I'm breaking some kind of "girl code," even if Jana and I aren't exactly friends. But dating her ex-husband? Taking this to the next level? I can say goodbye to the book deal, say goodbye to having Jana as my agent. She is the one chance I have to get my career going, to stand on my own two feet, out of the weight of Robyn's shadow. If I fuck this up, it's over.

So then don't fuck it up, I tell myself as I head out the door and down the outside staircase to the front, catching the scent of the geraniums. I walk along the pebbled driveway, past the flowering oleander and potted lemons, the heat bearing down on me and making me break a sweat, even though it's only ten a.m.

I cross the country road to the chapel, the rows of silvery olive trees climbing up the dusty hill behind it.

I've actually never been in it before. It's quite small, white, with two narrow slits for windows, and one glass door with a curtain. The door is open, the curtain billowing in the hot breeze.

I go up the stone path and pause outside the door.

"Claudio?" I ask, hearing the muffled sound of something being moved around.

"Shit," he swears from inside.

Swearing in a church? How uncouth.

217

"Are you okay?" I ask, not wanting to go inside in case he's, like, praying or something. I know the Italians are very religious, although the swearing has thrown me off.

Suddenly the curtain moves and Claudio pokes his head out.

He smiles, perfect white teeth glowing against his tanned skin, a thin sheen of sweat on his brow, and once again I feel my insides melt, my legs growing weak. All he has to do is just fucking appear and I'm a goner.

I'm *hopeless*.

"Good morning, *musa*," he says to me. "I was hoping you wouldn't discover where I am."

I frown. "Vanni gave up your whereabouts. What are you doing in there?"

He doesn't look impressed. "Did Vanni mention that he was supposed to keep it a surprise?"

I shake my head. "He didn't say much. What's the surprise?"

"Well, it's not done yet. I was planning to show you this afternoon."

"And the surprise is in the church?" I pause. "You're not planning to introduce me to God or something, are you?"

He smirks. "Not quite. More like God might find *you*."

Okay, now I'm really worried.

He chuckles warmly at the look on my face and then straightens up, pulling back the curtain. "Come on in, then."

I hesitate, because honestly I don't know if I'm about to walk into a religious intervention or what. That *would* be a surprise.

But I walk through the curtain and into the chapel.

I don't know what I was expecting, a church I guess, but this isn't it. It's a literal bedroom, complete with a queen-size bed that is pushed haphazardly against the wall. The walls are painted pale yellow and there's a nave at the center, a carved out arch where the altar would be, dotted with golden candles. An oil painting of Mary hangs in the middle. Handmade decorations in low relief line the side walls, and there's a velvet chaise lounge with golden legs and gilded trim.

In the middle of the room is a desk. It's large, made of dense dark wood. It looks very old and is covered in patches of dust.

"What is this?" I ask, and then my eyes are drawn to the ceiling. I gasp. There are frescoes along the curved ceiling, each one intricately painted.

"This," Claudio says, leaning against the desk, "was a chapel that Francesco Scatena built for his family in the 1880s. Before this was a hunting lodge, a family had a house here and this was a working olive farm."

"But what is it now?"

"Oh. It was renovated a long time ago to become a suite for the lodge. Naturally, it hasn't been used for a long time, unless I have a lot of family staying over. Now, I'm turning it into your office."

I stare at him, mouth open. "I'm sorry, what?"

"Your office," he repeats, wiping dust off the top of the desk with a smooth swipe of his hand. "Do you like it?"

"Like it?" I repeat, shaking my head. "I'm ... what do you mean this is my office?"

"Grace," he says patiently. "You know I tell no lies. This is your office now. I moved the desk in here, brought it out of storage. Now I just have to grab a chair from the house, move some things around, but yes, this is your office. I know you've been struggling with a place to write, so I figured..."

Holy shit.

219

I mean, maybe that's not the right thought for here but...
Yeah. Holy shit.

One of those bars around my heart is threatening to break. It's definitely bending, moving, feelings I'd never had before threatening to overtake me.

He did this ... for *me*?

"But," I say, still not believing it. "This is sacrilegious."

Claudio stares at me with wide eyes for a moment before he bursts into laughter.

"Sacrilegious? Oh, *musa*. No, no. There is nothing sacrilegious about art."

"That's not true. I'm writing a romance. At least, it's a book with sex in it."

A dark, smoldering look washes across his eyes. "I think you know how I feel about sex. Sex with you *is* an art. And I can't get much closer to heaven than when I'm buried deep inside you."

The flush returns to my cheeks, my body awash with goosebumps.

Damn.

He straightens up and walks over to me, cupping my cheek.

"This is all for you, Grace," he murmurs, running his thumb over my lower lip. "It is my gift for you. It is the least I can do for all the inspiration you have given me. I want you to be inspired too."

I stare up at him, his thumb rough against my lip, his hand warm. I'm lost in the intensity of his eyes. So lost, that almost all thoughts leave my brain so all I'm left with is the bare, basic version of myself. The version that wants nothing more than to be with him, forever and always.

But as that thought manages to make its way through

me, I'm struck with worry. That horrible realization that always follows a high.

"You did all this but I'm leaving so soon," I tell him quietly.

His Adam's apple bobs in his throat, a soft smile on his lips. "Who says you have to leave?" His hand leaves my face, trails to the back of my neck.

I blink. "Because..."

"Because you're supposed to be here for a month, *si*? But that is a date that Jana picked for you, because that's when she knew I'd come back. I am not coming back. I have been here all this time. So why can't you stay longer?"

I look away, trying to think. He starts running his fingers through my hair, making it hard to gather my thoughts. I close my eyes, giving into the sensation.

"Jana will think something is up if I stay."

"And what will she think is up?"

"That ... I don't know. Maybe she'll suspect the truth. That you're the reason I'm staying here."

"Uh huh," he says matter-of-factly. I open my eyes to look at him, his expression serious. "You don't think she would completely understand that you may need more time to finish your book? After all, you said you were here to get a lot done. What is wrong with telling her you'd rather finish it all in one spot?"

He's got a point there.

"And also," he says, making a light fist in my hair, "who cares what my ex-wife thinks? If she wants to think you're staying here because of me, let her."

I balk, giving him an incredulous look. How can he even think of saying that?

"Are you kidding me?"

He frowns, dropping his hand. He folds his arms across his chest, scrutinizing me. "What?"

"What do you mean, what? I can't have Jana know about us! How do you think she would react if she found out I was sleeping with her ex-husband?"

He has the audacity to shrug. "I don't think she'd care."

"You don't think she'd care?"

He considers that for a moment. "She wouldn't have her feelings hurt, if that's what you're worried about. She's not my biggest fan."

"I know that she's not in love with you. At least, that's what I gather. But that doesn't mean that her feelings won't be hurt. Pride is a feeling, isn't it?"

"Pride is a sin."

"Okay fine, whatever. It will hurt her pride. Her trust in me. That's breaking something between us, crossing a line. How do you think she would react if she found out that her troublesome client whom she sent down here to write ended up sleeping with her husband? With her child around!"

"Grace, you are worried about the wrong things."

"Then tell me the right things to worry about. Look, you know her better than anyone. Tell me she won't lash out at this. Tell me that I wouldn't be the one to suffer. She won't want to represent me anymore. She'll drop me. I'll be left on my own."

"Hey, hey," he says softly, putting his arms on my shoulders and pulling me against his chest. "Don't let that mind of yours run away on you. I understand your concerns but..."

"But nothing. Those concerns are everything."

I have to say, he actually looks hurt. Something pinches in my chest.

"Okay," he says. "Then we don't say anything to Jana. But you can still stay here, for as long as you want. Tell her you want to finish your book here and that will be the end of it. Is there any reason you need to go back to Edinburgh? Your apartment? Any plants that need to be watered?"

I sigh. "All my plants die within the first week of bringing them home. No, I don't need to be back."

The corner of his mouth lifts. "Then you will stay?"

I swallow. "For how long?"

"As long as you need. At least the summer."

The entire summer. Another month or two of being with Claudio, sleeping with Claudio. It was almost better when I knew the end of our affair was coming sooner, because that meant there was less time for my feelings to build and run away on me. A lot can change over two months. How can I protect my heart for that long?

"*Per favore*," he says gravely, holding my hand up to his mouth and placing a kiss on my knuckles, his eyes pinning me in place. "Please stay with me."

My whole body aches with his words.

I can't say no to this, I can't say no to him.

Despite the heartache I know will come down the line, the thought of passing this up seems unconscionable.

"I will stay," I tell him.

He smiles against my hand then pulls me in for a quick kiss.

"Okay, okay," he says excitedly, breaking away and turning his body to the room, his hands on his hips, surveying it. "I am not done. I have to get back to work."

"Don't rush on account of me."

He looks at me over his shoulder. "You must write, Grace. Besides, I want to get this done before I head to Carrara today."

With me as his muse, Claudio is almost done working on the clay mold for his sculpture. I've been sitting for him a few times this week while he sculpts, armed with roses. Now, with him nearing completion, he has to head to Carrara, which is an area north of here where they mine marble from the mountains. According to Claudio, Carrara marble is the best you can use, and the quarries have been used since Ancient Roman times.

"Are you sure you don't want to come?" he asks.

I shake my head. As much as a trip to the mountains up north sounds fun, I know I have to write. I figure with him gone, it will probably be easier too. The only problem is that he's planning on staying overnight at a friend's house, one of the guys who works at the quarry, which means I'll be alone with Vanni. He was invited but he passed it up, saying it was boring.

"I'm looking forward to getting some work done," I tell him. "Less distractions."

"Yes, well let's hope that Vanni stays out of your hair."

"He's a good kid. He knows when I have to work."

In fact, later, right after Claudio gets in his Range Rover and takes off for Carrara, Vanni turns to me and says, "Time for you to get to work. Go, go!"

I laugh and collect my laptop from my room. I have a few hours of writing left before I have to make dinner. Luckily, Vanni has volunteered to help, which should be a fun thing to do together. No doubt it won't be as good as Claudio's but if we make it ourselves, at least it means something.

Since Claudio finished my office right before he left, I know it's ready for me to use. I head across the road and step inside the door, taking in the room with respect.

It hums with silence in here, and the thick stone walls

keep out all the heat. It feels like a tomb in some ways, but it's comforting. There's enough good lighting so my eyes won't feel strained, and the lack of windows means I have even less distractions.

I open my laptop and get to work.

The time passes quickly, the words flowing freely. Every now and then I pause to have a sip from my water bottle, and I glance up at the Virgin Mary who is staring down at me. If anything, I feel her encouragement.

I stop for an early dinner, and Vanni and I make caprese sandwiches and eat them outside on the patio. I have a glass of wine that goes down too easily, but I need to keep my wits about me.

It's still oppressively hot, even after dinner, and Vanni wants to go swimming. Since I should supervise him anyway, I decide to join him. At first, I attempt to do some laps, but Vanni is playing shark and diving under at the last minute as I pass him by, grabbing my legs. So we end up having a splash fest, which then escalates once he brings out the pool noodles.

I know my experience with kids was lacking before I came here, but I have to say being around Vanni has really opened my eyes. I've never been sure I wanted kids before and, frankly, I'm still not. I get it when Claudio said that Jana wasn't maternal, because sometimes I think I'm the same way (and it does give me a bit of a pause, because Claudio is so well-suited to being a father).

But I really like being around Vanni. So much so that I think Claudio won't be the only one to break my heart when I eventually leave. I'm going to miss this kid, too.

At least we have the whole summer together now.

"Grace!" Vanni yells at me, snapping me to attention.

I have no time to react as the pool noodle goes *whack* right across my face.

"You're dead," I growl at him.

"*Italiano!*" he yells gleefully, swimming away.

"*Sei morto!*" I tell him, grabbing the nearest pool noodle and going after him.

~

LATER THAT NIGHT, I'M DEEP ASLEEP IN MY BED WHEN I hear something.

I sit up slowly, my eyes adjusting to the darkness of the bedroom.

The door creaks open.

I don't panic right away, because I assume it's Vanni. Maybe he's had a bad dream about being stuck in the wrong universe.

But then I notice a tall, dark figure stepping inside.

Oh my god.

I open my mouth to scream but hear, "Grace..."

Would a killer know my name?

They would if they were like Kathy Bates in *Misery*.

"It's me."

Claudio.

I exhale deeply, my heart thundering against my ribs. "What are you doing here?" I whisper.

The door quietly clicks shut and he walks across to my bed, standing at the end of it. "I came back. I couldn't stand to be away from you." His voice is raw and impassioned.

I lick my lips, instantly melting at the urgency in his words.

"It must be the middle of the night."

"It doesn't matter," he says. "I woke up on the couch at

my friend's and I thought, what am I doing? Why am I here? Why am I not with you? It doesn't matter that we have more time together now if I'm not going to use that time properly."

I lean over and switch on the bedside light.

There he is, his features seeming sharp and shadowed in the half light. My god, is this really the man I've been giving my body to? The man who seems to want so much more? How can he be so beautiful?

"I'm glad you're back," I tell him quietly. "It was a little lonely without you."

He doesn't say anything to that. The look on his face is so serious and smoldering that it makes my skin feel like it's being licked by flames.

We stare at each other for what feels like minutes and hours and then he's getting on the bed and prowling across it over to me.

"Why can't you sleep naked?" he whispers to me as his body rises above mine and I'm bracketed in by his large, strong frame, and his musky, sweet scent. His hand trails down over my breasts and then tugs at the hem of my t-shirt. "You know I come for you. You know I make you come."

I gulp. That he does.

And yet something feels different tonight. There's an intensity in the air, electric and alive, and the look in his eyes is nothing short of brooding. He wants me, that much is sure. Wants me so badly that he drove back to see me in the middle of the night.

For once, I feel like what we're doing is slipping beyond casual fucking.

This is becoming something so much bigger than that.

Fear flits through me again and I nearly clutch my chest, as if I could protect my heart from being squashed by him.

How will he not break me when this is all over? The path to destruction is inevitable.

But I raise my arms as he lifts the shirt over my head, my breasts bare, and then he works down my underwear, until I'm lying on the bed completely naked.

My mind is racing as I watch him, wondering what he's going to do, his gaze raking over my skin.

He lowers his head and his mouth licks over my breasts, his fingers pinching my nipples until I let out a cry of sweet pain, my face growing hot. My spine seems to buzz with each suck of his hot mouth over my cooler skin.

How can I leave this? How can this all be over one day? I don't want this to end and yet I know there is no alternative. We simply can't be together, so it's casual sex or nothing, but at the same time, this isn't casual. Not even a little. I want to be with him so badly that it scares me, makes my bones shake, makes my heart feel pinched and tight. If the yearning and the pining is already like this and he's *here*, what will it be like when he's not?

"You're thinking too much," he murmurs, and I look down to see his face moving down my stomach and back up, licking a path with a wide sweep of his tongue. His hands are at my thighs, digging into them, spreading them wide.

But he stops, tilting his head as he studies my face.

"W-what?" I manage to say, my throat feeling incredibly dry.

He wags a finger at me. "That brain of yours. The writer brain. What are you doing? Narrating? Or are you worrying?"

I close my eyes. It's so hard to turn it off sometimes. To be in the moment, no matter how beautiful the moment is.

"I know how to help you," he says after a beat. I feel him move off the bed.

He's gotten up, and he's going over to my wardrobe, flipping through the dresses. He finds a wide sash around one and whips the sash away from the dress, then he goes to the yellow and white dress I've been wearing while modeling for him, and removes the tie that goes around the waist.

He comes back to the bed, the tie and the sash in each hand.

"You like it when I spank you," he says to me, keeping his voice low. A comment, not a question. "You like the pain because it feels good, but also because it makes you focus. It brings you to the present. It quiets your mind. I can't get away with spanking you here — it will be too loud. But this should help do the same thing."

I don't know what he has in mind until he walks over to the side of the bed and nods at me. "Raise your arms, above your head."

I do as he says and watch him as he leans over and ties the yellow waist tie around my wrists, holding them above my head, bent against the headboard.

"There," he says, satisfied, his eyes sweeping over my body, leaving sparks in their wake. I've never been so exposed before.

I like it.

"That will help," he says. "And so will this."

He leans over me and places the sash over my eyes until I can't see.

Oh my god, he's blindfolding me.

"Lift your head," he murmurs, and I do so. He quickly ties the ends of the sash at the back, then slips his hand to the back of my neck and lowers my head to the pillow.

"There," he says. "Now your senses won't be so over-whelmed. You can't see me, and you won't need to think about what to do with your hands. You'll just focus on me, on me touching, licking, tasting every part of your body."

Oh Grace. You poor naïve romance novelist. Your first time being tied up.

I feel myself flush in anticipation. There's a scary thrill to this, but scary in a delicious way. With my hands tied and my sight blocked, I feel like every inch of my skin is hyper-sensitive and alive.

I'm a feast, a succulent dish, offered up on a platter to a god.

I hear him removing his clothing, and I suddenly wish I could see, because I can never pass up a chance to ogle his body. But then as he gets closer to the bed, I suck in my breath and hold it until my lungs grow tight, not knowing what he's going to do.

I feel the heat of his face as it comes over my chest, and then hot air blows against my breasts.

"Fuck," I cry out through a rough gasp, my back arching up, my wrists fighting against the string for a moment.

Claudio continues to blow, concentrating on one nipple, then the other, before heading down over my sides, toward my belly.

I feel his hands grip my upper thighs, thumbs digging in, and he spreads my legs again and starts blowing down, down, down, the stubble on his cheeks scratching against my skin, the air blowing on my clit.

Sweet Jesus!

"Claudio!" I cry out harshly, my hips bucking up toward his face, wanting so badly for this teasing to stop, to feel the soft purchase of his mouth. This is already driving me crazy.

He pulls back just a bit, enough for me to hold my

breath again, waiting, waiting ... where is he going to go next?

God, he was right when he said this would help me focus. I've never been so attuned to my body before, to every single need and craving it has. And it wants him to eat me out, lick every crevice, until his cock is crammed inside me.

"What are you thinking now?" he murmurs, still between my legs, his breath hot as he speaks just inches from where I am so very wet and desperate.

"I want to grab your hair and shove your face between my legs, make you devour me."

A pause. Then his warm chuckle.

"Very well."

His lips meet my clit in a second, a burst of pleasure shooting through me like lightning bolts, and my hips are rising off the bed and I am so fucking done for, I feel like I've been turned inside out.

Meanwhile, he shows no signs of slowing. He licks at me, tongue strong and hot, and I'm growing slicker and slicker, the sound getting messier and messier.

I don't even have time to prepare until I'm coming, my body shaking with tiny explosions.

"Holy fuck," I cry out softly, stifling my words into a whimper, and I'm coming in his mouth harder than I've ever come before. If Vanni wasn't across the hall, I think I would have *screamed*.

I'm still being torn by my release, still pulsing and sensitive, and totally wired, when I feel him shift onto the bed, grabbing my left leg and raising it up so it's straight and lying against his chest, then he's slamming his cock into me.

I barely have time to breathe. He slides into me with such slick, delicious ease that it makes my mouth water.

"Oh, Grace," he says through a tight moan as he pushes himself in and out, the rhythm quick but controlled. "What are you doing to me?"

What are you doing to me? I want to ask, since I've barely calmed down from my orgasm and he's already fucking me.

And the man knows how to fuck. His hips grind into me in small, quick circles, his cock hitting each sensitive nerve, and with my senses putting all the focus on us, on our bodies, on our pleasure, I can feel another orgasm building within me.

"Touch me," I whisper, no longer too sensitive.

I tense in anticipation, and then his thumb rubs against my clit, creating friction that will carry me through again. Pleasure overwhelms my senses, while my senses add to the pleasure.

The sound of his raspy breath and the gentle creak of the bed.

The feel of his cock as it rams inside me, the rough side of his thumb sliding over my sensitive flesh.

The smell of our sex, mixed with almonds and sunshine.

The taste of my own sweat on my upper lip.

I am so fucking alive.

And then ... then it's too much.

I silently beg for him to keep going. I'm so close, so close.

And then I'm there.

A mess of nonsense words choke inside my throat, and then my body is convulsing, shaking with ferocity. I am utterly boneless, my senses blown apart, and I see galaxies behind my eyes. If you were to see me right now, there wouldn't be just one Grace Harper, but many of her, all of them scattered like blissed-out confetti.

"Oh god," Claudio says through a quiet grunt, and then I'm squeezing him, trying to wring every last bit of energy from him. I feel his body still and tense up, and then with a low groan, he almost collapses on top of me, his breath loud and rough in the room.

We don't say anything for a few moments. He pulls out and lies down beside me, both of us trying to get back into our minds and bodies again.

Then he reaches over and removes the blindfold.

The dim light of the room feels like being on the sun.

I turn my head to see his dark eyes raking over me, then he leans over and unties my wrists.

I pull them down toward me, shaking them out. My arms had fallen asleep and I hadn't even noticed. I was numb to everything else but him.

I guess that was the point.

"Wow," I finally say, letting out a deep breath.

His smile is so sweet, like he's proud of himself. I suppose he should be. The man made me see stars.

"*You* were wow," he says, his finger drifting from the top of my head, down over my nose, over my lips, to my chin, his gaze following. His eyes are the most beautiful after sex, so lazy and heavy-lidded, filled with peace and something so, *so* tender that it often takes my breath away.

Like right now. I could die in his tenderness.

We stare at each other like this for a few minutes, just so incredibly happy in what we've created for each other. Then he sits up, swinging his legs over the bed.

"In a couple days, we are going to Elba," he says simply, eyeing me over his shoulder. "Try to get as much writing done as you can before then."

I stare blankly at him. "Elba? The island?"

He gets up and walks around the bed to pick up his briefs, slipping them on while I wait for an answer.

"Yes," he finally says, snapping his waistband against his sleek stomach. "To visit my parents. You and me and Vanni. You will enjoy it. It's good for you to get out of this house."

My chest warms at the idea of going on a trip with him, even if it is to see his parents.

That part scares me.

"Are you sure you want me to go?" I ask. "It sounds like I would be ruining a family trip."

And parents are serious business and are we even serious?

"You ruin nothing. Don't you see, Grace? You are everything to me. And I have a possessive heart. It wants only you."

It's hard to argue with that. Sometimes Claudio's emotions and feelings feel too big for me to handle, too much for my heart to take. But then, if I just let myself sink into them, revel in them, I can't get enough.

And I truly can't get enough of him, or his possessive heart.

"Okay. Yes. I would love to go," I tell him, breaking into a grin.

Oh, Grace. You are so screwed.

SIXTEEN

CLAUDIO

"Are you ready?"

I pause at the top of the stairs, listening for Grace's response.

Silence.

"Grace? It's only for three nights. You need as few clothes as possible." I pause. "In fact, the fewer the clothes, the better."

I wait a few moments, then hear her door slam. "I'm ready!"

I glance at my watch while I hear her thunder down the stairs, dragging her carry-on behind her. We're cutting it close to making the ferry, but I don't need to remind her of that again.

I lock up the house and stow the bags in the luggage shelf behind the seats of the Ferrari, securing them with the car's original leather straps. Then we're buckling up and zooming out of the driveway.

Things moved fast when Grace agreed to go to Elba with me. I called up my parents to let them know I wanted to come by with Vanni and that I was bringing a friend of mine. I never mentioned what type of friend, and I sure as hell didn't tell them that she is Jana's client. They, like my sisters, are not a fan of her whatsoever.

But when I broke the news to Vanni, he visibly shuddered. I guess spending a few days with us at his grandparents' house, no matter how grandiose the location, or how beautiful the island, was too much for him. He insisted that he be allowed to spend the time at Paolo's house.

After talking to Paolo's parents, they were more than happy for Paolo to have company for a few days.

Which meant that I had Grace all to myself.

Okay, so it isn't that simple. Of course we'll be staying at my parents, and Grace has noted a few times that she wants us to give the illusion of being friends. I tried to tell her that my parents don't care, but she seems to think the information will get back to Vanni or Jana, even though that's not the case at all.

I have to admit, I'm trying hard not to get frustrated or hurt when Grace seems to be keeping me at a distance. Everything with her is so focused on sex, and I'm not complaining, but obviously things are getting more complicated than that. I just keep telling myself that I know where she's coming from, and I have to remember that.

The ferry terminal to Elba is down the coast at the town of Piombino, and I spend most of our drive gunning it down the motorway so we can make the ferry on time. Of course, when we get to the terminal, it's a confusing mess of cars, but eventually we get in line and then drive onto the ferry.

Grace wants to explore, so we walk about the ferry, getting a glass of wine in the cafeteria before we hit the outer decks.

"Wow, the breeze feels so good," Grace says, smiling, her hair whipping across her sunglasses. She's leaning against the railing, watching the waves crashing below us. She points to the landmasses dotting the horizon. "That closest one, is that Elba?"

I nod, standing next to her, shoulder to shoulder. I can never get close enough.

"Sì. And that over there is the northern tip of Corsica."

"Have you ever been?"

I nod. "Yes, but I prefer Sardinia. Perhaps we can go one day."

She licks her lips for a moment, then gives a nod. "Aye. There are a lot of one days, aren't there?"

I slip my hand around her waist and pull her toward me, still marveling at how I'm allowed to touch her like this. "One days will always turn into the present, as long as you're with me," I tell her, nuzzling my face into her neck. I take in a deep breath of her orange and vanilla shampoo. She smells like happiness.

It's not long before the ferry motors along the rugged coast of Elba and pulls into the harbor, at the town of Porto-ferraio. Grace marvels at the colorful red-roofed houses clinging to the cliffs and the tower of the old fortress before we have to head down to the car.

"So, did you grow up here?" she asks once we've departed the ferry and are burning around the traffic circles leading out of town.

"I did," I tell her, adjusting my grip on the wheel. "Well, I was here until I was twelve. Then we moved to Lucca when my father decided to open the gallery. Not too far from where the villa is."

"That must have been nice, growing up on an island," she says.

"It had its moments," I tell her. "My father prefers to be submerged in nature, but I personally can't be too far from the city. My inspiration comes from people. Here, it is very beautiful, but there is a lot of peace and quiet. Even the tourists rarely find this place. They all go to Capri instead."

The road quickly goes from suburbs to farmland, and then starts twisting as it winds its way along the curves of interior mountains. Grace seems besotted with the journey, the window down, wind in her hair, ruffling the edge of her short blue dress. The scent of rosemary and dry grass wafting into the car, and Grace has her eyes closed, breathing it in.

The warmth in my chest spreads like a rising sun.

I am in trouble with this woman. I know I am. I can't even look at her anymore without having myself tested. And it's not just my body being tested, even if I can resist looking at her pale legs or the soft curves of her cleavage. It's my heart that's being tried.

I've always been confident around women, and I've never had any problems attracting them. I think my appeal isn't just my looks, but that I never seem to need anyone. And this is true. It's not an act. I don't play hard to get, per se, but my heart never seems to follow where my body does.

As a result, I've had just a few long-term relationships. I'm not even sure Jana counts, to be honest. She got pregnant with Vanni after that one night I had with her. I got a phone call from her six weeks later, telling me she was going to have an abortion.

I'll admit, my first thought was of relief. I was twenty-six and just coming into my own as an artist. I was afraid I would lose momentum if I got together with Jana, if she had the baby (though now looking back, perhaps this is what Grace feels when she thinks about us. The loss of her momentum).

But then the guilt set in. Good old Catholic guilt. I

thought about my parents, and as complicated as they are, they've always made me strive to do more with my morals. There was definitely some pressure as well, when I broke the news to them. I would persuade Jana to have the baby, then I would marry her. It was the right thing to do, and I was raised to do the right thing. I'd just never been tested like that before.

So I convinced Jana to have the baby. I asked her to marry me.

And while our marriage was brief, it did resemble a relationship of sorts.

But my heart never opened for her. It opened for Vanni, of course. The love I felt for my son when he was born blew me right open, like it brought me into another world I didn't even know existed.

That love was enough for me. The romantic, obsessive, head over heels love that I should feel for a woman? That didn't interest me anymore. And when Jana and I divorced, I carried that preference with me. Even with Marika, I loved her company, loved the sex, but I didn't love her. I didn't need it. My art was enough to keep me challenged and whole and happy.

But now? Now ... we'll, I don't know what's happening, but my art is starting to feel like it's not enough for me anymore. My art has always been about control. About creating an outcome with my own skill and persistence.

The way I feel about Grace? I have no control here. All I have is persistence, and the hope that however I feel about her, she might feel the same way. Right now we're at that stage where the sex is amazing and I'm overly infatuated with her, but I'm balancing on the edge that separates the now from the future, ready to fall for the first time.

She glances at me, her eyes hidden by her sunglasses. She grins. "You're thinking about me."

I can't hide from her. That's the other thing.

"I'm always thinking about you," I tell her. "You're the first thing I think about when I wake up, and the last thing I think about before I fall asleep. And you're in every single thought in-between."

She swallows, her shoulders relaxing. I know I come on strong. I wear my heart on my sleeve, I say things that perhaps are better suited to poets back in the day. But this is all part and parcel of me. I can't change that. I don't want to.

And it hasn't scared her away. Yet.

The drive through the interior of the island takes a while longer. Grace gasps appreciatively when slices of the Tyrrhenian Sea start appearing beyond the hills. Soon, the car is coasting along the bays that make up the south side of the island, the sea an ombre of colors from deep, jewel-like navy blue, to turquoise and pale azure.

The sea breeze sweeps through the open windows, blowing Grace's dress up just enough that I catch a glimpse of bare flesh.

"*Mio Dio*," I say, my throat already hoarse at the sight. "Please tell me you're wearing underwear."

She clamps the skirt of her dress down and gives me a sheepish smile. "We were in such a rush to catch the ferry ... I guess I forgot."

But from the way she's biting her lip, I know it was no accident.

I'm immediately hard.

Fuck.

"Show me," I tell her, my eyes going from the winding road ahead to her lap.

"Nooo," she says with a sly laugh. "You need to keep your eyes on the road."

"I know this road and this car like the back of my hand. I can see it with my eyes closed. Your pussy, however ... I'm afraid I need a little more experience." I lick my lips, feeling my skin buzz with power. "Show me."

She looks away, eyes on the cars ahead. Then she slowly slides her hands up her inner thighs, pushing her dress up until her pussy is bare for me to see, the sun coming through the windshield and hitting it just right.

My god.

I grip the steering wheel, bringing my eyes to the road as we handle another turn.

"Play with yourself," I tell her, my voice hoarse with want. Traffic starts to get heavy coming toward us, so I keep my attention focused straight ahead for a few moments, until we turn around a bend and the blue expanse of the sea appears again, sailboats bobbing in the distance.

But the view does nothing for me.

I look to Grace, and to my surprise, she's leaning her seat back, her legs spread wide, the fingers of her right hand sliding up and down over her clit.

I didn't think she'd do it, but now that she is, I realize what a mistake this is. This is pure torture, having to watch her do this and not have her myself, and I'm most likely going to drive this car right off a cliff.

I clear my throat. "Okay, you can stop," I tell her. "This isn't fair."

"It was your idea," she says. She opens her legs wider now and starts inserting her fingers inside. The sound is wet and lewd inside the car, her fingers shining. Her head rolls back against the seat and she lets out a low moan that I feel in the marrow of my bones.

I'm dead.

I tear my eyes away from her, my breath coming harsh now, while my cock is straining against the fly of my pants, growing tighter, bigger, and begging for attention. Heat courses through my veins, the temperature rising with each passing second.

"Oh," she moans.

My eyes pinch shut for a moment, opening in time to take another curve.

I steal a glance at her again, watching as she fucks herself with her fingers, the sight, the sound, her wet and open mouth, all of it about to make my heart explode.

"I'm so close," she says breathlessly, dragging out each word. I don't care if she's putting on a show or not, it's dangerously hot all the same.

"Fuck it," I growl.

I see a sliver of space on the side of the road, right below a rough cliffside of rosemary, and I yank the car over, slamming on the brakes. A cloud of dust rises up around the car, as other vehicles whiz past us, probably wondering why I would make such a harsh landing with a vintage Ferrari.

Because of Grace Harper, that's why.

"Claudio," she says, looking around.

I waste no time. I reach over and quickly unbuckle her seatbelt, then do the same to mine. Then I unzip my pants, my hand taking a firm hold of my cock as I pull it out, thick and hot in my grasp.

"Take off those sunglasses and come over here," I tell her, slamming my seat back to give her more room. "I can't stand another minute of this."

She's twisted in her seat to face me, but she doesn't move. Her mouth is open in shock. I reach out and take her sunglasses off her face, tossing them into the back seat.

Her wide blue eyes stare at me.

"Claudio," she says in a hush, eyes darting from me to the road. "We can't ... people can see."

"Fuck them," I growl. "And fuck me before I lose my damn mind." My smile is lazy but quick, fueled by this intense need to screw here right here, right now. I reach over and grab her hips, picking her up, and she easily slides across the low, smooth console, onto my lap, my cock stiff and ready for her.

"B-but we..." she says, her voice so small, unsure, and yet catching with her own lust.

"You don't think they haven't seen someone fuck in a Ferrari before? *Bella*, this is Italy," I tell her, wrapping my fingers around her waist and lifting her up so that the tip of my cock is pressed against her, already so wet and willing.

But I wait, letting her control how she wants to ride me. If It were up to me, I would fucking impale her with my cock right now, pull down her dress so that her tits bounce freely for all the passing cars to see. She's all mine, but it doesn't mean I don't want to show her off.

It takes all my strength to hold it together, my fingertips pressing tighter into her soft skin until I'm sure I'm leaving a mark.

She bites her lip, and I see the lust spread across her face and chest in flashes of delicate pink, like she's been dusted with rose petals. Her eyes keep looking to the road. While I find the idea of people watching us to be exciting, her natural bashfulness is coming through, and I can tell when her mind is about to run away on her.

"Hold on," I tell her. I reach over and flip open the console, taking out a silk scarf I use to wipe down the dash with. I give the black fabric a shake and then reach up, placing it against her eyes. "Remember what we did before?" I ask her. "Block it all out. Focus on me. On your pleasure."

She gives me a slight nod, her lower lip getting a real workout as she worries it between her teeth. I tie the scarf behind her head.

"There," I whisper. "There's nothing else but me."

She exhales and then grabs my cock, making my eyes roll back in my head.

I relax against the seat, and she slowly, carefully lowers herself onto me.

Fuck. Me.

She's so wet and needy, it's easy to slide into her. I have to temper my impatience and try to go slow, not only so I don't hurt her, but because I know if I just let myself do what I wanted, I'd be coming in less than a minute.

Not that we have all the time in the world. It might be risqué to have sex in a parked car beside a busy road, but it's also probably illegal.

"Oh god," she whispers, placing her hands on my shoulders to brace herself.

"Does that feel good?" I murmur, my voice rough and desperate. "Tell me it feels good."

"Yes." She breaks off into a gasp as she pushes herself down onto my shaft, harder this time. "Oh god, yes."

I want to slide into her one sweet beautiful inch at a time, but I don't think that's in the cards today. Instead I start thrusting upward, stiff, thick jabs that make her gasp for air, my hands going around her ass, nails digging in. We reach a sort of unity together, our rhythm matching each other as she bucks her hips into me, leaning back.

"I'm close," she manages to say, breaking off into a muffled cry.

I stick my thumb in my mouth, wetting it, then slide it down between us, over her clit, rubbing hard and fast.

"Fuck!" she cries out, her neck and back arched, her grip on my shoulders becoming vise-like. I watch the tremor pass through her, and even beneath the blindfold I can tell her eyes are pinched shut with exertion. Her pussy wraps tight around me, setting me off.

I let myself go, coming with a thundering groan. Her rhythm slows, and I feel like ... I don't even know. I'm tired, panting, coming down from the highest of highs.

A big truck roars past the car, making us shake, bringing me back to reality, that we're parked on the side of the road, on the way to meet my parents.

I push that all away.

I don't want to lose this feeling.

I cup her face in my hands, and I kiss her. I kiss her hard and sweet, and there are too many emotions rolling through me to make sense of them, but kissing her makes the most sense of all.

"I guess this isn't the first time you've had sex in here," she says against my lips. "This car is a chick magnet."

There's so much vulnerability in her voice that it breaks my heart. I reach out and take off the blindfold until she's blinking shyly at me.

"I've never had sex in this car before," I admit, adjusting myself, totally aware that I'm still inside her. I don't want to pull out, not yet. "You're the first one."

"Right."

"*Musa*," I whisper to her, kissing her again. I pull back, searching her eyes, feeling everything inside threatening to spill over. "I want you. I want this. Always. Not just for now. I want so much from you that I'm afraid to ask ... I don't even think I'm worthy of asking."

She swallows, staring right back at me, her eyes bright and glassy. They don't look fearful at all. "What do you want?" she asks after a beat.

I place my hands at her heart. I can't make myself say it but I hope that it's enough.

She gives me a small smile and then adjusts herself. I'm pretty much slipping out. "Oh boy," she says, looking down. "So I guess there was a good reason you haven't had sex in this car. We've made quite a mess."

I'm not proud to admit that a tiny part of me is cringing at the idea of having cum-stained leather in a million-dollar car, but I'm sure it will come out, and anyway, this was worth it.

She tries to wipe it off with her dress and then moves over to her seat.

"Okay," I say, zipping up my pants and pulling my seat forward. We both buckle up. "Now that we had a little, uh, rest break, how about we continue on to my parents?"

At that she looks worried, quickly reaching back and placing her sunglasses on, as if it will hide all her sins.

SEVENTEEN

GRACE

Who are you? I say to myself as I stare into my compact, wiping away any smudges of mascara from underneath my eyes. I totally look like I just had a wild shag. My face is flushed, my pupils huge, my lip liner smeared. My eye makeup is a mess from having the scarf over it.

And I have no idea who I am anymore.

Not that it's a bad thing, per se. I just know the Grace Harper of the past would never have sex in public. Twice. Doing it against those Roman ruins was one thing, but then fucking in his Ferrari on the side of the road? Who does that?

Robyn would have done that, I remind myself. *And she would have told you all about it, and you would have lived vicariously through her. Now you're doing the things she would have done. You're out here living.*

I dot powder on my shiny nose, blotting the perspiration on my forehead before I put the compact away. How is that the more sex I have with Claudio, the more alive I feel? Why didn't anyone tell me that sex was the secret to a more interesting life?

But, of course, it's more than that. If I can just focus on the sex for now, it will be easier.

"Almost there," Claudio says as the car takes another bend.

"Do you have, like, hand sanitizer or something?" I ask him. I wiggle my fingers at him. "I don't think I should be shaking your parents' hands."

He laughs. "Check the glove compartment."

I open it, and find a compact bottle of … leather cleaner. Well, at least it will come in handy for the stain I'm sure will remain on the seat. I take it out and spritz it onto my fingers anyway.

"You are crazy," he says, watching me.

"You keep your eyes on the road," I remind him. "This all happened because you couldn't stay focused."

He licks his lips. "Oh? And that was a bad thing?"

I look away, but I'm smiling.

Then my smile fades as he slows and exits left onto a smooth dirt road bracketed by shrubs. Dust rises up behind us and the scenery opens up until we're on a small peninsula, the shining blue sea spreading out on both sides.

"Down there, that's Cavoli," Claudio says, gesturing to the right. I stare down at the curving bay, the red-tiled roofs clinging to the hillside before they end at a pebbly beach, umbrellas and sun chairs lined up along it. The water is achingly blue, like a swimming pool, and everything looks like the quintessential Italian paradise.

"It's beautiful."

"There's a path that leads down there from their house. It's the only house on the whole peninsula. If you're not too stuffed from my mother's cooking, we can have an evening swim. The sun is out late."

I nod but start playing with the edge of my seatbelt, trying to work out my nerves.

"Hey," Claudio says, eyeing me. "It's going to be fine."

"You didn't tell them we are, you know..." I ask, even though we've already talked about this. I wanted to make this trip as low pressure as possible.

He slows the car down as we crawl past a few low, scrubby trees and the occasional cactus. "No. I said I was bringing a friend."

"But you didn't tell them I was a writer?"

He shrugs. "No."

"Why not?"

He wets his lips with his tongue, taking his time to respond. "They don't like Jana all that much. I don't want them to dismiss you off the bat with the association."

"But what happens when they ask me what I do and how we met and all that?"

"Let me handle it."

Hmmm. I don't like this. On one hand, I guess I'm asking Claudio to hide our physical relationship from them, like we're a pair of star-crossed lovers. On the other hand, I don't like that he's asking me to stay quiet about what I do. I mean, without my career, I'm pretty much ... nothing.

Finally, the dirt road turns to a gravel driveway and we pull into a parking spot beside a dark green Porsche 911. Vintage, naturally. Like father, like son.

We get out of the car and I get a quick look at the house —a white ranch-style, with an orange roof, framed by mounds of lavender, rosemary, and coral daisies—before a woman comes bounding out of it, her arms wide open.

"Claudio!" she calls out, making a beeline for him, and I'm struck by how she is the epitome of the Italian mother.

She's well-dressed in a yellow silk pantsuit, shoulder-length dark hair, with red lipstick. She pulls her son into an embrace, kissing both his cheeks over and over again, until Claudio is laughing, his hand on her bicep, trying to pull her off.

"*Mamma,*" he says. "*Per favore.*"

She grins at him and then suddenly her mood switches. She frowns and slaps him lightly across his face, and starts yelling at him about something in Italian.

Claudio rolls his eyes, and it's adorable how he's automatically gone back into parent-child mode. I know it's the same with me when I see my parents.

"I told you, he didn't want to come," he says to her with a sigh. "He is sick of me."

Ah, she asked about Vanni.

"Please," he adds and gestures to me, "speak in English for Grace."

Oh god. I shake my head, trying to smile. "No, it's okay. Please speak Italian. I am learning."

His mother looks at me, her frown deepening. "This is your *friend?*" she asks in disbelief.

Eeep. I sure hope Claudio at least told them I was a woman.

"Yes. Grace," he says. "Remember?"

"I remember," she says, giving me the once over.

Instinctively I smooth out my dress.

She walks over and stops just a foot away. Her perfume is heavy and smells like gardenias. "Grace," she says in her heavy accent. "Welcome to our home."

She places her hands on my shoulders, her bracelets jingling, and leans in to place a kiss on each cheek. I'm pretty sure her red lipstick marks are left behind, as they are all over Claudio.

"Let's get your bags," she says, turning around and heading to the Ferrari. "Then I'll show you to your rooms and we can have a nice aperitivo before dinner. Claudio, you know you will have to smoke a cigar with your father."

"Of course," he says.

We get our bags out of the car, and Claudio insists on carrying mine even though he's grumbling about how much I packed. But hey, I've never been here before. I know it's three days on Elba, but I'm better off packing six dresses just in case.

Once inside, I grab my bag, and his mother ushers me down one of the halls. "This is your room, the guest bedroom," she says. "Right next to our room. There's a bathroom right across the hall that's all yours."

The room is small and has a nice view of the lavender and rosemary out front.

"Where is Claudio's room?" I ask as I toss my bag onto the bed.

"He's down at the other end of the house," she says, pointing down the hall. "Growing up here, he was the only one with a room to himself and his own toilet. You can imagine his sisters weren't too happy about that. But he was the baby." She sighs and then shrugs as she looks at me. "What can you do?"

I want to hear more about Claudio as a child, but his mother tells me to freshen up and meet them on the terrace.

I take the opportunity to get out of my navy "Ferrari sex" dress and put on a gauzy white one with long sleeves and a macramé neckline, perfect for island dressing. This time I remember my underwear.

It's going to be kind of weird not being able to sneak into Claudio's room like we do at home. He said I was welcome to, and my room is the one we'd want to avoid being so close to his parents' room and all, but even so I don't want to risk it. I know it bothers him a little that I'm being so cagey about things, but it's just how I feel at the moment.

And I'm not sure if the moment will change while we're here.

I know that our fling is supposed to be no-strings attached, and meeting someone's parents and being introduced as more than a friend are strings. What would happen down the line when this is all over and I'm back in my sad flat in Edinburgh, and his parents wonder what happened to me? What happens if Vanni gets wind of that, the fact that we were together behind his back and didn't even tell him?

Then there's the fact that I care as much about his son's opinion as I do Jana's. He matters to me. So, as long as it can all stay a secret between Claudio and me, then we're good. But if it goes beyond that, things get tricky. Once again, we can't evolve into something more than sex. We can't get serious.

And I most definitely can't fall in love with him.

I swallow at that thought, my throat feeling caked in sawdust.

I try to give *that* word, *that* feeling, as little power as possible, in the event that I end up manifesting it, in the event I start believing it.

It will do neither of us any good.

But you'll still be powerless to stop it.

I ignore that and clear my throat, straighten my shoulders, smooth down my hair, and leave the room.

The house seemed to have one level at first, but there's an open area leading down to another floor which seems to bleed out onto a terrace, dotted with potted plants, an awning overhead. Some of Claudio's statues are in the corners, a pair of women rising from the waves. Four chairs are set up facing the sea, which sparkles between the bay below and the dark mound of Corsica in the distance. How neat that we're so close to France.

"There you are," Claudio says, twisting in his chair to look at me, a cigar hanging from his fingers. "The guest of the hour."

I walk across to them, smiling at his mother and father, both of them getting out of their chairs.

His father is the spitting image of him, just with white hair. A very handsome, distinguished looking man. Well-dressed too. He carries himself with a lot of confidence, his eyes sage and bright, but I guess that happens when you're a famous painter.

Sandro Romano.

"*Buona sera*," I tell him, since it's nearly seven o'clock.

"Ah yes. *Ciao.* Your Italian is very good, by the way," he tells me, kissing me on both cheeks, the smell of his cigar tickling my nose. "Please sit down."

"Can I get you something to drink?" his mother asks me as I sit down next to Claudio, quickly flashing him an appreciative smile. "Campari and soda?"

"That would be lovely," I tell her.

"That's a nice dress," Claudio comments. His words sound innocent, but there's no denying the glint of desire in his eyes.

"Thank you," I say innocently.

"So, Grace," his father says, and I turn my attention to him. "This is the first time you've been to Elba?"

"Yes. First time in Italy." I pause. "Actually, I was in Rome for one night, but I got food poisoning on the way over and didn't see any of the city."

"Ah, that's not good. Rome is a wonderful place sometimes. What month was this?"

"Uh, a few years ago. August."

He waves his hand at me and makes a dismissive noise. "Then you were better off. Rome in August is awful. Only tourists there. All the Romans are on holiday, they go elsewhere. Some even come here."

Well, that would have been good to know.

"It's just as well," I tell him. "My partner managed to see the Trevi Fountain early in the morning, but then both of us were flying out."

It takes me a moment to realize I've just mentioned Robyn.

"Partner? For work?" he asks, puffing on his cigar.

Shit.

"Aye," I tell him, hoping he'll leave it at that. "A work partner."

I glance quickly at Claudio, but he's looking across the sea, his hand dipping into a bowl of olives that sits between us.

A beat passes. "What kind of work do you do?" his father asks.

I give him a quick smile. Here it goes. Maybe I can tell the truth without Jana even having to come up.

"I'm an author."

"An author?" he exclaims, slapping his palm against his knee. "This is true? What do you write? What type of story?"

"Murder mystery. I have a series called the Sleuths of Stockbridge."

"Ah. I don't think I know it. You said you had a partner though?"

"Yes. I wrote them with someone. Her name was

254

Robyn. Together we were Robyn Grace. That's the pen name."

I'm tense, waiting for the blow. Usually when I tell people I've written with someone, they get ready to treat me like it doesn't count, like I got help with a book, that I didn't do it on my own.

But his father merely smiles. "That is fantastic. What a nice way to do art, is it not? To share the process of discovery with someone?" He sighs. "It is such a lonely profession. Even being a painter, it is so many hours in the studio or off on the land by yourself. You neglect every step of your life except the thing you're trying to create. Because, of course, if you neglect the thing you are trying to create, you may never create it! It is like the muse. You have to beg for her to show, and when she does, you have to show her so much attention so she doesn't leave you. Our life's work hinges on that muse." He pauses. "That fickle bitch."

I burst out laughing.

"*Papà*," Claudio chides him.

"What?" he asks, throwing his hands out. "It is true. Look at you, for example. You could be doing so much more work than you are, but you don't. You blame it on your muse. How she doesn't show for you." He shakes his head and looks away, sounding gruff now, in that way of fatherly disappointment I know too well. "You know, sometimes I think if you just tried a little harder, she might come to you more often."

"I am trying," Claudio says, his face darkening. "I have had so many commissions this year."

"But commissions don't put art into the store."

"There is too much art in the store as it is. There is no room."

His father waves him away and has a sip of his drink,

wiping his mouth with a napkin. "Bah. You know when I ran that store, we could hardly keep anything in stock."

"You can't compare the economy of the eighties to today."

His father shrugs.

Well, at least we managed to keep Jana from being mentioned, though it seems they have their little difficulties between them.

"Never mind them," his mother says, appearing with a sparkling red drink in a highball glass. She hands it to me, and I thank her as she sits down. "The two of them are always arguing about the same old things. The damn muse, as if she is the same for everyone."

I look to Claudio at that, and see him already staring deeply at me.

They don't know that I am his muse, and the fact that I am the muse, that I have the power to create his inspiration and his art, is a thrill that never leaves me.

That said, I am stumbling over what his father said. That you have to show the muse so much attention or else she'll leave for good. Is that why Claudio is so attracted to me? Because I promise him creation and success? If I didn't, would we even be here right now?

As if he can hear my thoughts, Claudio reaches up and taps the side of his head.

He mouths to me, "Stop."

I suppose my trepidation is on my face, as clear as anything.

THE NEXT DAY CLAUDIO KNOCKS ON MY DOOR EARLY,

telling me to get up and come with him to the beach for a morning swim. Seeing as we went to bed fairly early and in separate rooms, I don't want to pass it up. I need to be alone with him.

Except when we grab our towels and head down the steps, my flowing cover-up nearly making me trip and fall a bunch of times, we find we aren't the only people with that idea. There are quite a few people, old ones especially, heading into the water at this hour, the sun only now touching the beach on the other side of the bay.

And once I leave the towel and the caftan on the beach and walk along the smooth pebbles into the water, I realize that his parents have a clear view of us. In fact, when I look up at the cliffside, they're both sitting on the balcony, waving.

I wave back, grateful that I didn't do something stupid, like pinch Claudio's arse. *Just friends*, indeed.

"Ah," Claudio says, looking up and over his shoulder. "There they are." He gives me a look as he wades in. "I hope you weren't expecting privacy."

I shrug, following him, the sea cold at first, but warming up as it gets up to my knees, the water impossibly clear. I can even see a few fish darting around. "I'm happy I can just talk to you out of ear range," I tell him.

He steps forward a few feet, and I watch the bronzed muscles on his back as he pushes off the bottom and dives elegantly into the water with minimal splash.

I, on the other hand, take my time wading in until the water is chest-high and then I'm swimming toward him.

"I have a feeling you were once part fish," I tell him.

He spits out water and grins, his hair sticking to his forehead. "My mother can vouch for that. Living right there" —

257

he gestures to the house— "meant I could swim before I could walk. I think it was the only thing that kept me sane when growing up. And when we moved to Lucca, we had a pool there too. I was in it more than I was out of it. Before my art took hold ... it was the only way I could deal with life."

I cock my head, wondering what he had to deal with. "You don't strike me as a person who had a rough childhood. Your parents obviously love you very much."

"Yes," he says carefully, dark eyes watching the sun touch the water on the horizon, the sky slowly growing brighter. "They do. But you saw my father last night. I am always measured to him. It was worse when I wasn't making art. My sisters, they were allowed to do whatever, but I, well, I was expected to carry on the Romano name. The *genius*."

He turns around, facing me, slowly swimming backward. "When I was a child, my father did what he could to teach me how to paint like him. I tried. But I just ... I am not talented like him in that way. Just as he can't sculpt. We are both good at our own things. But I was young and I wanted to please him, and he demanded so much of me..." He swallows, eyeing his parents on the cliff for a moment, before meeting my gaze. "I grew up believing I would never be good enough. Perhaps I still carry some of that with me."

I shake my head. "How could your father even think that? I'm sure he doesn't. He seems so proud. I mean, look at your work. It's perfect. It's like ... I get why sculptors were so revered back in the day. They were almost like gods. Wasn't Michelangelo called The Divine One?"

His brows raise, impressed. "Oh. Someone has been doing some reading."

"Research is the best part of writing. Also the best way to get to know someone."

"I'm touched," he says. "But of course I am no Michelangelo. He could at least paint." He gives me a warm, patient smile as he treads water. "There's an old joke that sculpture is the thing you bump into when you back up to get a better look at a painting. If that doesn't sum up my relationship with my father and I, then I don't know what does."

He licks his lips, head tilted. "And even though artists like Michelangelo were revered in the day, can you name me any sculptors now? No. The art isn't dying but the interest in it is. It's just not sexy."

I laugh. "Sexy? I think watching you work is the sexiest thing. Your art is pure sex, the women you sculpt..."

He grins. "You are a bit biased, don't you think?"

"Maybe. But I mean it."

He exhales and looks away, the water glinting in his eyes. "I love what I do and I know that is good enough for me. But you know ... parents are hard to, how you say, negotiate, sometimes. Sometimes their opinions matter more than they should." He glances at me. "How about your father?"

My arms move faster to tread water, and I stare down through the clear depths at my wavering feet and the pebbled bottom just below. What about my father? Where to start?

I take in a deep breath, feeling as if I'm about to dive under. "As you know, he left my mom when I was about Vanni's age. Went to London. Fell in love and started a new family. Forgot all about me."

His face contorts in sympathy. "I am sure that must have been hard. Are you still in contact with him?"

"Sometimes." My voice sounds dull, like it always does when I talk about him. When I discuss Robyn, my voice goes all over the place and I get emotional through all the ups and downs. When I talk about my father, when I think about him, I feel nothing. I suppose because I stopped grieving him a long time ago.

What is the point of grieving someone who is still alive?

"He must be proud that his daughter is a famous author, yes?"

"Stop calling me that," I tell him. "I'm not famous. I'm barely an author. And that was his view on it too. Because I wrote with Robyn, it's like he attributed all my success to her. If we made a bestseller list, it was because of her. If we traveled for book signings, it was her. The money I made was because of her. He never believed I had any part of it, like he couldn't imagine that I had enough skill or talent or drive to actually write what I did and do a good job."

He watches me carefully for a few moments, then says, "Ah."

He starts swimming laps around me.

"Ah?"

"Yes. As in, ah, that makes sense."

"How so?"

An incredulous look comes across his brow, like he's dealing with an idiot here. "The way you view yourself as an author, your work, it's the same way your father does. No wonder this book has all this pressure riding on it. You're not only trying to prove something to your readers, or to Jana, or to yourself, but to your father as well. That kind of pressure will cause any artist to seize up."

Hmm. He has a point.

"And your mother?" he asks. "How is she?"

How is my mother? I've only exchanged a few emails

260

with her since I got to Italy, and mine have been very vague and brief. "She's good. A bit lonely, I think. She's still out in Ullapool, and I want her to move so badly. That little town is so beautiful yet so depressing. There are no good men there. She needs to at least get to Fort William."

"Maybe she should come to Italy."

"She's too stubborn, though I think it would do her some good." I pause, kicking my feet out so I'm floating on my back. "I should probably reach out to her more. It's hard, you know, when you get so wrapped up in work, or at least in *trying* to work. It's why I've been a pretty awful daughter, friend, and girlfriend."

"I think you're a wonderful girlfriend," he says.

And he says it so simply, so matter-of-fact, that it takes me a moment to realize what he's said.

"Girlfriend?" I ask.

He nods. "That is what you are to me. I can be whatever you want me to be to you: Italian lover, sexy artist, cock machine, but to me, you are my girlfriend." My heart is thudding in my chest, butterflies igniting every inch of my veins. He then frowns. "No. Girlfriend doesn't sound quite right, does it? How about *Dolcezza? Mi sono infatuato. Ho un debole per te. Mi hai cambiato la vita.*"

The lyrical, dulcet tone of his accent nearly drowns me and I have to fight to keep my head above water.

"I have no idea what you just said," I say breathlessly.

"It doesn't matter. Just know that I mean it." He starts swimming past me. "Come on, let's go back. My mother and father are no longer on the balcony, which means breakfast is ready." He glances at me over his shoulder. "Hope you worked up an appetite."

I nod and follow.

I worked up something alright.

But it isn't my appetite.

He called me his *girlfriend*.

And for once, I don't want to correct him.

Maybe I still don't know where we stand publicly, but if this is what we call each other in private, I kind of like it.

As hopeless as it seems.

EIGHTEEN
GRACE

AFTER YESTERDAY'S MORNING SWIM, WE SPENT THE rest of the day lounging on the beach and going up to the house for mealtimes, where his mother would spoil us with copious amounts of wonderful wine, and dishes fresh from the sea, like grilled seabass with fennel (can't get enough fennel!) and prawns cooked in white wine and sweet cherry tomatoes. We spent a little time exploring the bay around Cavoli Beach, but aside from some restaurants, gelato shops, and souvenir stores, there wasn't a lot to see.

But for our last day on Elba, Claudio decided we should go for a drive around the western tip, and then take a gondola up to the top of Mount Capanne, which I'm told is the highest peak on Elba. Then we'll go out with his parents for dinner to a trattoria on an olive farm, which is supposed to be one of the best on the island.

But first, alone time.

Being with Claudio around his parents reminded me a lot of the first days at Villa Rosa. I had to keep my attraction under wraps, be sly with my eye contact, pretend that I wasn't swooning over the things he said, or the way he looked.

Claudio has been doing the same, though he was a little more transparent. His eyes always sought mine no matter what room we were in, his smile was always overly warm, his focus was always on me. More than a few times I caught his mother shooting his father a look, but I couldn't read either of their expressions. It was *something*, though.

Regardless, this was much harder than our pre-coupling time at Villa Rosa, because we both knew how the other felt, and I mean that in both an emotional and physical way. We were used to having frequent (albeit secretive) sex and here it just wasn't an option. I was going fucking crazy. I couldn't even look at him without a torch igniting in my chest.

That said, I wasn't about to hop on him for another round of car sex, not on these roads.

"Oh my lord," I cry out, covering my eyes as Claudio guns the Ferrari and overtakes a line of cyclists. "How can they even cycle this? Are they crazy?"

"Very," he says, grinning into the wind, clearly enjoying himself.

I, on the other hand, with my fear of heights, didn't realize that the road around the western tip was up a precipitous mountainside. I was expecting leisurely winding around sparkling bays, not climbing along a narrow road, with a big drop off to your death on one side.

"You know, the scarf is in the console," he says cheekily. "Put it on if you don't want to look."

"No, thank you." I don't want to look but I feel I need to at the same time.

It feels like forever before the road stops being so nervewracking and heads more inland. We pull over into a busy gravel parking lot and then walk up to a café where a little old lady sells us tickets to ride the gondola.

Then we walk further up the mountain, the path thankfully shaded by tall trees. Even though it's morning, it's stinking hot again.

And that's when I see it.

I stop dead in my tracks. "What the hell is *that*?"

"The gondola?"

"No, *that*!"

I frantically wave my hand at the bright yellow cylindrical cages that are whisked around a vestibule and up the side of the mountain, two people standing in it per cage. There's no room to sit down, there's no seat. It's just people standing in open metal tubes, dangling from a continuous overhead wire.

"*That* is the gondola," he says.

"What? How? I thought it was like the Air Line that goes across the River Thames in London. Ten people can fit in it. There are seats. And glass windows. And, you know, safety precautions."

A bemused smile flits across his lips, his eyes crinkling at the corners. "Would you like to walk? I've done it a few times. It is no big deal."

I crane my head to look at the top of the distant craggy peak. "Up there? You want to walk up there? In this heat?"

"It's that or the gondola."

"Stop saying gondola. It's a human-sized birdcage hanging from a wire."

"Gondola is an Italian word."

"So gondola means the same thing as deathtrap?" I put my face in my hands for a moment and take a deep breath. I look up. The couple ahead of us are getting in and they're being whisked away and they look ... happy. Or stupid.

Definitely stupid.

"How high does it go above the ground?"

"Not high at all. I promise."

I sigh. I don't want to be a wuss. "Okay."

We walk up to the vestibule, give the man our tickets, and then we're waiting on the platform for the next birdcage to come around.

"This is shite," I mutter under my breath as the cage slows beside us, the cage door opening.

"Come on," Claudio says, grabbing my hand and pulling me inside.

Well, it's definitely intimate. There's enough room for both of us to turn around, and I'm sure you could maybe squeeze a child on it, but that's it.

And while the first few seconds as we get on, the cage door closing, are slow, now that we're away from the vestibule, we're moving faster, the wind in our hair.

"Ahhhh," I cry out, watching the ground drop away, my grip tight around the bar that rings the cage. I can feel my pulse starting to skyrocket, and I'm getting that pins and needles feeling in my veins, a sign of oncoming vertigo.

"Perhaps it's best if you look up," he says. "Don't look down."

"You said it doesn't go that high!"

He shrugs. "Maybe, I don't know."

"You jerk!" I say, swatting at him.

He lets me hit him, then grabs my wrists, pinning me in place. "No fighting on the gondola," he says with a smirk. "It's dangerous. Against the rules."

"Fuck the rules."

A flash of heat comes over his eyes, and he pulls me right up against his chest, kissing me. All it takes is the swift press of his lips against mine to unlock the hunger inside, the fact that we've only been able to sneak sweet little kisses here and there.

Now, all thoughts of where we are, hanging thirty feet in the air, don't seem to matter as much as the feel of him against me.

The kiss is both soft and hard, our lips lost to each other, sinking into the moment, this chance to let loose, to truly be alone. Claudio groans a little when I open my mouth to let him inside, and the sound goes straight to my bones.

I've missed this.

He lets go of my wrists, his hands going around to grab hold of my arse, pulling me up against him, his erection stiff against me, while I reach up and weave my fingers through his soft dark hair, holding on tight.

I want to fuck him right now, feel every inch of him inside, devour him until I have nothing left to give.

But this damn cage is too small for it to be comfortable, and the idea of rocking it back and forth makes that vertigo and panic come back.

No worries, though.

I pull away slightly, giving him a wicked smile, and then I drop to my knees.

"Grace," he murmurs, desire caught in his throat, making him hoarse.

I say nothing. I barely fit, but luckily my legs are short. The metal bottom of the cage digs into my knees, and the soles of my shoes are jammed flush against the sides. But I have room to do what I need to do.

I reach up and start to unzip his fly, until I see his black briefs.

He helps by reaching inside them and pulling out his cock.

God, it looks formidable in this light, especially after not seeing it for days.

I take hold of it, feeling it's weight, his skin feeling like hot velvet. In all my life I never knew I could appreciate a dick like I do his.

I wet my lips and stare up at him with big innocent eyes, and slowly push his tip through my mouth, the salt of his precum sliding over my tongue.

"Fuck," Claudio growls, his expression turning primal.

A thrill goes through me, that he loves that I'm doing this, that I have this power over him.

Still, this is the first time I'm giving him a blow job. I'm not quite sure what he likes.

I push his cock in and then slowly take it out, my teeth grazing his shaft a little. He plops out of my mouth with a lewd wet noise and I lick my lips as I stare at him.

"How do you like it?" I ask. "Tell me what you want."

He makes a fist at the base of his cock, eyes boring into mine, and says, "Suck." He bites his lip in anticipation. "Just suck."

Okay then. I have to appreciate how direct he is.

I put him back into my mouth, sucking at him, making my lips and fist a solid ring, and he starts pumping his hips into my face, harder and harder.

Things get messy pretty fast. It's very wet and slippery, his cock almost bobbing out of my mouth a few times, and sometimes my teeth get in the way. But all the while Claudio is watching me, hissing Italian expletives under his breath and groaning out my name. This is by far one of the sexiest and strangest things I've ever done. Thank god there is no one in the baskets ahead of us or behind us, and the few that have passed have been empty.

Wait ... have they?

I pause, wanting to turn my head to look around, but Claudio grabs my hair, tugging on it, holding me in place. His other hand then slips around the back of my head as he starts pushing my face forward, in time with the pumps of his hips.

"Oh ... fuck," he cries out as he rams his cock through my lips. He stiffens in my hands, and I look up to see his head fall back, his mouth open, face contorted in pleasure. "Fuck, fuck, fuck."

He shoots straight to the back of my throat, and I swallow it down without a second thought.

His pumping slows, and I regain control of his cock, pulling it from my lips. I wipe my mouth on my shoulder and then carefully try to get to my feet.

Even though I'm all buzzed out from sucking him off, I'm suddenly very aware that the cage is swinging slightly and moving higher up the mountain. All the trees have faded away to bare rock and, good timing, the next cage coming down toward us on the opposite side actually has people in it.

"You," he says gruffly as he slowly zips himself up with one hand, his other going to my cheek. "How will I ever deserve you?"

"You can start by not making me ride things like this," I tell him. I look down again, and we're at least seventy feet in the air now. Okay, so that was a good distraction for the time being, but I'm going to close my eyes for the rest of the ride.

It isn't until we finally reach the top and have a drink on the patio of what has to be the island's most isolated bar, that I finally relax.

"Hey," I tell him, in between sips of my beer. We've been sitting here lost in the view, which runs from one end

269

of Elba to the other. We're truly on top of the world here, a thousand meters above the blue Mediterranean.

Claudio's leaning back in his chair, hands behind his head and looking blissed out. "Mmm?" he says, face tipped to the sun.

I lean in closer. "There weren't people in the cages coming down, were there? I mean, when I was sucking you off..."

A tiny smile tugs at his lips.

Noooo.

I reach out and smack him. "Are you serious!?"

He laughs, and I want to pull his aviators off his face and see his eyes. "No, no one saw."

That's not quite what I asked.

And judging by the looks we get in the parking lot later, after we take the gondola back down, I'm pretty sure some people saw plenty.

WE TOOK OUR SWEET TIME GETTING BACK TO THE house. I made Claudio stop by a seaside town, where we were able to stroll, hand-in-hand, like a real couple. It was so nice, so easy, so natural, that I was hit with the inexplicable urge to tell him that I wanted to move here, to live in Italy with him forever. Have a wonderful little place by the sea, just him and me and Vanni. I could write novels in the early morning, watching the sun come up, Vanni and Claudio catching fresh fish for lunch, and we could swim in the ocean at dusk after a few glasses of wine.

I could see that future so clearly that it scared me.

That happiness, it was all there, in sight, and yet not

only did I think I wasn't deserving of a future like that, I knew it was hopeless.

All because of Vanni and Jana.

Maybe Vanni will change his mind. Maybe Jana won't care.

I've entertained these scenarios too. It's true that Vanni might come around, especially the more he gets to know me, and once he learns I'm not trying to be his mother or replace Jana. And then Jana, well, she might wish me well. And even if she doesn't, it might not matter enough for her to drop me as a client.

And if she does? If you lose her as an agent?

Well, I better be damn sure I'm making the right choice. I've lost so much in my life, the thought of going all in with Claudio and then having it fall apart is too much for me to handle.

I manage to shake those thoughts from my head as we drive inland. It would have been faster to go back around the island the way we came, but I wanted to see what driving over the mountain would be like. Apparently, all it took was a penis for me to overcome my fear of heights.

Who knew?

Eventually, we end up back at his parents' house, a little later than we had promised. His mother is running around, talking about the reservation and how we won't make it, while his father doesn't seem to care and thinks the fish place down at the beach is good enough.

I decide to keep my dress on, changing into nicer sandals, and then we're all cramming into his father's classic Porsche 911. The interior is as flawless as Claudio's is (or was until recently, *ahem*), but the backseats are tiny. I barely fit myself, while Claudio's knees are rammed right up against his mother's seat.

His father also drives like a maniac. I should be used to it by now, from the way that Claudio drives, and everyone else in this country, but his father seems to think he's a rally driver. We go flying around the corners, Claudio and I rammed up against each other, his mother, praying in Italian and doing the sign of the cross.

The restaurant is about twenty minutes away from the house. We go down a gravel road for a while, rows and rows of olive trees passing us, their leaves twisting to silver in the wind. Finally, we stop in front of what looks like an old country house, albeit with half a dozen cars parked out front.

"Here we are," his father says, slamming on the brakes so that Claudio and I nearly bonk our heads against the front seats. "Right on time."

We wait for them to step out of the car, taking their time, and Claudio discreetly reaches over and gives my hand a squeeze.

There's a lot more effort getting out of the car than getting into it, but soon we're entering the restaurant, greeted by a dashing older man who seems to know the Romanos very well.

He leads us to a table in the back of the restaurant, my eyes taking it all in. The restaurant has red tiles, a low white ceiling with dark wood exposed beams. There are rustic touches everywhere, from the antique framed photos on the walls, to the lace curtains, to the hanging sausages near the kitchen.

It's fairly small too, maybe seven tables, almost all of them occupied.

We sit down, and the waiter brings out a bowl of olives while we look through the menu.

"So, Grace," his mother says to me after a bottle of red

wine is ordered for the table. She folds her hands in front of her and gives me a sweet smile. "I know you are an artist like Claudio and my husband, because you don't like to talk about your work. But please, what is the name of your series again?"

I finish my sip of wine. "The Sleuths of Stockbridge."

"In Italian it is *I Detective Scozzesi*," Claudio says to her. "I've read them all. They're very good. You would like them."

My heart does a little flip at that.

"I have not heard of them, but that doesn't mean anything," she says. "And if you write these books with another author, where is she?"

I have another sip of wine before I answer that one. "She's dead."

Her eyes widen, and she exchanges a look with her husband. "Oh. I am so sorry."

I just nod. "She died over Christmas. Hit by a drunk driver. Suffice to say, I won't be continuing the series anymore."

The two of them lapse into silence, feeling sad. It's inevitable whenever Robyn is brought up. The tragedy. The unfairness of it all.

"But she is writing a book on her own," Claudio speaks up. "She won't let me read it yet, but I believe it is a romance."

"Oh?" his mother says, raising a single brow, that Romano talent. "I do like romance. Who doesn't?"

"You'd be surprised," I tell her.

She stares at me for me to go on.

I sigh. "As an author, you notice it. It's always over-looked for literary fiction, whatever that means. People always thumb their nose at the genre, even though romance finds its way into every good story, every good movie or TV show."

"Romance is art," Claudio says. "No one knows that better than the Italians. Your book will do very well here, Grace."

If I can finish it. I should be writing right now, instead of vacationing on Elba. But at least things are coming easier. I'm already at forty thousand words, which is a huge accomplishment. Now I'm just waiting for the right time to drop the sex scene. I can't torture my characters for too long.

Especially when I'm being tortured myself. Every so often, I feel Claudio's foot under the table, sliding up my calves, reminding me that I can't have him at the moment.

"So is that why you're here?" she asks after a moment.

I nod. "Aye. I thought Italy would give me some inspiration."

"And has it?" asks his father. He eyes his son briefly.

I swallow, trying to keep my cheeks from going hot. Perhaps I can blame the flush on the wine. "It has. It's, erm, very romantic here."

"You know," his mother says, a look of disdain on her face. "Claudio's ex-wife is an agent. Perhaps you've heard of her. Jana Lee? She represents many famous authors. I would suggest she represent you, but that wouldn't be a good idea."

Oh fuck. Here it is. Here is the moment.

I look at Claudio, fully expecting him to lie in order to sidestep a landmine, even though I think lying would be a bad idea in itself. What if word comes out down the line that Jana is my agent? All his mother needs to do is look me up on my long-neglected Twitter account and see that she's proudly listed there.

274

Claudio lifts his wine glass to his lips. "Actually, that's how we met. Jana *is* Grace's agent."

I try to keep my face from reacting, even though both of his parents look completely shocked.

"What?" his mother says, looking at the both of us. "She's your agent?"

I nod. "She's very good at what she does."

She makes a face. "I have no doubt. But you must understand, she hasn't been the best mother to Vanni."

"Which has nothing to do with Grace," Claudio says emphatically, pressing his fingers into the table. "And also, I'm his father. I am the judge. If I felt Jana wasn't being a good mother, or being enough, I would call her on it. Talk it out like adults. We may be exes, but we communicate ... well, usually." I can tell he's thinking of when Jana neglected to tell him I was using his house. "As it is, I think we've worked things out quite well."

His father shrugs, obviously not caring too much about any of this.

His mother sighs. "Well, then I trust you to know what is right."

After that, the Jana talk tapers off. I think we've escaped the worst of it, and telling the truth wasn't so bad after all. Topics go back to more neutral affairs.

Then the food comes. Squid ink risotto. Stuffed sardines. Wild boar pasta. Pappardelle with wild mushrooms. I have *guguglione*, which is a stew of peppers and aubergine, a local dish and the restaurant's most popular. I am in heaven.

By the end, all of us are in food comas, and we finish with glasses of Amaro, the sunset twinkling through the olive groves just outside our window, a fresh breeze coming in. Claudio's father is paying the bill, and I'm just about to tell him I'll be happy to pay my part (knowing he'll dismiss that), when Claudio's mother gasps. I look at her. Her eyes are wide and she's looking over Claudio's shoulder.

Claudio and I both turn at the same time.

There is a stunning woman in a very expensive looking black dress walking over to us, smiling with supermodel white teeth, and waving.

"*Ciao, ciao!*" she cries out.

There is a flurry of activity as Claudio and Claudio's mother get up from their chairs and embrace and kiss this gorgeous woman on the cheek.

I exchange a look with his father but he just shrugs and finishes signing the bill.

A flurry of Italian erupts from all three of them, and then Claudio sits back down.

He leans in close to me. "Old friend," he whispers.

I give him a pointed look. "Do all your old friends look like supermodels?"

He manages a smile and finishes the rest of his Amaro.

Then his mother sits down.

"Oh, that is Angelina," she says to me. "Isn't she gorgeous? Beautiful. Beautiful. You know, they grew up in Cavoli Beach. See, she is with her parents now. She was good friends with Claudio as a child." She throws her napkin down. "Oh, I wish we could stay and join their table."

"We are going home," his father grumbles.

"Angelina and Claudio would make such a good couple, don't you think?" she asks me.

Oh dear.

I give her a stiff smile, trying to hide my jealousy.

"They're certainly very attractive."

His father snorts, shaking his head. "She has been trying for years to set those two up."

"And Claudio has refused," she says, pouting. She gives her son a dirty look. "Every time I try and get them together, it's Claudio that says no."

The jealousy in my stomach starts to settle.

"Because I am not interested," he says plainly.

"But how can you not be?"

"Like this," he says, and then shrugs as an example.

"No, no," she says, shaking her hands, her bracelets jangling. "You told me once it's because Vanni wouldn't approve. But how would you know? How would he know? He's never met Angelina."

"I just know," he says, voice taking on an edge. "And anyway, it doesn't really matter. In the end, it is my decision. I don't have any interest in her."

"So you're going to stay single forever?"

Oh, I don't like this conversation and I don't like where it's going.

"Not forever," he says carefully.

"You are too tied to your art," she admonishes him with a wave of disappointment, leaning back in her chair. "No time for women. You will die alone."

"Or perhaps no woman is stupid enough to go out with him," his father says. "Who wants to come in third place? There is Vanni, there is art, and then there is this poor woman. She will always come in last."

I bite my tongue. Hard. I don't want them to know we're together, especially now, but it's really hard not to come to Claudio's defense.

I glance at him. He's *furious*, his eyes hard pinpricks as he stares at his father.

"First you say I don't work hard enough," Claudio says

277

through gritted teeth. "Then you say I don't have time for a woman. Which is it? I'll tell you what it is. Could it be that, until now, I hadn't found the right woman?"

Fuck.

"What do you mean, until now?" his mother asks.

He stiffens beside me.

Gives me an apologetic glance.

"Me and Grace are together. She is my girlfriend."

Oh my god. My eyes go wide, my face in flames.

"She is?" his mother asks, looking at me. "Is this true?"

I swallow. Obviously I'm not going to deny it.

But oh my god, how could he tell them this when I specifically told him not to, when I don't know what we are?!

"Of course it is true," his father says gruffly, getting out of his seat. "Don't be so naïve, Nina."

"I am not naïve," she protests. "I just … well, well."

Claudio is watching me, his eyes boring into the side of my face, but I can't look at him, not right now. Not when he told them that.

We get up and leave the restaurant.

Cram into the back of the car.

As we drive back, Claudio keeps reaching for my hand but...

I keep mine in my lap.

I'm so angry that he outed us.

That this relationship is out in the open and it's no longer in my control.

I had wanted to take things slow, and suddenly we're official? He's announced to his parents that we are boyfriend and girlfriend? What's next? Jana knowing? Vanni?

You know they're going to find out eventually. You

should at least prepare for that moment now. It's going to get bleak.

I sigh, the thoughts dwelling on me heavily, my anger coursing through me. I know I shouldn't be this upset over it and that I'm overreacting, but I can't help it.

When we get back to the house, Claudio and his parents go out onto the balcony to have some more drinks, but all I want to do is either yell at him (and there's no good place to do that), or just go to bed angry.

And as unhealthy and moody as it is, I decide on the latter.

NINETEEN

CLAUDIO

SHE WON'T EVEN LOOK AT ME.

I started this morning trying to pull that same shit with her. You know, you are mad at me, so I will be mad at you. I can usually play that game very well, my temper getting the best of me.

But it was impossible. How can I not look at her? She is my muse, my everything. My eyes are drawn to her everywhere she goes, as if they have a will of their own, wanting to drink in her beauty, like a man dying of thirst.

Even when I'm mad at her, I'm utterly captivated.

But the thing is, I'm not mad at her anymore. I'm just hurt. Hurt that she decided to clam up and ignore me. I know I shouldn't have said anything about us being together, I know it's opened up a proverbial can of worms. I know this is my fault.

And I know her fears.

I just wish she could choose *me* over her fears.

Right now her fear is winning, even when it's been explained to her, even when she knows why she is acting the way she is.

I get it, though. I really do. I have the same fears, the fear that Vanni may make me choose between her and him. Fears that once we move past the physical fling and start opening up to each other, there will be no turning back.

The fear that I could lose her.

But we're already at that point. I have chosen her over the fear.

I'm not sure she will do the same.

"You know, you can't ignore me forever," I tell her as we sit in the ferry lineup, waiting for the ship to pull in. It's been a long, quiet drive here. "I am right here in this car and soon we will be back at Villa Rosa, and I will be right there too."

She presses her lips together, but her eyes look wet, no longer angry. Just sad.

"I know this is an uncomfortable conversation, Grace," I say gently. "I know that you would rather run away from it and give me the silent treatment. But we need to talk about it. Together. We are both adults and we both care about each other very much. So, let's prove that, okay?"

She exhales loudly and looks down at her hands. "I'm sorry," she says.

"Okay. I am sorry too. I shouldn't have said anything."

Her head snaps up, a hint of anger in her eyes again. "No, you really shouldn't have."

I hold up my hands in peace. "I know it wasn't my place to say anything when you specifically told me not to. I just ... I had to defend myself. I had to defend you. What we have."

"But I don't know what we have," she cries out. "What we are."

I twist in my seat to look at her, trying to find the

patience. "What do you want? How about we start with you? What do you want from me? From us?"

She looks away, and I reach out, pressing my fingers under her chin until she turns her head to face me. I dip my head, searching her eyes. "Hey? What do you want? Do you just want us to fuck for the rest of the time you're here? That's it? Just the sex? Then fine. If that's what you want, I can do that. I don't want to, but I will do it for you. I respect you too much to go against your wishes."

She blinks. "What do *you* want?"

"No, no," I say, dropping my hand and placing my palm on her forearm, giving it a light squeeze. "This is about you right now."

"But you are part of it," she says. "Don't you see? I don't ... I can't trust how you feel about me."

I pull back, my heart squeezing. It feels like I've been slapped. "You can't trust me? How can you say that?"

"Because!" she cries out. "I'm your muse. I'm the model for your statue. You need me to inspire you, and when you're done creating art, then what? Then you'll tire of me. You won't want me anymore."

"Grace," I say roughly. "That is not true—"

"And you treat me as if I'm a problem to fix. Like a wounded bird that crashed into a window. Nursing my broken wing."

"But you're *my* bird."

"So you see, it's true!"

I breathe in sharply through my nose, trying to calm my thoughts. "I am not trying to fix you. We've talked about this. I am trying to help you. That's all. And I don't even need to help you anymore, or maybe I never did. You're coming out of your shell now, your wing is fixed. It was all in you this whole time. You just had to ... find yourself. And maybe you found yourself in me, or maybe you found it in yourself, or in this country, or at the bottom of a wine glass, but you've come so far. Can't you feel it? Can't you see that you don't have any broken wings?"

A long breath escapes her and she leans back against the seat, staring at the ceiling. I watch as her chest rises and falls.

Moments pass.

"*Musa*," I say softly. "I know this isn't easy for you. All I'm asking is to put the fear aside for now and take a chance on me. You say you're worried about Vanni and Jana, and I know you are. But I think ... I think if you take a moment you'll see that it goes deeper than that. Can you imagine, please, just for a moment, if Jana and Vanni weren't an issue? If they were happy for us? Can you then imagine you would let yourself be happy?"

Her jaw twitches, as if something I just said stoked a fire inside her.

I press on. "So you fear I will grow tired of you when you are no longer my muse, but that's not how this is. I will never grow tired of you. I will never stop wanting you and wanting to be around you. You have to let yourself believe that. You have to let yourself believe in your own happiness. You're so afraid of it. That's what you're scared of. All these scapegoats, and really you're just afraid to be happy. What is it that makes you push it away and say, no, that's not for me?"

I don't expect her to say anything, so it surprises me when she clears her throat and says, "Because it can be taken away."

I nod, wanting to reach for her again but trying to give her as much space in this cramped car as I can. "Because it makes you vulnerable. It makes me vulnerable too. Don't you know I find your vulnerability beautiful? It shows me who you really are. It lets me climb inside your soul and look around and be ... I am just so overwhelmed by you, Grace. By your deepest, darkest, purest parts. You have no idea how far your outer beauty bleeds inward." I exhale, my breath shaky. "I could drown in it. I *am* drowning in it. Drowning in you."

All this time I am gazing into her eyes, because even though I've never been this vulnerable with her before, I need her to see it. I need her to believe it.

I need it like the air I breathe.

Her beautiful blue eyes begin to swim with tears and she squeezes her eyes shut so they spill down her cheeks.

She's her purest, rawest self.

Something I'll never be able to capture in art.

Nothing can transcend her.

"I ... I..." she begins and then she starts to bawl. She throws her arms around me, and I put mine around her, holding her tight as she cries into my chest. Her sobs are loud and heaving, and I know this has been a long time coming. Sometimes I'll catch her looking weepy-eyed back home, holding back tears, trying to negotiate the loss of her friend. But nothing like this.

All this grief has had nowhere to go.

So I let her cry. I keep holding her, my hand at the back of her head, cradling her, and I murmur to her, telling her it's going to be okay, telling her I'm here for her, telling her that I always will be.

Whether she wants that or not.

Whether she believes it or not.

She cries for a long time until the cadence of her breath is more even and she's relaxing in my arms.

Eventually she lifts her head, wiping her nose with her hand. "Ugh, I'm so sorry."

"Shh, shh," I say softly, kissing her forehead. "No apologies. I am so glad that you cried."

"I'm not," she says glumly, pulling away and sitting back in her seat. I move closer so that my arm slips around her shoulders. I need to be touching her.

She raises her chin to meet my eyes. The whites of hers are red, her mascara in black streaks below, yet she's still so beautiful that she knocks the air from me.

"I guess I needed to do that," she says after a beat. She clears her throat. "And I guess I don't need to tell you that. You're so ... you *know* me, somehow, and so well."

"You have a lot of grief you've been carrying with you. Tell me, when was the last time you cried like that over Robyn?"

She gnaws on her lip and sniffs. "It was a long time. Back when it happened."

"Grief doesn't have a schedule. It doesn't follow patterns. It happens when it happens and the only thing you can do is let it flow through you. Fighting it does no good. It will only build and come out later, in a more destructive way." I pause, tucking a strand of silky hair behind her ear. "You miss Robyn and you always will. And you will move on with your life because you cannot sit in grief either. You feel guilty for writing on your own, for having your own career, maybe even for finding me, but you have to remind yourself, this is what Robyn wants for you. She wants you to continue writing. She wants you to stand on your own two feet. And maybe, just maybe, she wants you to meet a nice man with a magic cock who will set your heart on fire." I swallow. "Maybe that man could be me."

A delicate smile curves her lips, and she squints at me thoughtfully. "I would like that to be you," she whispers.

I want so badly to give my heart away to her. All of it. Saving none of it for later, unsure of what she'll do with it. No, I want her to have it all.

I don't know what stops me. Maybe that fear I said I would ignore.

Maybe I just don't want to ruin the moment. I feel like we just broke through something, something that we've both been battling for and battling against.

"It *is* me," I tell her, leaning in to kiss her on the lips. I whisper against her mouth. "But please, do me a favor."

"What?"

I bring my mouth to her neck, kissing her sweetly before I press my lips against her ear. "Please. If you find yourself falling in love with me, don't stop it. Don't hold back. Don't deny yourself that. Let yourself love me."

I pull back and pin her with my gaze, hoping she takes me seriously.

She's blinking at me, seeming like she wants to say yes.

Then there's a frantic tapping at the window, and I look up with a start.

A ferry worker is angrily motioning for us to go. During all of this, we completely missed the fact that we are supposed to be boarding.

"*Spiacente!*" I apologize to the worker and then quickly start the car, the engine roaring as we follow the line onto the lower deck of the ferry.

By the time we're able to park the car and then go to the upper decks, the subject of love has been dropped.

But I haven't forgotten.

~

I AM IN MY STUDIO, BUSYING MYSELF BY REARRANGING things before I can get back to work on my sculpture, when I hear a car honk from outside.

I grin.

My boy is home.

I drop what I'm doing and stride out of the front doors to see Paolo's mother waving goodbye to me as she drives off and Vanni running straight to me.

"*Papà!*" he yells, throwing himself around my waist and hugging me.

My chest absolutely aches. It's been so long since Vanni has hugged me like this, and every passing day with him I'm reminded that he is becoming less of a boy and more of a man, and that I'll never be able to go back in time and get my boy back. Perhaps in his world, time is something you can manipulate and control, but in this world, when you have a child, it moves entirely too fast.

"Hey, Vanni," I say to him, careful not to dote on him too much. I don't want his own affection to embarrass him. "It's good to see you. Did you miss me?"

He pulls back, looking awkward. "A little."

"A little is good enough for me. Are you hungry?"

"Yes!" he exclaims, running into the house. "I want to eat everything!"

"Vanni," I call out after him, looking down at my feet at his bag that he didn't bother to bring into the house. "Whatever." I shake my head and pick it up. He's becoming more of a man, but with none of the responsibility.

I carry his bag inside and head into the kitchen to find him staring with wild eyes into the fridge.

"Go relax. I'll make you something," I tell him.

He leans against the counter, grabbing a pear from the

fruit bowl. "Where is Grace? She didn't leave without saying goodbye, did she?"

He looks so worried that I almost laugh.

"No. She's upstairs having a nap."

"Whew," he says, exhaling. Then he manages a small smile. "Grandma and Grandpa talked her ear off, didn't they?"

"Actually, they weren't so bad." Especially after we got back from dinner. Grace wasn't talking and didn't come out to have drinks either. My parents could tell that something was wrong, but for once they didn't press me about it. This morning though, Grace went out of her way to help my mother with breakfast, so at least she left on a high note.

"They were upset that you weren't there," I add.

"Grandma is always upset. I see her all the time."

"Not all the time."

"Once a month. That is all the time."

"I thought you and time had a different relationship."

He shrugs. "It's all relative."

I make Vanni a sandwich, and he tells me all about his days at Paolo's. Apparently his parents just turned vegan, which is something Vanni didn't know about, so he was starving the whole time (nevermind the fact that we eat vegetarian many times a week). He had fun, but Paolo is a shade more introverted than he is, so by the end he was bored. Said he'd rather have stayed here and hung out with Emilio.

I toy with the idea of telling him about Grace, especially since my parents already know about us. But I know this is a decision I need to make with her. Even though he is my son, I know she would see this as a betrayal again.

And what are you to her? Did you even find out?

I guess for all our conversation in the ferry line-up, we

never really hammered out what this relationship is. Boyfriend and girlfriend, yes. But with a time limit and no clear future.

And, for now, still a secret in this house.

So after Vanni is done and says he's going to go sit by the pool and play a video game on his iPad all day (apparently Paolo also isn't allowed video games anymore), I decide to go upstairs and check on Grace. She seemed so tired when we finally got home. I'm sure crying like she did took it all out of her.

I knock gently on her door. "Grace?" I whisper.

I open it and poke my head in.

She's lying on top of her bed on her side, back to me. I take a moment to stare at the curve of her hips, the dip of her waist, the golden afternoon sun coming through the window.

Fuck it.

I'm in love with her.

The realization is so sharp, so swift, I feel like I've been stabbed in the heart with the sweetest blade.

Of course I am in love with her.

There was never any other way.

There was never another outcome.

She walked into my life, and I fell for her and that's the way our story is written.

With me on my knees.

I take a deep breath, trying to fight the feeling, needing for it to stay buried for a while. I might feel this way, but she doesn't. I can't afford to scare her again.

I'm about to close the door and leave the room when she lifts her head.

"Claudio?" she whispers.

Yes, my love?

I clear my throat. "I was just checking in on you."

She looks over her shoulder at me and then rolls over, yawning. She raises her arms above her head and then flops them down on the bed. "I was having such a strange dream."

I walk in the room, shutting the door behind me. "Good strange or bad strange?"

"Good strange," she says as I sit on the edge of the bed. She hoists herself up on her elbows. "You had finished your sculpture, but instead of being the model, I was the one encased in marble."

"That's terrifying."

"And then I was at the bottom of the sea, with all these fish around me."

"Even more terrifying."

"Except I was a mermaid. You know, also. Perhaps that can be your next project?"

"You'll inspire me forever, *la mia musa*, but your dream sounds more creepy than good."

"No, it was good. I was happy. At the end, I broke free of the marble and I swam away. With my mermaid tail."

I give her a warm smile, picturing her as a mermaid. She would definitely be one of those sirens that lures men into the sea.

"Did Vanni come back yet?" she asks.

"He did. I made him a sandwich. Dare I say the boy missed me. Or he missed my cooking. But I like to think he missed me."

"Of course he did," she says.

"He was very worried when he saw you weren't here."

"Oh. You told him I was napping?"

"*Sì*. But it got me thinking ... he's grown quite attached

to you. I know it doesn't seem like it, because he has his own way, but he's fond of you."

"You know how I feel about him."

"Yes," I say, climbing onto the bed and lying down next to her, my head propped up by my elbow. "I do. So ... when do you think we should tell him?"

Her eyes go round, brow furrowed in consternation. "Vanni? About us?"

"Yes. Only because my parents now know, and that went okay."

"That did *not* go okay," she says, narrowing her eyes.

"It went okay for them, is what I mean. And I think it will go okay for Vanni. But of course, how do we explain what we are when I don't even know? We never did come to an agreement."

"An agreement," she scoffs. "This isn't a negotiation."

"It kind of is. What are we? Where are we going?"

"You are persistent."

"Only about the things that matter."

"Well I..." She trails off and gives me a sweet smile. "I guess we are exclusive to each other."

"I told you I have a possessive heart."

"And I do too. So we are exclusive. Girlfriend and boyfriend, right? But no, you're right. That's such a juvenile term. Partners? More than lovers. And ... I want to stay here as long as I can."

"And then what happens?"

She looks down at the bedspread. "I don't know. What do we do when I have to leave?"

I place my hand on top of hers. "You don't leave."

"What if you came up to Edinburgh?"

It softens my heart that she would think that's an option, but at the same time she knows it's not. "I can't leave my gallery. I can't uproot Vanni from his home. He's been through that before, I..."

"I know," she says quickly. "And honestly, I don't want to go back home. I can't. I've never felt more alive than I do here. Edinburgh ... it doesn't even feel like my home anymore. That city belonged to the person I used to be, not the person I've become."

"Well, I'll tell you this much," I say, holding her hand and raising it to my lips. I murmur against her skin. "We don't have to decide anything now. We can just be."

She swallows and looks away.

I kiss her hand, her knuckles, her fingers, turning them over and placing my lips on her palm. "You're mine, Grace. More than my muse, more than a lover. I've never felt this way before about anything or anyone, and I ... I know that if you just trust me, if you give me your heart, I will carry it with me. I will be kind and gentle with it. I will always keep it tucked next to mine. So that whatever happens in the future, it doesn't matter. I'll have your heart and you'll have mine."

She turns and looks at me. Her fingers reach out and trail down the side of my face, her eyes big and gleaming as if she's trying to really see me. "You're a good man, Claudio Romano."

"I'm *your* man," I tell her. "That is what makes me good."

She stares at my lips for a moment and then leans in, kissing me. Her hand slides back into my hair and my mouth opens against hers. I feel myself getting lost again, all the feelings inside me bubbling up like sweet Prosecco. There is so much fucking *joy* being with her like this that it's become impossible to contain.

I find myself smiling as I kiss her, and then I roll over on top of her, pinning her below me. My cock lengthens between us.

"No blindfolds this time," I whisper to her, tugging up her dress. "I want to look into your eyes as you come. I want you to look into mine. I want you to see me." I run my thumb over her lip, feeling emotion catch in my throat. "I want you to see me as I really am, how I really feel, everything open. Nothing to hide. The real me."

She blinks at me. Of course I have been nothing but the real me with her. But even so, I know I'm holding back. I no longer want to keep it from her.

I love her.

I love her so damn much.

She nods slightly, her features serious, and she reaches down to unzip my pants, shrugging them down over my ass. I position myself beneath her and then push inside her, her thighs parting to let me in.

My eyes flutter closed as she holds me tight, so hot and wet and perfect.

We fit. We fit in such a way that it seems terribly cruel that we haven't found each other until now. We missed out on so much by not being together that we've spent our life wandering around, wondering if it was ever possible to feel this way.

Then again, if I had known her when I was younger, maybe we wouldn't fit like we do now. Maybe we're born whole and polished and unscathed, and then life slowly chips away at us. Some of those chips are deep, some are just surface scratches, but we carry them with us as we walk through life, becoming more and more worn.

Yet the flaws make us who we are. What we've been through make us who we are. This life, it's trial by fire. If we didn't go through it, we wouldn't be the people we are today, and we wouldn't fit like we do right now.

I slide into her with such ease that I know I've never belonged so much as I do now. Not just with her, but here, in the world. She makes everything make sense again.

I press my face into her neck and I'm *grinning,* buried in her hair. Letting it all wash over me.

I won't lose her, no matter what.

My pumps quicken, her short nails scratching at my back, wanting more from me, fevered and needy.

She whispers her desires.

Deeper.

Harder.

More.

She's so greedy she's insatiable, and then I'm slamming my hips against her, trying to give her what she wants, trying to hold on, my cock driving deeper. The headboard slams into the wall over and over again, and I can only hope Vanni is still outside by the pool, because we are being *loud.*

"Claudio," she says, her voice breaking as her eyes pinch shut, her pleasure threatening to overtake her. "I—"

"Don't close your eyes," I command. "Keep looking at me."

Her eyes fly open and then she's coming.

I watch as she becomes undone, a spool of thread unraveling, leaving something bare and bright and beautiful behind.

"Oh god!" she cries out, tears rushing to her eyes, her mouth open and wet as she keeps crying out my name. Her body rises off the bed, shuddering around me, and I give myself permission to let go.

I come with a deep groan, my back arching as the orgasm rips up my spine, rendering me boneless. I nearly collapse on top of her, bracketing her between my elbows. My head drops, limp, forehead resting against her chest. I can feel her heartbeat through her skin, slowly calming down. It's reassuring to feel her heart, to know it's there, to know that maybe one day it will be mine for good.

"I love you," I whisper hoarsely.

The words slip out.

They fall into the room like feathers, silent, hanging there.

If anything, her heartbeat gets louder.

I raise my head to see her staring at the ceiling, blinking.

Maybe she didn't hear me.

Maybe it doesn't matter.

"Grace?" I whisper, catching my breath.

She raises her head and looks at me. There is so much softness in her eyes that I can't seem to make heads or tails of it.

"You love me?" she whispers.

I give her a smile that says, *of course. Isn't it obvious?*

Her mouth closes, a wayward tear spilling out from the corner of her eye.

She rolls over on her side.

I go on mine so that I'm spooning her, holding her against me.

I suppose it should be awkward that she's not saying anything back. But that's not why I said it. I didn't say it to hear it. I said it because it's true.

That's all there is to it.

My truth.

She doesn't seem to know what to do with it, but she's not pushing it away, either.

Finally she says quietly, "I think we should tell Vanni."

"That I love you?"

She nods. "Well, no. That's not what I meant. I mean, I think we should tell Vanni about us. Soon. And maybe, if he knows you love me, maybe he'll understand."

I'm about to tell her I completely agree when she holds up her finger. "But first, I want to put some feelers out."

"*Feelers?*" I ask, confused by this strange word.

"Aye. I want to ask him some questions just to get an idea of how he'll take it. You know. So we'll be prepared."

I don't think that's necessary, but I want to give her what she wants.

"Okay. Put out your *feelers*," I say, tickling her, because this is what feelers should be.

She laughs, squirming away from me.

So I tickle her some more.

TWENTY

GRACE

For the first time, I wake up in Claudio's arms, in Claudio's bed.

Last night, after I did one final sculpting session in his studio, as he did the last touches on the clay model, we ended up back in his bedroom. It's like now that we've decided we're going to tell Vanni, we've been a little looser with our rules.

That said, we're still careful and cautious, and Vanni was fast asleep by then, so he didn't catch me sneaking in there.

But after it was all over, I didn't want to go back to my bedroom and Claudio didn't want me to leave.

So I stayed.

It helps that I know he loves me.

He *loves* me.

I still can't believe it.

I believe him, I truly do. I see it in his eyes, and through his eyes I can see his heart and I know that he's an amazing man with an incredible capacity for love.

But it still knocks me off-balance sometimes.

He loves me and he cares for me and he wants to be with me.

There's nothing else I want.

And yet...*yet.*

I'm still trying to sift through my own feelings, trying to figure out what's real and what's not. I hadn't counted on him falling in love with me, I hadn't counted on any of this. I don't even know what to do with the information, except hold it close to me, cradle it, indulge in it.

But how do I feel about him? How do I know I'm in love with him?

Sometimes I think I am. Sometimes I catch my heart tripping in my chest, the air stolen from my lungs, the butterflies fluttering in my belly, all because of something he says, or does, or just his smile.

God, his smile makes me melt into a puddle of goo.

So how do I figure out if what I'm feeling comes from the heart or if it's just my physical reaction to him, my lust? Lust and infatuation are easy things to slip into, but love feels like it takes time to build. And maybe because our personalities are quite different in that way—he's impulsive and ready to throw himself off the deep end, I'm reserved and unsure and cautious—maybe the way we fall is inherently different.

Or maybe you're just overthinking things, I tell myself as I stretch the muscles in my legs, my toes tangling in the sheets. *Maybe you just need to accept it and keep an open mind.*

Just remember to let go if you feel like you're falling.

"Good morning," Claudio murmurs from beside me. His arms are around me, and though I remember falling asleep with more distance between us, I suppose it's possible that we found ourselves back together in our sleep.

Like two magnets that can't be kept apart.

"Mmm you smell so good," he exclaims, his nose buried in my neck.

I laugh, his stubble tickling me. "That's not usually something you hear first thing in the morning."

"Oh, but it's true," he says, sniffing up and down my neck. "You smell like you. It is my favorite smell in the world, did you know that?"

"I do now."

"Make sure you write about it in your book," he says, kissing me beneath my ear. "I think the hero should love the way she smells. And definitely the way she tastes."

"I will make a note of it."

A few days have passed since we've returned from Elba, and on every single one of those days, I've been throwing myself into my book. All my complicated feelings have been poured out on the page, and for the first time in my life, writing feels like therapy. I'm starting to understand why some authors go in so deep, it's because they're trying to figure out their own shit in their own life.

There's something so vulnerable about it, too. Like my issues are going to be out there for the world to judge. Of course, no one will know how much of it is me. But I will. Probably another good reason not to ever read reviews.

But while the writing has been good, and the chapters have been ticking along, it's also been a convenient way to hold off talking to Vanni.

I know. I know I told Claudio I would put my feelers out, but hey, the muse is visiting *me* now, and like Sandro Romano said, she is a fickle bitch.

Still...

"Are you putting your *feelers* out today?" Claudio asks, exaggerating the word, making the motion to tickle me.

"For the last time," I say, swatting him away, "it doesn't mean to tickle someone. And yes. Eventually. I have to get through some writing first. I have all this dialogue that I need to get down. My characters won't stop talking to each other in my brain."

"I suppose you cannot interfere with the muse. What is it like, being a muse *and* having a muse?"

"Sometimes I think that being someone else's muse *is* the muse. It's inspiring enough."

Eventually I get out of bed and creep back to my room before Vanni wakes up, then I get ready for the day. The day of sitting around on my arse in my church-slash-office.

But by the time it's mid-afternoon and all my espresso shots have worn off, and my brain turns to mush, I decide I need a break. I head back into the house, get changed into my bathing suit, then grab my Kindle, needing a new book to cleanse the palette, and possibly inspire me. Sometimes reading something while writing can push you to do better, try harder. So long as the book is good.

I take my spot by the pool, a tall glass of mineral water beside me (I want wine or an Aperol Spritz, but I can wait until lunch). It's another lovely perfect day and I'm getting used to the heat now as the summer goes on.

I've gotten through a chapter in this new book, when Claudio emerges from the house, wiping his hands on an apron coated in fine white dust.

"Just started with the marble?" I ask him, shielding my eyes from the sun.

He nods. "First cuts. This is the beginning of a very, very long process."

From what he's told me, it takes from two-to-four months to complete the sculpture. It's weird to think that there might be a statue of me here after I'm gone.

The thought twists my stomach and I have to remind myself that everything will work out.

"*Allora*," he goes on. "I just talked to Maria on the phone. She and Sofia are coming here for dinner. Emilio will be here, too."

"Oh, great!" I liked Maria. And the more people over for dinner, the more Claudio tries to show off in his cooking.

"She's going to take you out for a coffee first," he hastily adds.

I jerk my chin in. "What?"

"Maria. She's going to take you for a coffee, probably after lunch. Or a drink, whatever. But just so you know so you can, uh, plan your schedule." He waves his fingers at me in a roundabout motion, as if the pool is part of my schedule.

"That's fine, but why does she want to take me out for coffee?"

"Maybe she wants to get to know you."

Hmmm. I have a strange lump in the pit of my stomach. Something about Claudio's expression is throwing me off. That man can't hide anything from me.

"Claudio..." I begin. "What is it?"

"Nothing."

"Why does she want to get to know me?"

"No reason."

"Claudio!"

He sighs, squeezing the bridge of his nose, leaving dusty white thumbprints on the bridge. "She knows about us."

"She knows!" I exclaim, throwing my Kindle down on the grass. "How does she know?"

He shrugs, like he doesn't have any stake in this. "My parents told her."

"They what?"

"They are very happy for me, happy for us. They like you a lot, Grace, even if you were a bit anti-social that last night."

I stare at nothing, shaking my head. I don't really care that Maria knows we're together, but I care even more now that she wants to talk to me.

Alone.

In private.

Just the two of us.

"She's not planning to murder me, is she?" I say, half-joking.

He laughs. "No. Honest. She wants to get to know you. If you are a part of my life, then she wants to know that part of my life."

I don't like this. I'm nervous now. Of his own sister. She just seems so wise, and headstrong, and ... damn intimidating. The way she roasted Jana? My god.

"It will be fine," he assures me.

But of course, I can't help but dwell on it for the rest of the morning, all the way through lunch.

I'm sitting outside on the patio, nursing a glass of wine, trying to calm my nerves when I hear the car doors slam, and then the raucous Italian to follow, getting louder and louder as Claudio and Maria step outside. In the background, Vanni and Sofia dart out from around the corner, and are running around the yard like they've just injected themselves with sugar.

"Grace," Maria says to me, throwing her arms out. Her voice is warm, even though her eyes are trickier to figure out. I get up and she embraces me, kissing me on both cheeks, as I do the same to her. "Are you ready?" she asks, and then nods at my drink. "I will take you to a bar that has the best wine in Lucca."

Okay, maybe this won't be *so* bad.

I get up and go upstairs to grab my purse, and then I'm out front and climbing in the passenger side of Maria's car.

"Sorry to disappoint you," she says as she buckles herself in. "But I don't have my brother's taste in cars."

"No, it's a relief," I tell her. I don't even know what kind of model hers is, it just looks old and reliable. "This is a car I can relate to. I can't relate to Claudio's collection. I feel like a bull in a china shop."

"I know that expression," she says as we quickly reverse out of the driveway and onto the narrow road, the rear of the car nearly smashing into the chapel, but we stop at the last minute. She drives like her brother, though. "Except the china isn't worth a million dollars."

My eyes nearly bug out of my head. "His cars are worth a million?"

"Not all, but that one is," she says, gesturing to the Ferrari out front as we leave Villa Rosa in a plume of dust.

"Wow," I say, unable to wrap my head around it.

"My brother is very successful, yes?" she says, smiling at me. "I can see from your expression you weren't sure how much."

"No," I say shaking my head. "I mean, I know he's successful. That is obvious. It's just ... that's a lot of money. He never seems to, well, give off the impression that he has that much."

"That is part of his charm, I suppose," she muses. "But that doesn't mean other people don't know. A lot of women have thrown themselves at him, do you know that?"

A hot coal of jealousy flares up inside me.

I swallow. "I can imagine."

My mind goes back to Marika, to Angelina. Who knows

what other gorgeous women are out there that have tried in vain to win Claudio's heart?

"They throw themselves at him, because they know he is rich," she goes on. "They are gold diggers, a lot of them. Or they fall in love with the idea of falling in love with an artist." She lets out a dry laugh. "Little do they know, but loving an artist isn't so easy. Of course, some say he is handsome too, but that is not for me to comment on."

I feel her eyes on me briefly, something on her mind.

She adds, "But these women, they don't have my brother's best interest at heart. You see, he's a very open person and I'm always so worried when I see them going after him. I don't want him to get hurt."

"I'm sure he takes care of himself," I say quietly.

"He does. Doesn't mean I don't worry."

I give her a look. "Well, I can assure you that I'm not one of those girls. His money means nothing to me. As for him being an artist, well it just means we have something in common."

I'm not about to add that I find her brother ridiculously hot and that the sex is absolutely wild.

She observes me for a moment, then brings her eyes back to the road, nodding. "I know that. I can tell. I just wanted to make sure."

"Is that why you're taking me out?"

"Yes," she admits, no qualms in being honest. "But also, I want to get to know you. You mean so much to my brother and, well, I just wanted to welcome you into the family."

I stiffen up at that.

"What is it?" she asks me.

"Not everyone in the family knows," I tell her. "Your parents do, and you do, and I'm sure your sisters do."

"I am sure everyone on Elba knows as well," she adds.

"Right. But there are two people who don't. One is Jana."

Now it's time for her to go stiff. "She is not part of the family."

"Not to you, but she is to Vanni. And Vanni is the other person. We haven't told either of them. We've been putting it off because it's just so new and, until now, it was just a vacation romance. We didn't know if we would have a future together. But now we have to tell them. I just don't think either of them are going to like it."

Maria starts to laugh. Her laugh is a lot like Claudio's, loud and boisterous and taking up space. If I wasn't so confused, I'd probably find it infectious.

"What?"

"Nothing. I'm just picturing Jana's reaction. Okay. Let us just get some drinks first, shall we?"

To my surprise, she doesn't take me to the walled city of Lucca, but to the space just beyond it, parking beside a restaurant that overlooks the Serchio River. We get a table outside overlooking the water, and the buildings of the walled city, including the famed Guinigi Tower, with its oak tree on top.

"This is lovely," I tell her as the waiter drops off some olives.

"I prefer it," she says. "Claudio is always dragging me to the gallery and to places in the city walls, but it's too much for me, too busy, too many tourists. Too hot." For emphasis, she picks up a menu and fans herself with it. "But here, it is peaceful. And I promise you, the wine is excellent."

I trust her on that, so when the waiter comes back, I let her do the ordering.

"You sure?" she asks.

"Please, I'm an author. I'll take whatever you got."

She laughs and gets us a bottle of white from Sicily.

"*Allora*," she says. "You were saying. You haven't told Jana or Vanni."

"No. I have been meaning to talk to Vanni..."

"That is Claudio's role, no?"

"It is. Definitely. But I just wanted to put my f-...I wanted to get a feel for things. I know that he's had issues with his father's girlfriends in the past, enough so that Claudio broke up with them."

"Ah yes, Marika. She was a nice girl but...Claudio didn't look at her the way that he looks at you. He is crazy for you, Grace. I know this seems so big and hard to understand when you're looking into a family from the outside, but even though Claudio will always do what's best for his son, that doesn't mean he can't do what's best for himself."

I nod, popping an olive in my mouth.

"Do you love him?"

I nearly choke on the olive, the brine tickling my throat.

"So you haven't told him, I take it," she comments.

I carefully chew the olive and then swallow it, buying time. "He told me he loves me."

"That much anyone can see. But what about you?"

I want to be honest with her. It strikes me right now, after all this time, that I haven't had a female friend to talk to since Robyn died. Everything I've been going through regarding Claudio, I've been going through alone. Thank god I've been channeling into my writing, otherwise I'd go insane.

But can I trust her? She is his sister, after all.

"I am close with Claudio," she says, reading my expression. "But I am not that close."

I nod, taking in a deep breath. "Well, I don't know. I think ... I think I'm falling in love with him. I just don't know how to separate it from infatuation. I've never been in love before ... or at least, I don't think."

"If you don't know, then you haven't," she says.

"So how will I?"

She just gives me a knowing smile. "When you know, you know. What they say is true. Perhaps you haven't let yourself fall yet. When you are so worried about the future and what other people will say, perhaps you are still protecting yourself. Once you move past all of that, once you feel safe and confident in your future, maybe then..."

Maybe then.

"Either way, this is Claudio's son and he knows what is best for him. Vanni, no matter how he feels, will come around eventually."

I exhale, sinking back in my chair. "I hope so. I understand exactly how Vanni feels, too. When my parents divorced, I wanted nothing more than for them to get back together. They didn't, and then my dad went and married someone else. And honestly, it made me feel like dirt. Like I was unwanted and forgotten."

"Well, was your father dirt?"

I laugh at the sincerity of her question. "We have a complicated relationship. I love him still, but he could have handled that a lot better."

Understatement of the year.

"But you turned out fine," she says.

"Did I? I'm a *writer*."

She chuckles. "Okay, so it was good for that. But I don't think Claudio is like your father, and as much as I don't like Jana, Vanni's relationship with her is very different. It does seem to work for them. I think, no matter what happens, let Vanni be Vanni. He's a smart kid. He'll want his father to be happy and you can't deny that he is, now that he's found you."

The waiter takes the opportunity to drop off the bottle of wine, pouring us each a glass. They take their jobs so seriously here, back in Edinburgh they'd plunk it on the table and leave.

We pick up our glasses and raise them to each other.

"And when it comes to Jana," Maria says to me, swirling the wine around in the glass. "You have to ask yourself, what it matters? If you can't hide it from her forever and it doesn't change how you feel about Claudio, then who cares? She can be mad if she wants, and maybe your career will hurt. But can you imagine caring so much that you leave Claudio behind? Can you imagine coming into success and having no one to share it with? Because that's what will happen and you'll end up feeling empty."

She raises the glass to her nose. "You are putting all your stock into the wrong person. Jana is just an agent. If you are a good writer, and I know you are, then you will find success no matter what happens. You will get another agent. But Claudio? There is no other Claudio. *Capisci?*"

There is no other Claudio.

He's one in a billion.

As am I.

"*Capisco*," I answer.

I understand.

She closes her eyes and breathes in the wine. "*Perfetto.*"

I do the same, the notes of lemon and apples and hay wafting in my nose. Then I sip. The wine tastes like gold.

In fact, the whole moment is golden.

Because what Maria said is the truth.

I have nothing to be afraid of anymore.

After a moment I say, "I will talk to Vanni later tonight."

"Good," she says. "And then tell Jana, and get it all over with so you can be with my brother. And maybe, somewhere along the way, you'll fall in love with him."

I give her a shy smile at that, because, I know I'm starting to fall.

~

IT'S AFTER DINNER WHEN MARIA AND SOFIA DRIVE OFF back home, and all the digestifs have been finished, that I decide to follow through with her advice and find Vanni.

He's not hard to find. After a day of running around with his cousin and splashing around in the pool, he's up on the couch, reading a book. The house is silent, aside from the occasional muffled drill coming from Claudio's studio.

"*Ciao* Vanni," I say to him, sitting beside him on the couch. "What are you reading?"

"Space time continuum," he says, glancing up at me from behind the book. "Though the author's voice is a little dry. You ever think about writing about time travel?"

I grin at him. "If I could understand it, maybe. Or I could make it a romance. Like Outlander."

He makes a face. "I told you. Outlander's science is all wrong and romance is gross."

Ah. This might actually make a good segue.

"You say that now Vanni, but in time, it won't be so gross to you."

He mumbles something in Italian, and shrugs. Probably the equivalent of *whatever*.

"I'm serious. One day you'll fall in love with someone and you won't find them so gross anymore. You'll want to spend all day with them. Play all your video games with them. You'll teach them about space stuff and time travel and they'll eat it all up, and then they'll tell you about things you'll find interesting. And you'll never want to let them go. You'll want to spend your life with them."

"And then marry her?" he adds. "And have a baby? And get divorced? I don't think so."

Well, shit. He has me there.

"But that doesn't always happen."

"It happened to my father."

I don't know how to tell him that his father never loved his mother and I'm not about to. So I just say, "Things happen. But your mother and father are very happy now, just not with each other. They have other people to love. Big careers. They're happy."

He shakes his head. "My father is not happy."

I swallow the lump in my throat. "I think he is."

"No," he says. "He isn't. The father in Gio's universe? He is happy. He never divorced. He is in love. And Gio is happy. That's why *this* is the darkest timeline. I got stuck in the wrong one. I should have been in the one where my parents are still together."

Crushed. I feel absolutely crushed. Not just that poor Vanni feels this way, but that the chances of him ever being accepting of me and Claudio have gone out the window. He will never accept us together. He will never understand.

"What if..." I begin, grasping for straws. "What if neither timeline is better than the other? What if there are good things and bad things in each one?"

He stares at me. I have his attention.

I clear my throat and go on. "They say the choices we make every day are the things that influence our life. Our timelines. There are so many choices, though. What to eat, what to wear, where to go. Each of those choices have a direct influence on each other. You know Jurassic Park?"

He sits up. "Which one?"

"Uh, the first one. Jeff Goldblum said that a butterfly flaps its wings in Shanghai and you get rain instead of snow in ... some other place. Okay, I don't remember the quote exactly, but it's the butterfly effect, right? So, with so many choices influencing our lives, aren't there infinite timelines and versions of ourselves? And if that's the case, can't it be true that at least more than one of them are...happy?"

He stares at me for a moment, and I think I might have gotten through to him.

Then he looks back to his book, shaking his head. "That makes no sense."

I sigh, giving up. I put my feelers out and the feelers came back saying "good fucking luck."

I make my way downstairs to give Claudio the bad news.

TWENTY-ONE

GRACE

We're going to Florence.

It was a completely impromptu, last-minute trip, and all Claudio's idea. After I told him about my talk with Vanni, he said he would talk to him personally and set him straight. Tell him the truth about us. I didn't want him to hurt Vanni's feelings in any way, but he's his father so I know I have to back off and give them space. He knows what's best.

But Claudio also thought a trip might make the news go down easier.

Plus, his friend I met at the gallery, Lorenzo Ducati, is playing in that weird violent sport thing, and apparently that's a big deal and something not to be missed.

We're currently in the Range Rover, zooming down the motorway through verdant hills and small towns, and I'm actually really excited. We're going for three nights, which Claudio says is just enough to get a taste of the famous city, and that we can always go back for more at any time. Florence is only an hour drive, though we have been making plenty of touristy stops on my behalf. The countryside is just begging to have its photo taken.

"There's the *Duomo!*" Vanni yells as the city appears. "Oh wait. That's another church. There's a lot of them."

We hit a bit of traffic and then try to find a parking space outside of the city. The parking situation is very strange and capricious in Florence, and even though the hotel has legal parking, Claudio decides to park elsewhere. I have a feeling he doesn't trust valets, even with his Range Rover.

Now I'm regretting my decision to pack so much. Claudio grunts as he picks it up, insisting he carry it to the hotel, which I think is just an excuse to complain about it.

Florence is hot as hell and absolutely alive with people. Even though it's lunchtime, everyone is drunk and wearing shirts in either white or red, beers in hand, shouting and chanting. The atmosphere is electric.

"They are all here for the game, Calcio Storico," Claudio explains as some guy gets in his face and yells something joyous, before running down the street, drink spilling. "That guy, he's in a red shirt, so he is cheering for his neighborhood, Santa Maria Novella. The white shirts represent Santo Spirito. Those are the teams that made it to the final."

"I am upset that San Giovanni isn't playing," Vanni says, pouting. "They are my namesake."

"They are the green team," Claudio says to me. "You may see some blue or green shirts here anyway, people who refuse to accept they lost."

"So, it's different Florentine neighborhoods competing?" I ask, trying to understand.

"That is correct. Each is named after the main church in that neighborhood. Don't worry. It will all make sense later. I think."

"Which neighborhood does Lorenzo play for?"

"He is from Santa Maria Novella. Red shirt. Which is fitting, because when he plays, he is out for blood."

"He's *barbaric*," Vanni whispers to me. "I've seen him play on the internet and..." He trails off, shaking his head in quiet disgust.

Okay, this game definitely sounds more interesting now.

Soon we arrive at our hotel, which is the nicest hotel I have ever stepped in. It's The Savoy, and it feels like you're walking into a palace. But as much as I want to luxuriate here and hunker down in a beautiful room with a cocktail, we're on a schedule today. We need to meet up with Lorenzo to get the tickets, then Claudio wants to take us to the famous *Duomo*, the Cathedral of Santa Maria del Fiore, all before the parade that starts at four p.m., with the game starting after.

We put our stuff away in our rooms (of course, I have a room to myself while Vanni and Claudio share a suite), and then we make our way out of the hotel. In the lobby I pass a couple of statues that seem to have Claudio's workmanship.

"Did you do those?" I whisper to him, jutting my thumb at the statues.

He shrugs, a humble smile on his lips. "Perhaps that's why I get a discount when I stay here?"

I laugh, and we step out into the stunning expanse of the Piazza della Repubblica. Claudio leads us across the street, holding both me and Vanni's hands because it is *so* busy here, holy crap, and then we see Lorenzo waiting by an old carousel.

"Claudio," Lorenzo says as they greet each other warmly. They embrace quickly, a few hearty slaps on the back. If Lorenzo hits Claudio any harder, I think he might jostle a few organs loose.

Lorenzo eyes me and nods. "*Ciao*. Grace, right?'"

I nod, smiling, and then he looks down to Vanni and holds his palm out for a high five.

"Vanni!' Lorenzo says. "*Il mio piccolo amico!*"

Vanni just stares and timidly gives him a high five. I don't think I've ever seen him speechless before, and it's adorable.

I also don't blame him.

Lorenzo is a tall, hunky hulk of a man with darkly tanned skin, tattoos, and brooding look to him. His nose has definitely been broken a few times, adding a touch of rugged danger.

He's also wearing billowing red pants that come to his knees, high red socks, and a red shirt that looks torn and dirty already. Not the most aerodynamic uniform.

"I only came to give you these," he says to Claudio, slipping him three tickets. "I have to go back before some crazy fucker in a white shirt tries to fight me right here."

"*Grazie*," Claudio says, putting the tickets away. "I will see you after the game, yes?"

"It depends if I still have my head," he says with a wild grin, and wags his brows at Vanni, who just gasps.

Then Lorenzo is off and running through the crowd.

"*Wow*," Vanni says after a moment. "It's like he's going off to war."

Claudio shrugs. "That isn't a bad analogy. There's a reason his nickname is The Warrior." He grabs Vanni's hand. "Come on, let's get some lunch and see the *Duomo* before the parade starts."

Vanni can never say no to food.

Florence feels hotter than Lucca, and there are so many more people packed in the tiny streets, I'm guessing even more so today. The streets are crowded and a little claustrophobic, and it's a relief when we find a restaurant on a quiet alley to have some lunch. We take our time, eating a few courses, drinking a bottle of wine and some cocktails.

Then, when we're refreshed, we head to the *Duomo*.

I remember the history of the cathedral quite well from my classes at university, so it's positively surreal to be standing just below the famous red dome and the green and white façade. There is so much history in this city, so many artists produced here, that it's a little overwhelming, and the Duomo is the focal point.

We decide to skip going inside the cathedral today, since the line is insanely long and we don't have that much time, so we just explore the outside. Vanni wants to climb the 463 steps to the top, but I'm not even doing that when we do have the time.

Finally it's time for the foot parade. Because it goes past the Duomo, we stand back in the shade and watch as men and boys come out in Renaissance style outfits, marching with drums, and throwing flags up in the air.

Then, Claudio takes us through tiny, winding streets to the Piazza di Santa Croce, where the game is held.

It is *insane*.

In front of a large, gilded cathedral with intricate architecture, is absolute chaos. I know that normally that church would be the focal point, but right now it's the large rectangular square packed with dirt that's surrounded by thousands of fans in red and white. The energy is off the charts.

"We will come back tomorrow and it will be quiet," Claudio says, nodding at the church. "The tombs of Michelangelo and Galileo are inside. I always try to pay tribute when I am here."

Then, with a steely grip on our hands, he leads me and Vanni through the pressing crowd until we find our seats on bleachers on the red side. We're at the back, but honestly that's good enough for me. I wouldn't want to get too close to the action if it's as dangerous as I think it is.

It's not long before the crowd starts chanting, waiting for the teams to come out. It's close to five p.m. now and it's hot as sin outside, made even hotter by all these people. Claudio tells me that almost seven thousand fans are gathered around us, most of them rabidly passionate for their neighborhood.

Finally, the men come out and the crowd erupts.

Twenty-seven players on each side.

Fifty-four of the roughest, toughest, most brutal looking men I've ever seen, nearly all of them shirtless and covered in tattoos. Surprisingly, there's a wide range of body types, from thin and wiry, to lean and athletic, to tall and hulking, to big and bear-like. Not surprisingly, they all look like they're about to murder someone.

"So, these are all professional athletes?" I ask Claudio, my voice barely audible above the crowd.

He shakes his head. "No. They train like they are, but they do not get paid to do this."

"What do they get out of it?"

"Glory. Honor. And their neighborhood gets a feast, so that's nice."

Nice? These men look like they're about to fight to the death, and all they get is some nice food to share? Wow.

"They are in it because their heart is in it," Claudio says. "And your heart can convince you to do anything."

His deep eyes linger on my face for a moment before he looks away, and I know he wasn't just talking about the warrior's hearts.

And so the game starts with a clash. The goal, I believe, is to get a ball in the net at either end, but in order to do that, you have to get through the players first. And that's where the rugby aspect comes in.

Except in rugby you are not allowed to kick people in the head.

Or punch them in the face.

Or wrestle them to the ground and pin them there.

Or use MMA moves.

All of these techniques and more are being used to try to get the ball to the other side, blood spilling everywhere, ultimate carnage.

It is the most intensely violent thing I've ever watched. I'm not even sure it can be called it a game, it really is a war, a battle, and within minutes, half the players are on the ground. Stretchers are constantly taking people off the dirt, and then those same players will run back on with broken noses and head wounds and black eyes.

"I told you," Vanni says to me, noting the grim expression on my face. "It is barbaric. Some play with broken ribs. Did you know that even popes used to play this game, but they were allowed to use swords? I'm not sure I could have watched that."

Me neither. And yet I can't look away.

Especially as Lorenzo is still playing. He's really good, and his strength and bulk make it easy for him to fight his way across, taking punches but giving them even better.

I take out my phone to try and capture it all on camera, when I notice I have a missed call.

My heart drops through my chest.

It's from *Jana*.

Jana hasn't even called me once since I got here, not even after the big mix-up at the beginning. We've emailed a few times, but that's been it. She's left me alone, and I've been grateful for it.

It's never good when your agent calls.

Unless it *is* good.

Hmmm.

Suddenly my mind is running away on me. Maybe this isn't about my deadline, and maybe it's not about Claudio or Vanni either, maybe we just sold movie rights or something like that.

"Is that my mother?" Vanni asks, peering at the missed call on the display.

Claudio immediately looks over, concerned. "Jana?"

"I missed her call," I say feebly. "I better go and call her back."

I don't want to call her back, but I won't be able to sit and watch the game if I don't. "I'll be back," I tell them, then I make my way through the crowded stands until I'm free.

When I find a spot in the shade away from the noise and the crowds, I take out the phone and press redial with shaking hands.

She picks up on the first ring, giving me no time to freak out.

"Grace," she says in her quick, clipped voice. "How are you?"

I swallow, trying to calm my racing heart. "I'm good. Sorry, I missed your call..."

"That's fine, I would have kept trying anyway. Listen, sweetheart, I have a free day tomorrow and I thought I would fly down to see you in Lucca."

No.

My heart drops even further.

"Uh..." I stammer. "Why?"

She laughs. "Why? Because I want to check up on you and see how you're doing. I feel so bad about you having to be there with my ex-husband and Vanni, I know Claudio can be such a pain in the neck sometimes."

No, not really.

"Plus, it would be good to hear about the book, face-to-face. And let's be honest here, I think a little accountability isn't a bad thing. Plus, I could use some sunshine, it's just been rubbish weather in London. We've had no summer at all. Meanwhile one of my clients is down south, soaking it all up."

I'm just blinking, trying to figure out what to say.

"Grace? Are you there?"

"Yes, yes, hi," I tell her quickly, feeling flustered. My face is going hot. "Well, that's great and all but we're not in Lucca right now."

"Where are you?"

"In Florence."

"Oh," she says. "*Firenze*. A day trip?"

"No. We're spending a few days here."

"You and Vanni and Claudio?"

"Yes." Then I hastily add, "And Lorenzo Ducati. You know, that calcium story player."

"Calcio Storico?" she corrects me. "And yes, I know him. He's a big muscley piece of man meat if I've ever seen one." Suddenly she gasps. "Oh, Grace. Are you together with him?"

"Claudio?" I squeak.

Another sharp laugh. "Good heavens, *no*. I mean Lorenzo."

I can hardly breathe. "No, no...he's nice, though." I say that last part a little warmly, hoping to throw her off track.

"Ah, *well then*," she says, and I know she's taken the bait. "That's great. He's a good guy. A little scary, but good. Why don't I come down to Florence tomorrow then, if

320

you're there for a few days. Where are you staying? The Savoy?"

"Yes..."

"Perfect. It will be easier for me to fly into Florence anyway. Listen, I'll call you when I land. Don't forget to warn the boys."

And then she hangs up.

Holy SHIT.

~

I DON'T SLEEP A WINK.

How can I when fucking Jana is coming to Florence!

After she called, I went to join Claudio and Vanni in the stands, but kept mum on the phone call. I tried to get back into the game, but it was pointless. All I could think about was Jana coming. I barely even noticed when the red team won, thanks to some winning moves by Lorenzo, who ended the game all bloody, beaten and triumphant.

With the game over, we stayed on the streets and partied and drank, until Vanni was tired and wanted to go home. Then, on the way back to the hotel, I finally spilled the news.

Vanni, of course, was all super excited to see his mother.

And Claudio? Well, he was concerned, but not as upset as I thought he would be. Or, at least, not as upset as I was.

I'm still upset. I'm lying in a gorgeous room in the Savoy hotel, a view of the Duomo from my window, feeling groggy and exhausted, and all I want to do is bury myself under the covers and never come out.

But then there's a knock at my door, spoiling those plans.

321

I slip a robe over my camisole and booty shorts, just in case it's room service, and I open the door.

It's Claudio, leaning against the doorway, looking effortlessly sexy and casual.

"*Buongiorno*," he says to me, his eyes resting briefly on my lips. I know what he's thinking. He wants to kiss me.

I poke my head out of the door, looking down the hall both ways, then push up on my toes to meet his mouth, giving him a quick kiss.

"I better do that now, because I sure as hell won't be able to do that later," I say.

He gives me a soft smile, eyes crinkling at the corner. "How are you doing?" he asks me. "You were pretty upset last night."

I exhale and throw my arms out as I head back into the room. "Why shouldn't I be?"

He closes the door softly behind me but keeps his distance. I suppose with Vanni right next door, he doesn't want to get pulled into anything and lose track of time. That's a bad habit of ours.

"Maybe this is all happening for a reason," he says calmly.

"So you're happy your ex-wife is showing up on our little vacation?"

He crosses his arms and frowns. "No. I am not happy. But Vanni is happy. And our little vacation includes him too."

I close my eyes, rubbing my thumb into my forehead. "Yes. I know. Of course. I just mean..."

"I know what you mean, Grace," he says. "This has taken me off-guard too. But it is happening and her plane should be landing right now. So, she'll be here soon, and then we'll have to deal with it."

"What do you suppose we should do?" I ask, looking at him for answers.

"Well, we could just continue on like we have been doing in front of Vanni, and we can pretend that we aren't together, and that I'm not madly in love with you."

My heart skips at those words. I'll never tire of hearing it.

"Or," he adds, "we can be adults and tell the both of them. Two birds with one sword."

"Stone. Two birds with one stone."

"I prefer sword. It's easier to stab them both at the same time," he says, making a jousting lunge.

"Right. I think that's a bad idea."

"I figured you would. Okay, so we just continue as we have. No problems. Okay?"

I nod but I know that it's not going to be that easy.

I have a bad feeling.

"Look, Vanni is almost ready and then we're going to head down for breakfast. It is really good here. Why don't you get dressed and come meet us?"

"Okay," I say softly, even though I can't imagine eating anything right now.

Of course, when I do get ready for the day, and I head downstairs to the restaurant, my stomach kicks into high gear. Walking past all the opulently set tables, spying all the food, I realize I could eat a horse.

I find Claudio and Vanni at a table in the back. Both of them look dashing in cream colored pants and red shirts, a silky polo for Claudio, a t-shirt for Vanni. Makes me wish I had packed a red dress.

"You guys match," I tell them as I sit down.

"It wasn't on purpose," Vanni grumbles through a bite of toast and Nutella.

"Vanni, don't talk with your mouth full. Not here, anyway."

Vanni reaches for a napkin and daintily wipes his lips with it, acting all posh.

I laugh. "Well, you both look great."

"So do you," Claudio says, eying me in my yellow and white dress. I know it will always remind him of his art. Perhaps I wore it on purpose today.

"And so does the food," I say, picking up the menu. I'm drooling over everything, but the first thing I need is a coffee.

It's when I'm nearly done with my latte that Vanni suddenly cries out, "*Mamma!*"

He bolts from his chair and we look over to see Jana walking past the restaurant, towing a tiny carry-on bag behind her.

"Vanni!" she cries out, dropping her suitcase and opening her arms and Vanni goes flying into them.

I have to say, it breaks my heart a little.

Not in a bad way, per se. It's just so sweet. And it makes me realize how much Vanni needs his mother, how much he loves her, and how much Jana cares about him. Even from a distance, it's not hard to see.

I glance beside me at Claudio and he's practically beaming as he watches them. It means so much to him too.

Jana picks her suitcase back up, and Vanni grabs her hand and leads her through the restaurant toward us, and she's waving at us as she comes near.

She looks great, actually. When I met her in London, she was so stern and sharp, but here she already seems relaxed, even though she's wearing a brown suit and black-framed eyeglasses. Her hair seems brighter and longer too, though still closely cropped.

"Jana," Claudio says warmly, while the both of us attempt to get up.

"No, no, no," she says, frantically waving her hands at us. "Don't get up. Enjoy your food. I'm going to go see if I can get an early check-in and change. They bloody hell better give me one, lord knows I have so many points racked up with this joint." She waves at Vanni and says. "I'll be down in a bit."

Then she hurries off toward reception, and no doubt there will be hell to pay with the clerk if she doesn't get her early check-in.

"Isn't this great?" Vanni says to us, smiling as he sits back down.

While Claudio's smile comes easy to him, it's rare to see it on Vanni.

He goes on. "This is like all the timelines are colliding into one super timeline."

Oh boy.

I exchange a look with Claudio. Vanni's happiness is contagious, but in a way it makes everything else that much harder.

When our food comes and we've finished, we leave the restaurant and see Jana waiting on a chair in the lobby. She gets up and comes over to us, heading straight for Claudio.

I step back and watch as they embrace, kiss each other on the cheek.

This is so weird.

It really is. I've tried to fit the image of them together in my mind so many times, even after seeing their wedding photos and whatnot, but to see it in the flesh is jarring. They're both attractive people, but they are *soooo* different, from their age, to their mannerisms, to their, I don't know, life essence or something.

But if they seem angry at each other, it doesn't show. They don't seem overly affectionate either, it's just very neutral and pleasant and strange.

Then Jana turns to me. "Grace," she says, pulling me into a quick, light hug, a few taps on the shoulder. She's skinny and it feels like I could crush her. "You're looking well. You've got quite the glow."

I try not to blush and add to that glow, because only Claudio and I know what that glow is really about.

"Okay," she says. "Before it gets too hot and crowded, let's go sight-seeing. Did you get to the Duomo yesterday?"

"*No*," Vanni says, "and I want to climb to the top and they don't want to."

He points accusatorily at us.

"Oh Vanni, no one wants to do that," she says to him. "They're spring chickens, but I am far too old. How about we go inside the cathedral for now?"

Jana is obviously exaggerating her age, but I'm not going to argue with her. I'm not going up there.

Vanni at least agrees to that, so we walk back to the Duomo, Jana holding Vanni's hand the whole way.

The line-up isn't as long as yesterday, but it's still an hour's wait. So the four of us stand in line, and talk about a whole range of stuff, though most of the time it's Vanni rambling on to his mother about space shit.

A couple of times I take the opportunity to be alone, and volunteer to go get gelatos for everyone. I wish Italy embraced the coffee to-go thing here, but they don't. So, I have an espresso while standing up at a counter, hoping the coffee will calm my nerves while knowing it's doing the opposite.

Finally, we finish our gelatos and get inside the cathedral.

It's absolutely stunning, and I'm taken by the vast gothic interior, feeling spacious even with all the people in it. It's surprisingly bare, but it adds to the sense of peace and tranquility inside.

We walk slowly toward one of the many circular stained-glass windows, Vanni and Jana ahead of us. They stop and Vanni points up, excitedly telling his mother something about it. It's probably a portal to another dimension or something.

I glance at Claudio who is standing right next to me, and he gives me a small yet reassuring smile. Briefly, very briefly, his fingers reach out for mine and we grasp the tips of each other's hand for a moment, before our hands fall away.

Even from that one instance of my skin against his, I feel my body grow heavy and warm and happy. He's grounded me.

We spend quite a bit of time inside the cathedral because there is a lot to see, and then we head back to where we were last night, a chance to go inside the Santa Croce church where the game was.

Here, Claudio pays his respects to the tomb of Michelangelo, and I feel his reverence for him, while Vanni lingers at the tomb of Galileo. Fittingly, when we leave the church, he wants to go to the Museo Galileo.

I'm tired on my feet though, so we have lunch first.

And this whole time, the topics of conversation have stayed very easy and neutral. A lot of questions on how I'm liking Italy, but Jana doesn't touch on how it's been to live with Claudio and vice versa, nor does she ask what I've been doing, or how the book is going.

But I know that's coming. That's one of the reasons she's here.

It isn't until later, when we're at a nice restaurant for dinner, eating outside in a quaint alleyway, that Jana turns her sights on me for real.

"So, Grace," she says over a sip of her wine. "Tell me, how is the book coming along?" She catches the expression on my face because she adds, "You knew this was coming."

I give her a cautious smile. "The book is actually doing really well."

Her eyes go round. "Really?"

I nod, spearing my linguine. "Really. I'm at chapter..."

"You're at chapter sixteen," Claudio fills in.

Now Jana is looking at him in surprise. "Oh? You've read it?"

"No." He shakes his head and has some of his wine. "I haven't. But we talk about the book often."

"He's good for bouncing ideas off of," I explain.

"I see," she says slowly. Then she smiles at me. "Well that is excellent news Grace. I am so excited for this book."

"Me too," I say. Then I blurt out, "But I thought you should know, it's a romance now."

"Gross," Vanni comments.

Jana adjusts her glasses and stares at me. "A romance?"

"Yes."

Oh shit. I see her disappointment.

I clear my throat. "See, I was stuck when it was women's fiction and it was so much pressure on myself to produce this big aching book and then I thought, you know what? I've gone through too much pain and misery lately, I don't want to write something that will make me feel worse. I want to write something happy. I wanted to write a romance with a happily-ever-after. And I figured, well, if I feel this way about the book, maybe that's what will make it good. Maybe others will want to feel good too. Close the book with a happy sigh and let that feeling carry them through the day."

I realize I'm rambling so I quickly shove a forkful of pasta into my mouth, just to shut myself up.

"Oh, okay," Jana says after a moment. She looks to Claudio. "You'll have to excuse me if I'm not picking up on her passion for the project, it's just very different than the book the publishers decided to buy from her."

"I'm aware," Claudio says smoothly, and I can tell that Jana doesn't like that. "But if the book is better this way, then I'm sure it will be okay."

"Claudio, darling, look. You don't know publishing."

"No, but I know a good writer when I see one and I think any publisher will want Grace's book."

She squints at him and then looks at me. "So, I see you've had a cheerleader this whole time" Meaning Claudio. "Listen, this is a lot to take in."

"I know. I'm sorry. But it will be fine," I tell her. "Because it's almost done. It will be finished soon. And it's more or less the exact same story, there are just fewer tears and more sex."

"But people want tears!" Jana exclaims.

"And people want sex," I counter.

"¡Basta!" Vanni yells, covering his ears with his napkins.

Claudio reaches over and lowers Vanni's arm, since he's attracting attention from the other tables.

"And who says there isn't both," I tell her, leaning forward. "It has all the ingredients the publishers want, it's just sexier and it ends happily. That's all. I am sure readers will go through the wringer regardless."

Claudio quickly reaches over and puts his own hands over Vanni's ears now. "And if they can get off on it, all the better," he adds with a cheeky smile.

Then he drops his hands. Vanni looks like he wants to hide under the table.

"You're not wrong," Jana eventually admits.

"*And* I'm happy for having written it. That counts for something."

"It counts for *everything*," Claudio says emphatically, his eyes locked on mine. "You come first, remember?"

I bite back a smile.

Jana exhales loudly, tilting her head as she moves her vegetables around on her plate. "I don't know what to tell you. I mean, I will give them the book and hope for the best. I suppose I should have known this would happen. How could you come to Italy and not want to write a romance? For all I know, you are living your own romance already."

Claudio and raise our brows at each other.

"Didn't you say you came here to see that Lorenzo?" Jana goes on, asking me. "The game was last night, wasn't it?"

"It was..." I say carefully.

"So, am I wrong in thinking there is something blossoming between you both?"

I'm looking at Claudio again, trying to find the words.

Then Vanni puts his fork down with a loud clatter, looks his mother dead in the eye, and says, "No. Grace is not in love with Lorenzo." He looks at me and then at Claudio. "Grace is in love with my father and he is in love with her. They are in love with each other!"

Jana blinks.

Claudio chokes on his water.

I feel the world *shift*.

TWENTY-TWO

GRACE

WHAT THE FUCK?

I feel like I'm about to fall off my chair.

Did Vanni really just say that? Did he really just tell his mother that Claudio and I are in love with each other?

"What is he talking about?" Jana asks, her voice shaking a little, her eyes darting between the two of us. "In love with each other? You? And *you*?"

I don't say anything. I can't. I press my lips together, hard, because I'm afraid I might vomit if I don't.

Jana doesn't look happy *at all*.

And Vanni?

Well, I can't figure the kid out.

"Vanni," Claudio says sternly after a moment. "What do you mean by that?"

Vanni sighs heavily, rolling his eyes. "Oh please. Do you think I'm stupid or something? It is *very* obvious."

More silence.

Vanni knows. He's probably known all this time.

We've been so busy trying to hide it, so busy worrying about him knowing, we never realized he was onto us. I'm quickly flipping through the days in my brain, trying to figure out when we were careless. God, I hope he didn't see anything...

I catch Claudio's eyes and he must be thinking the same thing because he says, "But *how* do you know?"

Vanni stares at him with a wry expression. "I just know. Besides, I got confirmation that I am right."

"From who?"

Vanni shrugs. "No one."

"*Sofia*," Claudio mutters.

"I'm saying nothing."

Sofia. Of course. Maria would have told her daughter, or her daughter would have overheard her talking about it to Claudio or her parents, and then the telephone game began.

"Is this true?" Jana asks, staring at me now. Her eyes are hard, and they're hurt too. "Grace. Are you in love with my ex-husband?"

Oh shit. Now I really don't want to say anything.

"I am in love with her," Claudio interjects, to which Jana gasps. "Vanni is right. And we are together. We are happy. We are *so* happy, Jana."

Jana shakes her head in disbelief. "I can't believe it." Her eyes snap to me again. "How could you do that to me? How could you make things so bloody complicated? You were supposed to come here to write, not screw my ex, my son's father. How *dare* you?"

My face grows hot, the tears threatening to come.

"*Hey*," Claudio says sharply, eyes blazing at her. "This isn't Grace's fault. It just happened. It wasn't planned. And if it makes you feel any better, we spent many sleepless nights trying to figure out how to tell you. The *both* of you."

"Oh sure. That's why they were sleepless. No," Jana says, getting to her feet and throwing her napkin down on her plate. "No. This isn't right. This is *humiliating*. I came down here to see you and meanwhile you're all secretly playing house? I don't think so…"

"Jana," Claudio says to her.

"I'm leaving," she says, grabbing her purse and marching through the restaurant, people turning their heads to watch her go.

"Fuck," Claudio swears. He gives me and Vanni an apologetic look and goes after her. I suppose someone has to. After the look she gave me, it sure as hell won't be me.

"Whoa," Vanni says, watching his father run down the street after her. "My mother is really angry."

"I know," I say quietly, my stomach turning in knots. This was my worst-case scenario, and it's happening right in front of me. The thing I was afraid of came true.

I'm over.

The book is over.

I won't have a career anymore.

I'm finished.

"Do you think she's coming back?" he asks with big eyes, worry all over his face.

"She will," I say, trying to reassure him, though I can't be sure. This might be the last time *I* ever see Jana Lee again. "She loves you, Vanni. She won't leave without saying goodbye."

He seems to calm at that. I take a large sip of wine, no longer hungry, my anxiety ripping through me. But even the wine doesn't seem to help.

"Hey," Vanni says to me. "Are you mad at me?"

I shake the doom from my heart and look at him in surprise. "Mad at you?"

"Yes. For saying something. Maybe you were keeping it

a secret from her, like you were keeping it from me." He cocks his brow for emphasis.

"Oh, Vanni," I say with a sigh, my heart heavy. "I am so sorry we didn't tell you sooner. Your father wanted to, but I was too afraid. It's my fault."

"Is that why you were trying to talk to me about romance the other day? Because that was a bit weird."

"Erm, yeah," I admit.

"Why didn't you just say something? I would have understood. I'm not a kid."

I'm not about to argue with him, that he *is* a kid, because right now, he's a lot more mature than I am.

"I was trying...I was so afraid to talk to you."

He contemplates that for a moment. "I suppose I am intimidating."

I laugh. "You are, Vanni, you are." I pause, biting my lip. "And, well...you kept talking about Gio's timeline and it was better because your mother and your father were together. So I figured...how can I compete with that universe?"

"That is true," he says slowly. Then he perks up. "But now it is better. This timeline is no longer the darkest. Now I'll have my father and mother and you'll be there too. The three of you can live together!"

"Vanni, what you're describing is polygamy. And that's not going to happen."

His face falls. "Oh."

"But that doesn't mean you won't have three people who love you very much. Your father, your mother, and me. Isn't that nice, to have three people in your life who you can call your family?"

Okay, I am probably overstepping my boundaries here, but I've got adrenaline coursing through my veins still. I know that Jana will punish me for this, the least I can do is make sure that Vanni doesn't hate me as well.

"I do have a lot of family already," he muses. "I suppose it doesn't hurt to have more."

"See. More people to adore you."

My words seem to have an impact on him. He nods slowly, his lips pursed as he mulls it over. "But my mother will still live in London?"

"She will. It will be just as before. But now your father is happy. Right? All you wanted was for him to be happy, now you *know* he is happy."

"Because he's in love with you..."

I smile softly and reach over and squeeze his hand. "Yes. He's in love with me and..." I take in a deep breath. "I'm in love with him."

I'm in love with him.

No point denying it anymore, no point in trying to figure it out.

What Maria said was true, when you know, you know....and I *know*. Maybe she was also right in that it took the truth to come out before I could recognize it, but it's there and shining inside me, loud and pure and true.

I love Claudio Romano.

"Gross," Vanni says under his breath, taking his hand away.

He goes back to eating his food, while I sit there feeling stunned and breathless.

No one ever said love would hit you like a frying pan to the face, scrambling your brain, making you feel dumbstruck.

But that's all I can feel right now. Like I've been shaken upside down and now I have to figure out how to get everything back in the right spot, or perhaps the beauty is that you don't. Love is chaotic and messy and maybe nothing will ever feel the same again, and maybe that's the point of it all. Maybe that's the best thing to ever happen to me.

I definitely know that Claudio is the best thing to ever happen to me.

I quickly reach into my purse and pull out my phone, going to the notes app.

"What are you doing?" Vanni asks in between bites of his food.

"I'm writing," I tell him, my fingers flying across the keyboard. "I think I know how to end the book."

"It's a romance," he says. "There's probably going to be kissing."

I break out into laughter, happiness flooding through me. "Yes, there is going to be kissing."

"And no time travel?"

"No time travel."

I know how the heroine is going to come to her senses, I know how they'll end up on their happily-ever-after. I know it and I can see the end so clear. I'm spurred on not only by my love of Claudio, but I feel like I have Robyn on my shoulder, showing me what to do and where to go. Even if Jana drops me as a client, I know I'm going to be okay.

I'm going to be okay, because even though writing can be the loneliest profession, you're never truly alone when you have people that love you.

"Can I get dessert?" Vanni asks me, after we've sat in silence for a while. "I don't think they're ever coming back."

I finish wrapping up a sentence and slide the phone away. There's a difference between being struck by inspiration and being rude. "Sure you can. Let's see..."

I'm bringing the menu over to us when I see Claudio come back into the restaurant, his expression grim.

Uh oh.

He sits down and gives us a quick smile, reaching for the last of the wine.

"How was it?" I ask him.

"I'll tell you later," he says before he has a big gulp.

"She's coming back, right?" Vanni asks.

He shakes his head, swallowing. "She's gone to her room. She has a headache. But you will see her when you go back. Perhaps you can download a movie and watch it together."

"Okay," Vanni says, seeming content with that.

But I feel *awful*.

"Hey," Claudio says to me gently.

He reaches across the table and places his hand on top of mine and holds it tight, our first public display of affection in front of Vanni.

Vanni just rolls his eyes and goes back to reading the dessert menu.

"It's going to be okay," Claudio says to me. "I promise."

I trust Claudio and all, but I don't see how *any* of that is going to be okay.

When we get back to the hotel, Vanni goes to Jana's room to watch a movie, and I'm alone in mine, staring out the window at the streets of Florence, watching the tourists move in the night. It's so much calmer after the sun goes down. I think I prefer it this way.

Finally, there's a knock at my door.

"Who is it?" I call out, walking over to it.

"Special delivery," an overly high-pitched voice says from the other side.

I can't help but smile.

I open the door.

Claudio is standing there holding a bottle of Prosecco

337

and a floral arrangement of pale taupe and pink roses in a vase.

"For you," he says, handing me the vase as he walks in the room. Then he shakes the bottle of Prosecco. "For us."

I sniff the roses, their scent mild. "Where did you get this?"

He shrugs. "I stole it from the display down the hall."

I laugh. "Well, they're very pretty. Not as pretty as yours, of course."

"Of course," he says, as he handles the Prosecco, his forearms popping as he untwists the wire around the cork. He glances up at me. "How are you feeling?"

I shrug one shoulder. "About as well as I can be." I go and sit on the edge of the bed, watching him open the bottle with a *pop*. "Alternating between relief and worry."

"This will help with the worry," he says, walking over to the bar area and pouring us two glasses.

He comes back over and hands one to me. He raises his glass and I do the same.

"Here is to coming clean," he says, staring down at me. "To no more hiding. We can finally be us."

I raise the glass and have a large gulp, the bubbles tickling my nose.

To love.

"So," I begin as he sits down on the bed next to me, our legs dangling off. "Are you going to tell me what happened?"

He nods as he links his foot around mine. "She is pissed."

I suck in my breath.

"And you knew that she would be, and I suppose I should have taken your fears more seriously," he adds.

I gulp. "Fuck."

"Yes. It's her pride that's hurt. I asked her if she still had feelings for me..."

Oh god.

I sit up straighter. "*And?*"

"She laughed. It was very bitter. I know she doesn't, but I had to be sure because I couldn't understand her reaction to us. But yes, it is her pride, which is more precious to her than I could have imagined. Something about you being younger than me, than her, and she is older, and you are a new client, and it was something a woman does not do to another woman. I don't know, here in Italy it is no big deal. But I guess it is over there. Once you are divorced, you are not allowed to find love again? I don't know."

Guilt creates knots in my stomach and I feel like keeling over.

"And so on and so on." He sighs, has another sip. "I told her that this has nothing to do with you, that if she has prob-lems to take it up with me. Oh, and she did that too. I got an earful, that I am a bastard and whatever. In the end, I told her that no matter what happens, I plan on being with you forever, so whether she decides to drop you as a client or not, she will always have to deal with you."

I blink. I'm stuck on what he just said.

Not about her dropping me as a client.

He plans on being with me *forever.*

"Oh no," he says, frowning as he searches my face. "I said the wrong thing."

I shake my head, trying to deal with that chaotic mess of feelings inside me. "You didn't," I whisper.

"I scared you. I said too much."

His expression is crumbling, so I quickly grab his hand and squeeze it. "No. You didn't scare me at all. I...that's what I want."

He stares at me in disbelief. "You do?"

"Yes. I don't want you for now. Or a few months from now. Or a year from now. I want you forever."

Claudio blinks, completely taken aback.

I put my hand on his cheek, his stubble rough against my warm palm. "Claudio. I felt myself falling and I didn't stop myself this time. I let it happen. I let myself fall in love with you." Hot tears prick my eyes. "I love you. I'm in love with you and it's scary, and it's chaotic, and it's messy, and I don't think I'll ever be the same again but...I love you. In this universe, and in the next one, and the next one."

A tear falls down Claudio's cheek and the next thing I know, he's pressing my face between his hands and kissing me. So hard, so passionate, rolling with such feeling that I feel my glass fall to the floor and his does the same, Prosecco spilling everywhere.

But I don't care.

I am in love.

And as a result, my brain has deserted me.

We roll back onto the bed and he crawls over me, and I don't think I'll ever get tired of seeing his large, tanned, muscular frame above my body.

My hands skim down the muscles of his back, pulling at his shirt.

His hands slide up my legs, bunching up my dress, pushing aside my underwear until he finds me soaked and bare and ready for him.

We don't have words tonight because all the words have been said for now.

All we have are our hearts and we're letting those lead the way, and make the choices, the way it always should be.

He continues to kiss me, soft lips and slick tongue that

gradually turns raw and wild, and it all means so much more now. Now that I know what I'm feeling, now that I know I *love* him, it takes this meeting of our bodies to another plane of existence, to another level. I don't want to just give him my body, I want to give him my heart and soul and every other piece of me.

And as he undoes his pants and pushes his cock inside of me, I know he's taking those pieces of me, savoring them, making them meld with everything he has to give.

Give and take.

He rocks into my hips, I buck up against him.

He slowly pulls himself out, I squeeze him as he goes.

His lips suck down my neck, my nails scratch at his back.

We fuck like this, soft and slow and sweet, both of us brimming with too many feelings, occasionally looking at each other in awe, like neither of us knew it could be *this good*.

But it is.

We come together, my orgasm crashing down on me like a tidal wave, spinning me in all directions. He cries out my name, sharp and loud in the room, as he shudders out his breath, his hips pressing hard against mine.

All the emotions of the day suddenly come flooding back at full strength, like I had barely been keeping the water back, and now the dam has caved in.

Shit.

I'm crying.

"*Musa?*" he whispers to me, still inside me. I never want him to leave.

He places his thumbs below my eyes and wipes away the tears.

"I love you," I cry out, feeling stupid.

His eyes glow with adoration as he gazes down at me. "Yes, I know. But please, don't stop saying it."

I pinch my eyes shut. The relief over telling Vanni, the fear that I'll lose Jana as an agent, that my book might be in jeopardy, all these feelings are swirling around, competing against each other for my attention.

But the fact that I love him, and that I have his love, is the biggest one of all.

And my heart has never felt so full.

No matter what happens, I'm going to be okay.

We're going to be okay.

After all, I know the ending.

TWENTY-THREE

CLAUDIO

It feels good to be in my own bed.

It feels even better to have Grace beside me.

No more sneaking around. Just the pure truth. Just us.

"Good morning," I whisper to her. She's curled on her side, head on the pillow, hair spilling around her. Her eyes slowly blink open and I'm caught in how startlingly blue they can seem first thing in the morning. I love this version of Grace, when her mind is quiet and she's in the moment. She looks at me and I know that I'm all she sees.

"Good morning," she says quietly. Her expression is so soft and sweet.

I'm falling more in love with her all the time.

"How did you sleep? You seemed like you were out right through the night."

She wets her lips. "I think so? I was so tired when we got home I just passed out the moment my head hit the pillow."

It's true. Once we arrived back to Villa Rosa from Florence it was fairly late, and we were all exhausted since we tried to cram so much in that last day. Even Vanni fell asleep in the car on the short drive home.

But with Vanni knowing about us, and giving us his approval, I knew that if Grace wanted to sleep in my bed, that we wouldn't have to hide it. I still want to keep things light in front of Vanni, for obvious reasons, and I'm a bit wary of even kissing her in front of him, but he didn't seem to notice she went to sleep in my room.

In *our* room.

Because that's what this is now.

"*Allora*," I say slowly, not wanting to scare her off. She might love me, but what I'm about to say to her could still come on too strongly for her. "When are you going to move in with me?"

She stills, staring up at me. "Move in here?"

"Yes. We talked about this before. You suggested I come up to Edinburgh..."

"Oh, I know. I know. And that's not an option. I just..."

"I'm coming on too strongly?"

She grins. "You are coming on just strong enough. You wouldn't be Claudio otherwise. You wouldn't be the man I fell in love with."

Fuck.

I can't get enough of those words. I'm aware that it's been only a couple of days since she first told me she loved me, but I have been reveling in them ever since.

She loves me.

My heart couldn't be more full. I have a son that loves me, and respects that Grace and I want to be together, and I have the love of an amazingly talented, inspiring, complicated woman who keeps me on my toes. I'm excited to go back to the marble statue today, and I know it's going to be one of my best pieces, all because of her.

I have everything I want.

Except I want her to move in with me.

And then marry me.

And then it will be complete.

"Besides," she goes on, "you told me the other day that you want me forever and I told you the same. Forever means I'm going to be moving in here. I just have to figure out the process." She pauses and sits up. "It definitely means I need to finish my book first before I get any more distracted."

Then she goes stiff.

I sit up beside her and put my hand on her shoulder. "Are you okay?"

She nods, her face pale. "Aye. I just realized...what's the point of finishing the book when I don't even know if I have an agent?"

Right.

After Jana found out about us, and I ended up arguing with her in the streets of Florence, it was unclear what Jana's plans were. She was pissed, that much was true, though she never outright told me that she didn't want to represent Grace anymore. Perhaps she knew if she did, then I'd really let my temper fly. We've had so many fights in the past that it gets pretty exhausting, and I don't think either of us wanted to deal with that.

All Jana wanted to do was see her son for the rest of that night, and then the next morning she flew back to London.

I haven't contacted her yet, knowing she needed a few days of space to clear her head and calm down. I know her pride was damaged, and the bear was poked, but I figure she'll eventually come to her senses.

At any rate, it's not Grace's job to contact her. She did nothing wrong.

"I'm going to call her today," I tell Grace.

"Oh no, don't," she cries out, her forehead creasing. "Please don't."

"Why not? She is my ex-wife. We had a fight and I need to make sure she's not punishing you for no reason."

"It's not for no reason..."

"Tell me, Grace, if you were in her shoes, how would you react?"

"I..." she rubs her lips together, thinking. "I would be taken aback. No doubt. But in the end, I think I would want you to be happy."

"Yes. That is the correct way to act. It doesn't matter anyway, I need to talk to her, because you're mine and you're going to move in with us here, and you'll continue to be a part of my life, and therefore you'll be a part of hers. It's in her best interest to behave. And remember, you're the talented one here. She represents you because you are good. If she drops you, you will find another agent, and things don't look so well for her, do they?"

She nods, looking down at her hands.

"What I am saying," I tell her, brushing her hair behind her shoulder, "is that you need to go and finish the book. That's all. It's just you and the book. I'll handle Jana, okay? Then when all is said and done, then we'll get you moved out of your flat in Edinburgh and everything else that follows. But for now...your job is to write. *Capisci?*"

"Okay," she says after a moment. Then she throws her shoulders back. "I'm going to write."

She hops out of bed, spry as anything.

"Where are you going?" I ask her. "It's early."

"I'm going to the loo," she says, heading to the toilet. "Then I'm going to my office."

"I'm going back to sleep," I tell her, flopping back down on the bed.

"No you're not!" she calls out. "You know I can't work without the espresso."

Damn. She'll never figure out that machine.

I groan loud enough so that she hears it, and then get out of bed to make her coffee.

THE DAY GOES SLOWLY.

Grace spends all her time in her office, riding a massive wave of inspiration. I see her occasionally when she comes back into the house for snacks or refreshments, but I give her space. She even writes through lunch, which blows Vanni's mind. "How could anyone pass up a meal?" he says.

I end up working on the statue, which probably seems like tedious work to anyone else, but to me it's a whole new world. I get so involved in what I am doing, chipping away at the marble to make it become something beautiful and real, that I also would work right through lunch.

Of course Vanni would never let that happen.

He's been in good spirits himself. I've asked him a few times, privately, if he really is okay with Grace and me being together. He said that he's slowly come around to the idea, as long as we promise never to break up. He doesn't want to get attached to Grace and then have her leave.

I promised him that would never happen. That we love each other too much, and that the three of us are on this ride together.

He seemed satisfied with that answer. He just wants to feel included, and I'll do anything to take all his fears away. At least I can trust my son to be honest with me, even when he does talk about my parenting in another dimension.

The last piece of the puzzle is Jana.

Right before I'm about to start dinner, I take a couple of shots of whisky, and then I'm in my study for privacy, ringing her up.

She doesn't answer right away. I have a feeling that my face and number showing up on her screen might make her pause.

But she does, right before it goes to voicemail.

"Claudio," she says stiffly.

"Jana," I say, trying to sound as warm as possible to counter that.

"Is everything okay? Is Vanni all right?"

"He is fine."

You know why I'm calling.

"Oh, good. It was so nice to see him."

She doesn't sound awkward at all.

"Yes. He misses you a lot," I tell her.

"I know."

"You need to come by more often. I mean that."

"I know." Pause. "Though I'm sure I won't matter much soon."

"What does that mean?"

"You. And Grace."

"What about us?"

She lets out a dry laugh. "Oh. You don't see how it is, do you? She's the new me, Claudio. She's the replacement."

"You never said that about any of my other ex-girl-friends," I point out. "You never said that about Marika."

"Because you didn't love Marika. Certainly not the way that you love Grace. Oh, I know that Vanni spilled the bloody beans, but it was quite obvious even before that. I saw the looks you gave each other, looks that *we* never exchanged, and I just...I didn't want to believe it. I didn't want to believe that I was being replaced with a younger, prettier version of myself."

Now I'm laughing.

"Don't be a wanker," she swears.

"I'm not. I'm not trying to be. Listen, Jana, she is younger than you yes, and you are both very beautiful, strong women. But you are nothing alike. So don't think that she is the same version of you. She isn't. She is who she is, and you are who you are. And you are happy, aren't you? Are you not still with William?"

"I am. And we're happy."

"So, what does it matter about us?"

Silence falls over the line.

"Claudio," she says after a beat. "I don't want to lose my son."

"You won't lose your son," I say tiredly. "He will always be your son. That will never, ever change. But...please. You saw how happy he was when he saw you. He loves and misses you. You need to be here more. Call him more. Be more involved in his life. Being a mother doesn't mean you get all the privileges for doing none of the work. You still have to work at being in his life. It's not fair to anyone otherwise, especially not him. You love him; show him that by being there."

She lets out a huff of air. "You know, you're right."

"I know I am."

"I should do more...no excuses."

"Good. Because he needs you, and I need you to be his mother."

"But, eventually, he'll want to be with Grace."

"You will always be his mother," I tell her sternly. "And Grace, she will one day be my wife. But we can all make this work together."

"You're going to marry her," she says, more of a statement than a question.

"I will. When the time is right, and when she's moved in, and the dust has settled. Yes. I'm going to ask her to marry me. Jana, I want to spend the rest of my life with her."

"Oh bloody hell. That makes me a matchmaker, doesn't it?"

"Did you send her here hoping she would meet me?"

"Hell no."

"Then you can't claim that. But if it weren't for you taking an interest in her talent and her writing and the state of her mind, then no, perhaps we wouldn't have met." I wait a beat. "Speaking of, you know you really need to talk to her and apologize."

"I know."

"I mean it. She has been worried sick these last couple of days, thinking you're going to drop her as a client."

"Oh, come now. I'm not going to drop her as a client. She's gold."

"She is gold. But she doesn't always know that. Or she chooses not to believe it."

"*Writers*," she mutters under her breath.

"You can say that again."

"So I suppose we have more than Vanni in common now," she muses.

I grin into the phone. "That we do. And I know we both care a lot about her. So please, call her and talk to her and let her know that everything is going to be okay."

"I will call her tonight. How about that?"

"Good."

"Claudio," she says.

"Yes?"

"Make sure she finishes that book, okay? I really think it's going to change her life."

"I hope so," I tell her. "Because she's already changed mine."

∾

LATER THAT NIGHT, GRACE GETS THE PHONE CALL from Jana. She goes into her office chapel for almost an hour, and when she returns, she's looking relieved. She heads straight to the bar and I mix her up a Negroni. We take the drinks to the patio and watch the sun set. In the distance, Emilio is inspecting the lemon trees, filling his basket full. We will soon have lemons for days.

"So how was it?" I ask Grace.

She gives me a wide, breathtaking grin. "Good. Really good."

I take a sip of my drink and wait for her to go on, delighting in how beautiful she looks and how good she must feel.

"I read some of the book to her on the phone, then I emailed the rest. She's going to read it this week to give me feedback on it, plus I'm going to send some to that author friend I told you about, Kat Manning? I'm going to see if she'll be a critique partner. Obviously Robyn was mine before, but now I need someone else."

"That's a great idea," I say encouragingly.

She nods, has some of her drink. "Aye. And Jana said that she has a good feeling about it. She's going to contact the editor today and tell her that the genre changed but that we can still sell it as women's fiction, if needed. Just because it's women's fiction, doesn't mean it has to have a miserable ending. But she has a feeling they might be up to the romance. I hope so. It would be nice to have a publishing company stand behind it and back that genre up. She says people will definitely read it. I might even need to make it a wee more sexy."

"More sexy?" I question. "How is that even possible?"

She shrugs. "I can always try." She gives me sly eyes and looks me up and down. "Besides, I have the best inspiration right here."

I puff out my chest and grab my dick. "That you do."

She bursts out laughing, spilling some of her drink on her dress. She stares down at the stain and then shrugs. I'm sure she has a replacement dress somewhere.

"So, I know I've asked you this before, but do you have a name for your book yet?" I ask.

She beams. "Yes. I've finally decided on one."

"And so? What is it?"

"When Tomorrow Comes."

I frown. "Okay. What does it mean?"

"I don't know...but it sounds good."

I laugh. "That's what counts."

At least when it comes to us, we know what tomorrow will bring.

More of this.

More of *us*.

EPILOGUE

Grace
One Year Later – London, England

"I HAVE TO TELL YOU, I'M YOUR BIGGEST FAN!" THE girl standing in front of me says, clutching a copy of *When Tomorrow Comes* to her chest.

"Thank you," I tell her, though in the back of my head I'm trying to understand how she could be my biggest fan if she's only read this one book.

"I've read all of the Sleuths of Stockbridge series a million times," she goes on, sounding panicky. "You really can write it all."

I slowly hold out my hand for the book. "You mean, you've read *everything*?"

She nods violently, handing it to me. "Yes. It's all so good. Sorry, I'm shaking."

I stare at her for a moment, letting it sink in. I've been signing books for an hour and it's been so perfect so far, really everything I could have dreamed of. I'm signing in Waterstones off Piccadilly in London, there's a line of people, my romance released to both critical success and sales. Maybe not as many sales as my publisher hoped for, but this reader aside, readers don't always follow you when you switch genres.

And yet, through all of this, I've had that imposter syndrome snaking through my veins. Whispering in my ear.

You're not good at this.

This was a fluke.

You only got this because of your agent.

No one will read your backlist.

Robyn should be signing with you.

And some of this is true, of course. My agent did help me land this deal, most people won't read my backlist, and Robyn *should* be here.

But sometimes I find myself wondering if Robyn and I were meant to write together forever anyway. It's hard to speculate after someone dies, because you really don't know what direction their life would have gone in. There are so many choices we have to make along the way, each choice pushing us down a different path, as slight as it may be. It's like my poorly worded Dr. Ian Malcolm analogy from *Jurassic Park*. A butterfly flaps its wings in Scotland and suddenly our world is different.

I still think, though, that Robyn would be with me at this signing if she were alive. Perhaps we would have branched out on our own at this point, but we would have remained the best of friends. And she would be here, either hovering over my shoulder, running outside to get me Starbucks, or hiding in the back row, watching me with a smile on her face. In fact, sometimes when I look up, I swear I see her. I feel her, at any rate.

And she's proud of me.

The reader is still staring down at me expectantly, shaking slightly, and I snap back into it. I can't afford to let my thoughts drift when I'm signing books, I can barely afford to talk. I've spelt quite a few names wrong because I've been distracted.

I open the cover and look at the dedication page.

To Robyn, my muse.

Because she really was my muse all this time. Someone's whole life can inspire you, even after they're gone.

My throat grows tight with suppressed tears, and I quickly flip the page back and sign my name just below the title, *When Tomorrow Comes.* I've looked at that dedication page over and over again today, but right now, right now it really hits.

I take my time making sure my writing looks neat (it doesn't) and then hand the book back to the reader. She gives me a funny look, perhaps worried that I have tears in my eyes, but then again, she has tears in her eyes too, just for different reasons.

Then she comes around the table and we smile for a picture that Claudio takes of us.

"Say *formaggio,*" he says, grinning his perfect white smile as he peers into the girl's iPhone.

"*Formaggio,*" the reader says, giggling. I just smile, staring more at him than the lens. As you can imagine, I have been saying *formaggio* all day. Claudio really needs to mix it up.

"Thank you so much," the reader says. I remind myself that the name I signed was Sarah, and that I'll try to remember her later, but of course my absent-minded brain probably won't comply.

"Wait, wait," Claudio says, switching to his phone. "One for us."

The reader looks thrilled as she poses with me again, smiling. "*Formaggio!*"

It was Claudio's idea. He thought that we should document every person that comes to the table and put the pictures on my website, or maybe a scrapbook or something. I don't know anyone who makes scrapbooks anymore (I certainly don't have the time), but the intention is good. He said since it's my first solo signing, that in some ways, it's my first one, and that we have to capture the memories.

Little does he know that I've been mentally capturing the memories for a year now. Before I go to bed at night, I take out my journal and I write down moments from the day. Every moment with Claudio, every second, is so precious to me, I can't afford to lose any of them.

I am so in love with you, I think, staring at him with doe eyes as he steps back and lets the next person in line come through. *I can't wait to be your wife.*

Ah yes. Aside from my book finally being published (publishing takes eons), another big change has happened since Claudio and Vanni found me naked in their swimming pool. We're getting married!

He proposed only a month ago, so it's all very fresh in my mind. It wasn't much of a surprise, because we already knew we'd get married when I agreed to move in with him at Villa Rosa. But because of Vanni, because Claudio had been married before, we agreed to take it slow.

Even now, our wedding isn't planned for at least another year, which is fine by me. I'm in no rush. Plus, after my book tour is over, I've got two books to finish by the end of the year...and it's already August! So planning a wedding will have to take the backseat for a bit.

Though I don't think I'll be doing much planning, to be honest. Carla, who works at the gallery, has become one of my good friends and she, along with Maria, have joined forces and taken over the whole wedding planning thing. Sometimes Nina, my future mother-in-law, tries to get in on it too. Once a week they try to get me to answer some questions about the wedding: where do you want it to be, how many people, when do we start looking for the dress, what color scheme do you want, and so on, and so on.

Even Jana will occasionally email me things she saw in *Brides* magazine or something. You know, when she's not sending me emails wondering where the book is and if I have to ask for another extension.

Some things never change.

Speaking of Jana, while I'm nodding at the next reader while they talk to me, trying to figure out the spelling of their name, I see Jana squeeze along the side of the line, Vanni in tow. She had just taken him to a museum, I'm assuming, because he's carrying a huge bag that says The Science Museum, which I am sure is crammed with things I won't understand.

They go right up to Claudio and start talking, and Vanni opens the bag to show his father what he got.

My heart swells at the sight. I knew it wasn't going to be easy coming into a fractured family like this, but if anything, we've all grown closer because of it, and Jana has gotten more involved with Vanni. I'm sure there's a part of her that feels intimidated by me, which is a weird thought, since I'm usually intimidated by her, as both Vanni's mother and my powerhouse agent. But Claudio's theory is that she feels her role in Vanni's life might be slipping, which has spurred her on to be more attentive.

That's not true, at all. She's not slipping. I'm not trying

to replace her, and I think everyone knows that. I'm just an addition. That doesn't mean that I don't have to act like a mother half the time. I get along with Vanni like he's a younger brother, and I adore the kid, but I do have to put my foot down from time to time and attempt to do some parenting. Luckily, he doesn't give me much pushback about that, although sometimes he'll pull that "but I thought you were my friend" thing.

At any rate, Jana comes and visits us once a month in Lucca, and sometimes we'll all come up here to London, like we're doing now, or we'll all go up to Scotland to see my mother.

The book tour kicks off here and then all of us (except Jana) are on the road for a few weeks. With Vanni on summer vacation still, it's the perfect time to travel as a family. Thankfully, Jana is taking care of Vanni tonight, so that Claudio and I can have some alone time and celebrate my first signing.

In fact, he went and got us a "pre-honeymoon suite" at The Ritz. I'm not sure if the hotel calls it that, but Claudio does, and even though I've been having fun signing, I can't wait to stop talking and being social and enjoy some alone time with my husband-to-be.

I wave at Vanni and Jana, and then Claudio comes back to take some more pictures. Jana and Vanni wait for a bit, watching me. Jana looks very proud. Vanni looks...very bored. They only watch for about five minutes before I can tell Vanni is complaining about dropping dopamine levels or something.

Jana quickly comes around my table to me, crouching down. "Do you need anything?" she asks me. "How are they treating you? You don't have any more coffee, do you need a coffee? They should be offering you coffee."

I laugh. "It sounds like *you* don't need any more coffee. And I'm fine. I have Claudio."

"Okay," she says warily. "But the bookstore should be stepping up. They should realize who you are. Grace Harper, bestselling author."

"I think they know who I am," I say, gesturing to all the signage around the store, pictures of the cover, and also my blown-up face from the one headshot I like.

"Oh but *I* did all that," she says. And then she points to the rows of bookshelves. "See? I got you end placement on all those rows. For a romance, that is rare."

Jana has been telling me all the things she's gotten for me for months now, so I'm always aware of how much power she has. I'm also very appreciative.

"I see. It looks great."

"Good," she says, getting back up and giving my shoulder a squeeze. "I'm going to take Vanni to the zoo now. I'll see you tomorrow." Pause. "Remember to have fun!"

I give her a big smile to show her how much fun I'm having.

"Wait, wait," Claudio says, whipping his phone out. "Jana, go back there."

Jana sighs and dutifully comes back beside me and we both smile for the camera. I know she acts like she doesn't like photos, but she secretly loves it.

Then Vanni waves goodbye to me and off they go.

I watch them leave, then turn my attention to the line.

Holy moly, did it just get bigger?

I take a quick glance at my phone. Just another hour. My hand is cramping up from signing and my mouth hurts from talking, but I get back into the zone, and welcome the next person in line.

~

"So where do you want to go?" Claudio asks me as we leave the bookstore. He's holding my hand, but doesn't know what direction to take me. "We could go to Buckingham Palace, Camden Market, walk in the steps of Jack the Ripper in Shoreditch."

"Claudio," I say to him with a sigh. "I'm Scottish. I've done these things. Let's go back to the hotel. This is our last chance to be alone before a month of travel happens. We should take advantage of it."

"You don't have to tell me twice," he says, and we head in the direction of the hotel, which isn't too far.

When we get there, we have a drink at the swanky bar and I take a few moments to just breathe and decompress and enjoy the quiet. Claudio keeps his arm around me, making me feel safe, but doesn't press me for conversation.

My mind is sluggish but keeps trying to go over the day. How lucky I was to have that signing, how fortunate I am that the book actually got finished and published, and that (most) people love it. And how amazing it is that I have Claudio by my side, that we're going to be married one day, and that I will love him forever.

"What are you thinking about?" he asks me quietly, his fingers playing with my hair. We've sat in silence for a long time.

"Everything," I tell him. "But mainly you."

He angles his face toward me, smiles his beautiful smile, and then kisses me on the cheek. His lips are soft and lingering, causing a thrill to run up my spine.

I pick up my glass and finish my cocktail. Aperol Spritz, naturally, even though it's not as good as the ones Claudio makes for me back home.

Home, I think, and it makes me sad for a moment. I'm excited to travel, and to do these events, but I'm going to miss Villa Rosa. It really is the best spot on earth, a place that both inspires me *and* makes me feel grounded. A place to belong to.

Though, when I think about it, a part of me will be there even when I'm not. The marble statue of me with the roses sits just beside the bar downstairs. It was Claudio's joke to have her guarding the wine.

I think it's funny, but also she's beautiful. She's like me, but she isn't me, and every time I pass by her I'm reminded of his days sculpting me, and how we got together. It will remind me of the beginning of our love for the rest of my life. He named the statue, "Your Precious Heart," taken from the lyrics of an INXS song.

"Let's go back to the room," I tell him.

He wags his brows at me. He knows what I mean. He finishes his cocktail and then we're going up the elevator to our room near the top floor.

Our room is pretty swanky and happens to have a balcony overlooking London. It's a funny city in that when you're at street level, things kind of feel like a maze, but when you have a chance to be up high, then the city really opens up.

Right now it's shining and golden and beautiful, matching how I feel on the inside. Like anything and everything is possible and I can't wait for what's next.

While I'm staring at the view, Claudio closes the door behind us, and then grabs me by the elbows spinning me around into a kiss.

I sink deeply into his arms, falling into the kiss, our mouths opening against each other with tenderness that will soon morph into hunger. We fit so well together, it's amazing we're even able to come apart. My hands go to the small of his back, pulling up his shirt so that I can slide my palms over his smooth, hot skin. I love the feel of him, that even after a year, I never get tired of this. It's like I need this connection with him to feel alive and whole.

He pulls away, cupping my face, his head resting against my forehead. "I am so proud of you," he murmurs. "You did so good today."

"Because I had you there."

"No," he says. He gazes deep into my eyes and I am lost in the dark depths of his. "Because you are *you*, Grace Harper. This is who you are. Who you were born to be. I merely showed you this. You were already there." He places a gentle kiss on my forehead. "*Musa*. And now, you inspire so many others, not just me."

I close my eyes and let it wash over me, knowing how much we belong to each other, and that our future together is only just starting.

I am his, and he is mine.

Inspired, desired, and completely in love.

THE END

WHAT TO READ AFTER ONE HOT ITALIAN SUMMER

If you're looking for something else to read from me that's similar to *One Hot Italian Summer*, do I have some recommended books for you!

The Forbidden Man - After moving to Madrid to become the first female physiotherapist for the Real Madrid football team, Thalia must resist the temptation of the much younger player Alejo Albarado. Steamy, sensual and highly emotional, this book will sweep you off to Spain, break your heart and put it back together.

Tropes: Forbidden romance, sports romance, younger man/older woman

Love, in English - 23 yr-old Vera Miles doesn't know what she wants from life, but she's hoping to find it when she embarks on a two-week course in the Spanish countryside. What she doesn't expect is the love of her life, Mateo Casalles, who she strikes up a deep relationship with. Of course, Mateo can never be hers if he belongs to someone else...

Tropes: Forbidden romance, older man/younger woman, slow-burn

Before I Ever Met You - Growing up, Jackie always knew Will McAllister as her father's good friend. When single mom Jackie ends up moving back to her hometown of Vancouver, looking for a job, she gets hired at her father's company - as Will's assistant. But the heat rises and sparks fly as Will and Jackie fall head over heels for each other, doing their best to deny it...and failing.

Tropes: Dad's best friend, older man/younger woman, single mom, office romance

My Life in Shambles - When Valerie Stephens made

the resolution to say yes to new adventures, she never thought she'd end up in the tiny Irish town of Shambles, fake engaged to one of Ireland's top rugby players, Padraig McCarthy. But there's a first time for everything...including losing your heart.

Tropes: Fake relationship, sports romance, emotional tearjerker

ACKNOWLEDGMENTS

They say writing is the loneliest profession.

No, you didn't start reading this book over again (that's also the first sentence), it's just the truth. But just because writing tends to attract weird introverted hermits like myself, doesn't mean that I do it all on my own. There is always a team of people in the wings, supporting me, believing in my work, and encouraging me.

Believe me...if you've picked up anything from being in Grace's POV, it's that we writers are a neurotic mess and we LIVE on encouragement.

So...One Hot Italian Summer had a lot of cheerleaders as I wrote and in particular I would like to thank Tarryn Fisher, Kathleen Tucker, Jay Crownover, Angie McKeon, Heather Brown, Dawn Sousa , Elsi Gabrielsen and of course, Nina Grinstead and the Valentine PR team (and Charlie!).

More thanks to my beta readers Pavlina Michou, Sarah Symonds, Sarah Sentz, Heather Pollack.

Hang Le, thanks again for this cover. We've been a team

for six years and countless covers and I definitely can't do this without you!

Sandra, you're the MVP.

And *Grazie* to the REAL Marika Nespoli for help with my Italian!

PS I've been with my agent Taylor Haggerty of Root Literary since 2014 and I consider her a champion of my work and a friend. Taylor, I will not sleep with any ex-husbands of yours :P

PPS Scott you are my muse and I wouldn't be doing this without you. You're my greatest fan, and the best cook in the world (you feed me AND my soul), and thank you for loving my artist heart with your artist heart.

CONNECT WITH THE AUTHOR

Hey! Nice you meet you :) If you want to connect with me, you can always find me on Instagram (where I post travel photos, fashion, teasers, etc, IG IS MY LIFE and the easiest place to find me online...plus you'll be able to see ALL the pictures I took of Lucca, Elba, Florence and the EXACT places that appear in the book!)

-> or in my Facebook Group (we're a fun & friendly bunch and would love to have you join. I do lots of exclusives and share behind the scenes, have giveaways, etc)

-> Otherwise, feel free to signup for my mailing list (it comes once a month) and Bookbub alerts!

ALSO BY KARINA HALLE

A Nordic King

Nothing Personal

My Life in Shambles

Discretion

Disarm

Disavow

The Royal Rogue

The Forbidden Man

Lovewrecked

One Hot Italian Summer

Romantic Suspense Novels by Karina Halle

Sins and Needles (The Artists Trilogy #1)

On Every Street (An Artists Trilogy Novella #0.5)

Shooting Scars (The Artists Trilogy #2)

Bold Tricks (The Artists Trilogy #3)

Dirty Angels (Dirty Angels #1)

Dirty Deeds (Dirty Angels #2)

Dirty Promises (Dirty Angels #3)

Black Hearts (Sins Duet #1)

Dirty Souls (Sins Duet #2)

Horror Romance

Darkhouse (EIT #1)

Red Fox (EIT #2)

The Benson (EIT #2.5)

Dead Sky Morning (EIT #3)

ABOUT THE AUTHOR

Karina Halle is a screenwriter, a former music & travel journalist, and the *New York Times*, *Wall Street Journal*, and *USA Today* bestselling author of *The Pact*, *A Nordic King*, and *Sins & Needles*, as well as sixty other wild and romantic reads.

She, her musician husband, and their adopted pit bull, Bruce, live in a rainforest on an island off the coast of British Columbia, where they operate Raven Ridge, a B&B that's perfect for writers' retreats and romantic getaways.

In the winter, you can often find them in California or on their beloved island of Kauai, soaking up as much sun (and getting as much inspiration) as possible. For more information, visit www.authorkarinahalle.com/books.

Printed in Great Britain
by Amazon

84945470R00222